DANCE OF THE EARTH

DANCE OF THE EARTH

ANNA M HOLMES

The
Book
Guild

First published in Great Britain in 2025 by
The Book Guild Ltd
Unit E2 Airfield Business Park,
Harrison Road, Market Harborough,
Leicestershire. LE16 7UL
Tel: 0116 2792299
www.bookguild.co.uk
Email: info@bookguild.co.uk

The manufacturer's authorised representative in the EU
for product safety is Authorised Rep Compliance Ltd,
71 Lower Baggot Street, Dublin D02 P593 Ireland (www.arccompliance.com)

This is a work of fiction.

Typeset in 12pt Adobe Jenson Pro

Printed and bound by CPI Group (UK) Ltd, Croydon, CR0 4YY

ISBN 978 1835743 102

British Library Cataloguing in Publication Data.
A catalogue record for this book is available from the British Library.

MIX
Paper | Supporting
responsible forestry
FSC
www.fsc.org
FSC® C013604

With love and gratitude to my one-and-only ballet teacher, Michelle Robinson, for opening the world of dance to me and for continuing to inspire new generations.

Contents

PRELUDE

1875

ONSTAGE, AMIDST SPECTACULAR SNOWDRIFT SCENERY, the Ice King cavorts with dozens of *corps de ballet* fiends set to freeze to death a hapless traveller. Then, in a dazzle of limelight, the Snow Queen magically appears from a frozen waterfall. To gasps and applause, a safely harnessed Madame Pitteri hovers, a sparkling white-tutued snowflake. She will put an end to this torment.

At the back of the theatre – sounds of orchestra muted – the stage door manager hears mewling and doesn't give it a thought. He opens the door, just enough, for the theatre cat.

'In y' come…' But it's only cold night air that brushes his ankles. He pushes the door wider. At his feet is an old wicker basket, the type found at Covent Garden market, but it doesn't hold cabbages. Stepping around it and into the dark empty street, he looks about. What's he supposed to do? He hesitates, then picks up the abandoned thing and heads back in. Setting it on the counter, he stares at it for some minutes. He could replace it; pretend he never saw it…

'Out of m' way!' Clutching the basket, he pushes through a crush of evil-looking green demons, painted faces made more fearsome by flickering yellow gas lights.

Among a gabble of shrill voices, one calls, 'Tommy. What you got there?'

No time for an answer. Dozens hurry on, soft ballet shoes pattering on stone floor, fingers unpinning spangled headdresses. In upstairs dressing rooms, floaty costumes hang

3

ready – fuchsias, tulips, tiger-lilies. There's Act Two to come, where, in a sunrise of Aurora-like displays, beauty – and love – will prevail.

Further along the corridor, Tommy squeezes past the Majiltons: the three shock-headed acrobats, still in their multicoloured tight-fitting outfits, idle with other turns, all done for the night. In the basket, what had been a mewl has risen in volume. Curious, they follow him to the Green Room, an all-purpose place to meet and mend.

At a large table strewn with damaged costumes and headdresses, Molly, a seamstress, is repairing a crimson velvet jacket.

'What on earth…?' She jerks at the sound, pricking her finger, then sweeps aside clutter, making room. 'Oh, my goodness!' She peers at a red-tipped nose of a tightly swaddled baby.

They gather – doorman, artistes, seamstresses, a carpenter nursing a bandaged hand…

Molly removes the bundle and begins unpeeling layers of sacking and woollies, then a dark purple silk shawl. She peeps under a makeshift nappy, declaring, 'A girl, and not long born.' As she prepares to rewrap the wee thing, the shawl catches her attention. 'I recognise this.' So instead, the babe is made snug in the velvet jacket – sharp needle removed.

Shaking out the square shawl, Molly folds it into a triangle and drapes it over her shoulders. Her fingers explore clusters of tiny pricks in the fabric where it had been drawn together and artificial flowers pinned to a bodiced bosom.

'That Spanish ballet, remember?'

Another seamstress takes it saying: 'And didn't we use it in *Beauties of the Harem?*' She slings it low around her hips, loosely knotting it at the side.

'Who,' Molly speculates, 'left the *corps de ballet* all of a sudden?'

'I let out Alice's costume – twice,' a seamstress recalls.

'Miscarried,' Molly says. 'She's behind the bar at The Crown now.'

'What about that slip of a girl from up north?' Tommy asks. 'Haven't seen her for a while.'

'Died some weeks back,' Molly says. 'Her lungs.'

More names crop up; names are dismissed.

Word spreads of the unexpected arrival, and more crowd in. Loudly they proclaim their astonishment at this baby lying among bits of fabric, gilt-foil, and sequins.

'Who'll take her to the Foundling Hospital?' someone asks. No one offers.

Molly cradles the baby, now sucking its thumb. 'Oh, the wee mite's starving.' She gulps, feeling something tug in her stomach.

'Poor bebe, let me 'old her,' Madame Pitteri says. The plump, golden-haired ballerina arrives, still wearing her Act Two, Queen Snowdrop, costume. 'She must 'ave a name.' She searches for a note tucked in the shabby basket, then, finding none, insists: 'I gift my own, Giovannina.'

'Giovannina,' Molly tries.

'Rather long for a tiny girl,' someone says.

'And not very *English*,' another whispers.

'Victoria, after Her Majesty? Vicky?'

And still they arrive. What seems the entire *corps de ballet* shrugs off tiredness, cramming in. Musicians, instruments packed, pause before heading into the cold November night.

A broad-brimmed hat with an ostrich feather is produced, into which slips of paper are deposited. A scrap of paper is retrieved and unfolded.

'Rosalinde!'

'Ah.' A violinist claps. He's a fan of *Die Fledermaus*. 'Dear baby Rosalinde!'

'Rosa perhaps?'

'Perhaps.'

No one recalls how Rose is settled upon. No one knows why she isn't handed over to the authorities who deal with abandoned babies. No one – least of all Molly – recalls why she, a young single woman, forever repairing costumes from Monsieur Alias's atelier, takes the baby home. Did everyone, including the theatre manager, rush away, leaving others, eventually her, to deal with the unwanted problem? Had something of *The Flower Queen* ballet's magic seeped backstage to cast a spell protecting this little thing?

Whatever the case, the die is cast. Rose, cared for by Molly, becomes the first-born child of the jewel of London's theatreland: the Alhambra Palace Theatre, Leicester Square.

ACT 1

1880–1895

How welcome is the relief of a spectacle which professes to be no more than merely beautiful… which provides, in short, the one escape into fairy-land which is permitted by that tyranny of the real world which is the worst tyranny of modern life.

THE SAVOY, 5 SEPTEMBER 1896

1

THE MUCKY, SOOTY STREETS OF WHITECHAPEL couldn't claim Rose. While she lived with Molly in an upstairs flat on Commercial Road, she belonged to a different world. A world – a tram ride away – smelling of gas, tobacco, warm greasepaint, and sweaty costumes.

Stepping through the stage door, she let go of Molly's hand. 'Hello, Mr Hobbs.'

He looked up from mail he was sorting. 'Morning, pest… Molly.'

'I'll take that, Tommy.' Molly picked up a soft-looking package.

'Ah. Just the lady.' Monsieur Alias, heading out, stopped to ask: 'Those dresses. Delivered in good order?' He tucked a silk scarf inside velvet lapels.

'Mostly, Monsieur, but the braid on Kath's lot don't match the rest,' Molly would be unpicking and restitching today, 'and only a hundred and sixty.'

He tutted, saying he'd get the other half chased up. Impatient for his attention, Rose tugged at his coat tail.

'M'sieur!' She slipped off her own coat, revealing her dress, and gave a twirl.

'Ah! You are exquisite today.' Tiny, dapper Monsieur

Alias peered through his monocle, admiring a combination of prawn pink and lime green. 'If memory serves, this is from *Dolly Varden's Lovers*, and this, *The Enchanted Forest*.' She wore, she discovered, the history of their ballets. 'Making you, ma chérie,' he tapped her nose, 'a very important person.' He tipped his hat and left.

'Right, love,' Molly said, 'you know where to find me. Keep out of the way and don't cross the magic lines.' With a peck on the cheek, Molly set off for the Green Room, with that uneven gait of hers due to the special boot she had to wear.

The grand front of house glass doors onto Leicester Square were one boundary, and with Mr Hobbs guarding the drab stage door, she was never in danger of straying beyond that.

'Magic lines,' she repeated, then skipped into her playground.

Come evening, with her vivid dresses and hair ribbons, she'd be *almost* invisible amongst hundreds of brightly costumed dancers and visiting artistes. Daytime was different. With everyone in workaday drab outfits she stood out and wasn't *always* welcome.

On hearing a growled, 'Who's that girl?' she ducked into a dressing room, hiding behind sour-smelling costumes hanging on hooks. Pretending to be a statue, she waited, listening for the twirly moustached manager's footsteps to recede. This was a game she played, but she wasn't sure *he* was playing. Other times there'd be a, 'Why's she still here?' But the moment passed, or that manager left, a new one arriving. 'You want me to lose my job?' a flustered Molly might say. Or 'Nap time,' Molly taking her firmly by the hand, leading her to the Green Room. Here, as every afternoon, she made a nest in the remnant pile stacked in a corner, where, to the rhythmic clacks of sewing machines and jawing people, she slept. There'd be a long evening ahead.

In the wings, she sat huddled against the wall under a dangling fire bucket, catching glimpses of a painted world lit by limelight. Frothy dresses fluttered as lines of high-kicking dancers showed their legs all the way to their knickers. Hard-soled shoes tapped out Irish jigs and hornpipes. She'd inch forwards for a better view. Closer. Closer still…

'Out of the way, child!' A stampede threatened to engulf her. 'God's sake, Rose!' – a crush of breathless dancers hurtling to dressing rooms.

Opposite her, in the impossibly crowded prompt side wing, the stage manager oversaw everything that mattered: rows of brass buttons and bells ordering lights to change and curtains to drop; props and bits of costumes that must be found *immediately*; people, mysteriously missing, needed onstage *now!* Behind him, quick-change artists scurried to discard costumes in a narrow space only to speed back onto stage, transformed.

There was nothing she'd not seen, nowhere she'd not been. On one memorable under-stage visit, she'd been buckled into a harness and launched through a trapdoor, hovering above the stage where carpenters were fixing some scenery. 'Again. Do it again!' she'd shrieked.

The Alhambra conjured magic, and she was under its spell.

School became a necessity, and Rose reluctantly fitted it in. She had little in common with children whose fathers were costermongers, bricklayers and drivers; children who played outside, whatever the weather. When they'd be going to sleep, in a bed shared with brothers and sisters, she'd be waking from a nap, ready for the show.

When wearing a new dress to school, she was crushed hearing, 'They're just bits of rags, stitched together.' Molly was indignant on hearing that. 'Rags! They're special – off-cuts, mind – but each holds a story. You tell them, from me.' Rose didn't pass on the message and future dresses, while colourful, weren't quite as gaudy.

'Who's your ma?' a shabby girl taunted in the playground. 'Or your pa? Can't say, can you, 'cos you're a *foundling*.' That girl had bruises on her arms, but she also had parents.

'I've got Molly and everyone at the Hammy.' The Babyish name slipped out.

'Not the same.'

It put doubt in her mind, where there had been none.

One December morning, having just turned seven, she arrived at the school gate to see an older girl running towards her.

'Rose! Ma's wondering what Molly's going to do now.' Bessy's eyes shone bright, as they do when there's drama to share, and you're the one in charge. 'Don't you know?' Seeing her blank stare, Bessy continued, 'Gone – your precious theatre – burned down.'

'Can't have.'

'Has too, Ma said so. And Pa's been out all night. Still there.' Rose knew he was a fireman, so there was authority behind those shocking words. Vaguely, she was aware a teacher had stepped out the door ringing a handbell; aware of children scuttling into untidy lines ready to march in…

'Rose! Where're you going? What shall I say?'

But she was already running fast, reaching into a pocket for the tram fare.

At Leicester Square, she couldn't stop coughing for the smoke. Desperate to see, she elbowed her way through a throng to the cordoned-off site, police patrolling, firemen still active beyond. She stared, not quite believing. Just two smoke-stained towers remained. Gone, the gilded staircases; gone, the domed, pale-blue ceiling scattered with golden stars. And the crystal chandeliers? Peering at the smouldering, sodden ruin, she sought for sparkles but could only see sparking cinders. Along with the taste of gritty smoke came a different, bitter, taste. Ever after, she blamed Bessy, feeling that big girl was responsible.

If buildings could suddenly disappear, so could people. She spun around, eyes seeking, not knowing where Molly might be. She raced to Monsieur Alias's Soho Square premises. Not there. Back again. She was a ruin, hat lost, neatly plaited hair come loose, breakfast churning in her stomach. Then…

'Molly!' There she was, amongst others in the Strand, guarding all sorts of bits and pieces that had been rescued. 'Molly! Molly!' She streaked up, hugging Molly's ample waist.

Molly didn't seem surprised to see her and didn't ask where her hat was. 'Oh love, what a thing. The costumes are gone, but Mr Jacobi's scores are saved. What are we to do?'

She clung tighter, great gobs of sobs rising.

Molly started to pat her back, but her mind was elsewhere. 'We don't know what we're going to do. All of us.'

It dawned on her then, what Bessy had been saying. It wasn't just the theatre that had gone… 'And the dancers?'

'Out of work with the rest of us,' Molly managed to say.

And then a terrible thought. A picture of ragamuffin children at Whitechapel market took hold – children she tried *not* to see. One boy always huddled in the same doorway: skinny, scabby face, feet bound in rags. Molly would spot him. 'Poor mite, give him this.' And Rose would take the penny, making the transaction quickly, trying not to allow a clean glove to become dirtied. Backing away, she would reach for the comfort of Molly's hand and tug her. One day, Molly didn't see the waif, so asked about. 'Dead,' they were told by a costermonger by his barrow of potatoes, carrots and turnips. 'When I set up, I thought it was a pile of rags, but no, it was him curled up in the doorway, stiff as you like and light as a feather. Poor lad.' Molly shook her head. 'Poor little mite,' then gave her a long hard look. At that, Rose's heart hammered, and she gripped Molly's hand.

Near the ruins of the Alhambra, surrounded by newly out-of-work men and women, Rose asked, 'And me?' She could hardly breathe, then she sicked-up her breakfast, splattering her dress and shoes. 'Don't leave me, Molly, don't ever leave me!'

As her worries spilt out, Molly gently shook her. 'Don't be so daft. I'm not going anywhere and I'm not planning to give you away. As if!'

Days later, Molly not-so-gently pushed her away. 'You're a ruddy shadow, and you're getting under my feet.'

In time, she stopped worrying about *that*. But everything else? One day, visiting Monsieur Alias's, the costumier surprised her.

'But yes, a new theatre shall rise from the ashes and be magnificent... Come.'

With dainty steps, he led her to a room lined with shelves holding books of all sizes, where, standing on a stool, he reached for a particular book. After flicking through pages, he pointed to a black and white drawing.

'What do you see?' An odd-looking bird was spreading its wings, trying to escape a fierce fire burning all around it.

'Poor bird,' she said.

'Happy bird,' he corrected. 'It is, um, ressuscité – reborn from the ashes. I have yet to be called upon to design such a costume, but,' he adjusted his monocle, 'I see a glorious creature in silky cinnabar and flaming reds and oranges. But the beak?' He pursed his lips. 'What colour might this magical bird have?'

'Green, *emerald* green,' she clarified. Colours were not just red, but scarlet, crimson, burgundy. Never blue, but navy, cerulean.

'Very well. I will remember.' He took her hand, leading her to the foot of a flight of stairs. From above came a steady rackety sound of many sewing machines where Molly was working on a contract for another theatre. Stepping aside, she made space for two women to pass downstairs, arms laden with multicoloured flounced skirts. 'You see, ma chérie, life continues.'

Within a year, on the gutted site, a glorious new Alhambra opened: a cerulean, domed ceiling and lantern skylight as perfect – if not more so – than the old; intricately decorated tiered balconies and boxes, easily as ravishing. Before long, familiar smells seeped into walls and fabrics making themselves at home. And so did Rose.

When *The Swans* opened, Rose had just turned nine. She waited outside Emma Palladino's dressing room, curtsied, whispering a shy, 'Hello, Madame,' to the ballerina, before trailing after her admiring her wasp-like figure with rounded bosom, cinched waist, and ballooning tutu to her knees.

Week after week, from her place in the wings, she experienced every step their Swan Queen danced. By curtain call she was wrung out, emotionally drained. Near her would be two fellows adjusting their pantomime horse outfit and burlesque acrobats limbering up for the following turn. She was ready for a good laugh by then.

One afternoon, she knocked on Madame Palladino's dressing room door, the dresser letting her in.

'Please, Madame.' She held out a posy of violets to her adored ballerina, now sitting bundled in rugs.

'Darling child.' With her red nose streaming, Madame

Palladino looked decidedly unlovely. 'What a pet.' A clammy hand touched her cheek. Then Madame reached for a hanky and gave her nose a good blow. At that moment, Rose understood it was not the earthly woman she had fallen in love with, but the heroines she inhabited onstage, and she had to be part of it.

That Sunday at home, with Molly settling in her comfy chair, twisted foot resting on a pouf, she raised the subject.

'Molly. I want to leave school. I want to start.'

'When you're ten we can talk about it—'

'Can't wait.'

'That's the law. And you might change your mind and decide you want some more schooling.'

'I won't. Never. I can read, anyway.' She flicked her eyes towards a pile of dog-eared penny dreadfuls: stories of vampires and highwaymen. As Molly couldn't read, she stumbled through, sounding out words or guessing.

Seeing Molly looking doubtful, she pressed her case. 'Wouldn't you like seeing me make people happy? You know, maybe sad and weepy, or have them laugh. You'd like that, wouldn't you?'

'Put that way…'

'Please, Molly.'

'Sure you're sure?'

'Really, truly.' Palms pressed her heart.

'Well, I won't say no to some of your wages after all this time. And I'm only just getting back on my feet.' After the fire, she would mean, when times had been hard.

If there was any legal arrangement to being looked after by Molly, Rose never thought to ask. What Molly had said was, 'That night, it felt I was your blooming fairy godmother. I couldn't give you away, could I, it was like something had happened.'

'*I* happened!' she'd insist.

Another time, Molly said, 'When my ma died, my older sisters were already in service, so it was just me and my so-called uncle at home, and he started to act funny.' When Rose said that sounded fun, Molly said it wasn't. Molly also said, 'Being a little girl alone in the world isn't nice, and I didn't want you ending up like those wretched waifs we see.'

Unthinkable!

'I'll put in a word with Madame Cormani,' Molly said. 'She'll say yes – always needs dancers to train. You'll be needing a muslin petticoat – plain, mind you, no frills – so, let's get started.' She indicated her nearby sewing basket: woven lid rarely closed, padded satin lining stuck through with pins. From among a neatly arranged array of coloured thread, darning wool, scissors, thimble, and a pincushion, Rose took out the measuring tape.

Under Madame Cormani's tutelage, Rose learnt to march and gallop and keep in time with the other girls. Never once did she regret leaving school early. Alhambra ballets taught her everything she needed: hornpipes from England, reels from Scotland, jigs from Ireland. And tarantellas 'are from *my* country,' their teacher reminded them. Sometimes in newspapers she spotted headlines of trouble brewing but was incurious, her eyes sliding to the entertainment listings. Theatres of far-away wars that troubled politicians only touched her theatre in cheerful ways. She knew being British – *English* – was the best thing in the world, and her queen ruled a lot of that.

Le Bivouac, celebrating Her Majesty's armed forces, marked Rose's debut. As one of nearly two hundred dancers packed tight, and positioned near the back, she couldn't really be seen or see much – too many taller girls in front. She was a back row dancer, among daughters and nieces of the theatre's carpenters or firemen, and older dancers who were no longer 'as pretty as in my heyday,' they'd say, but could still kick up a leg. Not that there was room for that. Jammed shoulder to shoulder with girls either side, she marched in tightly drilled patterns, a rifle clutched to her side. Above the stamp of feet came clapping from beyond the footlights and she imagined how the older, shapelier, girls must dazzle in their short snug-fitting military-style tunics, long legs in tights and high boots. Butterflies in her stomach began a little jig.

At a swagged box nearest the stage, she glimpsed a man in a tailored evening suit lean close to a lady sitting upright with silky flowers fixed to her elaborate hairdo. Her corseted evening dress might, surely, have a large silk rosette at the back of the waist, and her flounced silk skirt would be spread, trailing to the floor.

Those butterflies were fluttering around her heart now. She wanted that lady to see her, wanted to hear applause, just for *her*.

2

By seventeen, Rose was well established as a front row dancer. With eleven other girls, she shared a cramped dressing room lined with hooks and shelves, a sour smell of damp costumes and body odours pervading. One morning, just as she was bending down to her locker, a rat scurried across the dimly lit floor. She leapt back.

'You see it? Bigger than yesterday's, I swear!' The only furry creatures with skinny tales she tolerated were costumed in pantomime.

'And look at this.' Evelyn held up the remains of a sandwich, wrapping paper nibbled through. 'I've had enough. Come on, Rose – and you others. We're *all* going.'

'Where?'

'To see Mr Gilmer, that's where.'

Rose watched her friend knock at the door, then, hearing a gruff, 'Come in,' steeled herself and crossed the threshold, beckoning the rest of her reluctant posse. Mr Gilmer was perusing a design for the front cover of a forthcoming programme, a part-smoked cigar resting on an ashtray.

'Sorry to bother you, Mr Gilmer, but look here.' Evelyn brandished her sandwich. 'A rat got to this before I could. Would you have your daughter in a room like ours? It's not right. We're working girls—'

'If you want to stay "working girls", you should mind your tongue.' The manager rammed the cigar in his mouth, looking startled. Rose watched Evelyn shift from foot to foot, fearing what was to come. She tugged at Evelyn's skirt, whispering, 'Let's go,' but her friend would have her say.

'Covent Garden ain't so bad. Nor the Empire. The girls there say they've the rat catcher in. Regular. And we're the Alhambra. The best, ain't we?' She met his gaze.

Mr Gilmer sucked on his cigar as he sucked on the implication.

Next day, rat catchers got to work, and Rose got on with the business of advancing.

One Sunday at home, needing another practice outfit, Rose stretched her arms wide as Molly encircled her chest with a measuring tape.

'My word.' Molly double-checked the measurement. 'You're becoming quite a special rose.'

She sighed; the butter-ball figure of Emma Palladino was not to be hers. 'You think I'm growing too tall? Too *big*? I'm never cast as nymphs and fairies, always ruddy sailors or soldiers.'

'Womanly, that's what you are. Signor Coppi will have his eye on you for new ballets.' Molly extended the measuring tape from waist to knee, making a note on a scrap of paper. 'And you've lovely legs, mind. You'll shine, mark my words.'

Molly admired nice legs, and pretty feet. 'If I can't be pretty,' Molly used to say, 'you will be.' While Molly favoured simple dresses, insisting, 'I don't like to draw attention to myself,' she had sewn startling rainbow outfits for Rose when she was little.

A look passed over Molly's eyes. 'Those stage-door Johnnies will be after you.'

'I'm not headed down that route.'

'When I first started work with Monsieur Alias, I was shocked. Girls slipping away between ballets. Sitting about in the under-stage canteen, dressing gowns thrown over costumes, in full make-up looking like harlots. Men knew where to find girls, and girls knew where to find men who'd buy them a drink.'

Rose hated to think her own mother might have been one of those feckless sorts. 'You've told me, Molly, but it's not like that now.'

'I've seen girls legless by the last ballet of the evening.'

'Not now. They'd be thrown out, pronto. And like I said,' she kissed Molly's head, 'no need to worry about me.'

She set her sights higher than some random fellow up in the West End for the evening. She was after a prince. Not like Prince Rudolf of Austria, wherever that was, who'd killed himself. And although she was not entrapped by an evil magician or held captive by a nasty foreign type, a *Swan Lake* or *Sleeping Beauty* kind of prince would suit. Or, given that a prince was unlikely, a heroic man, handsome and wealthy. Her sweetheart would be English – that went without saying.

Molly sighed. 'I sometimes worry about you, that's all. Anyway, what colour petticoat shall I make? I can get hold of a nice salmon pink.'

'Purple edging would go well.'

'I'll see what I can find.'

With her new petticoat, she wore a bodice trimmed with frills, and, on colder mornings, a scarlet jacket with puffed sleeves and cinched waist. Signor Coppi, their plump little Italian ballet master, was noticing her.

'*Brava*, Banbury!' He stood at the front of the stage banging his stick keeping all his dancing girls stepping in time. She caught his eye and kicked a little higher. Moments later,

Signor darted forwards to demonstrate a step – 'So, so, so' – before returning to his position. *Thump, thump* marked his stick and up went her leg.

In two nightly ballets, Rose's natural beauty – enhanced by rouged cheeks and carmine lips – shone beyond the footlights. One night, with curtain calls for *Chicago* over, she fought her way through the crush to reach her dressing room.

'Hurry up, Ivy, will you.' She was bone-tired and wanting her bed. She'd removed her make-up, dressed in street clothes, irritated Ivy was taking ages. They lived near each other so took the tram together before dashing in different directions. There had been no more outrage about the Ripper, but even so, they took the last leg home at a gallop.

She and Ivy said goodnight to Tommy – still in his job – and stepped out the stage door.

'Miss Banbury!'

Rose turned to see a young man step forwards.

Ivy nudged her, whispering, 'Oi, oi.'

'How d'you know my name?' The likes of her weren't in programmes.

'A chap can ask about, can't he?' He gave a little cough. 'Front row, second from right.'

Ivy couldn't resist. 'Didn't know you could see so well from the sixpenny seats.'

The fellow attempted a smile. 'Just wanted to say hello, introduce myself. Gerald. Perhaps I can take you and your friend…'

'Ivy.'

'…for *supper*.' He said "supper" as if it was a word he'd practised.

'Nah. It's late.'

'Another evening?' This fellow, Gerald, might be early twenties by the look of him, and judging by his frayed cuffs, he didn't have money to flash. And judging by his east London vowels, not too different to her own – though she was working on that – he didn't seem such a catch.

'Thanks anyway, Gerald, but I go straight home after work.' She turned away but Ivy caught her sleeve.

'If you've a friend who'd like to join us…' Ivy dropped a hint.

It was arranged. A foursome.

The Crown, a pub in Charing Cross Road where everyone from Theatreland gathered, was crowded, and she knew most people in the noisy, fuggy bar reeking of spilt beer. She noticed Gerald counting out coins, checking the change carefully before making his way to where they sat.

'Thanks so much, Gerald.' He handed her a pale ale without slopping a drop. 'So, what's your line of work?'

'A shipping clerk, that's me. Good prospects.' He settled next to her, smiling shyly.

Half an hour passed easily enough, though Gerald's friend had little to say for himself, and before long Ivy was making faces indicating it was time to leave.

Next day, Rose picked things over with Ivy. 'I dunno. What do you think?'

'His nails are bitten to the quick, all ragged. Seems a bit of a nervy sort to me.' That hadn't passed Rose by. 'A decent sort though. What more do you want?'

'To have my name inked on Alhambra playbills for all the world to see, that's what. Not a ballerina, never that, but a principal artiste.' She stretched an arm, tracing imagined letters. 'Miss Rose Banbury.'

'Good luck.' Ivy was shorter, plumper, and not nearly as pretty. 'If I fancied Gerald, I'd take him over from you, it's just that I don't.'

She met Gerald one more time before sending him packing. A sweetheart might be nice, but one that was fitting for an aspiring principal artiste.

Brandishing a folded copy of *The Globe*, Rose burst into her dressing room. 'Look at this, will you!'

Tousled heads looked up – yawning girls preparing for class – then they clustered around. She pointed to the entertainment column's review of *Don Quixote*.

'And here he writes, "The ever-popular Miss Rose Banbury…" Hear that? My first mention!' It was thrilling seeing her name in a newspaper. Promotion on the bill was only a matter of time.

'He must've enjoyed your little turn as a lady of Spain,' said Ivy.

'Or your legs,' came an envious voice.

'Now, now.' Evelyn raised a hand. 'That's lovely, Rose, happy for you. I know you want to get on. Me, I'm thinking of getting out.'

'Out?' Rose was startled. 'But you love dancing.'

'I'm fed up with the nights. Regular hours would be nice – selling hats or gloves. A department store, I'm thinking.'

Conversation turned to Evelyn's potential departure while Rose searched for her scissors. She'd clip out the article for Molly to add to the scrapbook.

It wasn't just *The Globe* reviewer noticing her. Across Mr Jacobi's raised baton – their musical director looking immaculate in his dress suit, moustache and beard well-clipped – Rose spotted a man in a three-pound front row seat, top hat perched on lap, who seemed to enjoy looking at her. She began to look out for him.

It was early December, she'd just turned eighteen, when she saw him waiting outside, standing apart from other stage-door Johnnies. Poised, leaning on a cane, he ignored girls who'd paused to call saucily, 'You waitin' for me, darlin'? I'm ready for a drink if you are.'

He caught her eye, tipping his silk top hat. He was tall, and not bad-looking, if he did have a rather narrow face and longish nose. Despite the chilly evening, his knee-length frock coat was open, revealing a very nice silk cravat and pin at his throat and an equally nice double-breasted waistcoat. Rose's eyes travelled down his length, taking in tailored striped trousers ending with polished shoes. She knew a thing or two about fashion and the cut of cloth, and this gentleman with a waxed moustache looked just the ticket, and he was looking at her.

'Good evening, Miss,' he said. 'I enjoyed the show enormously, and your contribution to it.'

Rose was a quick learner: well-spoken, well-dressed, ten or so years her senior.

'You noticed me then?' she postured, chin tilted, hip angled.

'You shine across the footlights. I am only surprised you have not yet been promoted. A girl such as you...' A kid-leather gloved hand waved vaguely.

She glanced at Ivy, who raised an eyebrow in an "are-you-coming-or-not?" way, but the gentleman was in no rush to leave. Neither was she.

'Arthur Roberts,' he offered. 'May I call tomorrow evening? There's a club we might—'

'We?' Ivy chipped in. 'Rose and me stick together.'

'Delighted. I have discovered Miss Banbury's name—'

'Oh, have you!' Rose looked at him under her lashes.

'And yours is...?' He smiled effortlessly at Ivy and Rose noticed his teeth weren't snaggly. This gentleman, with a lovely warm voice, was entirely presentable and passed muster at the first hurdle.

She angled her hat and smiled. 'A *club*, did you say?'

The following night, the show went well. From the wings, she watched Mr Grais's baboon and donkey circus act, amazed how well the pompadoured, striped-shirted showman trained his troupe of animals. He was a clever juggler too, rarely dropping a club. She hoped Mr Roberts was enjoying it. Then, with animals herded off, sweepers and cleaners moved on, bucket and mop in hand.

Taking her place onstage for *Chicago* – still running after all those months – she detected the lingering whiff of animals and disinfectant with top notes of floral perfumes she and other girls had doused themselves with. Rose tried to spot Mr Roberts, making sure a leg was artfully displayed through the high-cut slit of her costume when she posed.

In her dressing room, after smearing cold cream on her face and wiping off stage make-up, Rose dressed carefully in a new red jacket with leg-of-mutton sleeves and tight waist. Her green woollen skirt was flared over a pale-yellow petticoat and bum roll, and her small hat, trimmed with flowers and stiff bows, was quite the thing. When she and Ivy stepped out of the stage door, she was fashionably attired – with a distinctive feel for colour that was all her own – with only the tips of her shoes peeping out with each step.

She waved. 'Mr Roberts. Here we are!'

Arthur Roberts strode forwards. 'What a lucky man. Two ladies!' Arm in arm, they walked in the direction of Soho and in Dean Street stopped at the iron railing outside Blacks. 'Shall we?' he said.

Mr Roberts handed over his top hat and cloak. 'Evening, Watkins. Would you be so kind as to ensure a cab is waiting in an hour?' He peeled a note from a wad, returning the wallet to his pocket. 'This way, ladies.' He stood back, allowing her and Ivy to precede him. Rose took Ivy's hand and with backs straight, chins lifted, walked in.

She sniffed expensive leather upholstery and cigars. Her feet sunk into deep pile carpet without a hint of beer about it. Waiters carrying silver platters with crystal decanters attended to clients in the panel-lined room.

'Do you care for oysters?' Mr Roberts asked.

Ivy was ditched after that first evening. She trusted Mr Roberts – Arthur – not to try anything funny.

Late in December, in the Café Royal, Regent Street – its gilded ceiling and walls making it their favourite – Arthur produced a small, gift-wrapped box.

'I do hope you like this. A Christmas present, if you will.'

Inside, Rose found an enamel brooch of a single red rose with clusters of tiny clear stones. 'Oh, this is so pretty, thank you, Arthur.' She pinned it to her bodice, thinking she'd never been given anything as valuable… if they *were* diamonds.

'A rose for my Rose.' Arthur squeezed her hand, and his eyes looked kindly at her. 'Now, what shall we have?' A waiter, a long white apron around his middle, was at their table.

Christmas came and went, then in the New Year she asked to be taken dancing. Having Arthur's hand around her waist, her right hand held in his left, was delicious. Together they galloped, two-stepped and waltzed giddily around the floor. Twice a week, Arthur would wait for her at the stage door, and they'd head off for supper followed by dancing. Heavenly.

Once, at a hotel for an afternoon tango tea, Arthur taught her the Argentinian dance, vague about where he had learnt it. With her hip touching his and the beat – dum-da-dum-da – throbbing through her, she longed to unbutton the high collar of her cotton blouse.

'Rose by name, rose by nature.' Arthur laughed, touching her dimpled chin. Then, with one hand supporting her waist, the other holding her hand, he expertly dipped her into a daring swoop, looking like he might ravish her. Delicious!

Flushed, and back on both feet, she could no longer resist unbuttoning her collar button. 'Oh, I do so love dancing with you, and I imagine I've years ahead of me at the Alhambra.'

'I imagine you have!' Arthur agreed.

'That is, unless I marry.' She laughed lightly.

'Marry? Why, then I must lose you!'

Her laugh became tighter. 'Don't be silly.'

'Dear Rose, you mustn't marry too soon, as then I'd never see you.' Seeing her crestfallen face, it was his turn to look shocked. 'Oh, my dearest. I assumed... I had not thought to trouble you with... Shall we...?'

With the orchestra playing and laughing dancers swirling past, she sat next to Arthur, listening to the bare bones of his private life.

'I've mentioned I live in Esher – yes? Always that last train to catch. Did you imagine I live alone?'

'Well, family, parents...' It came to her; she'd been rather incurious and had not enquired. 'Didn't you say you went to church with your family?'

'Family, yes.' Arthur blinked rapidly. 'My, my wife... Beatrice... Bea.'

'Bea,' Rose repeated, stung by the sound. If there was a wife, then... Her breath caught in her throat, but she must know. 'And has she, have you, any chi—'

'No, no. None.' Arthur's mouth twitched and she waited for him to say more, but he moved on quickly. A detached house; a substantial garden with an orchard; the convenience to the station... Rose half listened, imagining a bumble bee taking flight from that big garden and disappearing for good... 'Rose. Rose. Are you all right, dear?' Arthur moved his chair closer still, squeezing her hands.

'Yes, Arthur.'

'Don't we have fun together?' Leaning closer, eyes sincere.

'Oh yes, Arthur.'

'You know you are special to me. You bring a great deal of joy to my life. You do believe me, don't you?'

She nodded. Then, with a silk hanky, Arthur dabbed the corners of her moist eyes, and with those unshed tears, her dreams of societal betterment dissolved. She must focus on her career more than ever.

'Molly. You think I should throw him over? It can't lead to anything.'

Molly knitted, whisking stitch after stitch from one clicking needle to another. 'In time, that would be best. I don't want you going off the rails...'

Neither did she.

'...but on the other hand, I do so love seeing my Rose growing up and becoming a lady. I never had the chance to dance.' She sighed as she stuck out a malformed foot.

'Did you ever hope to marry, Molly? You've never said.'

Molly paused, a far-away look in her eyes. 'There was a boy—'

'Oh, Molly.'

Molly held up the partly knitted bolero to ward off interruptions. 'We were sweet on each other. Went off to sea, he did.'

'Drowned? Killed?'

'Nothing like. I waited three years. By the time he came home, you'd taken up residence, and he didn't believe my story: you being a foundling—'

'What!'

'Thought I'd got fed up waiting.'

'You've never said!' Rose was aghast. 'People from the Alhambra would've backed you up.'

'Those pedlars in make-believe! Those storytellers!' Molly pursed her mouth.

Rose, rooted to the spot, whispered: 'I spoiled your life.'

'Bygones, love.' Molly set aside her knitting and got to her feet. 'And I wouldn't change a thing. Whatever love is in me, I poured into you.' She picked up the patchwork cushion she'd been leaning against and looked at it. 'And the Alhambra. Love at first sight, that was.'

'Here.' Rose took the gaudy cushion and shook up the stuffing.

'We do all right, don't we?' Molly said.

'Oh yes! We have a nice life all right, and nice things.'

It wasn't just cushions. Fabrics covering armchairs were from Monsieur Alias's remnant pile: vibrant velvets and satins, random in nature with no two chairs alike, while antimacassars were edged in lacy off-cuts. On a shelf, atop lacey doilies, Molly kept a small collection of porcelain shepherdesses.

Molly caught her eye. 'The thing is, Rose, all these suppers and dances aren't for nothing. Arthur will be wanting more from you. I don't want you to, well, you know...'

There had been chaste damp kisses on her cheek, gazing into eyes – Arthur's a watery light blue – and many soft squeezes of the hand, but in all their meetings, Arthur had not presumed more.

'There are plenty of floozies around if *that's* all he's after.' Rose jutted her chin. She liked Arthur very much and knew he enjoyed her company. That could be enough between a man and his sweetheart – couldn't it? What *did* she want of Arthur? She asked that question of herself constantly and could not see beyond the excitement of rushing offstage, changing into street clothes and knowing there would be a rendezvous with him. "Rendezvous". That was the word he used, and it sent a delicious shiver up her spine. There was something naughty about it.

'Floozy?' Molly smiled. 'No, love, that's not you.'

'I've told you he's married, no kiddies though. He's got some sort of banking job. Commutes from Esher—'

'Very nice, I should think.'

'Said I should go to the races at Esher one day. And I said, "Not likely. Why would I want to travel out of London?" And you know, he laughed at that, saying, "A short train ride from Waterloo," calling me a "funny sweet thing". But I told him the next time he bets on a winner, he can buy me a fur coat.'

In early 1894, Rose's name appeared on the bill in *Revolt of the Daughters*. She was cast as one of four modern sisters – very sporty girls – who also danced the can-can in one scene. Alhambra productions liked to include this.

'A keepsake, Arthur.' She made sure he took evidence of her success away with him, when often he left playbills behind at the end of an evening.

'I'll find a safe place for it,' he assured her. And with her eyes still on him, Arthur folded the playbill and slipped it in his jacket. 'My Rosy-Posy is making her way up, and I couldn't be prouder.'

One June evening, after the show Arthur was waiting for her in his usual spot a short distance from the stage door.

'I wonder, darling' – he had taken to calling her this, or Rosy-Posy – 'shall we take a stroll?' Rose slipped her arm into the crook of his elbow. She was his girl. 'You'll be hungry,' Arthur said. 'Supper?'

At the Café Royal, Arthur seemed preoccupied and barely ate while she tucked into her meal and chit-chatted. Did he spot her especially fierce face in the demon dance in *Sita*? Had he caught her winking just for him?

'Darling,' he said. 'I'd like to show you something – a small flat actually – close by.' Seeing her draw back, he placed a hand over hers and hurried on. 'No, no. Perfectly fine, I assure you. You see, I've been thinking. It would be rather useful if I had a place in town, and this isn't far from the theatre, so you might like to rest there.'

'That's a kind thought.' Rose was touched. The period between rehearsals and evening shows could drag if she didn't have shopping or a matinee at her own theatre or another show in the West End she wanted to catch.

'I rented it just the other week. Not far.' He stood and helped her from her chair. 'Would you care to see it?'

Once outside, his hand was on her back, propelling her forwards. They didn't have to walk far – just into Frith Street – where Arthur paused at a greengrocer shop with a door to the left.

'Handy should I fancy something to eat. Don't you agree?'

She nodded, taking close interest in a window display of a variety of apples.

'Up here,' he said, producing a key and leading her upstairs.

Inside his rented flat, Arthur hurried past the small kitchen, saying, 'Not likely to use this much, but please feel free.' She wondered if he would allow her to invite Ivy and some of the other girls.

The sitting room had two comfortable chairs and a table, though not much else. When he pushed open a door to another room, she was confronted by a solid iron-framed bed with thick sagging mattress. The pillows looked fresh enough, though the blankets needed a good shaking by the looks.

'I may stay over some nights,' Arthur said casually. 'Jolly handy if I've a late night.'

'Yes, I imagine so.'

'Racing to catch the last train can be, well, a little tiresome.'

'Tiresome,' Rose agreed. 'And tiring. You mustn't get ill, Arthur dear. I'd hate that.'

His eyes were tender. 'So sweet of you to be concerned.' As he kissed her ear, his moustache tickled, making her giggle.

They didn't stay long, and the flat was barely mentioned between them for some weeks. Rose had a key but didn't like to make use of the place.

Soon after, a parcel arrived, delivered to Rose at the theatre: a capelet of plush black velvet edged with fur.

'Arthur must've won on the horses. Very nice, don't you think?'

'I'd say.' Ivy fingered the expensive fabric.

Rose draped it over her shoulders. 'I'd like a photo portrait.'

'Well, he won't be able to keep it. His wife and all.'

'For me, then. I'd like it.' She caught sight of herself in the mirror. 'Blimey, I could be a real duchess—'

'A princess!'

She smiled, liking the idea. 'A princess in my gilded palace. That's me!'

3

THAT SUMMER, ROSE FOLLOWED *THE WESTMINSTER Gazette's* coverage of Fred Storey's court case: his agent suing him for commission he believed was owed for Fred's engagement at the Alhambra. A detail jumped out. 'Fifteen pounds a week!' To think Fred was earning that unthinkable amount for acting the fool of the Don in their adaptation of Cervante's story. The agent had been canny in the terms of the agreement.

It got her thinking. Perhaps it was time to have a chat with the Alhambra's manager when her contract was due to renew. But what about with Arthur? Should she throw him over? Or might she negotiate some sort of "arrangement"? She needed to negotiate very carefully. Arthur was no fool, and she was not a loose woman. How to steer a path and keep the best of everything?

One Saturday evening in August, Arthur was at the stage door as expected. The theatre had been unbearably hot, and Rose hurried out, fanning her face.

'Oh Arthur, get me a drink before I melt!'

At the Café Royal again, she gulped down a glass of chilled punch and before their supper arrived, they'd both ordered a second glass. Arthur never talked about his wife – naturally

– and she had no interest in the world of finance. Neither did she care to know what their prime minister's new government was up to – Arthur had discovered early on that politics wasn't for her – so she prattled about her day and the performances that evening with Arthur agreeing, 'Oh yes, darling, you were magnificent at *that* moment! And just so you know how much I admire you.' He slid a slim jewellery case across the table.

'Oh!' She admired the creamy strand of pearls resting on black velvet. 'My goodness, what a lucky girl I am.'

Arthur was on his feet, attaching it around her throat. 'Beautiful, my darling.'

Before she had time to order a second Peach Melba – those slippery peaches, raspberry sauce and ice cream far too tempting – he had paid the bill. Outside, cabs stood waiting. Somehow it seemed way too much trouble to travel home, and Arthur didn't suggest it. Without saying a word, she tucked her hand into his elbow and walked north. Outside the Lyric in Shaftesbury Avenue, they paused at the poster, *Little Christopher Columbus.*

'Have you been?' Arthur asked.

'I've so little time, though I'm sure I'd like it. Perhaps we can go togeth—'

'I'm told it's very funny.'

'We've never seen a show together. I'm free next Monday.'

They walked on, then, as if a greater force tugged them, they turned into Frith Street, and somehow they were standing at the greengrocer, looking at displayed fruit and vegetables.

'Ah, my little flat!' Arthur looked surprised as if the door had materialised from thin air.

'So it is,' Rose agreed.

Arthur hesitated. 'Shall we, my Rosy-Posy?'

She mustn't. She shouldn't. But… but… Arthur looked so handsome, and he was so kind to her.

'Why not?' She giggled, allowing herself to be guided up the stairs. With Arthur's hand on her back, she wondered if he could feel her heart racing.

Inside, nothing seemed changed. It didn't appear he was bringing fancy girls here – that went through her mind – so he managed to catch the last train to Esher of an evening. Slipping the summer shawl from her shoulders, she couldn't resist flirting.

Before she knew it, the shawl was tied around her swaying hips, arms raised, with Arthur clapping and singing. Before she knew it, she'd pulled him to his feet, and they were hip to hip in an oily tango. Before she knew it, he had danced her around the small sitting room once, twice, then through the door to the bedroom. Before she knew it, she had thrown herself on the flocky-soft mattress, perspiring, laughing her head off.

There was the heat of rapid breath as Arthur kissed her throat, the sensation of his moustache tickling her chin, whispering, 'So adorable.' His fingers began to undo buttons at the throat of her blouse. She sat up, flustered and sticky.

'No, no, wait!' She should go home to Molly, but Arthur's hands had begun to explore the line of her almost-exposed breasts all the while moaning, repeating she was simply adorable.

This was not something Rose could withstand. At that moment, she decided he must leave his wife for her. Arthur was the hero – *her* hero – and she was every maiden that ballerinas had portrayed so convincingly on the Alhambra's stage.

Rose's first disappointment was seeing Arthur undressed. Without his expensively tailored jackets and coats, despite his good height, his chest was shallow. Between his legs, his *thing* was not a surprise. Countless dressing-room doors were left ajar – mistakenly or on purpose – hasty costume changes within. More than once she'd witnessed fumbles and pokes in backstage nooks. There had been one time a member of a visiting acrobatic act flashed *his* member at her. Over the years, she'd seen them marching upright – as now – or slackly at ease. Allowing her eyes to travel down, scrutinising Arthur's body, she noted his legs were long but lacked the athletic thighs and shapely calf muscles she expected of a leading man. Arthur's limbs were spindly.

Rose's second disappointment was the act of love itself. She did not swoon, nor did raptures carry her away. 'It's a sticky business,' girls had said. 'You get used to it though, and it becomes fun.' No one had told her it might hurt – there must be something wrong with her. And she felt soiled – that was the worst of it – no longer a rosebud.

Tears would not stop. At first, they slid down her cheeks then she sat up. Gulped hiccups becoming heaving sobs.

'Darling, did I hurt you? I would not dream…' In turn, Arthur was inconsolable. 'You are adorable, I would not upset you for the world.'

After considerable petting and comforting, Rose regained her composure.

'Oh, Arthur. You won't throw me over, will you?'

'What a goose you are!' He patted her bare knee. 'I'm very fond of you. Very fond, Rosy-Posy.'

That aside, another worry *must* be talked about. 'I've not gone off the rails, have I? You know, getting in the family way.'

A blotchy rash appeared on Arthur's neck, and he began to stammer. 'You see… w-w-well…' He took a deep breath. 'You can be sure that won't happen, darling. I swear I would have taken precautions – I'm not that kind of a fellow. You, er, you know we haven't children, Bea and I…'

Rose glanced away. She hated any reference to his wife.

Arthur clasped her hands, determined to continue. 'She consulted a specialist, you see, and there's nothing wrong with her female… parts, so it must be me.' An embarrassed laugh escaped him. 'Not very manly to admit to such a thing, but in the circumstances…'

Rose withdrew her hands, not sure what to think.

'Darling, you won't throw *me* over, will you? My ballet girl means the world to me.'

A fingertip gently stroked the dimple in her chin, and sincere blue eyes looked deeply into hers, welling again with tears. 'Like soft caramels,' Arthur whispered, kissing a damp cheek.

As August progressed, Rose discovered the act that had hurt the first time did not hurt the more she and Arthur practised. Summer evenings with Arthur – and occasional afternoons – were utterly blissful and she forgave his physical shortcomings, giving herself over to the joys of loving. In that little flat, she danced burlesque stripteases that Madame Cormani had never taught her but came naturally. She peeled off a glove, flung to where Arthur sat, almost drooling. The power! He groaned, and she teased him, pressing a stockinged foot into his chest. 'Wait, you greedy boy.' Hooks must be undone, and layers of clothes removed. Rose had never imagined that naked bodies could give so much pleasure.

September progressed with an inkling something was not quite as it should be. Come October, Rose was sure. The problem must be with his wife. She was proof Arthur could sire a child, and it terrified her. Several times she tried telling Molly, only to lose her nerve. Knowing she had let Molly down was the worst of it, so she kept putting it off until one morning…

'When were you planning on telling me?' Molly's voice

cut through retching sounds as Rose hunched over the sink. Breakfast had not stayed down. Molly wrung out a cloth, passing it to her. 'What does *he* have to say about it?' Molly dried a plate, tracing the rim slowly.

Rose hadn't introduced Arthur to Molly, their worlds too far apart. She shared fun things – what they'd eaten for supper and where they'd been dancing – but she'd not told Molly of the flat.

'He doesn't know. I've not—'

'Doesn't know!' Molly banged the plate down. 'What were you thinking? You've allowed that fellow – *married*, I might add – to have his way. Really, Rose, after everything I've done for you.'

'I wanted to be sure before telling Arthur.'

The two of them sat in silence facing each other across the oil-cloth tabletop.

'Should I have done something, said something, to warn you better about *men*?' Molly said. 'I brought you up, after all.'

'No, Molly, don't blame yourself. It's me.'

'Let's see you.' Molly, all practical again, was on her feet, drawing Rose to stand, hands sliding over the rise of her stomach as if assessing her for a dress. Molly tsked.

'Here you are, not yet nineteen, unmarried and growing a child in your belly that, I'd say, is three months cooked.'

'I'd say that's about right.' When being fitted for a new costume, the seamstress, a mouthful of pins, muttered about Rose putting on weight. 'Arthur and his missus don't have children. Thought it was his problem.'

'And you believed him? Well, *this* is his problem. You've got to tell him, Rose.'

'I'm working up to it.'

In her fantasies, she imagined Arthur divorcing and marrying her. He longed for a son; he told her so. But when she tried to imagine herself in suburban Surrey filling her day with children, baking, and housework, waiting for Arthur to come home, it seemed a lonely life. Each day at the Alhambra, she could count on being among four hundred souls milling about backstage. Worse, the imagined Esher life didn't sound romantic.

'Perhaps he needn't know, Molly. Some of the girls have got rid of theirs. I was thinking, you know…'

Molly needed something to occupy her hands. She fetched her knitting. While the needles began a familiar click, click, Molly spoke carefully. 'I wish you'd said earlier. It's easier earlier. I do know someone, but it won't be, well, very nice…'

Rose met her gaze and nodded for Molly to continue.

'I can enquire. But you've got to tell Arthur—'

'No. I don't want—'

'These things cost, and Arthur should do the decent thing.'

Rose had another plan. She would pawn the beautiful rose brooch Arthur had given her. 'Pawn, mind,' she stressed to Molly. 'I want it back. You know Signor Coppi has plans for me—'

'Plans?'

'I'll no longer be billed as a "lesser artiste".' It was her destiny to be an Alhambra star, and this was a mere stumbling block. 'Might be time to look for an agent.'

'One step at a time.' Molly caught her eye. 'I'll get in touch with Mabel, then.'

'It won't hurt, will it?'

'How should I know?'

Rose turned into a narrow street off Brick Lane, terraced houses, bricks stained black with soot, snotty-nosed kids kicking a ball – and each other. She knocked at number eight.

A thin girl opened the door, staring blank-eyed. 'You're wanting Ma?'

'If she's Mabel.'

As the girl stepped back, Rose took a deep breath and crossed the threshold.

In Mabel's dingy sitting room, listening to the cries of some unfortunate having a procedure in the adjoining room, Rose felt her resolve slipping. On seeing the whey-faced female stagger out, knees buckling before dropping into a faint, Rose caught sight of a skinny woman with thinning hair shoot out, apron sploshed with blood. Mabel, then.

'Don't just stand there,' Mabel yelled, 'help her up!' But Rose backed away, turned and bolted. It would have to be a life in Esher after all, as soon as the current Mrs Roberts could be dislodged.

Arthur's face formed into an expression of shock Mr Agoust, the Alhambra's best mime artist, would be proud of. It was freezing in his flat, but at least it was private.

'Pregnant? But, Rose, darling. This is impossible. I've told you, I can't—'

'Oh, but you can, Arthur—'

'Aside from me, have there been—'

'Excuse me!' Arthur had the decency to colour as she went on. 'I'll have the baby then carry on dancing.'

Arthur nodded, saying, 'Good, good.'

They sat in silence. While she'd had time to get used to the idea, small movements in Arthur's face – cheeks twitching, eyes flickering – suggested fluttering thoughts.

Finally: 'I don't know what to suggest, Rose.'

She knew what. 'But, of course, you'll have to get a divorce and marry me.'

Arthur sat forwards. 'Impossible. Rose, how could you

imagine such a thing? When have I ever suggested marriage?'

'But the baby. This changes things.' Rose was confused. 'You've told me you wanted a family.'

'It was my dearest wish that Bea could conceive. She is my wife, Rose. I love her. You and I could never...'

Whatever else Arthur was saying escaped her. She watched his mouth moving but a buzzing sound filled her ears, while the words "love her" repeated over and over in her brain. It was true Arthur had never used those words when indulging her with a gift or fondling her breasts on the bed a few yards away. "Fond of you", Arthur might say, or "silly over you". It dawned on Rose she would never be Mrs Roberts. She recalled her thoughts about contractual arrangements. Fool! She had nothing in place. She stroked her rounded stomach. *Silly goose.*

Arthur needed time to absorb the shock and think things over. Understandable.

The next time they met, he had a plan.

'Forgive me, darling, for my earlier behaviour and anything I said that might have hurt you.' They were strolling along the Embankment. Despite it being a cold January day, Arthur favoured being somewhere public. 'So, we stay civil with each other, as we discuss our little problem.' Possibly he thought she might fly at him and scratch his face.

She glanced at the filthy Thames, wondering if he hoped she'd throw herself in. That would solve his little problem. But, of course, he didn't – too much a gentleman – and she would never. Such violent dramatic acts were best left for the stage.

'I'll not leave you wanting.' His look was tender. 'I promise I'll provide for you, and the precious child.' Rose let out a breath she hadn't realised she was holding as Arthur continued. 'I've met with my lawyer. We'll put something in place for you – regular payments – and perhaps you may like to continue with the flat. In which case, I would visit.'

Rose listened to his plan with a sinking heart. Arthur could afford to be generous, and she would not starve, but living alone with a child in that dingy flat filled her with dread.

'Let me think on it, Arthur.'

'Yes, darling.'

They were as careful with each other as if handling eggs. Arthur kissed her lightly on the forehead, tipped his hat, and they parted.

Over the coming weeks, the nearest thing to a contract was agreed. There would be a quarterly bank note she could collect from Quince and Fairfield, lawyers in Essex Street, off the Strand. The flat was hers to use, and Arthur hoped to continue to see her "down the line".

Arthur's attendances at the Alhambra tailed off. He saw one or two performances of *Ali Baba* but the broad comedy that had Rose chuckling was not for him. Mr Agoust's turn as a comic donkey did not, he said, 'Tickle my funny bone, but all those coloured electric lights: what a spectacle! And naturally,' he assured her, 'it's always a joy to see you shine across the footlights.'

There was to be no attendance at the early March opening of *A Day Out*, nor later during the run. By now, Rose was five months gone. She was discretely moved to the second row of the *corps de ballet*, and shortly after, further demoted to the back row. She did not see out the run of *A Day Out*, nor could she be cast in the summer production of *Titania*.

'But,' she assured Signor Coppi, 'I'll be back in autumn. Please keep a good part for me.'

The ballet master kissed her hand. 'There ez always a place for you in my ballets and in my 'art.'

Somehow Mrs Roberts got wind of her husband's *theatrical adventures*, as Arthur wrote, and while she could not stop monetary arrangements agreed with his lawyer, she insisted the lease on the Soho flat must be relinquished.

Rose didn't care about the flat, the scene of her undoing, but it was everything else Mrs Roberts insisted on that made her quake.

> *It is not just the flat I must give up, it is you too, Rose. I have sworn I will not see you again. It is painful, I acknowledge, but I must rebuild my marriage. I have adored my time with you, and you have my word I will not renege on my monetary arrangement for you and our child.*
>
> *My very best wishes to you, my darling, and safe passage through life.*
>
> *Your Arthur.*

Rose screwed up the letter, too shocked to cry. Had something terrible like this happened with her own mother? She could never imagine that woman as a flesh and blood person who laughed and cried. But one thing was clear, that woman – girl, perhaps – had fallen on hard times.

But she was *special*. Hadn't Madame Pitteri held her that cold evening she'd been dumped outside the theatre? Almost a *blessing*. Hadn't Molly cherished her? Wasn't she destined for a glorious life onstage? Life without dancing was unthinkable. The word that came to mind was "careless". She, who was always so careful when dusting Molly's porcelain figurines, had been remarkably careless when it mattered most, in handling herself.

During the last months of her pregnancy, Molly put in a word for her with Monsieur Alias.

'Rose, how lovely to see you!' the costumier welcomed her. Every inch of his Aladdin's cave was known to her as much as backstage Alhambra. Racks holding dozens of the same costume and labelled trunks filled rooms. Up one storey, a library piled with books on architecture, archaeology, interior designs and period dress stimulated creative ideas. Another room startled with its vibrant colours. Shelves holding bolts of soft woollens, satins, tulles; cards wrapped in yards of ribbon and cord; artificial flowers – lilies, roses, sprigs of ivy – spilled from boxes.

'This way!' The little man indicated the stairs. 'We're in the middle of a run of fairy outfits.'

Step by step, the clack of sewing machines drew her upwards.

She became one of many women preparing costumes for *Titania*, due to open in July. She mourned she would not be part of it but cheered herself up, knowing she would soon be back, treading the boards.

4

ROSE WAS ALONE AT HOME WHEN A CONTRACTION deep in her abdomen made her gasp. This was expected, but still a shock. A plan had been agreed: the woman a few doors along would fetch a midwife and send for Molly. If, at first, she'd gone off the rails, she was back on them now, an unwilling passenger on a train chugging to its destination: *you-can-not-get-off*; *you-can-not-get-off*. 'Oh, shut up. I know!'

She hoisted her right foot onto the chair, widening her knee into a deep plié that might have pleased Madame Cormani. Reaching across the mound of her belly, she could just manage the buttons of her ankle boot. She blew her cheeks as the next contraction spasmed through her body. Fumbling with a button on the left boot, she found her fingers trembling. Too much.

It was the end of May – still a sharp nip in the air. She thrust her arms through sleeves of a bright plaid jacket. It fitted across her back and shoulders with the edges halting either side of her bosom and belly. Her dress was a drab, second-hand garment, never one she'd normally wear, but it fitted. She didn't bother with a hat. Making her way down, she felt the tread of each stair.

As she paused at her neighbour's door, hand raised to

knock, an urge to be elsewhere tugged her heart as surely as this baby tugged to be born. She hesitated then turned away. With palms pressed into the aching small of her back, the short walk to the High Street had never been so long. When she got there, it was teeming. Jostling women eager to get their hands on early season strawberries and rhubarb; a whelkman, dipping low into the barrel balanced in his wheelbarrow, scooping out measure after measure for waiting customers. At the jellied eel stand, normally a feast she was greedy for, her stomach turned.

'Oh!' she yelped and leant against a barrow as a contraction took hold.

'I'll toss it all off, shall I? Give you a lift?' The costermonger gestured to his barrow holding baskets of cabbages and carrots, his tone jocular. She didn't bother answering. 'You all right, love?' An edge to his voice now. Seeing him start towards her, she gestured him away. 'The stop's not far, I can manage.'

But he accompanied her anyway, waited, then helped her navigate the steep steps.

Once on the crowded omnibus, she tried to hold herself in, arms across her belly, horrified of making a scene. Those jolts as the horses clattered onwards were too much. Walk then. Waddle, more like. Sweat trickled down her back and her armpits were clammy.

In the Strand, she gratefully accepted the arm of a woman. 'Leicester Square. Alhambra,' she said as of giving directly to a cab driver.

'Must be a good bill tonight,' the woman chuckled, 'that's all I can say.'

Laughter was beyond her. 'Wait!' Rose rested a hand against a wall, winching at a whacking ache.

'Going to get much worse before it gets better.' The woman was matter-of-fact. 'Let's get you inside.' Others were pausing to look, concerned she was about to squat in the street. The woman's hand was on her back. 'Sure I can't get a cab? Might be best, don't you think? Or here?' She indicated a pub two doors along.

Rose shook her head, clamped her lips. 'Thanks so much. I'll manage from here.' She headed towards the back of the Alhambra. It would be mortifying to be spotted by well-dressed patrons at the grand entrance who might remember seeing her onstage. Within minutes, she pushed through an unassuming door and rapped on the counter.

'Tommy! Tommy!'

'Miss Rose!' He was out from behind his desk to greet her. 'Oh my goodness.' Tommy stared as warm water pooled at her feet. 'Never mind, we'll get a mop to it. Come on now.'

He steered her through backstage corridors squeezing past musicians carrying instrument cases, performers – men, women, children, dogs – costumed and ready for the early evening show.

'Molly!'

'Rose! What on earth are you doing here?' Molly bustled forwards with that loping limp of hers, the front of her bodice stuck through with dress pins for any passing seam or hem coming adrift.

Rose found herself transferred to Molly's care and steered to the Green Room where a sewing machine clattered away.

'Quick girls, a screen!'

Feet running, doing Molly's bidding. Molly unfastened her sodden woollen dress, and Rose allowed it to be pulled off. The petticoat would remain.

'There. Over there.' She gestured to the pile of cut-offs in a corner. Both in the old Alhambra and the new, this pile was a constant. She settled herself.

'Bloody hell!' A fresh pain jagged through her, legs contracting.

Someone was loosening her bodice, bloated breasts freed from their confine, belly set to pop.

In the moment of the door opening and closing, Rose heard a bar or two of music drift in. She tried to place it. Hummed it, then just when she thought she had it, the tune escaped.

'Up you come.' Hands supported under her armpits, and with turned-out feet planted wide, she was hoisted to something like a vertical position, then steered from her nest to the large table.

Many hands scooped aside dark green cambric, pattern pieces pinned, ready for cutting.

'Robin Hood and his flaming merry men,' Molly said. 'We done the stockings.' She nodded towards dozens of long knitted stockings, dyed a uniform forest green, hanging on a line. 'Rush job. Poor Annie's taken ill.'

Rose found herself flat on her back, knees bent, inspected by Molly, four girls at a discrete distance. Molly turned to a seamstress.

'Ask front of house if any of our doctor regulars are in tonight. And be quick about it. And girls,' this to others hovering wide-eyed, 'you're going to have a lesson tonight I hope you'll never forget.'

A strong contraction shot through her body and sweat beaded her forehead. 'Wedge the door open,' she begged. 'Let me hear some life.'

Molly understood.

Passing in the corridor, a woman gave a trilling laugh as she headed to the stage. Two men were arguing: one wanted to throw something new in their turn, the other urging caution: 'Why change things if it ain't broke?' When the backstage door opened, the faintest brass section drifted up to where Rose lay like a bloater at Billingsgate market.

She reclined on cushions. Royal purples and crimson with tassels, from Ali Baba's palace no doubt. Freshly laundered towels were stacked nearby, a basin of water, cloths. A bucket appeared. 'In case you get caught short.'

'Glory be, it *hurts!*' she yelled.

As news of her predicament spread, dozens of ballet girls pressed in, chattering and jostling. Black-rimmed eyes and rouged cheeks pressed close.

Molly wasn't having any of it. 'This ain't a sideshow. One at a time. In fact, thinking on it, only one. Who's it to be, Rose?'

So Ivy, wearing her *Ali Baba* harem costume, sat chatting. 'Me and Peggy are going to The Crown later. Meeting—'

'Agh!'

'Think I told you about Alf. He's—'

'Ohh!' She dug her nails into Ivy's wrist.

'They're loving the aerial ballet—'

'Alf?'

'No, you idiot – the audience. Wish I could learn to do that, flying on wires. You should see them, Rose… Oh… Must dash.' Ivy pecked her on the cheek. 'Best of luck, old thing. Hope you're done when I get back.'

Another earthquake passed through her. She spasmed, shrieked, blasting and blinding – not so much a fish now as a coster-girl – falling back against her royal cushions.

Just then, a well-dressed gentleman appeared at the door, escorted by Tommy. He must have received an earful.

'Doctor Friedman,' the man offered. 'I received a message at my box. You, I believe,' his eyes rested on her, 'require my services. May I?' He took a step forwards.

'Evening, Doctor,' Molly beckoned him. 'Ever so pleased to see you… Girls!' She clapped her hands, and the doctor's top hat, cloak, cane, and gloves were taken from him.

The doctor – and Rose trusted he was a man of medicine

and not some quack who'd come to inspect her for his own dubious pleasure – did a quick examination.

'You'll have done this before, I'm supposing, Doctor?'

'Once or twice.' Was that a wink he gave? His eyes slid to her left hand, without a wedding ring, back to her face, where he made firm eye contact. 'And you know, Miss, er…'

'Rose. I'm Rose.'

'Miss Rose. Babies have a way of knowing what they're doing. So do mothers-to-be. I'm here to conduct the orchestra. Think of it like that.'

'Get it out of me,' she screamed.

'Wait… Wait…' the doctor urged, peering at her nether end as Molly mopped her sweating brow.

And on it went.

Ivy reappeared dressed for the next ballet and gave her another peck on the cheek. 'Do get on with it, Rose.'

Her eyes bulged, the veins in her neck stood out.

'Arrgh…'

With a ferocity that seemed to split her in two, a baby shot into the world. Molly handed shears to the doctor – no shortage of those in this room – and with the umbilical cord cut, the newborn girl made her presence known.

'Miss Rose, I'm not sure we have another dancer on our hands. Perhaps with these lungs we have a future opera diva to rival beloved Nellie Melba.'

'More likely Marie Lloyd.' Molly towelled the newborn of its waxy coating.

The doctor checked the babe, then, with flailing limbs controlled within a towel, Rose accepted the wrapped bundle into her arms. Above a pink squished face was a mass of dark spikey hair. That much she noticed. And powerful lungs.

Rose felt agitated, fresh cramps snatching her breath away.

'Normal, quite normal,' the doctor assured her. 'Still a bit more to expel. The placenta, you know.'

Rose winced. This was not nice. She squeezed her eyes, grunted, pushed. There was a slurp, and she caught a glimpse of a dark, livery, sinewy mass expelled into a carefully positioned basin. Not so much Billingsgate – more Smithfield and the knackers' yards.

Everything was too much. She lay back on her cushions, the doctor peering between her thighs. 'A small tear; it will soon mend,' he was saying.

'Have you a name in mind?' the doctor asked casually as he washed his hands. Other faces turned to her.

'Pierina,' Rose whispered. She was glad it was a girl and had drawn up a list of favourite ballerinas.

'Pierina?'

'Italian,' said Molly. 'Madame Legnani was our reigning ballerina for a time.'

'Ah, yes. I recall Madame. How she could spin like a top.'

'*Fouettés*,' Rose managed to find the word.

'I was quite enraptured. Understandable she might be honoured in this way.' The doctor pursed his lips. 'It's an unusual name, don't you agree?'

Rose had been so certain. Now she shrank into herself, suddenly defensive.

'Rina?' Voice soft.

The doctor beamed. 'A lovely name. Nina—'

'*Rina*.'

'Yes, yes. Nina. Perhaps now,' the doctor gestured to cups of tea, long gone cold, 'we might celebrate with something stronger. Don't you agree?'

'Anything can be found in a theatre, doctor, onstage or off,' said Molly, and it didn't take long for bottles and glasses to appear. Soon a party was in full swing with more artistes, stagehands and dressers arriving. Rose watched as her baby – no longer crying – was passed from hand to hand and cooed over.

'Nina!' A toast rang out, drinking vessels raised. 'To the latest addition to our Alhambra family! Nina!'

Maybe this child *should* be Nina. After all hadn't that older ballerina, Giovannina Pitteri, asked to gift her own name to her?

With the baby resettled on her chest, she felt, fully, the responsibility of motherhood. Then she felt something more tangible. She gasped, sweat beading her forehead as fresh pains shot through her.

A whimper became a cry, 'Doctor! I'm dying!'

Molly was at her side looking panicked, hands fluttering. 'You'll be all right. Everything'll be all right, love.' She took the baby from her. 'Oh… Oh… Doctor!'

But Rose knew, just knew, life was slipping away.

She was centre stage; the stage manager ordering lights to dim.

'Not yet!' she yelled. Could he hear?

The heavy stage curtain was dropping…

'Please. No!'

'Rose, love. What is it?' Molly's voice had an edge to it.

…had dropped; hem dragging on floorboards.

A trapdoor opened beneath her, and she was plummeting, fate determined to drag her low.

'No!' A cry tore from her heart. She reached up with both hands, clawing at that gossamer palace of dreams, then, as fresh tugs dragged deep in her belly, groans rose in her throat, and she gave in to the inevitable.

The doctor's voice from afar: 'Ah, I see we're not done yet!'

ACT 2

1905–1913

She will dance not in the form of a nymph, nor fairy, nor coquette, but in the form of a woman in its greatest and purest expression.

The Dancer of the Future, Isadora Duncan

5

It was early January when Walter sat next to Father watching *Peter Pan* at the Duke of York's theatre. They hadn't managed opening week, as the best tickets had been booked solid. He understood why. It was the most thrilling thing he had *ever* experienced. He longed to be Peter, or better, one of the Darling boys. There was John in pyjamas rising high above his bed, exactly, *exactly* as in his recurring dreams where he floats high in the sky, with sounds of Mother's piano playing the thread that keeps him from drifting away.

When Captain Hook peered from beneath black greasy ringlets, raving, 'Do you want a touch of the cat before you walk the plank?' Walter wiggled in discomfort. But when a laugh emanated from deep in his devilish belly and out through crimson lips stretched wide, Walter was truly terrified. But there was Father laughing heartily at his side, slapping his thigh. Seeing that villainous captain place a dagger between his teeth all the better to wield his sword, Walter screamed, 'Look out, Peter!' He knew it was make-believe, but he could almost be one of the children cutting and thrusting. 'Look out! Look out!' He shot to his feet.

'Sit down!' Father hissed. 'Or I'll have to take you out.' Walter plumped straight back into his seat. This must not be missed, no matter how terrifying. He was in awe. His senses overloaded.

Afterwards, at a fancy café that Father used to visit as a young man, they ordered cake and cocoa and Father cautioned, 'I think, son, it might be better if we spare Mother the details of our fun and frolics. We know her views on theatre and we don't want her to put the kibosh on this. She might feel you'll become over-excited.'

'I'll just say we had a pleasant time.'

'That's the ticket.'

A doctor had advised that the scarlet fever he'd survived might weaken his heart, but Father had said, 'Your heart's strong enough to withstand the excitement of a theatre show, wouldn't you say?'

Walter placed a hand over his heart, making Father smile. 'Still ticking?' Then Father became the crocodile, making ticking noises with his tongue, pretend-pouncing across the table and Walter squealed, almost upending his cup.

'I wish we could have more days like this.'

'But then they wouldn't be special. Think on *that*. Come along, darling boy, we've a train to catch.'

He slipped his hand into the safety of Father's.

Walter could not fathom why he was to be sent away to school. He appealed, begged, but Mother and Father were resolute. Again, that word Father was becoming fond of, "mollycoddling".

'Being a boarder rather than a day boy will be just the ticket,' he told Walter. 'It must get lonely with just Mother and me.'

He tried his best to dissuade them. Tears with Mother rarely worked. Her reasoning as to why he must leave home appeared vague, though increasingly he sensed her indifference.

It was the little things: a tightening between the shoulders when she felt expected to take an interest in something he said. Or a rebuff – 'I can manage quite well' – when he asked to turn the pages of her music. Once, memorably, Gregory, his piano tutor, had said, 'I say, Mrs Roberts, you'll have some competition before you know it, the speed at which your son is progressing.'

'Really?' Mother looked surprised. 'Splendid.'

'He must take after you.'

Mother gave her cool smile.

Walter was admitted to St John's, Leatherhead not as a foundationer – those boys voted to receive a free education – but as a fee-paying student. He feared, just as with his new uniform – a size too big – he would never grow into his school. St John's was an austere red-brick building set back from the road, offering little comfort, its classrooms chilly. Not a speck of colour by way of flower beds in the grounds gave joy – just a bare grassy field, torn up by rugby boots and sharp knees brought low by a tackle. Seeing a boy land face down on the greasy pitch, the air knocked out of him, he winced.

His past illness meant he was excused games. But he was not spared twice-weekly gym lessons, their ferocious drill master seemingly to delight when dividing them into teams and pouring scorn on losing sides who were slower or weaker. He was always one of the last to be selected.

Clambering over the box horse, he felt a hand cuff his head. 'Really, Roberts,' the older boy leading his team said. 'My sister could do it. She's six!'

'Sorry,' he panted, looking at smirking faces.

He baulked at climbing onto a roof to retrieve a ball, hearing a whispered, 'Cowardy, cowardy custard.' So another boy shinnied up a drain, boys cheering him on.

Music was his sanctuary. As a church school there was Chapel, and Walter, with his crystal-clear soprano, was in the choir. And then there was the piano. Mr Reed, his music master, freely admitted he was, 'An organ and choral man, but I'll do my best to push you along.' At these piano lessons, Walter would look in despair at his master's chubby fingers navigating the keyboard. He liked Mr Reed, but the hands were not elegant, not nearly as pleasing to watch as his former piano tutor's. Mr Reed was older than Father, perhaps in his fifties, Walter speculated, and here too he was no match for Gregory's handsome youthfulness.

For all Mr Reed's deficiencies at the keyboard, he knew his theory and soon introduced his pupils to a well-thumbed thick orchestral score, Beethoven's *Symphony No 5 in C Minor*. He ran a finger down the page, whistling the opening bars of the clarinet melody, past the silent trumpets and timpani to the violins.

'See this, boys? That someone can separate all these voices while keeping the overall structure in one's head.' Mr Reed rapped his skull with his knuckles. 'Admirable. Wouldn't you agree?' Walter followed his teacher's finger tracing from left to right across the staves, humming the opening, 'Da-da- da-dum,' repeating with a lower, 'da-da-da-duuum… You, boy,' he pointed, 'are a viola, and you, a bassoon. And I think, Radcliff, you should manage the cello. If you're not sure, go to the piano.'

Walter was transfixed at the complexity, the tricksiness.

Music became the paddle helping him navigate the uncertain waters of school.

At home for summer, he played all three of Erik Satie's *Gymnopédies* for Gregory with the devotion of a true disciple.

'Very nice, indeed. You're developing a real feel.' Gregory patted his hand.

'Gregory...' Walter hesitated. 'You know I've told you about Mr Reed, our music master? He's good at arranging choral parts, you know...'

From under a pile, he drew out pages of sheet music, handwritten musical notes on the staves, *Gymnopedie Number One* in careful cursive at the top of page one.

'What have we here?' Gregory turned the pages. 'Did Mr Reed arrange this?'

'*I* did. Mr Reed helped. It's for four hands, you know.'

'As I see.' Gregory tested a phrase or two, smiling. 'Let's give it a whirl!' He handed Walter his part.

Sitting side by side, Walter kept up the steadying lower register pulse, while Gregory lightly played the melody. He felt the brush of electricity on his wrist on those occasions Gregory's left wrist crossed his right. *Almost* intertwined.

'Well,' Gregory said, after they'd stumbled through. 'That was enormous fun. Well done! Let's play this again next time.'

'Yes please!'

Some weeks earlier, Walter had been curious about the strange name Satie had given his three piano pieces. Mr Reed, who had answers for what fugues, concertos or sonatas were, and ready explanations why sonatas might be called the Moonlight or the Tempest, could only raise his eyebrows. 'I've no idea. If you care to look into it, then please inform me.' He winked.

In the school's library, Walter stood on a stepladder and reached down a volume of an encyclopaedia with "G" on the spine.

The name "gymnopédie", he learnt, derived from ancient Greece where young male athletes – from a place called Sparta – would dance naked with each other in some sort of religious festival. He read it twice then snapped the dictionary shut and quickly levered it back onto the shelf. He did not tell Mr Reed the results of his research and his master did not enquire, either having forgotten, or – Walter blushed – knowing without being told.

A new dream filled his nights. He was one of those naked dancing boys.

6

'ROBERTS. TO MY OFFICE.' REVERENT RUTTY WORE HIS stern trouble-brewing face before swivelling, black robe swishing, and striding away. Walter's brain froze. What had he done? Slowly, he closed his Latin prep and followed the headmaster.

'Sit down, Roberts.' The headmaster settled behind his desk, indicating a chair opposite.

Walter hesitated, trying to read his headmaster's face between the sideburns: drooping lids, mouth pulled down by jowly cheeks. Perhaps he was not to be punished for a yet-unknown misdemeanour. Legs trembling, he sat.

'Roberts… Walter…'

He had never been called by his Christian name. A feeling of foreboding grew.

'Your mother telephoned earlier. I'm afraid she has sad news and it's fallen on me to share it with you.'

If Mother had phoned, then… 'Father?' Walter whispered.

He was met with a nod from the old man, who was, Walter realised, looking compassionate.

'Your father. Yes. An accident. One of those dratted trams collided with a cab. Driver safe, passenger and horse not so fortunate.'

'Sir, is he hurt?'

'He was injured. Taken to hospital... No, lad.' Seeing hope in Walter's eyes, it had to be spelt out. 'His injuries were severe. He is dead.'

Dead. Such a wasteland of a word. Life squashed from it.

His headmaster was by his side, a hand squeezing a shoulder. 'I'm so sorry to be the one to share this unfortunate news.'

News was reported in newspapers. Polar explorations. Strife and war. Inventions. Father dying was not *news*; it was a catastrophe.

'Rest assured your father will be at the good Lord's side. We must face our trials bravely, Roberts. I lost my mother at a young age. God guided me, and that early misfortune did not prevent me from being determined to get on with life. You must do the same.'

Walter looked around the room and wondered if this was what he was meant to aspire to. The walls of the office – school's eagle crest next to a photo of a youthful Reverent Rutty receiving a diploma, shelves with folders and crammed bookcases – began to shimmy, slip, and slope.

A memory: with Father rowing a small boat on the River Wey. 'Off adventuring, we two boys.' Father had chuckled. They'd sung "Away Away, My Heart's On Fire".

At home, Mother had song sheets from Gilbert and Sullivan's operettas she might play on rare occasions, so Walter knew the lyrics. But Father knew songs, which Mother certainly did *not*. While he rowed, Father sang in a high silly voice: *'Oh Mr Porter, what shall I do? I want to go to Birmingham and they're taking me to Crewe. Take me back to London, as quickly as you can. Oh! Mr Porter, what a silly girl I am.'*

'Silly girl to get on the wrong train,' Walter said, and Father had laughingly shrugged.

'It can happen. We all make mistakes in life.'

They had returned to the riverbank, where Mother waited with a picnic.

Walter found himself a bystander at Father's funeral. Gathered outside St Mary and St Nicholas, an ancient church, he mingled with men and women in mourning dress. Mother's face was covered with a black veil falling from her hat. Her black gown, touching the ground, was empty apart from a glistening jet brooch at her throat. It was March, still chilly. High in a holly tree, magpies squawked then one took flight, a black and white flash against grey clouds, while around him, shadowy people made their way into church.

Among the mourners were three top-hatted, well-dressed men – Father's colleagues, they told him – who attended the service but did not wait for the burial. One of them pressed a five-pound note in his hand, saying, 'Buy something memorable with it. Remember your father had a fun side to him.' He winked. 'We've been out on the town dancing, more than once.' Walter was surprised by the gesture and the comment. His memories of Father were of him arriving home each evening looking tired and not very talkative.

Father's brother, who'd travelled from Cardiff, wore a suit smelling of mothballs. He squeezed Walter's shoulder, urging him to, 'Bear up.' Father's mother was dead and his father, a preacher, too unwell to travel. For some reason, he'd never visited Wales.

His grandmother, from Exeter, was walking with Mother. 'What are your plans for the boy, Bea?' Grandmother was becoming deaf and what she thought was a whisper carried easily to where Walter stood staring at his feet.

'And Arthur's will?' one of Mother's sisters asked. 'What provisions for you and the boy?'

Never *Walter*. Why was no one using his name? And what did provisions mean? He crept nearer.

'I spoke to Mr Quince the other day,' Mother said. 'Everything is watertight, as one would expect with Arthur.'

He stepped nearer and took Mother's gloved hand in his. She started, then managed a tight smile. 'We must manage alone now, Walter.'

Some days later, he returned to school and gave back, unread, Wordsworth's volume of poems that Mr Rutty had thought might comfort him.

Music was his comfort.

For their Lent service, Mr Reed asked him to sing a solo verse in "O Love, How Deep, How Broad, How High".

'But I'm not good enough,' Walter said.

'Leave that for me to decide.'

For a week, he agonised. 'I've a sore throat,' he tried.

'Matron's lemon and ginger beverage does wonders,' Mr Reed said.

On the day of the service, stomach cramping, he hid in a toilet. *Cowardy custard*, he taunted himself. *Sissy*. There was no escape.

At a raised hand and seeing his choir master take an inbreath, his mouth drawing together to make a "F" sound, he began in his clear soprano:

'*For us he prayed; for us he taught; for us his daily works he wrought…*'

He wrote Mother letters, telling her of his choir and piano lessons. She replied once. Reverent Rutty telephoned home, learning, 'Your mother's a little unwell, nothing to worry about, she assures me, and,' he blinked, 'she said to be sure to tell you she's looking forward to seeing you when school breaks up.'

'Thank you, sir.' That was a relief.

'I very much enjoyed your solo, Roberts. Mr Reed speaks highly of your commitment.'

'Thank you, sir.'

The moment Walter opened the squeaky gate and walked up the path to the house, he sensed a change that his eyes would soon confirm. Inside he found wooden crates and wicker packing cases already sealed, with others open and partly filled. Dora's voice called through the house: 'What do you want doing with these, Ma'am?' before she came into sight holding two porcelain fruit bowls.

He stood transfixed in the disrupted parlour, belongings everywhere. 'The piano! It's not here!' He felt his heart clattering. 'Stop, Dora. What are you doing? Where's Mother?'

'Walter!' The maid's eyes widened. 'We hadn't expected you till later.' She placed the bowls down and stepped forwards to greet him.

'What are you doing?' He pulled away to shout upstairs. 'Mother!'

'Don't you know?' Dora looked shocked, uncertain. 'Your mother's mov—'

'Moving? Where?' He shook Dora's shoulders. She was small, they were eye level, and he saw she was fearful.

'Oh, Walter. I thought you must know. She wants to be close to her own family—'

'*I'm* her family,' Walter cried.

'Her Exeter family.'

Walter dropped down onto a packed case as Dora disappeared. He heard her voice calling, 'Mrs Roberts? Mrs Roberts! Walter's here.'

Mother, when she came in, removing her gardening hat, was remarkably gentle.

'Walter.' She moved forwards to hug him. 'We've a lot to

talk about. Dora, refreshments, I think.'

Dora nodded and hurried to the kitchen as Mother led him by the hand towards chairs stacked with things to pack. They moved aside a pile of cushions and settled not quite side by side, not quite facing each other.

'I am moving, Walter. This will be a big change for us both. You will not be coming with me.'

Her eyes were not cruel. She was stating a fact he must absorb. Against the sounds of Dora pottering in the kitchen and gushing water filling the kettle, Walter listened to things he could never have imagined.

'You are not my child, you see.' Mother sat very straight, hands folded on her lap. 'Arthur, Father, was your father, but I am not your real mother.'

Mother was quickly at his side, holding him steady.

'Oh, I have done this badly. I don't mean to hurt you. I didn't know how best to talk about this.' Mother's hands were trembling as much as his own. 'I'm sorry this is all a shock.' She settled back in her chair and crossed her hands on her lap. 'Now that you are twelve, you are old enough to absorb some of the truth of the world. I must tell you, no matter how painful.'

He felt a skittering in his ribs, his heart no longer keeping strict rhythm. That same heart that Mother – the woman by his side – had told him must be *especially* protected after scarlet fever. His lips clamped shut.

'Take a deep breath, Walter. Breathe deeply. You're very pale.'

She drew her chair closer, their knees almost touching.

'When you were a baby, no more than nine months, you came to live with us – we have a photo from then.' That same framed family photo – Mother sitting, a baby (him) on her lap, Father standing, one hand on her shoulder – had taken pride of place on Father's desk, in the small room he called his office. Was it packed away? Put aside now? He would check later. 'That photograph was soon after we had moved here from our old house in Esher. A fresh start in Leatherhead, only several miles away, both with good train services into London for Father. No one suspected you weren't mine.' Mother stroked her stomach, biting her lower lip.

'Who?' he squeaked. Then he cleared his throat, before repeating, 'Who is she – my real mother?'

'I never met her. But, yes…' Mother paused as Dora coughed discreetly, holding a tray with cups of tea and sandwiches. 'Just place it down.' Seeing Dora looking around for somewhere to leave their luncheon, Mother – still Mother, surely – instructed, 'The floor will do.'

Once Dora left, Mother took a breath. 'She was a performer – music halls.' Her lips pressed tight.

An image of a lithe acrobat flashed before his eyes, followed by a pretty songstress. 'A singer…?'

'A *dancing girl*!' Walter felt a drop of salivary venom hit his cheek. 'A cheap kind of girl. Don't ask me where she danced. I never asked, and your father didn't say.'

Cheap. The word sounded nasty. Nothing he associated with Father, or Mother. Or him!

'Your mother found it hard to cope, and as we didn't have children,' a blotchy patch coloured Mother's neck, 'your father requested that I… that I become your mother.'

Before Walter could think what to ask, she spoke quickly, as if releasing a secret held tight for far too long. 'I tried, but your father sinned. I did my Christian duty. I did my best.'

Duty? Is that what he was to her?

They stared at Dora's tray, neither of them inclined to eat or drink.

'Shall we go into the garden, Walter?'

Walking back and forth along the paved path edged with lavender and well-kept borders, Walter came to understand something of her struggles, and in those moments of loving her a little more came a loathing for Father. How could he do this to her? Then: how could Father do this to *him*?

Under an apple tree, he dropped to the grass, legs curled tightly into his stomach.

'We'll talk later.' Mother lightly squeezed a shoulder, then left.

After the sobbing subsided, Walter rolled onto his back and, through blurred eyes, stared upwards to where soft clouds broke up the gentle sky. He recalled Peter Pan standing legs astride, hand on hips, saying with bravado, 'Don't have a mother.' Might he find that special place for lost boys? 'Second to the right and straight on till morning.' But he was no longer a little boy on the edge of Neverland.

Mother, he found later, would be leaving to live with a sister. He had a week to decide which of his possessions he wanted to keep.

'Can't I come to Exeter?' So forlorn, it was scarcely a question.

'I considered it, Walter. Truly I did, but no, I'm sorry.' Mother sighed. 'In time, you might wish to establish relationships with your father's side of the family.'

Unlikely, Walter thought. His grandfather was a staunch Methodist, and he suspected the small amount of contact there *had* been was due to Father's "mistake".

'You're to meet Father's lawyer, Mr Quince, tomorrow. He's expecting you.'

'You'll come with me?' Voice breathless.

'I have confidence you'll not get lost. You're a big boy now, Walter.'

Second to the right, and straight on till morning.

70

Waterloo Station was busier than Walter remembered when he'd held Father's hand. In the huge concourse, he stood just under the big clock, back to a pillar, getting his bearings, anxious he wouldn't know which platform the Leatherhead train left from. Outside the station, in the commotion of dozens of horse-drawn and motorised cabs crammed together, picking up or disgorging passengers, his anxiety increased. London was impossibly big.

Again, he unfolded the map Mother had drawn, paper damp from clammy hands. He took a steadying breath and set off in what he trusted was the right direction.

He crossed the Thames and walked along the Strand. Here he counted the side streets until he reached Essex Street. Once there he easily found a sign, Quince & Fairfield, hanging above a shabby black door. It had been simpler than he'd feared.

Inside, an elderly clerk sat behind a desk covered with folders, piles of paper, inkstand and pens. Leading off were two dark, varnished doors. To the right, Mr Angus Fairfield Esq. was written in faded gold. The door to the left was marked as the territory of Mr Quince. The clerk gestured to it.

Mr Quince had a ring of grey hair circling a bald head. He wore pince-nez and cultivated a bushy moustache.

'Bang on time, Master Roberts.' He slipped his watch into a waistcoat pocket resting snuggly on his belly. 'I'm looking forward to our chat.' He came around his desk and gripped Walter's hand.

'Yes, sir.' Walter wasn't sure he was looking forward to anything the lawyer might say. He perched on the chair indicated and Mr Quince returned to his own. Behind glass cabinet doors of a dark wood bookcase were thick leather-bound tomes grouped in matching colours of brown or mossy green. A sideboard held a tray with an array of partly filled crystal decanters and drinking glasses. On the desk was a thick cardboard file, and what looked like an old shoebox, a peeling label on the side.

'These, young sir,' the lawyer patted the box and the file, 'are of particular interest to us today. You're asking why that is?'

Walter hadn't said a word.

Mr Quince narrowed his eyes, peering through his lenses. 'I have met you once before, you know.'

'Really, sir? I don't recall.'

'You wouldn't. You were just a babe in your mother's arms. For clarification, your *birth* mother sat exactly where you sit now.'

Walter squirmed, discomforted to learn this. The distant past touching the seat of his trousers.

'Why was she here, you're asking?' Mr Quince continued. 'This very office, that very spot where you sit now, was where you changed hands. From your mother's care to your father's. How about that!' He beamed.

'Father was here?'

'Oh yes. And to my knowledge, that was the last time they met, unless they broke the terms of the agreement – with Mrs Roberts, that is. But your father was an honourable man.'

Walter felt tongue-tied. Question piled onto question in his mind.

'A glass of cordial? If you were a darned sight older, I'd offer you a snifter.'

Walter found himself nursing a raspberry cordial while, after settling back in his chair, Mr Quince swirled a generous shot of an amber liquid in his own glass.

'Now, where to start? How about this box?' The lawyer blew dust off the lid and opened it. 'Would you like to see a photograph of your mother?' He drew out a cardboard frame, keeping the image to his chest. 'Yes?' The lawyer was either teasing or not wanting to overwhelm him.

'All right,' Walter answered, heart hammering.

With shaking hands, he accepted the photo. He took a sharp inbreath seeing a young woman, smiling, head tilted, gazing off to her right beyond the camera.

'Meet Rose. This is Rose Banbury.'

Walter traced the soft curve of a cheek with his finger.

'Pretty, you're thinking. I've seen your mother perform, I'll have you know.'

He met the lawyer's eyes.

'If things had gone differently for her, she could have become quite a star. There was something about Miss Banbury, those times I saw her shining in the front row of the *corps de ballet*.'

'You saw her perform, more than once?'

Mr Quince tugged on an ear, his mind drifting back to earlier days. 'With your father, on occasion. We had regular tickets for the Alhambra Theatre.'

'The Alhambra...' Walter was astounded at a hidden world revealing itself.

In the photo, Rose was sitting very straight, the portrait capturing her from the top of her wide-brimmed hat to just beyond the waist. She was all soft curves. Rounded cheeks, a dimple on her chin, a string of pearls encircling her throat. The white blouse she wore had a wide lacey collar exposing her upper chest, soft gathered fabric covered the rise of her bosom (he blushed, thinking of the word) down to her narrow waist. Draped across her shoulders was a dark velvety cape edged with fur. It was with enormous relief that Walter saw she didn't look cheap.

'Well, we must get on.' Mr Quince had taken out his watch and grunted. 'Having introduced you to the lovely Rose – we will return to that subject later – let's discuss the matter of your immediate future. Where are you to live, you're asking?'

'Yes, sir. I am.' Walter felt like a cloud pushed here and there at the whim of the wind.

'Your father made provisions, not just for your mother – and by this I refer to Rose Banbury – but for his wife – and here I refer to Beatrice Roberts, the woman you have known as your mother. And for his offspring. And here I mean you. Let's talk first of schooling. Your father intends – or I should say intended, dear man – for you to have a first-rate education. You will therefore stay at St John's for the remainder of your school days as a boarder. Are we agreed on that?'

'Yes, sir.' What else might he say?

'And during the holidays, you will board with Miss Reed, beloved sister of your music master. She has not married and keeps a good house, I am reliably told. You—'

'But I don't know her!'

'A meeting will be arranged, and I promise, if you do not see eye to eye, then we will come to another arrangement. I am doing my best to navigate a difficult passage with various interests at stake. I am your legal guardian till you reach the age of twenty-one. I represent *your* best interests as I represented your father's. Not Miss Banbury's. Not Mrs Roberts'. Yours. Are we agreed on *that*?'

Walter nodded.

'It's all here.' Mr Quince opened the folder to reveal a wadge of papers. He flicked through closely written pages and what looked like invoices or bank statements with figures scrawled on them. 'I can show you anything you care to see.'

'No, thank you, sir.'

'Excellent. Quite right. But any time, should you wish… There is not a fortune – not by any standard – but there is ample for school fees and to support you in further study. Or the steps into your manhood – whatever path you choose. Clear?' Mr Quince tilted his head.

'I think so, sir. Will I see you again?'

'Regularly. And by all means, write or telephone with any concern.'

One concern raised itself immediately. 'I'm learning piano.'

'And impressively, a little bird has told me.' Mr Quince tapped his nose. 'Let's just say that Miss Reed has something in her parlour that may interest you. And let's just say that it's an upright and tuned regularly, I am assured.'

Walter felt assured.

'Furthermore, during term time, I am informed by Mr Reed, the school, of its own volition, is employing another music master – a *professional* pianist. No doubt he will tell you.'

There was so much to remember, he wanted to hear it all over again.

'About your real mother.' Mr Quince stood, looking at the photo Walter was clutching in both hands. 'You are not required ever to meet her, but if you did wish to, she has indicated her willingness – indeed, her great desire – to meet you. Bear that in mind.'

'Yes, sir.' Walter stood and held out the photo of Rose.

'You may keep it.'

Walter imagined the dorm at school and the ragging he would receive from the boys. It might even be stolen by one of them as a prank, even destroyed.

'I'd like you to keep it, sir. I've nowhere to put it.'

'Very well.' The lawyer was about to place it back in the shoebox, then paused. 'There's a great deal to take in, I understand. But before you go, there is something more.' He reached into the box and took out a plummy-coloured scrap of fabric with twisted tassels. He shook it out, and Walter saw it was part of a shawl a woman might wear. It was old, and for some reason had been cut in half. He had no idea what this was about.

'A keepsake,' Mr Quince said. 'Your mother, Rose, wanted you to have something of her should she die. She is not dead, I repeat, but if she had died, she wanted you to have this photo of her, and this piece of shawl. Why, you're asking?'

He had been about to.

'It was very hard for her to part with you, you should understand that, but she could not give you the type of life your father could offer. This shawl,' he shook it, so it rippled, 'held some meaning for her. If you wish to meet her, you may enquire, and—'

'No, sir. I don't ever want to.'

'But later, should you decide to.'

'But why has she left me that?' This lady that gave him away. Rejected him. 'It's ruined.'

'Not ruined. Shared.' Once again, Mr Quince held it out. 'This is yours. The other half, I assume, is with your sister, Nina. Your twin.'

Walter felt the chair tilt, the floor rising to meet him.

7

Nina was ablaze, legs pumping, arms windmilling, signalling to a friend ahead of her.

'Edith!'

Having cut through Cecil Court passage, she was scampering along St Martin's Lane to get to the theatre before the half-past-two curtain-up. The Duke of York's foyer was almost empty, most people in their seats.

Edith headed up the stairs. 'Cutting it fine!'

'Sorry, sorry, couldn't get away.' Nina was close behind, overtaking. 'Come on! Keep up!' And upwards they sped to the side slips in the upper gallery.

There was no theatre in the West End Nina was not acquainted with. There was not one front of house manager she had not sussed: which of them might let her dart past with a wink, which might let her in late to watch the second half of a show for free in a hard-backed seat. There was not one lane or shortcut between theatres she couldn't find on the foggiest night.

'Had to stay behind after class,' Nina panted. 'Audition for something… missed lunch… bunked off character class, said I had a sore tummy, said—'

'Nina!'

'Had to!' That was true. Miss Stedman was not keen on her girls being corrupted by what she'd called "American dance ideas", requiring Nina to be devious.

They dropped into front-row slip seats just as the curtain rose.

'Phew!' A laugh ripped through her, earning a sharp tap on the shoulder from someone behind. She shrugged the hand off and leant her elbows on the railings, peering down at expensive seats in the circle. 'Not quite full, let's sneak down when the first dance is over,' she whispered, making a mental note of row numbers, counting seats in from the aisle.

They were here to see Isadora Duncan and find out what all the fuss was about. The American had visited before, but that was when Nina was small.

It had been an exhausting July, very hot, with every Saturday afternoon racing to one performance or other. Or, at least, when Nina could earn the price of a ticket. Twelfth birthday money from Ma and Mo had long since run out. 'You're like a blooming sponge,' Mo would say when Nina rattled off that day's show. Matinees she was allowed to attend with a friend – usually Edith – and evenings she would go with Ma, too young to travel home alone at night.

At the sound of a collective "ahh", Nina craned forwards. Their seats had limited views of the left side of the stage. Sure enough, Miss Duncan was walking to upstage centre. Here she posed in her heavy robes that reached the floor, lifting her chest, chin, arms, looking like one of those marble statues. The stage lighting was rather dim and the drapes somewhat drab. Apart from a piano and the pianist, the stage was bare, and Miss Duncan's arms, legs, feet were bare too. When the pianist began, Miss Duncan ran downstage towards the footlights, head back, arms wide, and there wasn't much by the way of undergarments under the dancer's draperies. *Interesting!*

An hour into the programme, neither she nor Edith were sure this was for them. Miss Duncan had a soft look about her, very rubbery and bendy – Nina glanced at her own knobbly elbows resting on the rail – and Miss Duncan looked so serious, even when she smiled. But there was something… something… Nina frowned, trying to decide. Seeing that curtain calls might go on for some time, she and Edith pushed past knees and took the stairs at a gallop.

'What did you like best?' Nina said.

'Different. Not ballet.'

'Definitely not ballet!'

A woman was walking far too slowly in front of her. As Nina sidestepped to pass, she accidently trod on her hem. 'Sorry!'

A scowl. 'Do watch where you're going!'

'Pick up your skirt, why don't you!' Nina shot past her. But not before hearing an indignant, 'Impudent girl!'

Out on the pavement, after a hurried goodbye to Edith, Nina raced away imitating Miss Duncan's swoops and dips. Ah! That's what the "something" was: Miss Duncan wasn't being told *what* to dance or *how* to dance. She hitched up her skirt, leaping along the pavement not caring what people thought. Maybe that's what Miss Stedman was afraid of. Her girls getting ideas of their own.

She swept into the Alhambra with an "'ello" to the stage door manager, then came to a halt, pushing back damp tendrils of hair. Those sequins were waiting to be sewn, but first Mo. No harm in a quick chat.

These days, Molly was a dresser for the Alhambra's new ballerina, Maria Bordin. 'There had been a scramble,' Ma had said, 'to get another star on board after years of drought.' Nina was usually, though not always, welcomed in the star dressing room and on occasion helped Mo, whose eyes were getting bad, though she refused to let on in case management got rid of her.

Nina knocked on the Number One dressing room. 'It's me. Can I come in?' Receiving no reply, she opened the door. Neither the ballerina nor Mo was there, so Nina didn't dare go in.

Signorina Bordin's dressing table was carefully arranged with greasepaint sticks, tubs of powder, cold cream, hairbrushes, hairpins. New pointe shoes lay nearby, trailing half-stitched ribbons. From a screen, coat hangers held a knee-length tutu and a flowing draped costume, ready for the last ballet of the evening: *L'Amour*. And with these familiar sights came smells: fresh roses and lilies in vases, slight whiffs of body odour from practice clothes flung over a chair. She inhaled a lingering hint of a perfume she knew to be from Paris. The signorina said so when she dabbed a drop behind Nina's ears one day. 'We ladies must smell delicious.'

Nina closed the door and made her way downstairs from the principals' dressing rooms. She stood back, allowing an artiste to pass with a bunch of yappy dogs in clown costumes, then made her way to the Green Room where three seamstresses were busy at it.

'Well?' Ma looked up from a sewing machine, yards of tarlatan either side of her.

'You wouldn't have liked it.' Nina perched on a table. 'For starters, it was long and there was no scenery.'

'Sounds dull.'

'And you wouldn't have liked Miss Duncan's boobies bobbing about under her robe.'

'Nina!'

She shrugged. 'It's true. I'm sure she wouldn't mind me saying so. She seemed to like her body. Not in a showy-off way but in a sort of comfortable way, if you know what I mean.'

She hopped off the table and imitated one or two moves she remembered, swaying left then right, angling her neck. Then, not attempting anything graceful, she dived into Ma's bag, where she'd find sandwiches, an apple and a bottle of cordial. She was starving.

'Tell you something, Ma. You and she could be sisters. You're about the same height and build, I should think. Definitely "no sylph!"' She laughed, repeating her teacher's favourite admonishment for galumphing pupils attempting grace.

'A sylph?' Ma looked deflated. 'I never was, and less so these days.'

For as long as she could remember, Ma had been one of Monsieur Alias's cutters and sewers. She loved visiting the little Frenchman's workshop, just a hop and skip from the theatre, where he might dart to a shelf stuffed full of rolls of fancy fabrics, asking, 'What do you think of this?' In an upper room behind rows of sewing machines, she sometimes found Ma churning out costumes. But on occasion – as today – Ma was backstage.

There had been a time when Nina had loved dressing in bits of white tarlatan, begging to have gauzy wings attached to the back of her waist and fixing a wreath of flowers to her head. She couldn't remember when that ambition died, but it had done, thread by thread.

'The only thing I'd like about being a sylph is if I could have wire attached and fly across the stage. That'd be fun.' Arms outstretched, she flung herself across the room, upending a mannequin with a half-stitched costume.

'Watch yourself, why don't you!' One of the sewing women glared at her.

'Sorry.' She set the thing upright, adjusting shoulder straps on the tacked bodice.

Today was a chock-full Saturday. Shortly, she and Ma were going to the Palace to see Maud Allan. It had taken ages to get tickets, always sold out. 'Men!' Ma grumbled. 'Bound to be men buying all the best seats when *real* dance-lovers can't buy tickets for love nor money.' The playbills showed Miss Allan looking exotic and romantic, a scanty costume covering just the bits that mattered. There'd been a rash of dancers unveiling themselves this summer, wiggling their bottoms onstage.

'You'd best get moving.' Ma nodded to tins of different colour sequins waiting to be fixed to the pile of costumes, then she rolled the edges of the fabric she was hemming, her feet beginning a rhythmic tread. Listlessly, Nina searched for a needle and unwound a length of thread. Adding sparkle to costumes would pay Ma back for the Maud Allan show, but it would take forever. Tomorrow she'd share her stories with Mo.

Neither Mo nor Ma was fussed about church, so she could look forward to a relaxing Sunday morning, all of them slopping around in dressing gowns, drinking cup after cup of tea with the only decision being which jam for the toast.

Ma 'n' Mo were almost one, and equal in importance. They'd always been in her life. If Nina were forced to choose which of them to rescue from a burning building, she doubted she could decide. She'd simply have to sacrifice herself. Die alongside them.

Twice a week, Nina took dance classes at the Stedman Ballet Academy off Tottenham Court Road. Ballet, naturally, and a range of stage dance styles.

'The Hippodrome's doing *Treasure Ship Under the Sea*,' Miss Stedman said, her upright posture demonstrating the benefits of ballet. 'I've arranged an audition for you.'

Nina was cast as a slithery sea creature. Another time, she impressed those auditioning with her springiness and became a jumping bean in *Jack and the Beanstalk*. The Academy took its cut, and the rest of her wages, bar an amount to Ma and Mo, went on theatre tickets.

If she and Ma had their differences – a growing list these days – they were united in worshiping the delectable Anna Pavlova. Three times the two of them sat, awed, in the Palace Theatre's cheap seats as the Russian ballerina flitted across the stage or flirted with her partner in a *Bacchanale*.

'She makes it such fun,' Nina whispered.

'So light,' Ma breathed. 'She might float away. And my goodness, look at *his* thighs!'

No one could help but notice Mr Mordkin's bare muscley legs. Nina admitted to a bit of a crush.

'Bet you never did anything like that.' She nudged Ma and giggled as he lifted his slender partner high above him. She found it hilarious that Ma had once played male roles.

'Well,' Ma whispered, 'we never had the training, you see. Different over there with the Czar himself supporting *real* ballet.' Schools and companies in Moscow and St Petersburg, Nina knew, with special theatres. What an idea!

Nina clapped like mad as Madame Pavlova, accepting massive bouquets, cradled them to her chest, a warm smile lighting her delicate face, Mr Mordkin bowing by her side. And the way she ran off: a lesson in artistry all its own. Here she was, back again. More and more curtain calls, Nina's palms stung. When the following act, The Musical Tramp, clattered onstage, an array of instruments strapped to his body, Nina scowled. There was no way she'd be following in Ma's footsteps into Variety theatre. Her dance world – her entire world – would be bigger and better.

8

Mr Monroe, the new piano teacher at St John's, was in his thirties and his clothes smelt of tobacco. He was more of a Beethoven man, Walter decided, watching his big frame almost obscuring the piano, massive hands pounding the keyboard.

Walter waited till Mr Monroe finished a particularly forceful passage before asking, 'You were a professional player, I was told?' Though it was hard to picture him with a full orchestra. He lacked the polish.

'Not *was*. *Am*. But don't expect a recital at Bechstein Hall any time soon.' Mr Monroe's laugh was full-throated. 'Between teaching and playing I make my living. Electric theatres.'

'Oh?'

'Mr Pyke employs me for his circuit. Shows for children in the afternoon, grown-ups at night. You'll find me at Pleasure Land, The American Bioscope, the—'

'The cinema?' Walter's eyes widened. This was something for working-class children, not St John's boys. A tutor who played in the cinema!

'New ones opening all the time. I'm in demand.' Mr Monroe grinned roguishly, turned back to the keyboard, improvising. 'What do you see on screen, Roberts?'

'I'm sorry, sir?'

'Here you are in the dark. There I am at the front, keeping up with the action.' His fingers ran away, thumping and thrumming at tremendous speed.

'A race maybe?'

'A chase! Precisely. Now what?' Mr Monroe's body swayed and from his hands came gentle tinkling runs and trills that surprised Walter by their delicacy.

'I don't know, sir.'

'Imagine, boy! You want to be a pianist. You must feel the moment. Feel the emotion you want to convey. Shut your eyes. What do you see?'

He scrunched his eyes closed. 'I'm not sure, sir.'

'An ardent lover, possibly?'

Immediately, Gregory's face floated into view. His eyes snapped open. 'Not really, sir. But it's nice.'

Mr Monroe's face dropped. 'I was hoping to touch something deeper.' He pounded his own chest.

Seeing the next of Mr Monroe's waiting pupils, sheet music tucked under an elbow, Walter gathered his books. 'Mr Monroe. Might I come one day? When you're playing?'

'To the electric theatre?' He was surprised. 'I take it you've never been.'

'Father and I were going to go,' Walter lied.

'Delighted! I'll speak to your housemaster. Perhaps invite one or two of the boys to accompany you.' Mr Monroe frowned. 'Some theatres are not in what you might call the most salubrious parts of town. Nor the audience the best behaved. I'll give thought to the best time and place.'

One Saturday, Walter walked across the grassy garden of Leicester Square with Mr Reed. It wasn't at all seedy but prettily laid out with a central fountain. The men and women sitting on benches were dressed smartly, and children running around weren't rough-looking. He glanced guiltily at the grandeur of the Alhambra with its elaborate towers, knowing something of the secrets it held, before hurrying to the next-door Bioscope.

Mr Reed had been before. 'Viewing newsreels and such. Keeping up with world affairs.'

Following refreshments in the tearoom, they went through to the small theatre, pausing to chat with Mr Monroe where he was settling behind a piano. Mr Reed looked with distrust at the long row of seats to the right of the aisle, instead guiding Walter to paired seat arrangements to the left. 'Better just the two of us. No one will disturb us in the dark.' *Should I worry about pickpockets?* Walter wondered, patting to check his coins were still there. Seeing courting couples fill the seats in front and behind and begin to cuddle, he stopped worrying about dextrous fingers reaching into his pocket.

First, there was a news reel with clips of Austrian soldiers in Bosnia and Herzegovina and King George and Queen Mary at a garden party. Then there was a comedy, *Deceived Slumming Party*. Every so often, Walter took his eyes off the screen to watch Mr Monroe hunched over the piano, glancing at the screen as if it were a conductor, indicating how he should play. Walter watched as big dogs and small dogs, one by one, were lifted and fed into a pretend grinder, Mr Monroe making crunching sounds. With a wheel turning, a string of sausages emerged. Hearing Mr Reed laughing loudly, Walter allowed himself to let go. First came small, squashed laughs that didn't know how to be out in the world, then a loud laugh from deep in his chest his choral master seemed pleased to hear.

Outside the cinema, blinking at the brightness of the day, he stopped to have a good look at the Alhambra.

Mr Reed was watching him keenly.

'Any time, Walter. Just say. Mr Quince believes she still works here.' He nodded to the imposing theatre. 'If you wish to meet her.'

Maybe she was one of the women heading through the big doors, or maybe that was her – the one who'd just come out and was now stepping up into a cab. And his sister? What of her? It was odd to think that Father had come here often. And Mr Quince. Even teachers from his school – Mr Monroe and Mr Reed – came to entertain or be entertained. If they all came, then the West End couldn't be *that* wicked.

'Just say the word,' Mr Reed said again as they set off in the direction of Waterloo station.

Glancing back at the Alhambra, he felt a prickling on his skin. Mother would not approve, but then Mother had abandoned him, just as Rose had done.

He allowed school life to engulf him. Mr Quince wrote, enquiring after his health and ending with the same question: if he felt ready to meet Rose, he may. Walter considered it for a week, before replying politely, 'No thank you.'

9

'Ma, take a look!' Nina flourished the latest edition of *Votes for Women*, with news from the National Women's Social and Political Union, under Ma's nose. She flipped through the pages. 'See! I want to join!'

'What? You expect me to collect you from a police station for chucking a brick through a window?'

'Not *them*. This.' She pointed to an advert. 'Mrs Holt's classes aren't difficult to get to. And she trained with Raymond Duncan, Isadora's brother. She says, "Grace and supplement of movement are necessary for a woman's well-being and charm."'

'Are they indeed,' Ma said. 'No harm trying.'

Wearing flowing draperies, her *passion* became bare-foot dancing, learning to ebb and flow. Her plump teacher would stand hand to heart and begin her stories, 'When Mr Duncan said...' so that Nina felt a mere breath away from his famous sister. In the church hall that Mrs Holt hired, Nina would lift her chest and arms, leaping in unbounded skips – 'Feel the breath in your lungs, filling your heart, girls' – gaining height with each inhalation. Then she'd exhale, sinking into poses only to breathe and gather herself again. Locating her solar plexus under a knobbly rib cage was tricky, and any level of grace an ongoing endeavour. But Nina was nothing if not an enthusiastic pupil. For a time.

She longed to canter ahead, unseen roots holding her back.

On her fourteenth birthday, Ma and Mo sang, 'Happy birthday, dear Nina 'n' Walter…' and there were two cakes as always. This brother who'd been given away was a shadowy figure featuring every 29th May only to disappear for another year. Walter's cake would be sent to him, Ma used to insist. Some years earlier, it had been a surprise when a child from a big family down the street called out, 'Mama says to tell your ma, thanks for the cake!' that Nina realised where Walter's cake really went. Then she'd learnt the full story from Ma: how she'd been in love, how there'd been a handsome man, how she'd not managed to keep Walter… Once the story was told, Nina didn't think of it again.

One day, the front door banged shut and Ma yelled, 'Molly? You here?'

'Just me,' she called out.

When Ma appeared, she didn't look quite herself. 'Oh. Oh!' was all she could say. Whatever had happened had sent Ma into a spin. 'Walter's asked to meet.' Her eyes were bright. 'Mr Quince sent word—'

'Who's Mr Quince when he's at home?'

'A lawyer. Your father's. I can't believe it. I'm so excited! After all this time!'

'Oh.'

While Ma jigged about, Nina felt heavy, as if there was a stone in her stomach. It was one thing to have a brother with a cake baked for him each year. It was another thing to have him claim a part of Ma.

Ma talked on about where to meet and what she might

wear, whether she should have her hair done and what he might look like. 'I'll tell you all about it.'

'I'm coming too, Ma!'

'Not the first time, love. This will just be me and Walter.'

'I want to come. Why can't I come?'

'Mr Quince says so. And I say so. That'll be best.'

'Well, don't bring him here! I don't want him here!'

'Oh, no, love. It'll be somewhere else.'

The corners of Nina's mouth drew down. She wished this Walter Roberts had not piped up but had left them alone. *Me, Ma 'n' Mo.* That was enough. Had always been.

She was resolute. From now on, she hated Walter.

10

'WALTER! MY OWN DARLING BOY!'

Walter met her eyes and instantly saw this was a terrible mistake.

A frizz of orange hair, which could not be natural, was piled high on her head, and her broad-brimmed red hat was festooned with pink roses. As the woman pushed back her chair and got to her feet, a striped lavender and yellow dress was revealed with a high lacey collar, upper sleeves puffed, waist encircled by a wide red sash with a rosette. He took an involuntary step back. Were ladies' day fashions so bold? Mother dressed soberly. A glance around the café suggested not *all* ladies were as colourful. With her corseted bosom, she was like a prow of a ship bearing down on him. 'Excusie, excuse me,' she was saying to those in her way. This couldn't be the same pretty lady in the studio portrait. Could it? But of course, this was Rose. This was his real mother. That dimple on her chin now almost buried in plumpness. It must be years since that posed photograph, and the woman before him had changed.

A few minutes earlier, when approaching the Café Royal, he recalled that special time with Father following *Peter Pan*. 'I used to dine here as a young man,' Father had said. With *her*!

Now he stood rooted, just inside the door.

Run! Flee! But too much trouble had been taken for this. First, the decision: 'Where might they rendezvous?' as Mr Quince had put it. Did he want to meet at their office? Too stuffy, Walter decided. 'School?' Mr Reed had suggested. Definitely not! So Rose Banbury had named this place and Walter hadn't registered it. She would recognise him by his school uniform, and he would recognise her from her photograph. 'Well, that's decided.' Mr Reed had smiled at Walter. 'Now let's go over some of the questions you may like to ask. If you feel flustered, they may fly from your mind.'

'Oh, Walter, my boy, I've waited so long for this.' At the touch of her hand to his cheek, he jerked back. *Don't touch me*, he wanted to yell. But could not. Could only endure.

'Come, come, I've ordered tea!' She led him back to the table where she'd left her coat – 'Excuse us. Excusie' – and diners scraped chairs to make way.

They faced one another across the small table, he with his hands folded on his lap, body pushed back, she with elbows on the table, face craning forwards.

'What should I call you?' Walter asked.

'Oh, listen to your lovely voice! Nina calls me Ma. You're welcome to do the same.'

The casualness with which she mentioned his sister's name caught him unawares. Mr Quince had mentioned Nina, but Walter had packed that thought away in the shoebox and left it with the lawyer along with the photo and the tatty shawl.

'Ma...'

Seeing his reluctance, she hurried on. 'But you're welcome to call me Rose. I wouldn't mind, you know. After all, we don't know each other. Not yet. But, oh, Walter...' Rose's eyes became rounder as she fought back tears. 'You must know I never stopped thinking of you. Never!'

The tiniest chink opened in his heart. That was a nice thought. But so much better if it were Mother, in Exeter.

A bustle as a tray of tea and a tiered plate of dainty sandwiches and cakes arrived in the hands of an elderly waiter.

'Here you are, Rose darlin'. And this handsome young fellow must be your Walter.'

'And doesn't he remind you of Arthur?'

Did everyone know his business? His cheeks flamed. Then Rose grabbed his hand, which he must have removed from his lap and placed on the table. He felt fingers on a wrist where it showed below a cuff.

'And I reckon he'll shoot up before long. How tall are you, Walter? Nina's nearly reached me now. Let's see you.'

To his horror, Rose removed her hat and tugged him to his feet. There, amid the potted palms, the nicely dressed men and women enjoying afternoon tea, she had him standing back-to-back while the waiter, who must have been born there, measured them. Before placing the empty tray on Rose's head, he wiped it on his white waist apron.

'You're wearing heels, Rose. That's cheating.'

'I'll bend my knees a bit.' Walter felt her slide down a little, and the waiter gave his verdict.

'An inch or two to go!'

Rose was delighted. 'I've not been totally left behind. Come now, this tea will be stewed.'

Why must tea and sandwiches feature when there are difficult things to discuss? He managed a sip of tea but, with a knot in his stomach, could not begin on a triangular egg-filled sandwich.

'Where to begin, Walter?' Rose asked, reaching for a cream-filled cake, with icing and a cherry on top. 'I'm tempted by this. Don't let me eat them all. Do have one.'

He took a breath and began. 'I… I want to know why you gave me away.'

'Oh, my, no mucking around!' Rose jerked back. 'You're a one, aren't you?' She toyed with her cup, a nervous giggle, almost a sigh. 'The thing is, Walter, I never had any chance of marrying your father. I wanted to, of course, but that wasn't to be.'

He nodded. Father was married to Mother.

'Looking after one baby is tough, but looking after two is well-nigh impossible. Molly helped but—'

'Molly?' Another sister?

'She brought me up. You'll meet her,' Walter planned not to, 'but I wanted to continue as a ballet girl. Perhaps they've told you?' Rose tilted her head, lifting an arm elegantly above her.

Walter could not imagine her flitting around the stage, but he nodded, encouragingly.

'Your father wanted the best for you, which I couldn't offer. Simple as that.' Rose sighed. 'I had to agree to his wife's demands. So I didn't ever get to see you, and if Arthur hadn't died, poor man, I never would.' Rose grasped both his hands in hers and squeezed them. 'Oh, you don't know how often I've dreamt of this moment. Nina wanted to come, you know, had to fight her off. Just you and me for this special day.'

Rose chatted easily, as if they'd always known each other. All Walter could do was nod. Her dancing days were long behind her, he learnt, but his sister danced.

'My contribution to the Alhambra is costumes, these days. And you, Walter. I long to hear.'

He didn't want to tell her much. 'Well, Mr Monroe, my piano teacher, thinks I'm coming along nicely.'

'You must have inherited that from me. I was a highly musical dancer. Mind you, your father was a lovely dancer and had a fine voice. But you know that.'

Was he? Had he? Walter realised how little he knew about Father. When he was younger, he'd imagined he'd inherited Mother's musical talents. He sank further into his chair.

He tried to remember other questions he had rehearsed with Mr Reed, but his mind was blank. He longed to leave and retreat to the orderly life of St John's: a place that, over time, he had grown into.

He stared at his mother in her gaudy outfit with those East End flattened vowels. Tears pricked his eyes, and he silently prayed, *Dear Lord. Why her?* There was no getting away from it: Rose was *common*. Just as Mother had said.

'Rose so enjoyed meeting you,' Mr Quince said when he telephoned. 'You are thinking another meeting is in order?'

'I'm rather busy, sir. Not yet.'

A month later came a letter, the lawyer explaining the next financial arrangement, before ending: *Furthermore, have you considered another meeting with Rose, or your sister? Oh dear! I am in danger of following that wily Cato the Elder's example. You may recall how that statesman ended his debates, whatever the subject: "Furthermore, I consider that Carthage must be destroyed." But I am encouraged, as we know how persistence paid off.*

Walter refused again. And again.

Music was his retreat. Claude Debussy's *Clair de Lune* rose dreamily from his hands at the keyboard, and he would spend hours working on Gabriel Fauré's moody *Nocturnes*. The French composers suited his tastes, and he began to explore the music of Maurice Ravel. That aside, French lessons were worth paying attention to. He imagined studying in Paris when he was older, and for that he needed to be fluent.

Images of Gregory's beauty filled his mind, and he pushed out unwanted, unnatural thoughts. Gregory in a flowing white shirt open to the waist, pearly white-skinned chest revealed, sitting next to him at a piano, body swaying in rapture. He woke distressed and ashamed from a dream where he and Gregory cuddled in bed, both in fleecy pyjamas. He had no idea where Gregory was these days; like so many others – Father, Mother – Gregory was no longer in his life.

There had been a school visit to the British Museum where a sniggering classmate drew him to a Roman statue, eye level with a marble penis. The visit passed quickly. As he became familiar with London, he found occasion to visit the museum by himself. In the galleries, he took his time drinking in the beauty of the male form, staring frankly at full-frontal statues. Was it *normal* to be naked in antiquity? At a Greek discus thrower, caught in the action of throwing, muscled chest rippling, Walter pictured dancing naked together. Sensing a museum guard staring, he moved on.

When he returned to school, he glanced up at the school motto carved into a stone arch. *Quae Sursum sunt quaerite.* "Seek those things that are above". Those words etched deeper into his soul.

At a piano he played Satie's three *Gymnopédies* over and over. Thinking of those statues. Thinking of Gregory's delicate hands. Thinking what Gregory's undressed body might look like as he peeled off his outer clothing.

Music was the gift he had been granted, and he wanted to reach into the very soul of it. Here was beauty. Here was something pure if only he could rid himself of the rest.

11

'Poor King. I'd like to pay my respects.' Rose had been heartbroken at news of his death – barely nine years on the throne. 'Will you come with me, Molly?'

'Not sure I'm up to standing so long, and you know, my eyes and all.'

Molly had started bumping into things, vision blurred. 'A bit worried about keeping my job,' she'd said one night, so they'd visited a doctor, only to be told, 'It's likely to get worse.' Amongst other things, Rose fretted about Molly.

In her broad-brimmed black hat, her body stuffed into her best black dress, mackintosh buttoned up, she set off in the rain. From under her umbrella, she peered at a street clogged with animals and machines. She never knew if she'd be getting a horse bus or a motor bus. Even, for a short time, she had ridden an electric one. The world was in such a rush these days.

Approaching the Palace of Westminster, she joined a long queue. 'Here, have one of my buns before they turn to pulp,' someone offered. 'How far've you come?' they asked each other. To take her mind off soaking feet, she sang along with the military band to "Praise, My Soul, the King of Heaven".

Inside Westminster Hall, shuffling forwards, until there

she was, Rose Banbury, in the presence of His Majesty. There he was, King Edward, raised high on a dais, two crowns atop the draped coffin. Scarlet-uniformed guards and Beefeaters in full regalia, standing to attention, heads bowed. This was theatre and Rose wouldn't have missed it for the world. She had a moment to pause, place her hands together, curtsey and whisper, 'God bless, Your Majesty,' then it was over.

As she trudged home from the bus stop, her umbrella barely protecting her from the driving rain, her thoughts turned from the royal family in mourning to her own. Still no word. Every so often, she would drop by Mr Quince's office and before the words were out of her mouth, the lawyer would say, 'Ah, Miss Banbury. You're asking if Walter has spoken of you? The answer is no. You're wondering if we have enquired of him? Yes, regularly. Walter prefers that we write and in turn he keeps us informed of his studies, and you'll be pleased to know your young fellow is progressing admirably. We must not force these other matters.'

These 'other matters' were Walter wanting, surely *longing*, to get to know her, curious to meet Nina. But he resisted, and it hurt. More than anything, she wanted to be loved by this stranger. When a letter arrived from Mr Quince with something extra about Arthur's estate, her heart fluttered, hoping the envelope hid another from Walter. She imagined it starting, "Dearest Mother, forgive me…" from a son "sorrowful" or "remorseful" on not being dutiful. *You're a blooming idiot,* she'd tell herself.

It was ten months since she'd met Walter, and Rose could acknowledge it had not gone well. She had wanted it to be perfect, but they were out of joint and his embarrassment obvious. Thinking back on it – as she did frequently – her eyes welled up and she wanted the doldrums to be over. 'Self-pity never served anyone,' Molly would say.

Nina was a different kettle of fish. Her daughter showed no interest in meeting Walter. 'Ma, you should forget about him. He thinks he's too grand to be part of our family. And no more cakes for him on birthdays. I'm not having my day spoilt.'

Children! Her daughter barely needed her, and her son was invisible. Nina had been brought up to be independent and from an early age had a key to the front door. She would organise her own clothes, schoolwork, get herself off to dance class, now she earned a living on the boards. When she or Molly tried to agree how far Nina was allowed to travel by herself, they would hear, 'Oh, I've already been there, it's the end of the tram line,' or, 'Oh, I saw that last week. Didn't I tell you?' when discussing suitable shows. And maybe she had. Rose was often too tired to keep up. And Nina's ideas! Rose felt herself out of step with her daughter.

Since attending Miss Holt's classes, Nina insisted: 'It's so freeing, Ma, dancing barefoot without corsets. I do wish you'd get rid of yours.' Nina had prodded her upholstered waist. 'You're so old-fashioned, Ma, and you're not old. I wish you'd let me choose your dresses – lovely high waists and long lines.'

'I'm happy as I am, thanks,' she said.

'You could still wear lighter corsets.'

'Leave me be.'

Nina was a survivor, but Rose fretted on and on about the son who eluded her.

As soon as she'd given birth to Nina backstage at the Alhambra, she had been lifted and deposited back on the cutting table, swept clear of bottles and glasses, and it all began again. The second baby came quickly, without too much pain and fuss. 'This wee man was sleeping through the show,' the doctor told her cheerfully. And the baby was calm. Smaller than his sister, with the same shock of dark hair.

And Rose was in shock. Suddenly frightened at what she begun those many months earlier. She was quite sober but the well-wishers – helpers and hangers-on – were in no mood to stop partying.

'Twins!'

'My Lord, girl, you don't do things by half!'

'Any more up there to come out, heh, Rose?'

'Whatcha goin' to call this one?'

She looked blankly at the sleeping baby in her arms. All her favourites from ballets and operettas were girls' names. There was Hubert, she supposed. She recalled Madame Marie, in travesty, taking the prince's role in their Christmas production of *The Sleeping Beauty*. She adored that ballet – and she'd been promoted to the front line of *the corps de ballet* – but the name didn't appeal.

'May I?' Doctor Friedman spoke softly. 'Miss Rose, might I offer my name?' He seemed overcome by shyness. 'Walter.'

'Why not.' Rose shrugged. 'It's as good as anything. That'll do.'

If Doctor Friedman was taken aback by her lack of enthusiasm, he was too polite to show it.

'A toast then. To Master Walter, and the delectable Miss Nina...'

'Rina,' she tried again. But the party had grown since word had spread that drink was flowing, and her voice was not heard.

'...and may their journey through life be joyous and healthful,' the doctor concluded.

'And better luck than yours, eh Rose!' some wag offered.

Rose found herself with two babies in her arms, exhausted and out of her depth.

After Walter had been taken to live with Arthur, she had dared hope she might continue dancing. Dear Signor Coppi had welcomed her enthusiastically. 'I think a Dryad, yes, that will suit, then I need more Canadian Troopers. Excellent!' And there she was back onstage in *Victoria and Merrie England* – music by Mr Arthur Sullivan himself. Remembering all those marches and processions on the jam-packed stage made her smile.

Nina was two by then and Rose was taken off guard to find stagehands yelling to, 'Get that flaming kid outta here!' Once, a carpenter nailed Nina into a box to shut her up. Rose pulled the nails out with the heel of her shoe and took her screaming child to Molly.

'I don't understand! Everyone was kind to me when I was little.'

Molly snorted. 'Memories play tricks. You were tolerated. But things have changed since them days.' Molly went on ironing, a dresser now, taking care of principal dancers like Louise Agoust and Lina Campana.

One day, the stage manager appeared at the dressing room Rose shared, a squawking child under an arm.

'Miss Banbury,' the puce-face man gasped, gripping his top hat as one of Nina's flailing arms connected with the rim. 'I deal with performing dogs, seals, monkeys, but unless this child has a licence to perform, she cannot, *must* not, be here.'

With her stomach dropping, Rose accepted Nina into her arms. It was a terrible moment: Nina sobbing, for whatever reason, and tears pouring down her own face. Failure is horrible to confront. Launching herself up back onto the stage was a momentary flight of fancy she could not sustain. She stroked Nina's hair, whispering, 'There, there,' consoling her distressed child. 'There, there.' She rocked back and forth consoling herself.

Soon after, she moved from dancer to seamstress for Monsieur Alias at Soho Square, turning out costumes at an industrial pace, just as Mr Ford was doing with his motor cars in Detroit.

Reaching her door after the King's funeral, Rose shook and closed her umbrella. Despite herself, she couldn't help but hope there might be a "Dearest Mother" letter waiting. She didn't have gentleman admirers so looked to her distant son. With his birthday less than two weeks away, she was hoping he might suggest a get-together. She stepped into her house of women, calling, 'I'm home,' hoping someone had the tea started. 'His coffin! Oh, you should have been there!'

But Nina was not home, nor was Molly, nor was there a letter on the doormat – just a demand to pay the gas bill. Bending to remove her boots, Rose noticed dog shit clinging to a sole. 'Typical!'

Standing in sodden stockings, she considered that no matter how high she aimed, something nasty pulled her down. She seemed destined to be a woman of the earth.

12

One Saturday afternoon, Nina was due at her usual ballet class.

'I'll meet you there,' Ma said. 'Been ages since I watched you. We'll shop afterwards.' Nina's coat was far too skimpy.

In centre practice, Nina was standing next to a dance friend, Hilda, keeping her balance in a slow *adagio* sequence, unfolding her left leg in a *développé*. When she'd negotiated that, she moved to stand, front leg extended, touching the ground in a *tendu*, arms in high fourth.

'Breathe into the tips of your fingers,' Miss Stedman urged as their regular pianist played a flowing tune. With her head turned towards what had been an audience of one – her teacher – she spotted that Ma was slipping into one of the wooden chairs at the front. And there was someone with her: a young man – no, a boy. Ma patted the seat next to her, but he didn't sit. She stared at the slender youth. He was about her age, fidgeting with the buttons on his jacket, stealing glances at the girls in the studio. Briefly, he met her gaze before his eyes flickered away. Nina jerked back, feeling as if someone had walloped her in the stomach.

Her face turned a fiery beetroot. Treachery! There had been a time when she'd wanted to meet Walter, then she wanted to forget him, wanted Ma to forget him. Something had been brewing, and she had been left out. *Excluded.* Ma must have met with Walter without her knowing. How dare she! And Mo? Was she part of this conspiracy? Half listening to Miss Stedman reel off an enchainment – hands mimicking the chain of steps she wanted her pupils to stitch together – Nina's brain whirled.

Here were the two of them together. No, the *three* of them in the same room for the first time in fifteen years. Nina was trapped, could not storm out. Thank goodness the wobbly bits of class had ended. She breathed deeply. This was a good time to locate her solar plexus and centre herself. While whipping around in a pirouette, she noticed Walter had edged nearer the piano, taking more interest in the music than the perspiring, aspiring clutch of girls in white practice dresses, broad ribbons around their foreheads. Hmm! If he *had* to be here, he could at least be watching *her.*

Finally, class ended. She managed a tight-lipped reverence – a wooden-armed *port de bras*, dipping into a hasty curtsey, muttering, 'Thank you, Miss Stedman,' called, 'Bye,' to Hilda, then stalked out, chin lifted, refusing to meet Ma's eyes.

'Nina! Please come and meet—'

But she was gone, letting the door slam behind her.

Nina avoided her mother for a week. One day she hung around outside the Alhambra's stage door having a smoke – she daren't let Ma know she was experimenting – then headed to the star dressing room. A performance was in full swing, so Mo was clearing away used costumes and preparing the next ballet.

'Stop mucking around with Madame's make-up.' Mo slapped her hand away. 'If she catches you, I'll be for it.' Mo peered over her round-framed spectacles. 'Not like you to sulk. Let's have it.'

But she could feel her lower lip protruding. Pathetic at her age! She longed to be grown up yet hold on to what was familiar. But change was happening – not just in her own body, but at the Alhambra. The current crop of ballets were feeble affairs to her mind – the latest a skit set on a beach that mocked her beloved Madame Pavlova and Monsieur Mordkin. When she watched from the highest tiers, it was clear that audiences no longer flocked to their theatre. There were better, more entertaining offerings elsewhere. Ma 'n' Mo acknowledged it, harking back to the good old days. 'It's a question of what dies first,' Mo said, 'ballets at the Alhambra or me backstage or home in my bed – God willing.' That made Nina anxious. Mo wasn't old but she had terrible headaches and complained about her eyes.

Mo, damp cloth in hand, wiped sweat stains from the armpits of a discarded tutu, and Nina felt a stirring of tenderness for this woman who was as much of a grandmother as anyone could be.

'Here, let me.' She took the long tutu and hung it up. Mo leant heavily against a counter, then plumped into a chair.

'Look, love,' Mo began, 'I know what's bothering you and you're being selfish. Don't give me that look.'

'Selfish? How can you?'

'Don't you dare dash out! I can't chase you.'

Instead, she crossed her arms and leant against the door, mouth shut.

'Think of your ma—'

'I do!'

'Shut up and let me speak!' Now Mo folded her arms. 'I don't hold with notions of shame and sin – unless we're talking murder. It was enough my poor ma was accused of sinning to cause this.' Mo stuck out a sturdy support boot. 'If I had believed such a foolish thing – about sin, I mean –

it would've been the Foundling Hospital for your ma who might've become, well... Thing is, Nina, we done our best to bring you up properly. And we done all right, ain't we?'

She nodded. Years earlier, she'd learnt what "bastard" meant and gave the girl who called her that a black eye. She knew many girls from better-off, respectable families. She also knew grimy-necked children who were far worse off, who didn't know where the next meal would come from.

And then there was the Alhambra. Other girls would listen wide-eyed to her backstage gossip. What's more, she charged her non-theatre friends for autographs from starry performers. Once, she'd stolen a cravat she swore had been worn by Basil Hallam, and that money went towards Miss St Denis's show at the Scala.

'Your ma has hankered for Walter for as many years as you've been on this earth. You think it was easy for her to give up a child?'

"Course not.'

'But she wanted the best for you both, and Arthur Roberts offered Walter that chance.'

'And he's had a fine old life, hasn't he?' Nina couldn't keep the envy from her voice.

'Some things are very fine, as far as I know.' Mo pressed her lips together. 'Others not so fine.'

'Him and Ma, how many times have they met?' She felt like a jealous wife curious about an affair.

'One other occasion.'

That was a relief. Nina had been imagining them meeting time after time, laughing and chatting, sharing tea and cakes at a fancy café.

'It was that lawyer who got things moving,' Mo chuckled, 'your ma pestered him, and he gave your brother a good talking to. So there you are. Thing is, Nina, your ma wants you and

Walter to get to know each other. He agreed to that, so—'

'All right. What's next then?'

'Blimey. That's a quick turnaround.'

'May as well get on with it. You tell Ma, or shall I?'

'You're a one!' Mo chuckled. 'Come here.' She spread her arms.

She crossed to where Mo sat, knelt, accepting her hug, and squeezed her in return.

In Mr Quince's office, Nina, wearing a new ankle-length hobble skirt, stood barely a foot from her brother, who wore his jacket fully buttoned. She accepted his extended hand. His clasp was rather soft, so she squeezed his fingers, enjoying seeing him flinch.

'Well, well. What a day this is! What a day, indeed!' Mr Quince's voice rang out.

'Oh, my children!' Within seconds, Ma had wrapped her arms around them both, as if she would never let them go.

She sensed Walter tighten and inwardly smiled. He would have to get used to their ways, as Ma and Mo were huggers. She counted three seconds till Walter extracted himself, stepped back and tidied his hair.

'I think we can agree that a celebration is called for.' The decanters were indicated. 'Wine? Sherry? I have some excellent Madeira. We are all quite grown enough – Master Walter and Miss Nina – wouldn't you say, Miss Banbury?' Mr Quince raised an eyebrow at Ma as if Ma had the slightest authority over her son.

Ma nodded. 'Yes, yes. No harm.'

Nina had sampled a fair range of alcohol: artistes backstage, ever ready to share a drink and their woes or tales of glory days, even with a child.

'A Madeira for me, if you please.' Nina spoke in what she hoped was a "good" voice.

'And I will have the same, thank you, sir.'

Her eyes widened. Walter spoke so nicely. How could they be kin?

With a sherry in Ma's hand, and what smelt like whisky in the lawyer's, the four of them stood in a small circle. Whereas Mr Quince beamed, at ease, Nina felt she'd been thrust onto stage without learning her steps. Ma and Walter looked as if they felt the same.

'A toast.' Mr Quince raised his glass. 'To reuniting the Banbury and Roberts faction of this family. You will all be thinking what a thrill this is, and I couldn't agree more. The family!'

'The family,' they echoed dutifully, and sipped. Walter looked like he might choke on the words, but Ma was beaming.

Mr Quince drew Ma aside, asking her about the latest productions at the Alhambra. Crafty man! She could talk about that all afternoon. Nina was left facing her brother, both fiddling with the stems of their glasses, occasionally taking tiny sips.

They were about the same height, she noticed. She had reached her full height of five foot six – a little shorter than Ma – while he, likely, still had some growing to do. Boys generally did at their age. *Their* age! How odd to know exactly when and where this stranger was born. She observed they had the same long faces, and similar shaped, quite sharp, noses. Nothing like Ma. Maybe they took after Arthur Roberts, but Nina had never seen a photo of him. Walter's eyes were sky blue, hers had coronas of flecked hazel. She was forever trying to tame her dark tresses, whereas his black hair, falling forwards on his brow, was much finer and his skin pale and freckled. He didn't look robust, and she liked people with loads of energy to match her own. She couldn't imagine being friends, but she'd promised Ma 'n' Mo, and herself, she'd be on her best behaviour.

She kicked it off, remembering to speak nicely. 'What do you like doing?'

'Oh, you know, the usual.'

She raised her eyebrows.

'Cricket. Not much of a player, but I follow it. And music. Piano specifically.'

'Ah yes, Ma mentioned you used to play.'

'Still do!' He became animated. 'When I finish school, I hope to study. I rather hope to go to Paris Conservatoire. Make a career of it.'

'Good for you.' *Conservatoire?* She determined to match him. 'I already have a career on the stage.' Nina suppressed a giggle.

Walter nodded. 'I prefer opera. Do you have a favourite?'

'Ballet? Currently I like—'

'Sorry, opera. I mean opera.'

'No. Can't say I do.'

In silence, they sipped their sweet wine. Nina glanced away, hoping to catch Ma's eye, but the lawyer could be heard saying, 'How fascinating, Miss Banbury, do tell me more!'

So she and Walter stood on the rug, twiddling their glasses.

'Perhaps,' Walter said tentatively, 'you may wish to attend a concert with me.'

'Perhaps.' Nina was cautious. 'Or you might like to attend a ballet performance?'

'That would be splendid. I shall look forward to it.'

They turned towards Mr Quince, both sets of eyes urging the lawyer to come to their rescue.

Nina did not make good her offer to Walter – made under the duress of excessive politeness – and her life grew busier. She kept an eye out for auditions in *The Stage*, which led to a tour with an exuberant troupe of Russian folk dancers.

The Russians – men and women – drank their way through England from Lincoln, Manchester, Leeds, and by the time they reached Newcastle, the show was beyond "wild and excessive"; it was "bacchanalian". Locals joined the visitors in late-night parties, no one understanding the other. After one drunken brawl, two of the troupe ended up in hospital. Another night, Nina – panting, scratching and breaking fingernails – fought off a beery Cossack grasping her small breasts. A kick in the groin ended that encounter. Enough!

She fled the troupe, her passion for all things Russian significantly dampened. Back home, Miss Stedman showed little sympathy. 'Better to allow me to arrange suitable engagements. This is not what I want my girls to be associated with.'

Then an odd thing happened. Ma suggested she audition for the Alhambra *corps de ballet*. 'You'll have no trouble getting in.'

'But I don't want *your* old life.'

'Nothing wrong with the Alhambra. It's work, isn't it? Dance work.'

She was allocated the same dressing room Ma had used, years earlier. Dumping down her bag of practice clothes, she gave it a kick, wondering if she could ever break away. This was not where she belonged.

Ma met Walter one more time, but Nina stayed away. With the ice broken, no one in the Banbury-Roberts family seemed in a rush to let the waters flow. It might freeze over, which could be a good thing. Their worlds were far apart.

13

Occasionally, Walter thought of Rose and Nina, his London family – his *only* family. He asked Mr Quince if Mother enquired about him and learnt she received six-monthly reports, 'Largely of a financial nature, with a supplementary on your progress. You may like to know she has married and is no longer Mrs Roberts.'

'I didn't know.' His brain whirled. 'Might she want to see—'

'No, no!' Mr Quince wagged a finger. 'Put that behind you. But, Walter, just as you wish your adopted mother to ask after you, you continue to spurn requests from your real mother. Think on it.' Mr Quince stared into his eyes. It had been that admonishment that forced Walter to look into his soul. He would not be a hypocrite. He no longer minded the idea of meeting Rose again – perhaps twice a year would be enough to satisfy her – but Nina he had only met the once.

His sister had appeared so worldly, while he must have sounded, well, *prissy*. He flinched. Hadn't he said "splendid" or something awful, just like Mother – and hadn't he boasted of following cricket to sound more manly? Ridiculous!

His seventeenth birthday celebrations were a quiet affair. The day before had been a discussion of arrangements for the coming year with Mr Quince, who, after finances had been

111

settled, said, 'And, you may like to know, tomorrow is opening night at the Alhambra – some concoction from Moscow, *The Dance Dream*, in which Miss Nina Banbury features. How about that? Your mother has tickets. Might you care to join me?'

Walter had a ready excuse. 'Sorry. Another time. Something's been arranged, you see.'

'A pity.'

'Yes, a pity,' Walter agreed, happy to duck the occasion.

Instead, Walter ate at the best restaurant in Leatherhead with Mr and Miss Reed. Over a meal of overcooked steak and roasted vegetables, Miss Reed repeated, 'So kind, Walter, so very kind!'

And Mr Reed scraped his plate clean of every morsel of treacle pudding, dabbing his moustache with his napkin, exclaiming, 'The best meal ever!'

Walter endured. Perhaps the Moscow ballet people would have been more entertaining.

With summer vacation starting, he expected to spend more time away from Miss Reed's home. He had good friends at school now and could bank on being invited to various family homes for days or a week at a time. Chilcott was a good fellow – they got on well – and Walter enjoyed the novelty of being thrust into a large family with boys and girls tumbling about. He was finding his feet.

On learning Mr Quince had been trying to contact him, Walter telephoned. 'Is anything the matter?'

'It is always up to me, you might agree, to be the one to bang heads together,' the lawyer's voice boomed. 'You, my boy, are joining the two Miss Banburys for an evening at Covent Garden Opera House. No, no! All arranged, I won't hear of any argument...' Walter hadn't said a word. 'Miss Nina has chosen the programme.'

Walter's eyes lit up. Nina's tastes must be maturing. 'Which opera, sir?'

'You misunderstand me. Ballet! The Russian Ballet is something of a craze. All those wonderful dancers Mr Diaghilev has tempted away from the Imperial Theatres. Paris last year; now it's our turn. The summer season!'

Walter's heart sank. Must he endure an evening of folly better suited to the halls?

'The Russians have come, and I am tempted to join you!'

'Of course, sir, you'd be welcome.' Walter thought it might even be better. Should conversation flag, Mr Quince could be banked upon to keep it going.

'Oh no, one lion amongst the ladies is quite enough. One-guinea seats, circle, third row. I'm sure your father would allow this small luxury from his funds. Wouldn't you say?'

'Just look at you!' Rose's gloved hand lightly brushed his lapel, her face radiating pleasure. 'Oh, Walter, you look so handsome.'

With his top hat and cloak in the cloak room, he knew he cut a fine figure in his tailored evening suit. If not quite a lion, he was no longer a cub, and he noted with satisfaction he was a little taller than both his mother and sister, despite their heels.

Instantly, he had recognised the opera cape Rose wore from her long-ago photo. Though smelling a little of camphor, it was quite beautiful.

'From your father.' She twirled around for him to admire and touched a strand of pearls at her throat. 'I see,' he said, troubled by the secret stories and intimacy such gifts hinted at and knowing she had treasured them for years when she might have pawned or sold them. The cape looked barely used and he imagined it stored in tissue paper. He was relieved to note Rose's hair, no longer a shrill orange but a fading brown beneath a flowery headdress.

And his sister? She was fanning herself with the programme, looking about, determined to be stand-offish. She wore a mauve, high-waisted evening dress, white lace at the cuffs. Noticing his eyes on her, she felt the need to say something.

'Latest fashion, you know. Ma 'n' Mo ran it up for me.' She tossed her head adding, 'And new shoes.' Beneath the ankle-length hem, trimmed in lace, he noticed fashionably pointed shoes with a sparkly buckle.

It was a Saturday evening, mid-July, in Covent Garden Opera House's circle bar, the three of them waiting with a crush of others. They were a fashionable lot: carefully set bouffant hair encircled with tiaras; diamonds and coloured gems at ears and throats; cut-glass accents lifted from women's rosy mouths and men's neatly sculpted beards.

'Don't they look tip-top?' Rose said.

'Splen— We all do,' he said gallantly, and meant it. 'Shall we go in?'

They moved towards the opened doors, ushers waiting to escort them down the carpeted isle, where Walter seated himself between his mother and sister. Shortly, the house lights dimmed, chatter subsided, and with a smattering of applause, the conductor took his place at the front of the waiting orchestra.

At the raise of the baton, Chopin's "Prelude" began, and Walter settled himself. With the heavy curtain still lowered, listening to the overture, he decided if he did not enjoy the dancing, he could close his eyes and lose himself in the music.

From the moment the curtain lifted to reveal a posed group – one male dancer, a short muscular lion amongst a dozen or more ladies in long white tutus – Walter understood there would be nothing cheap or shoddy about this programme. He could almost feel the mist in the air rising from the moonlit glade. Chopin's "Nocturne" swelled, reaching to where he sat, ears and eyes open to receive.

'No silly story,' Nina whispered, 'just Mr Fokine's choreography. I'm not usually one for sylphs, but I'm liking these.'

Walter did too. He admired Vaslav Nijinsky partnering first one then another of the delicate creatures. Throughout, he was aware of Rose sighing and cooing. She squeezed his hand.

'Thank you for coming, son, this means a lot to me.'

He smiled, touched by her honesty. Watching the ballet, he began to appreciate how movement could be linked and shaped to create a mood just as a score sought to achieve harmony of many parts. *Les Sylphides* was love at first sight.

Weber's *Invitation to the Dance*, used for *Le Spectre de la Rose*, he knew well, its dreaminess lulling him... 'Oh!' At crashing chords, Walter startled. Mr Nijinsky, the Rose, leapt – no, floated – through the open French window and commenced a dance with Miss Karsavina that was melting yet manly.

'That was,' Rose said as the curtain closed, 'just my cup of tea.'

'And mine,' he responded truthfully.

'You know your father was a lovely dancer, Walter. It reminded me of the many evenings we waltzed together.'

'Even the night we were conceived, isn't that right, Ma?' Nina was leaning across, speaking to her mother but looking directly at him. He felt himself blush but refused to rise to her bait by expressing shock.

'Oh, we liked to dance.' Rose waved her hand vaguely. 'Let's leave it at that.'

Next, he and all those seated witnessed a Russian scene where a chorus of voices swelled in Borodin's *Prince Igor* and savage tribespeople leapt. He saw that Nina was alert, taut, sitting forwards. She gripped his arm, then pulled away, muttering, 'Sorry.' But he didn't mind. Minutes later, she tapped his arm, and he turned to see her eyes bright as she hissed, 'This is what I want to do! I want to be there. With them. At that camp. Please, someone, let me gallop away—'

'Best learn to ride, then,' Rose whispered. 'Hope those London hacks are up to it. Saw a horse auction the other day—'

'Shh, Ma! Walter, isn't this marvellous?'

He managed to nod, resisting "splendid" again, but it *was* splendid. Adolf Bolm, the principal dancer, was well-built: not cool hard marble, but a man of bone, muscle, flesh. Walter loosened the collar threatening to choke him. That this frenzy was deemed fit to be on the revered Opera House stage amazed him.

He was on his feet, palms beating, voices cheering – all of them whipped into a near hysteria. Curtain call followed curtain call, not allowing those exhausted artists to leave the stage. Huge bouquets were presented to ballerinas, and from those seated in boxes, roses flew and scattered onto the stage.

'Well.' Nina raised an eyebrow. 'It looks like you enjoyed that.'

'I did, thank you. I'm so very pleased you suggested Mr Quince contact me.'

'Welcome to my world, brother.' She pressed her lips together. 'At least, the world I want.' Momentarily, he sensed her uncertainty, body slumping, then she jumped to her feet. 'Let's go.'

Rose gathered her bag. 'I could get used to the best seats. Lovely! I must thank Mr Quince – or, at least, Arthur's savings – for the treat. My goodness, hasn't Mr Diaghilev fielded a good crop?' She fanned herself. 'Not as many as *we* fielded in my day, mind you—'

'Ma! Don't go on. You can't seriously compare the Alhambra's *corps* with this!' Nina slapped Rose's arm with her programme. 'Good, you say? They were excellent. *Excellent!* All of them, not just the principals.'

'Yes, yes, but we had our stars. You never saw Emma—'

'Oh, Ma. Really!'

'You weren't there. You didn't see them.' Rose flicked the back of a glove against Nina's arm, and Walter suspected this was an ongoing squabble.

After that evening, there could be no turning back. A switch had been thrown, binding Walter to these two women with an electric charge.

He did not attend another performance that summer, though Nina refused to miss *Scheherazade*. He knew this because she wrote and told him so and had included another page filled with vibrant splashes of water paint in reds, blues and greens, *to give you an idea of the colours.* He smiled at her brief letter. No turning back.

Late November, another letter from Nina arrived. He recognised the scrawled writing on the envelope and the stamp stuck on awry. Inside he unfolded a page torn out of a notebook. Reading the terse message, he wondered if his sister had ever learnt letter-writing etiquette.

Walter

If you want to catch Scheherazade meet on Saturday. Got tickets. Hilda can't come. Gallery, unreserved. We'll need to queue so don't be late. If I don't see you I'll grab someone off the street!

Nina

Oh, not opera dress where we're sitting!

A long line snaked its way around the block from the Opera House doors.

'Here! Over here!'

He spotted his sister near the front of the queue waving her arms above her head, and goodness, that was quite a headdress she was wearing. He joined her and shuffled forwards among men and women huddled in winter coats, hats, and muffs, none deterred by a chilly overcast evening threatening rain. On reaching the stairs, Nina cantered up, lifting her skirt with one hand, clasping his hand in the other.

'Come on, I know just where I want to sit.'

Seeing from high above – the dancers diminished on the far-away stage – was not, obviously, as satisfactory as his introduction to the ballet. When he hinted as such, she pinched his arm. 'You pay next time, why don't you.' And he promised he would.

Rimsky-Korsakov's score had been turned into a vivid ballet, set in a harem – all fabulous garish cushions and rugs. With the Sultan away, what had begun as a party – those platters of fruit, wine and incense – becomes wilder. He glanced at a man just along from them, neck stretching forwards. Onstage, women beat tambourines and twirled, sheer fabric clinging to bodies: brilliant oranges and yellows, and scarlet patterns. And there was Nijinsky, a slave, coiled ready to spring, with a pulsating seductive Queen Zobeide egging him on.

He himself was goggle-eyed, whispering: 'I've never seen anything so exotic—'

'And thrilling! Vibrant!' Nina added, chin thrusting, accentuating each word.

Those colours were not solely confined to the stage. Above a mass of dark curls, Nina wore a paisley-printed turban, in shades of purple and magenta, like a flowering plant from Mother's conservatory. A spray of peacock feathers rose from the crown to an alarming height, and he pitied the person sitting behind. Around her neck trailed a long silky scarf – ostrich-feather motifs a brilliant orange, purple, and turquoise. She looked extraordinary – in an exquisite way – but he couldn't find the words to say so.

At the end of the programme, as they headed down the stairs from the Gallery, Nina caught his arm.

'Almost forgot. Ma wonders what you're doing at Christmas. Wonders if you might like to come to ours. Nothing special but you'd get to meet Mo.'

Walter stared, utterly surprised. He managed to stammer, 'I... I...' then fell into an uncomfortable silence.

Nina shrugged, turning away. 'Never mind. I told her it was a stupid idea, and you'd have something better planned. Wouldn't want—'

'Wait. Wait.'

Her strides were long and purposeful despite the narrowness of her skirt. He elbowed through the crush around the entrance, a smell of unwashed winter clothes and cheap perfume. When he reached Bow Street, he found Nina had not waited.

'Fool!' he hissed at himself, eyes darting, seeking her among the crowd. He spotted peacock feathers bobbing above hats several yards away. 'Nina! Please.' He ran, pushing past an overweight man, made bulkier by a fur coat, gripped her shoulder, forcing her to turn. 'Please tell your moth—'

'She's your ma too!' Her gaze was fierce, daring him to deny it, to deny her.

He tried again. 'Please tell Rose, *our* mother, I would be delighted to accept her invitation.'

A bloom spread over Nina's cheeks, and her mouth stretched into a wide grin. 'I'll tell her!' She spun on her heels, lifted her skirt, and was off.

'Wait! Where? Your address.'

'Got to dash. We'll write!'

Between a couple ambling arm in arm and an elderly man with a cane, Walter watched his sister dart forwards, her energy and heat palpable as she vanished up the street.

My sister. My family. He repeated the words to himself as he crossed Waterloo Bridge, making slowly for the station.

14

The days leading up to Christmas had them in a flurry.

'Do you think he'll like goose and apple stuffing?' Ma asked.

'What about a nice bit of tongue?' Mo suggested.

'And *please*,' Nina eyed the pile of darning, 'let's get rid of this.' They'd all be on display. From the lower drawer, where best linen was stored, she selected the white tablecloth edged with flowers, thinking it could do with an iron. Mo went to town polishing and scrubbing, and all of them set about baking and boiling.

On the day, Mo helped arrange her hair, gathered in loose curls at the nape of her neck, a broad blue satin ribbon encircling her head. Ma wore her special rose brooch and strand of pearls, as always. Hearing a knock, she fluffed the cushions one more time.

'Coming, son!' Ma called out.

Nina shot a look at Mo. 'Here goes.' But Mo wasn't listening, she was limping to greet Walter, one hand, two hands, extended.

'Lovely to see you, at last.' Mo bobbed her head as she clasped Walter's hands, then, with the smallest hesitation, wrapped her arms around him in a hug. 'Hope you don't mind.'

If he minded, he wasn't showing it. 'Lovely to meet you too,' he said.

Ma took his arm. 'Hope you're hungry; we've enough to feed a battalion.'

They settled at the table – best plates laden with roast pork, chicken, potatoes and greens. Her brother did his duty, eating everything on his plate, complimenting the cooks. She relaxed, deciding she didn't mind him visiting her home. Then a wicked thought came to her as Ma served the steamed pudding.

'Tell him, Ma 'n' Mo, stories about us – being born backstage and everything.' She turned to her brother. 'Wouldn't you like to hear?'

He put down his spoon. Blinked. 'If you wish.'

Ma laughed, 'Oh, well, I was bursting, but had to get there—'

'Alhambra, that is,' Mo said.

'You're both blood of my blood and bone of my bone,' Ma said. 'I swear I left a bit of myself on the Green Room floor...'

Nina watched Walter's face from under her lashes, wondering what it might take to make him show his feelings. They were so different, she couldn't imagine caring for him much, but for Ma's sake, she didn't mind sharing Christmas.

Five months later, Nina received a card written in carefully formed copperplate and a birthday gift, a delicate summer scarf of blues and greens, which pleased her enormously.

'Lovely,' Ma said. 'These colours suit you. I sent him greetings, did you?' She felt a stab of remorse. According to Ma, he was doing exceptionally well in his studies. 'And to think we've never heard him play!'

'Take him to the pub.'

'That old piano? It's got bung keys.'

'We'll have to wait then.' That suited her. She wanted to be proud of herself before listening to her brother. He'd been accepted for a music college in London – she'd not taken too much notice which one – so expected she'd see more of him then. She was jealous that Walter had a special place in Ma's heart and, another stab, he was steaming ahead. As were others.

Hilda had returned from touring America with Mr Mordkin's company, under the fancy title of the Imperial Russian Ballet, and Nina couldn't help but be envious.

'Oh, Nina, you can't imagine how big the Metropolitan stage is. Everything's big in New York.'

She regretted not auditioning, for once heeding Ma's caution: 'America! You're too young to go so far.'

'Hilda's younger—'

'Why would you want to leave London when you've a steady job?'

She was persuaded by that argument. She did have work. Until she didn't. In summer, her *corps de ballet* days ended. The Alhambra's licence was changing from variety to revue, so ballet was given the chop. Their final production, *The Pool*, closed, and she fell into a slump.

'I should've auditioned. Gone to America,' she sobbed, glaring at Ma. 'And stayed there.'

Ma patted her back. 'Something else will be around the corner. In the meantime, you can take your mind off things – I see Diaghilev's lot are back for the summer.'

'Oh, I'm going, you can be sure of that.'

'I was going to say, invite Walter.'

'Not this time.' She didn't fancy seeing her brother when she felt so low.

Nina perched on a seat in the upper circle at the Opera House, giving herself over to *The Firebird*. The creature flashed across the stage. A dazzle of colour. Gone! She waited… There, again, streaking the other direction – *grand jetés* this time – and off!

Tamara Karsavina wore a magnificent headdress – long flaming feathers quivering – a bodice of brilliant reds and oranges, pelts of white feathers and feathers swirling from her hips. Below this, forest-green sheer trousers ended mid-calf. She adored the exotic creature.

And as for Stravinsky's score, she'd never heard anything like it. Harsh rumbles gave way to eery, creepy sounds conjuring mystery and otherness. She leant forwards, not blinking, memorising the way the ballerina's arms framed her face, fingers sharp and fluttering, snapping her head sharply, lips drawn back, bared teeth, angry eyes. It came to her: this firebird was *her* – Nina – aflame, all sharp angles, radiating determination never to be trapped.

On leaving the Opera House, she passed through the arched walkways of Covent Garden. Glancing at women in filthy dresses, ferreting through remnants of fruit and discarded cabbage leaves, she shivered. They were a sharp reminder she was out of work. Then the memory of *The Firebird* spurred her. With hastened steps, she determined to blaze through life, in a hurry to live.

The advert was in *The Stage*. Someone called E J Kuryyo was teaching the "Russian Ballet, Pavlova and Nijinsky style". Immediately, Nina signed up for classes.

Meanwhile, a company headed by a husband-and-wife team, Theodore Kosloff and Alexandra Baldina, had a season planned.

'It's at the Coliseum,' Hilda said. 'And they need dancers. I'm sure they'll see you.'

In late summer, within a heartbeat of Diaghilev's *Scheherazade* ending at the Opera House with Madame Karsavina in the role of Zobeide, Nina and Hilda shared the vast London Coliseum stage with Madame Baldina in the main role. It mattered little that their twice-daily performances of *Scheherazade* were sandwiched between "My Old Dutch" and other ditties and sketches. It mattered little that when Madame Baldina became ill, Hilda took her part, with rapid adjustments to make the costume fit. The audience didn't seem to notice and roared their approval at curtain calls. What mattered was that Nina was sharing a stage with real Russian stars.

'Let's invite Walter up to watch,' Ma said on her third visit to see the show. 'I'm sure he'd love it.'

'I'm sure he would not.' She felt her almost-professional musician brother wouldn't approve the way Rimsky-Korsakov's score had been truncated. 'Didn't you read the *Bystander*? "The production vulgar and trite with all the aristocratic values of the Russian Ballet at Covent Garden absent."'

Ma hadn't kept that review but had cut out the accompanying photo of Nina and another dancer in their harem costumes: lying on their stomachs, propped on their elbows, chins on hands, legs bent up behind them.

Following a Saturday matinee, Ma appeared at her dressing room door. 'You decent? Look who we have here,' and Ma tugged Walter into view.

There was a communal squeak as Nina's fellow ladies of the harem grabbed something to cover half-naked bodies. In the time it took Nina to blink, Walter had disappeared.

'He'll wait outside.' Ma laughed. 'Second thoughts. You don't want me hanging around. You youngsters enjoy yourself. I'm off!'

A crowd of them piled into one of the cafés lining St Martin's Lane. Nina with Hilda and a bunch of English,

Polish and Russian dancers. And Walter. Amidst the chatter and high spirits of the just-offstage-performers, Nina was barely aware of Walter shrinking into himself.

'So, you're Nina's twin. What did you think of the show?' Hilda asked. 'Do you think I made a fair go at Zobeide? Was I compelling?' She lifted a scarf and peered over it, fluttering her eyes at Walter.

Nina watched Walter's colour rise. 'I, um… I can't really judge ballet. Sorry,' he said. 'But I thought it spirited,' he added, before withdrawing a cigarette from a slim silver case.

'And? The manly slaves? Were we spirited?' Alexei, one of the young Russian dancers, leant across, cupped Walter's visibly shaking hands and lit the cigarette.

Walter looked away, flustered. 'Oh, you know, yes, splendid. The whole thing was splendid.' He flourished his hand, wafting smoke.

Alexei looked at him keenly. '*Splendid.* Good word.'

'Please! Enough!' Nina threw up her arms. 'We are far from splendid, but we can agree we are spirited. Let's toast to that.' She raised her teacup.

'Spirited!' Glasses and teacups raised and clattered.

'Move up.' Nina shifted places to sit next to Walter and helped herself to one of his cigarettes. 'You managing with Miss Reed? Ma says she's being a pain.'

'A pain… I wouldn't put it that way. She's put up with me from the time I was a child. I think she'd like some peace. All that noise, you know.' Walter played an imaginary keyboard.

'You practise most days?'

'Of course. At school during the week, then Sundays at Miss Reed's.'

'Even Sundays… rest day and all of that? How much?' Nina squinted at him.

'Oh, you know. A few hours… Several.'

'Several, as in five…? Eight?' Seeing him nod, Nina began to appreciate her brother's determination matched her own.

'We hear you play?' It was Alexei, stretching an arm around Walter's shoulder. Walter coloured as Nina's friends tapped spoons to plates and cups, urging him.

'Oh yes, let's hear you!'

'Yes, do Walter. Let's go back.' Nina stood, leading the noisy troupe to the Coliseum where they dragged Walter to the rehearsal room and plonked him behind the old upright piano.

'Play! Play!' they encouraged.

Walter rubbed his hands on his trouser legs, then, with hands poised on the keyboard, waited for quiet. Nina was struck dumb. The piano became his companion in whatever game Walter was imagining and he barely glanced at his hands on the keyboard.

'Arabesque,' Walter told them as he continued. 'It's a ballet term, isn't it?'

'Oh!' Nina squeezed his shoulder. 'It's beautiful!'

Walter glanced at her with a small smile. 'I'm particularly fond of Debussy.'

He gave himself to the music, eyes closed, swaying, lost in the airy world of his creation. Three quiet notes and then a final chord.

'Nina's brother!'

'Walter, so clever!'

'Well, how delectable!'

She watched Walter being drawn to his feet and congratulated.

Hilda was at her side. 'Why on earth have you been hiding him?'

Nina was as mystified as her friend. 'I don't know.' Why had she? Had she been jealous, wanting to drag him down to the grime of Whitechapel? Had she wanted to wait until she was famous so she could lord it over him? Well, that wasn't going to happen.

She extracted Walter – the still point around whom her jabbering friends clamoured –wrapping an arm around his waist. 'My brother. My twin!' She ruffled his hair and laughed openly, happy to have finally claimed him. 'Oh!' She held him at arm's length, a sudden inspiration: 'Shall I send you postcards?'

'Will you remember?' Walter looked dubious, and Nina knew her letter-writing track record was not brilliant.

'I'll make sure she does,' Hilda assured him.

'I promise.' Nina looked Walter in the eye, placing her hand to her heart.

Before long, Kosloff's entourage would be off touring England, ending in Edinburgh, after which there'd be a special train back to Kings Cross en-route to Vienna. Before returning to the Coliseum, she was about to see a little of the world, feet no longer entangled in East End roots.

15

It was rare for any of the boys to be summoned to the phone, but his sister had said it was an emergency, so Walter dashed to the office fearing something terrible must have happened. As the man – or near man – in this family, he was anxious about what might be required of him.

Through the earpiece came Nina's hurried voice. 'Ma wants to come too. Has to be a Monday for me. All right?'

He nodded and mumbled, 'Yes.'

'What did you say, Walter? Speak up!'

Aware his housemaster was within range, Walter brought the mouthpiece closer, stretching his features into what he hoped was a serious expression. 'When did you get back?' he whispered. Already rehearsing how he might explain away this unusual summons: something serious but not life-threatening.

'A couple of weeks ago. Back at the Coliseum… I'll sort it, bound to be booked out, but the good old Ways and Means Committee will get us in.' His sister's confident laugh rang out.

It was not tickets for *their* version of *Scheherazade* Nina was urging him to watch. Diaghilev's Ballets Russes had returned for a brief season at the Opera House.

One mid-February evening, Walter met with Rose and Nina for an early supper at a place on the Strand.

A peck on the cheek, 'How are you, Walter?' from Rose.

'Well, thank you, and you?' from him.

A grin from Nina with a, 'Glad you could make it.' And over the meal, Nina entertaining them, dipping into stories of her travels as she dipped into her food – quick, sampling, moving on. 'Honestly, those Russians and Polish boys.' Nina rolled her eyes. 'You'd think they were made of money the way they go about losing it. Can't see a pack of cards without dragging you into a game of poker.'

'Don't you get drawn in,' Rose said.

'Once bitten, Ma. Lost a day's wages, so not falling for that again.' Nina laughed. 'And that Alexei's a terror – I hear him coming, rattling dice in his pocket ready to chance his luck. Oh, by the way, he was asking after you.'

'Me?' Rose looked surprised.

'No, Walter!' It was Walter's turn to look surprised. 'Alexei was wondering if you were coming to see our show, now we're back in town. We had a jolly time, didn't we?'

'Yes, we did.' Recalling the ease with which Alexei had draped an arm around his shoulder made Walter's heart race.

He had fond memories of that time around the piano with Nina's friends. They'd asked if he knew modern tunes and he'd tried his hand at "Maple Leaf Rag" as Mr Monroe had shown him, earning appreciative "wows". He'd enjoyed watching several of them grab partners and giddily spin around the room.

He had fonder memories from when Nina had been dragged away to sit with a gaggle of girls, leaving just Alexei and one or two others. Then just Alexei. When Walter made a move to put down the piano lid, Alexei stilled him, fetched another chair, and sat close.

'What songs do you know, Walter?' he asked.

At first, he demurred, then, when pressed, for the first time outside of choir, he was emboldened to play and sing in public, for some reason choosing "Shine On, Harvest Moon".

Alexei had watched him, saying, 'You sing like an angel. You know that?' And he had blushed.

It had been magical. He sang another song, drawing everyone back to the piano to sing along. Between songs, Alexei had lit a cigarette and shared it with him, back and forth.

'Well?' Nina tapped his arm. 'Will you be coming to see us?'

'I'm not sure,' he said. In truth, he was fearful the beautiful memory he harboured might be fractured by crass reality. Probably those moments – and he himself – meant nothing to the talented Russian dancer. 'I'm so busy. Really, I shouldn't be here tonight. But—'

Nina shrugged. 'Suit yourself.'

'If I can manage, then I'd like to come up again.'

Another shrug from Nina, and she began talking about Kosloff's hopes for another tour to the Continent.

He felt dull and childish beside his sister, his main contribution to the conversation being to confirm he was studying hard, which earned him a pat on the hand and Rose's, 'Good boy.'

Once in the Opera House, Walter sat by himself for the opening ballets so Nina and Rose could sit together, several rows ahead. Nina had not managed to get three seats next to each other. At an interval, Nina swapped, and Walter sat next to his mother.

With the opening bars of *L'après-midi d'un Faune* drifting through the air like a subtle perfume, shivers of anticipation rippled through him, the orchestra unfurling Debussy's

"Prelude" with great delicacy. A glissando on harp was the cue for the curtain to rise on Leon Bakst's dreamlike, impressionistic backcloth, and his eyes rested on the creature reclining on a rock: Nijinsky, part-man, part-goat.

It was a slight piece Walter didn't take much notice of, until the ending. Fleeing nymphs dropped a scarf, leaving the Faun with the captured treasure. Back atop his rock, Nijinsky held the silky fabric aloft, pressed it to his face, down his body – mouth wide, head back. Walter held his breath as the Faun lowered himself – hips thrust forwards, chest lifted – onto the outspread scarf. At a cymbal's *ting*, the dancer's taut body jerked upwards and, with diminishing strings and brass, Walter watched Nijinsky – the Faun – motionless, done, savouring the moment. Savouring the ecstasy.

The curtain lowered.

Conscious of his own throbbing penis and his mother sitting next him, Walter swallowed, dug fingers into his palms. He crossed his legs, willing himself to think of ugly things: boiled wilted cabbage, vomit, waddling overweight wheezing dogs, but Nijinsky stayed with him.

'What did you make of it?' Rose was clapping politely, and Walter remembered to clap, stinging palms momentarily distracting him. 'They're loving it.' Rose was turning left and right and looking up at the balcony.

Onstage, the company of nymphs stepped forwards, bowing. There was Nijinsky in his yellowy leotard with brown markings, looking so ordinary, a man you wouldn't glance twice at, yet moments before he'd been an artist absorbed.

'Well?' Rose nudged him.

'I liked it well enough,' he offered. 'There was something poetic about it, don't you think?'

'Poetic? That's not ballet.'

Whatever Rose's opinion, the rest of the audience were

enthusiastic, and with each curtain call, their rapture grew – 'Bravo. Encore!' – everyone on their feet clapping and stamping. Cautiously, Walter stood, his unwanted erection wilting.

The stage curtains closed, only to draw back into ruched drapes revealing the cast. Closed. Open. Walter lost count of the times the artists kissed and bowed to their cheering audience who would not let them go.

A pause, then Walter understood the ballet was to be repeated. All of it.

As it reached its climax again, an image of a young man's face formed in Walter's mind: Alexei. He felt, again, those casual moments of connection: a hand on his arm when Alexei was excited, wanting to say something but unable to find the English words. A thigh jigging against his own in time with the rhythm of the song. Each touch a fizz of electricity, Alexei's face close as he passed a cigarette to his lips. Alexei had been very tactile, Walter found, but was this simply an expression of "the theatrical temperament"? Rose and Nina were like that too, so Walter hadn't known what to make of it. Yet, Nina said, Alexei had *asked* after him…

Oh! Walter jerked, aware of a warm damp sensation at his groin. He crossed his legs, mortified and disgusted, feeling every bit the brutish goat. With the ballet at its conclusion, he stood wrestling to get his arms through the sleeves of his coat then drew it tightly around him to hide his shame.

'Walter?'

'Must go,' he spluttered. 'Sorry, Rose.'

'Go? But, Walter, there's still another ballet, you—'

'Train to catch. I must.'

'But don't you want to talk with Nina?'

'Sorry… Sorry.' He pushed passed knees, mumbling and stumbling out into the cool evening air then ran, down to the Strand, over the Thames, arriving at Waterloo station sweating and panting.

On the Leatherhead train, anxiety gnawed his gut. He stared out the window as the lights of south London receded.

Memory: flicking candles in his dorm, three poetry-loving pyjamaed boys cross-legged on beds. Chilcott, book in hand, mouth shaping the words he read aloud in a whispered voice: *"'...And joy is in the throbbing tide, whose intricate fingers beat and glide in felt bewildering harmonies of trembling touch...'"*

Still on the train, Walter extracted a volume of poetry and turned to a page marked with one of Nina's postcards – that same Rupert Brooke poem:

"In a cool curving world he lies And ripples with dark ecstasies..."

It was he, Walter, who had requested Chilcott read "The Fish" that time.

His nose clogged and eyes stung with tears he was determined to hold back. He thrust the book back into his bag. While his mind longed for beauty and aesthetics, his base part had grown to claim him, to torture him. He had a twisted, sinful soul. Knowing this was one thing, doing something about it was another. He did not know how to change, and feared it was beyond him.

ACT 3

1913

All the fever and fecundity of the hour seemed to be captured by the Russian Ballet.

PROUD TOWER, BARBARA W. TUCHMAN

16

Porters hefted trunks from carriages onto waiting trolleys on the platform. With just one suitcase, Nina did not need help. Clutching her bag in both hands, she staggered out of the station along with the other recruits. Sweet-smelling jasmine and flowers she didn't know the names of tumbled down stone walls, their scent on the breeze. Above, an open car with a laughing couple, the man at the wheel, turning a corner. Out of sight, the vehicle spluttered, struggling up the winding road into pine-covered hills, away from Monte Carlo. Below, pleasure crafts at anchor in the bay, rippling waves glinting in sharp Mediterranean sun.

She was here, yet still Nina doubted. 'I hope no one's made a mistake and sends me home. I couldn't bear it!'

'Why should they? Don't be daft,' Hilda said. 'You've got your contract, same as the rest of us.'

Nina gripped the handle of her suitcase. Between layers of clothes, she'd packed away her precious contract in a brown envelope, assuring her a place in this modernist vanguard.

'You're right!' She lifted her chin. 'Why should they. Unless I mess up, and I have no intention of doing that.'

'This way... I think.' Hilda held a scrap of paper with a pencil-drawn street map, an encircled "X" marking a spot.

'Come on, girls! Let's not be late on our first day.'

Nina followed, Anna and Doris clattered behind, shrill-voiced and breathless, hauling crammed, firmly buckled suitcases through narrow streets to what would be their lodgings.

But before class, Nina and other new girls had to meet Serge Grigoriev, Diaghilev's man in charge.

The previous weeks had been a whirlwind.

'Diaghilev might give audition,' Nicholai had said one Saturday on arriving at the Coliseum. 'Russian dancers caput. Polish, can't get.'

'Vacancies? Are you sure?' Nina asked.

'Vacancies. Yes. Me and Alexei he will see. But he need girls. Diaghilev don't think much of English dancers, but… well.' Nicholai shrugged.

Nina understood that it wasn't so easy for Diaghilev to get well-trained dancers, as more Russians from St Petersburg and Moscow were setting up companies of their own.

'Nicholai, you mean I can *request* an audition? Just like that?'

'Think so. Go see Grigoriev. Diaghilev likes young and pretty. Girls and boys.' Nicholai grinned.

As soon as she could, she went to meet Diaghilev's fixer in the Green Room at the Theatre Royal where he'd set himself up in a comfortable chair, notebook in hand. Serge Grigoriev, tall, dark-haired, narrow face, had been a dancer with the Imperial Ballet but now was devoted to Diaghilev's cause. He was also the gatekeeper, the man who ran the company doing whatever Diaghilev required to keep the show on the road. He explained in broken English about upcoming tours requiring an immediate start, then began to write down her details.

'Who? Where?' He frowned, pen paused where he'd written her name and age.

'Stedman's Ballet Academy. It's very well-respected, and I've studied with Monsieur Kuryyo.'

'Ah!'

Unsure what he may be thinking, she hurried on listing engagements, '...Including with a very highly thought of *Russian* folk troupe, and now, of course, contracted with Monsieur *Kosloff*—'

'Kosloff, yes,' his eyes narrowed, 'I see a performance, Miss...' He glanced at his notes.

'Banbury.'

'Miss Banbury. I am not sure you are ready—'

'Give me a chance. I'm *definitely* ready. I've watched all your productions. All! And I'm a fast learner.' Seeing her start to remove her coat, Grigoriev hastily held out a hand. 'No, no, sit,' alarmed she might spin around in front of him. And she would have. She was ready to beg if necessary. 'Anyone as persistent as you deserves a chance,' he conceded, after looking singularly unimpressed by her list of achievements.

Nina was not a morning person, none of them were, yet Monday, at ten o'clock, she was onstage at Covent Garden Opera House with Hilda and some of the others from Kosloff's company, all in practice clothes, all ready to impress. She stood shivering on the cold stage, reluctant to discard her wrap, while in the wings, stagehands clunked, not bothering to lower their voices.

Five empty chairs were lined in front of the safety curtain waiting for the terrifying selection committee's bottoms to rest upon them. A heavy wing curtain moved, voices, and in they filed, led by Grigoriev.

'Maestro Cecchetti,' Hilda whispered as the Italian ballet master took his seat along with his wife. She stared hard at the short, elderly man, whose balding head, circled in a grey fuzz of hair, gave no hint of greatness. Her gaze shifted to two figures entering from a front wing, Hilda's wheezing gasp matching her own. Nina barely glanced at Nijinsky, looking small and pale. It was the large man next to him, the man whose enterprise this was, that commanded attention.

Sergei Diaghilev walked onstage, his solid presence mesmerising. That large domed head, that oiled black brush of hair with a badger streak of white, that monocle. Diaghilev settled his bulky frame in a hard chair, back upright, hands resting on a cane. He adjusted his eyeglass, inspecting the line of dancers before him like a horse auction.

'Bonjour.' The single word of greeting was deep, resonating.

'Good morning, sir.' As Nina curtsied and the boys bowed, she caught sight of her shabby dancing shoes while Hilda's feet gleamed in shiny new pink ones. Blast! She felt disadvantaged before they began.

It was Grigoriev who took charge. 'So, we are ready… yes…? What will you show us?'

Nina scampered to a prearranged place and Nicholai counted them in to a sequence from *Scheherazade*. Not Fokine's version, naturally, but Kosloff's, the only one they knew. Without Rimsky-Korsakov's driving music, Nina struggled to find the spirit and essence of the drama. Without a piano, let alone an orchestra, there was nothing to help them keep time or muffle the soft thud of each landing and the sound of their breath. There was no magic.

Thud! Hilda hit the stage, was up again, her face pink with mortification, finding her way back into the group. Nina caught her eye, and they set off into a perfectly synchronised sequence. *Thud!* Hilda was down again. Now a fresh fear paralysed Nina. With the stage so slippery, she could no longer dance with abandon. At Hilda's third catastrophe, and with the female harem in disarray, the two male slaves looking hopelessly at a loss, Grigoriev clapped his hands.

'Enough! Much enough!' He turned to Enrico Cecchetti. 'Maestro, steps and simple sequences, if you will.'

The renowned ballet master was on his feet, rubbing his hands. Within minutes, he created order where there had been none. Chairs were found, and, using these as a barre, Nina followed instructions. By now she was not thinking clearly and happy that Hilda was positioned in front of her, executing speedy *battement frappés* and other exercises. Then, chairs removed, Cecchetti faced them, neat feet beating together in a sequence of *échappés* and *sautés*, and Nina marvelled at the elderly Italian's bounciness. Their turn next. At his counts, she sprung again and again. As a child, she had leapt into the middle of a swinging rope, two friends either end, chanting, 'Butterfly, butterfly, turn around. Butterfly, butterfly...' She would jump and jump. Stumbling meant ceding her place and taking the end of the rope for other girls. She held the record among her friends: a hundred and eighty-one skips. Now on this famous stage, she willed herself to greater heights. Beside her, she sensed Nicholai and Alexei's sinewy bodies pushing every fibre to defy gravity.

Cecchetti turned to Diaghilev. 'Have you seen enough?' In turn, Diaghilev spoke softly to Nijinsky.

She and the rest of the sweaty, panting would-be recruits weren't sure what to do. Try to read Diaghilev's mouth? Hopeless; she had no Russian and minimal French. Chat amongst themselves? Disrespectful. She stood with her heels together and toes turned out, hands clasped in front of her, eyes roving from one whispering committee member to the other as they leant across themselves to consult. A chair scraped and Diaghilev stood, audition over. She curtsied and watched his retreating back, the impresario leaving an essence of himself in the space he had just occupied: hair pomade, but something else besides. She touched her heart, fearful that another boat was about to sail without her. She was far from the best female dancer auditioning but she had a small head, a lean body, and was pretty enough, if you liked sharp features. Besides, no one could ever accuse her of not trying.

That evening at the Coliseum, Nicholai burst into the girls' dressing room brandishing a letter. 'We're in! Well, not all…'

'You? Who else?' Nina grabbed it from him, others pressing in. He and Alexei had been offered places and, despite her tumbles, so had Hilda; after all, she'd been promoted to play Zobeide and was a promising dancer. She scanned the names. Doris Faithful. Anna Broomfield. Pausing at a misspelt "Buntbury" instead of "Banbury". 'That's me, isn't it?' She shrieked, passing the letter for others to see. 'Must be better than I thought.'

'Or they're desperate,' a disappointed girl chipped in, turning aside.

'How's your French? Nina…?' Hilda shook her.

'Oh Lord, how will I manage?'

'*Kat tvoy russkiy?*' Nicholai asked.

'*Der'mo!* None, unless you count Russian swear words.' Overcome by the craziness that she would be sharing stages with the world's greatest dancers, she whooped. 'Where are my silver shoes. I'm on my way!'

'What?' Nicholai said.

In Monte Carlo, mornings started with Cecchetti's class, where he made it clear how much was to be learnt. She dreaded the touch of his cane correcting a raised leg or arm. Her brain ached at each step's function and quality. He spoke in a mix of languages she was becoming accustomed to. Without an academy – let alone the Imperial Ballet school – to feed the company, Cecchetti's classes provided the bedrock for Diaghilev.

There was little time to work in fresh recruits, from England

142

and Poland. During rehearsal, an impatient hand shoved her, 'Stand here,' a haughty face making her feel insignificant – worse, an imposter. As a child, though not much of a reader, *The Wonderful Wizard of Oz* had captured her imagination. She was Dorothy skipping along that yellow brick road to the Emerald City, telling Ma 'n' Mo, 'I'd not be in a rush to get back to a boring farm.' Any time she expected Diaghilev to see her for what she was: a girl who had no right to wear silver shoes in his glittering world.

And Diaghilev did watch – her and all of them. Sitting at the front of the rehearsal room, face impassive, he watched while Grigoriev drilled them into Fokine's steps.

She was slotted into the *corps de ballet* for *Scheherazade*, *Cleopatra*, *Petrushka*, and, on actual opening day, Grigoriev showed them their steps for *Prince Igor*. 'A horde – wild people,' Grigoriev urged, leaping, snarling. As he spun, she stepped back from a shower of spittle – something they were all learning to avoid from their regisseur.

In the wings, in a costume she'd seen on other dancers and now adjusted for her, she listened for the cue.

'Here goes,' she muttered, racing onto the stage, wanting to laugh out loud with the joy of it.

She embraced Monte Carlo. Here were palm trees and a wide terrace above which the casino and theatre complex dominated: gleaming white façade more elaborate than the Alhambra she knew so well. Her own home-made clothes she stuffed into her suitcase, inadequate, and begged for loans and favours from friends then spent with abandon. Diaghilev expected his company to be elegant onstage and off. She joined those strolling along the bay. Men in straw boaters, blazers, cream flannel trousers, canes in hand. Perfume wafted in her direction as women in elegant afternoon outfits, lacy parasol aloft, passed by.

At a kiosk, she chose a postcard with a photo of the theatre's luxurious interior and, standing there, wrote to Ma 'n' Mo: *Opening week spectacular and I haven't made a fool of myself! I get to be in a gypsy camp – a Tatar camp – after all! Not a fan of the new ballet. Hope you are well. Nina.*

That new ballet, *The Rite of Spring*, was the bane of her life – hers and everyone else's – and the Paris opening was not far off.

She watched local boys gambolling in the water, two swimming out to a fishing boat. She meant to learn to swim and had bought a costume in readiness. Tilting her chin upwards, she allowed the fierce spring sun to touch her face beneath the brim of her hat. She sucked in Monte Carlo's sea air, feeling herself reborn, sloughing off the old skin, her London skin.

17

WEARING A NEW HAT – NAVY BLUE, SMALL-RIMMED, generous bunches of artificial lilacs centre stage – Rose's step had an almost forgotten spring to it. She was meeting Sid to see a film. Something funny, he'd said – she'd not asked what.

At thirty-seven, Rose was blossoming, and she had Sid to thank for it. There had been other men in the years since Arthur, but none to sing about and some far too rough with a belly full of drink. There were times she'd lied to Nina, saying she'd walked into a door to explain away a black eye. 'Again?' her daughter had said, and Mo would suck her teeth: *don't go off the rails*. Sid wasn't one of those. They'd met backstage at the Alhambra when he sang in *Kill that Fly!* He toured the provinces, up and down the country, with occasional contracts in London's halls. And sometimes – like now – he was between work or "resting", leaner spells when he might be short of a bob or two and she would pay. She didn't mind.

She spotted Sid in the queue looking dapper – couldn't miss his blue checked suit. He was a gentleman, rarely keeping her waiting. She liked that about him.

'Sid! Yoo-hoo!' She quickened her pace.

'All right, love?' His kiss landed with a smack on her cheek.

'Yeah, I'm good. How was Ipswich?'

'Loved us! We *worked* that crowd. Wouldn't let us go. Two encores!' He tipped his homburg to the back of his head, while his feet did a tippy-tappy dance. *'Oh I wouldn't give you tuppence for your old watch chain, old iron, old iron...'*

Nearby in the queue, they started to laugh and point. A pro in their midst.

'Don't give 'em any more for free, Sid.'

He doffed his hat, giving the ladies a wink. Anything for an audience.

'How's Molly?' That was another thing Rose liked about Sid: he always asked after Molly.

'Fine, thanks. She says to say hello.'

Sid had become a frequent visitor at home – but after that unfortunate occurrence with the other fellow, he did not sleep over. Not that Nina was around these days – or would care – and she wondered if Molly minded, but Rose liked to keep things cosy at home. Molly went to an effort if Sid was expected; she'd be at the sink, hands peeling extra spuds, presenting a buttery pile of mash with a good cut of meat. And a steamed pudding, that too. Afterwards, they might play cards, or he might sing. He had a fine baritone when he wasn't putting on his Cockney routine.

'I have to sing for my supper, eh?' He'd wink at Molly.

'You're a regular Tommy Tucker, you are,' Molly would say, enjoying his cheek.

'Ah, you spoil me, you two girls.' Sid would lean back, unbutton his waistband. 'I know what side my bread's buttered.' He had a bag-full of patter and could carry on for ages.

Once in the picture house, she and Sid took their seats. The last time she'd been to the cinema was to see *The Miracle*. She'd been astounded by the nun chucking things in to run off with a knight. The hand-coloured film made her feel she was watching something onstage, and she might reach out to touch those on-screen people. Every time she came to see a film, there was some innovation. She rummaged into a pocket to reach for a bag of toffees, mindful a tooth might give way at the slightest. Better a toffee than visiting the dentist.

'What's on tonight then?'

After *Calamity Anne's Beauty*, she and Sid grabbed a bite to eat and set off to his lodgings for the main entertainment of the evening.

Sex was something she'd almost forgotten, but Sid made her feel a woman again, and she would always thank him for that, even if she never saw him again. He treated lovemaking like he might a turn. A bit of banter to warm up the audience before a well-practised routine that made her laugh or sometimes cry out. And he might prop his hand on an elbow, wink at her and ask, 'Up for an encore, love?'

Tonight, she undressed unhurriedly. Her petticoat and undergarments lay folded on a chair, and she raised her leg to remove a stocking while he stared, admiring all of her.

Smack! Sid's hand landed on her bare bottom, and he chuckled at her.

'Ow! Wait, wait.' She pushed him away. From her bag, she took out her diaphragm, raised a leg and inserted it. Twice she'd been a visitor at Mabel's dismal parlour; twice she'd had a tube inserted and the beginnings of babies sucked out. No more of that, and she didn't trust any man, not even Sid, to look out for her.

Once sorted, they lay side by side in a close embrace, her fingers curling in a mass of furry chest hair. She felt his hands sliding over her back, her thighs, then a finger explored inside her. 'Just a little trick I learnt,' he'd told her, and she liked this trick – the best warm-up act she'd ever experienced. She was blooming.

He extracted his damp finger, sniffed, then tasted her. 'Tangy. Like being at the seaside.'

'No, salt of the earth, me. Earthy.' Rose the woman, as much as rose the flower, needed muck to grow. She had travelled far from the girl who loved tulle tutus and satin bows.

'Salt of the earth? Yeah, that's about right, Rosie love.' Sid rolled her over, positioning himself behind, cock hard against her buttocks, breath loud as he nibbled an ear before moving smoothly towards the middle part of their regular routine.

When Rose arrived exhausted for work next morning, she wondered, not for the first time, whether she and Sid should limit their hanky-panky to Fridays or Saturdays. She was not a young thing anymore. And the Alhambra needed her. A home of revue these days, management still producing small ballets and sketches that needed new costumes, or, more likely – as today – old ones refreshed.

'Come on.' Rose grabbed another seamstress and together they tripped up to the storage attics with small sooty windows, switching on dim lights.

'So musty.' The girl wrinkled her nose at the racks of mothballed covered costumes and ancient hampers. 'Gives me goosebumps. Ghosts and all.'

'Really?' Rose was surprised. She breathed in these stale smells: traces of past performers and artistic endeavour.

'Let's get on.' The girl, eager to be done, headed to a stacked aisle to their right.

'This way.' She headed left, scanning labels: "men's' robes" "fairy wings (pink, blue, white)" "helmets – knights". She soon found it: "ladies temple costumes". Exotics were in demand. Her fingers pulled at dry cracked leather to unbuckle the strap, then she opened the wicker lid and dug through tissue-wrapped layers of musty costumes. She handed them to the girl and together they spread out a multicoloured treasure, counting, assessing what needed altering to turn Assyrian costumes into the designer's idea of Egyptian.

She glanced at the disinterested, pimply girl next to her. This sewing job was just that to her – a job – and she'd move on to something else before long.

'These'll do,' Rose told her.

The girl grabbed a pile and headed down, relieved to be out, while Rose took lingering breaths, savouring the old days, lifting and laying more costumes across her arms as so many layers of her life.

That evening, arriving home, she found Molly squinting through her magnifying glass at the latest postcard from Monte Carlo. Over her shoulder, Rose saw a picture of the terrace outside the Casino, a glimpse of bay beyond.

'Very fancy!'

'What's she got to say for herself?' Molly flipped the card over.

'Not much,' Rose said, seeing Nina's scrawl angled across the space, that other, more determined writers, would fill more carefully. '*The new ballet, about a sacrifice is so* – underlined – *blooming difficult. Not enjoying. Treated to supper last night at the very posh Café de Paris, you can just see it at the edge of the photo! Don't expect I'll be eating there often.*'

'She sounds as if she's enjoying herself. That's the main thing.' Molly nodded. 'Doesn't say who bought supper.'

'Mind your own beeswax, she'd say.'

Molly chuckled. 'She'd talk about anything, that one, but when it comes to some things…'

'Matters of the heart?'

'She can be secretive. Still, I trust her.'

Rose smiled. 'Not to go off the rails.'

'There's more steel in that girl than is good for anyone, and I pity any man that falls for her.'

'That's harsh!'

'That's the truth! But she'll take care of herself.'

'Oh yes.' Rose nodded. 'I've no doubt.' It had been Nina who'd introduced her to Marie Stopes' family planning methods, which Rose had been shocked by but was now grateful – for herself and her nearly adult daughter. The journals Nina read were full of this sort of thing. 'No, I'm not worried about Nina. She's a weed that'll grow in a crack in the pavement. But Walter, now. If ever a boy was a hothouse plant…'

'He's a sweet boy, your Walter. Boys take longer. He'll turn out hardy.'

'And aren't they doing well? Couldn't be prouder.'

'Aren't they just.' Molly reached for her knitting. Simple garments these days, this one a scarf. As she shook it out across her lap, Rose noticed a dropped stitch further down, too far to unpick. She'd not say; it would only upset her. She must remember to fix it later when Molly had gone to bed.

She found a space on the kitchen wall amongst the postcards and stuck a drawing pin through the corner of Monte Carlo where an ornamental gas lamp reached to a blue sky. Nice to see, but she had no ambition to travel to foreign parts.

17

Sitting in an upstairs prep room, Walter picked up a dog-eared copy of Thucydides and found the page marked with Nina's postcard.

Hellish! We must make something of this new ballet about a spring sacrifice or I've promised to eat my hat (it's new and I don't want to!). Everything else going swimmingly. (I have a stylish new swimming costume by the way.) All the best, Nina

It was impossible to imagine the sophisticated life his sister was living without envy. It had happened so quickly, now there she was rubbing shoulders with the elite of the arts world while he was still a schoolboy. Stravinsky! What he would give to be in a rehearsal room. Having heard *Petrushka* and *Firebird* played at full throttle at Covent Garden, he imagined the new score might blend Russian folk melodies with the composer's own brand of dissonance. His heart remained firmly with the French Romantics, so while recognising the brilliance of Stravinsky, he was not likely to ever *love* him.

'Bloody thing!' A boy was rattling the window, trying to block a draft.

'Don't bother,' Walter called out. For all the years he'd been here, school rooms and dorms had always been freezing. He allowed himself to be distracted by the determined boy wrestling with the sash window, let his eye linger on the image of the Mediterranean town Nina had posted, then got back to work.

There would be an exam question on Thucydides – *History of the Peloponnesian War*. That war, Walter concluded, had been an atrocity, Athens enslaving and slaughtering right, left and centre. It was, he would say in the essay he was sure to be set in his exam, *an assertion of rights by an unbridled power that could never happen these days*. That was ancient history they had learnt from.

Parades on the school grounds were now twice-weekly affairs. Full kit and rifles. Those of Walter's friends who had decided on a military career had been channelled into the Special Form study course, embedded in army and navy officer training that would take them to India, Malta, Rhodesia, and other outposts. He, on the other hand, was focused on his Cambridge School Certificate. Assuming he passed, then he'd be done with school. Walter bit the end of his pen. A place at the Royal College of Music was offered, but not certain. There was the question of fees, Mr Quince uncharacteristically cautious.

At a recent meeting, the lawyer laced his fingers, tapping his thumbs, a frown deepening between bushy eyebrows. 'We are, Master Roberts, heading for difficult times.' He gestured to the folded *Times* and the *Evening Standard* on his desk. 'The stock market is under pressure, as you know.' Walter did not. Why would he? 'Your father had shares in various enterprises – foreign railway stock included – and what rain hits Wall Street soon finds its way to the City.' Hearing a sigh, Walter supposed the lawyer too had money invested.

'You mention an unsettled outlook?' Walter wasn't sure what was troubling the markets.

'Why, in Europe!' Mr Quince looked surprised. 'You must read the news – even in Surrey.'

'Not much time really...' Upper sixth reading lists of

examinable texts featured highly; newspapers did not. 'Is there something I should be aware of?'

Mr Quince grunted. 'School prepares one for colleges, then upwards into solid careers, but I am apt to wonder if some consideration might be given to world affairs as they happen, not simply the world that has passed.' The lawyer's index finger followed the small print in a column. '"Unsettled on account of uncertainties of the European outlook. So far a violent disturbance has been avoided…"'

Listening to the lawyer read, he tried to imagine a future him, an older Walter. Married, bewhiskered, pipe between teeth, confidently predicting stock market movement or political fortunes rising or falling.

'"…and it is hoped that an improvement in the political situation, of which there have been indications recently, will speedily restore financial conditions." Hear that, my lad. We must not be gloomy.'

He hadn't been gloomy so far. 'Are you saying my music study is uncertain?' His voice cracked into a falsetto at "music study", returning to a deeper "uncertain". Heat tingled his cheeks.

'Turbulent times, I fear. But with prudent management of your finances, I believe we may see a way through. One year at a time.'

'A way through, sir? What do you mean?'

'Only that you may consider bolstering your earnings. No, let me be blunt. You will need part-time employment to supplement what can be provided from your father's depleting assets.'

'Oh!' Walter could not bring himself to ask *how* depleted. 'I can offer private teaching lessons – I'm sure.'

'That, yes, or you may consider playing for the cinema. Could be fun. Grand picture houses are opening every week.'

An image formed of Mr Monroe hunched over the keyboard in a passion, capturing an on-screen duel or embrace. But could he see himself in a smoky theatre on a badly tuned piano? He had attended film shows, his friends making leud remarks about bow-lipped ringleted ladies or fancying themselves cowboys. While they lost themselves in the stories, he was aware of pungent smells around him: the proximity of unwashed bodies in clothes needing laundering.

'Not something I've considered, sir.'

'I don't see why not. It's perfectly legitimate. No shame in this or any theatrical endeavour. You have learnt that, at least.' Mr Quince's gaze challenged him.

'Of course. I'm so impressed with Nina—'

'Spilling over with pride, I'm sure. And your mother. Don't forget Rose's achievements.'

'Of course... I didn't mean...' What didn't he mean? Getting to know and learning to like Rose was one thing, but professing her career at the Alhambra was anything to be proud of...? Walter caught Mr Quince's glinting eye and chuckle.

'It's all right, my boy, quite all right.' He put aside the newspaper. 'Now we have settled our affairs, a snifter, you're suggesting? I have a new single malt.'

'Please, a finger.'

He had loathed the smell and taste of whisky on his first sip but was acquiring a liking for the smoky amber. If many aspects of manliness were yet out of reach, he was comforted that, outwardly, he was cultivating an armour that would serve him: holding a cigarette between fingers, just so, and able to drink with fellows without spluttering.

Mr Quince handed him a glass. 'To your future, young sir.'

18

Postcards to Ma 'n' Mo or to Walter might be chipper, but under the surface she was brittle, ready to snap. This was a baptism of fire, and she feared she might catch and start to burn.

Nina repeated the sequences of twos, fives, sevens, elevens. One: forearms across chest, elbows jutting. Two: right arm crossed over head, left arm flung upwards. Three... she angled arms into *precise* shapes on *precise* counts: an arithmetical puzzle. They were working on the opening of Act Two of *Rite* where the Chosen One is selected for sacrifice.

'No, Nina. On *second* repeat, you take your head back. Again. Quicker.'

It was just Mim and her in the studio: the eurhythmics expert demonstrating slowly, as you would to a beginner. Marie Rambert had been brought in to assist Nijinsky with the choreography. The woman was a saviour, *and* she spoke English.

A large chalk circle marked the floor, which they moved along anticlockwise in small toes-turned-in steps. Nina walked flat-footed, then on half pointe, arms semaphoring into *her* pattern. Each of them would be doing something slightly different, so there was no chance of copying. Her crepe-dechine rehearsal dress clung to her, and weary legs refused to obey her scrambled brain.

She groaned. 'It looks so easy till you try it. How could he have thought this up?'

'Genius! Mr Nijinsky is a genius.' Nina had seen how devoted Mim was, refusing to hear anything said against him. And plenty *was* said. Everyone knew Diaghilev was pushing his star dancer – his lover – to fill the shoes of Fokine, their last choreographer. How jealously the director guarded him, fearful one of the other dancers – male or female – would snap him up. Nijinsky was an odd fish who ignored her completely. Still, Diaghilev had faith in him, and so, day by day, they were plodding through the murk of the dratted ballet.

As Nina practised a sequence, she considered that if Isadora Duncan had sought to tear through a veil, then Stravinsky and Nijinsky were shredding the fabric completely, breaking it down to smaller and smaller bits then stitching it up again.

Up. Down. Skip. Step. Interweave. She was a cog in some giant structure, threatening always to jam the machinery. Mortifying. If she'd forgotten a step in one or other ballet, she might improvise, and no one was any the wiser. But this…

'Faster now,' Mim was explaining. 'We stamp, we'll hear boom, boom of drum…'

Nina stamped, copying Mim's pistoning arms: up, down, across…

'Now the jumps, but not reaching-to-the-sky jumps. Centre of gravity low, must feel the earth under our feet. Six, seven. Now!'

They leapt in unison: once; twice, punching the air.

At a pause, Nina reached for a towel, wiping her sweltering face and neck. 'Mim, I don't want to let everyone down. My head's spinning. I can't remember, and there's all the other ballets I've rehearsed – all sloshing in my head.' *Rite* was the hill at which she was stumbling, looking for a patch of grass to die on.

'You'll remember,' Mim said.

'I'm scared Diaghilev will get rid of me, I—'

'Poosh!' Mim laughed, poking her in the chest. 'You? I think you never scared.' She lifted her arms high then flipped upside down in a perfect cartwheel. It was Nina's turn to laugh. The day earlier, a group of them had competed to see who could do the most cartwheels. Mim had won, but Nina was a close second. Everyone saw she was competitive.

'I'll write the counts down, like the other girls. That may help.'

But before she could reach her notebook, Mim grabbed it, tossing it aside. 'No, no, better to remember with your muscles.' She glanced at the clock. 'Come, we've time before the others arrive. Once more.'

Shortly they'd all be rehearsing the frenzied Dance of the Earth section that brought the curtain down for the end of Act One. It had to be finalised, and today everyone would be present. *Everyone.*

'This, this, and this!' Igor Stravinsky's fist thumped Kolossel's shoulder, urging their rehearsal pianist's beleaguered fingers to greater speed. *'Jouer au tempo écrit… Écoutez!'* The slightly built composer hauled the huge man to his feet and, remaining standing, threw himself into the form of his own score – hands pounding keys, feet stamping, singing snatches, sounds as they should be rendered.

'That fast?' Nina whispered to Hilda. They stared at each other. This was double the speed they'd been rehearsing. Stravinsky returned to a second piano and the two men began a four-handed cacophony.

Away from the musicians, two other men, equally large and small, equally at odds: Diaghilev and Nijinsky huddled in battle, the impresario's head thrust forwards, palms upwards. 'Vaslav,' Nina heard him say, his voice raised a pitch as it was whenever he was angry, and she could only imagine what he might be appealing. But the dancer appeared not to heed. He stood in his practice clothes – belted, tight-fitting trousers buttoned below the calf, white sports shirt with open collar and long sleeves – eerily still, picking his nails. And between them, Nina watched Grigoriev scuttle back and forth, spit flying, urging them to sort things out. And there was Mim, clutching that Bible of a notebook, sketches and sequences of complicated counts that looked like algebra. 'Marie, please...' Diaghilev replaced his monocle he'd allowed to drop and beckoned. The Polish woman darted to join them.

'Pray to God,' a Polish dancer with some English whispered to Nina, '*Rhythmichka* will sort the... um...' She pointed to her head.

'Block,' Nina offered.

'Block, yes, in Vaslav's head. I do very much wish *we* block this choreography.'

But which bit? That was the problem. It was all fragments with gaps where no one knew what came next. Roughly working out – blocking – the floor patterns and movements would give guidance.

Nina, with the rest of them, waited for the next thing to be resolved. They were leaving for Paris in a few days and there were many sections they didn't have the faintest idea about. The original name of this ballet, *The Great Sacrifice*, was apt. It wasn't just the maiden who'd be sacrificed for some fertility god, Nina feared the Paris reviewers might slaughter them all for the mess of it.

Grigoriev clapped his hands. 'Places, please. We are ready.'

'Bearskin men here,' Mim called, and Nijinsky began pushing men into formation – impatience palpable – demonstrating contorted body positions, trying to share what was locked in his brain.

She heard his exasperated cry, 'You are deliberately obstructing me!' as, yet again, dancers were unable to, instantly, execute a step to perfection.

Sucking in a juddering breath, she feared for her own limitations.

'Red women there.' Mim hurried to divert attention, and Nina moved into place. She was beginning to understand if there were to be a failure, it would be all of them who'd get roasted. She was a tiny part of this ambitious production: music, dance, sets and costume. No one was interested in Nina Banbury. No individuals here. No stars. She clustered with other dancers, comforted by their presence.

The day before they were due to leave for Paris, she was packing her sodden rehearsal clothes in her bag when she heard Grigoriev's voice: 'Ah, Miss Banbury, Diaghilev wishes you to attend him in the Green Room.'

Her heart contracted. This was it. She didn't think Diaghilev even noticed her all those times he watched classes and rehearsals. Certainly, he'd never spoken with her. Always when their director entered the studio or a room with his entourage, everything stopped. If a female was favoured with some quiet words, she curtsied; if he addressed one or other of the men, there was a click of heels, a stiff bow, ramrod straight. Had Diaghilev decided she was not up to scratch?

Willing her voice to be steady, she asked, 'Just me?'

'First you. Do you know where the other English girls are?'

'I think they're still in the changing room.' She watched Grigoriev retreating. Poor Hilda. Poor Doris and Anna. That didn't seem fair, and Hilda was progressing wonderfully. Nina dragged her feet to where Diaghilev waited and rapped on the door.

'*Entrez.*' The deep voice was unmistakable.

Inside, she found Diaghilev standing, back to her, hands behind his back, emitting that curious mixture of power and scent of hair oil. To find him alone was unheard of, and to find him unoccupied – or preoccupied? – was unusual. He turned as she stepped in, as if he'd forgotten he'd asked for her.

She willed her voice to be steady. 'Sergei Pavlovich, you wished to see me?'

'*Je vais apporter quelques modifications* – some changes – *avant la saison Parisienne.*' English was not something he had mastered so preferred not to try, while her French was still rudimentary. He adjusted his monocle, peering at her. 'The English…' He shook his big head, looking perplexed.

It was coming… Coming… Any moment… Behind her back, Nina dug her nails into her palms, her feet leaden.

'*J'ai bien réfléchi.*' Her director touched his temple. '*Banbury doit partir.*'

The blow had come.

'Must go!' A wail. She would beg, if not on her hands and knees then with hands clasped in front of her, pleading with the man who held her future in his. 'Oh, Sergei Pavlovich, please don't fire me. I've been working hard. *Rite* is challenging. I'm trying not to muck it up. I'll work harder. I've—'

'Quiet!' He held out a hand, shocked. 'Please…' He indicated chairs, and they sat – he upright as always, she on the very edge, legs trembling – the Chosen Maiden to be sacrificed. No. No. No!

She forced herself to meet his gaze as he said, '*Je ne regrette pas de t'avoir donne une place…*'

So he *didn't* regret having her here?

'...but Banbury must be left behind,' he continued in carefully enunciated English.

She swallowed hard. Maybe it would be better if he spoke French, and she would follow as best she could.

'Ballets Russes is *Russian!*' The "R" rolled with a passion she knew he harboured for his country yet was separated from. 'So, Banbury must go, and I give you a new name. A *Russian* name. "Nina" I approve, but "Banbury"? No... No.' He scrutinised her as if a more fitting name might be written on her face.

Relief flooded over her. She was staying! Diaghilev wanted her! She threw herself off her chair and hugged him. For a split second he tensed, then laughed, a deep genuine belt of laughter. Then he and she gathered themselves and sat again.

She didn't fancy a long complicated Russian name. It was only for the playbills, after all, so that Diaghilev could present the company as genuinely Russian to the public and press.

They tried one or two names but rejected them. It was easy in the end.

'Banbury was your father's name?'

'No, he was Arthur Roberts.' She did not say they weren't married.

'Roberts.' Diaghilev wrinkled his nose. 'Mother?'

'Rose Banbury.'

'Rose.' He nodded. 'Rosa... Rosova... Nina Rosova?'

Her face lit up. 'Nina Rosova. I like it very much. Oh, thank you, Sergei Pavlovich.' She jumped up and bobbed a curtsey. For a moment, she felt a hand touch her hair. A blessing, a baptism? She doubted there would be another intimate moment between them. Diaghilev was not a man to compliment his dancers – rarely the principals and certainly not the ensemble.

In the corridor she found the quaking English girls.

'Well?' Three sets of eyes drilled hers. She was bursting to tell them, but bit her lip, shaking her head. Doris grabbed her arm, but she shook herself free and hurried away, fearful the sparkle in her eyes would reveal the fire in her heart. Let them suffer a little as she had done. Let them find out for themselves.

Out of sight, she doubled over, body shaking, half laughing, half crying, feeling she might vomit. She must never doubt herself. She could reinvent the girl from Whitechapel. Nina-bloody-Rosova; the world had better watch out!

19

THIS TIME IT WAS A TELEGRAPH, NINA'S MODE OF communication even terser than her postcards:

RITE PREMIERE 29th. OUR BIRTHDAY. COME.

Walter read it again. Paris? His sister wanted him to travel to watch her dance, under the pretext it would coincide with their eighteenth birthday? Here was he deep in revisions for exams and she expected him to drop everything. He screwed the paper into a ball and binned it, annoyed she could think of herself and her glory.

A week later, his housemaster tossed him an envelope. 'Roberts, you're popular.'

PARIS IN SPRING!

More in curiosity than anything, Walter asked around. Boat train from Charing Cross, they said, steamer from Dover, train…

Nina's third message: LODGINGS SORTED. BE HERE!

Today was a Thursday, exactly a week till the premiere.

What to do? If the Paris ballet season had been months earlier, or months later, he would've jumped at the chance. Paris – the centre of art. He pictured himself at concert halls, visiting the Louvre, imagining the awe Notre-Dame might inspire in him, and so much more.

'You know, Roberts, it could be done.' Mr Reed pored over timetables. 'Best would be the overnight steamer. You could always take Pythagoras and trigonometry with you, books being highly portable. And, naturally, you'd get practice conjugating French verbs.'

Walter laughed, expecting Mr Reed to do the same. But no. Why would this master who'd guided him for so many years try to scupper his chances of betterment at this final hurdle of school life?

'Sir?'

'There are different ways to prepare for exams, Roberts, prepare for life! You've been tucked away in these brick walls for years. If your masters haven't drilled in everything by now, then God help our reputation. In my opinion, last-minute cramming won't make the slightest difference. It's the same with musical scores. The notes don't pass from fingers to brain in one or two practices, unless you're Mozart, which neither of us are. You allow the music to seep into your marrow over time. Go. Go, I say.'

Walter took a breath and dared think it possible. 'You really think so?'

'Ask yourself this. Are you set on Oxford or Cambridge? Are you likely to pass with First Class?'

'You know that's not what I aspire to. Second Class at most, I imagine. Possibly distinction in History.'

'There you are. And you've a place at the Academy, pending even a Third-Class pass?'

Walter nodded.

Mr Reed laid a hand on his shoulder. 'Music is your future. Discuss this with your Housemaster—'

'And if he doesn't—'

'Why then, take it up with Reverent Downes.'

The Head, who had replaced Reverent Rutty, must be consulted in any case.

'Actually, Roberts, I'll speak to him myself. I'll stress what an opportunity this is. A once-in-a-lifetime, not-to-be-missed opportunity. A premiere, no less! It may not be to my taste, or yours, but you can learn from him.' Mr Reed was not thinking of the choreographer but the composer. 'When you return—'

'If I go...'

'*When* you return, I want to hear everything. What you make of the orchestration, and the orchestra – over a hundred in the pit, so I read.' Mr Reed looked like he'd go himself, given the chance. 'Stravinsky's an unusual fellow. Highly irregular musical ideas, as you know.' They had analysed *Petrushka*. 'I believe the theatre has sold out, but your sister will have reserved a seat?'

'I imagine so. She's always managed to in the past.'

'Excellent! You've not travelled beyond these shores, so we must arrange for a passport quickly. I'll speak with Mr Quince.'

'But we don't know if I can go!'

'Nonsense, Roberts!'

The following day, Walter went to the Post Office and sent his first telegraph:

ARRIVING WEDNESDAY. WHERE SHALL I GO?

It was a sweltering day when Walter arrived in Paris. The Theatre des Champs-Elysées was a newly built, squat and solid-looking affair from the outside. He passed the entrance and made his way to the stage door.

'*Excuse-moi. Je suis ici pour rencontrer ma soeur*, Nina Banbury.' How delicious to speak French as if it were the most natural thing in the world.

'*Pardon?*' The stage door manager barely raised his eyes.

'*A danseur dans la compagnie.* Um, *Anglaise*. Nina Banbury. *Elle m'attend.*' He enunciated each word carefully.

The man ran his finger down a list of names, 'Banbury… Banbury…' shaking his head. For a moment, Walter's confidence deserted him. He was sure he had the right day, and it was five o'clock on the dot. He tried again but was met with indifference.

'Nina's twin! Welcome.' Alexei was limping towards him, leaning heavily on a cane.

'Alexei! So pleased to see you. I thought I'd got it wrong. He doesn't know her! Nina, I mean. I thought—'

Alexei lightly kissed first his left then right cheek, stopping Walter in his tracks.

The dancer exchanged words with the man and, with further shrugs, Walter understood that "Mademoiselle Rosova" was indeed expecting him.

'My sister has transformed?' Walter exchanged a grin with Alexei.

'Oh yes, quite transformed!' Alexei eyed his suitcase. 'Leave that here. I am ordered to look after you and I expect the dress rehearsal to go on and on.' He shook his head. 'Giving birth to *Rite* is troublesome and sadly I am not a part. I would like…' He extended a leg, a thick bandage binding an ankle. 'That English dancer, Doris, she has big feet. Boomph.' He thumped his hands together, and Walter pictured the calamity of tangled bodies on the floor.

'I'm so sorry. You must be terribly disappointed.'

'Fate.' The dancer shrugged. 'Two, three days, then better…

Come.' Walter followed a hobbling Alexei out. 'Coffee?'

'I just had… I'm fine, thank you, but if you would like—'

'We sit then.' He raised his cane and pointed towards the Seine.

'Shouldn't you rest?'

'When I die, Walter, when I die!'

He smiled, loving the sound of his name in Alexei's voice, a slight "V" sound to the "W". Alexei's mother was English but he had been born and brought up in St Petersburg, fluent in both languages with a command of French.

They found a bench overlooking the river, flowing through the heart of the city. It was Walter's fate to spend time with his injured friend – a situation he could not have imagined. Alexei asked about his studies, his music, and Walter talked freely, sensing the dancer's genuine interest. In turn, he asked about company life and how Nina was doing.

'She has spark. We like our jokes, she and I… Your birthday tomorrow, no?'

'Eighteen.'

'So young!' Alexei touched his cheek, laughing.

'You're not old!'

'Twenty-two, but I feel I have lived a long time.' He flexed his ankle. 'After tomorrow's performance, we celebrate. All arranged.'

'Oh! That will be splendid.'

'Yes, splendid!' Alexei repeated in precise English. Walter grimaced, knowing he sounded a prude, but Alexei reached out and tapped the tip of his nose. 'So sweet, Nina's brother. So sweet.'

He did not dare move.

'Alexei. I haven't got Nina anything for her birthday. I should.'

'You must!' Alexei's eyes sparkled. 'What shall we buy?'

'A scarf… something soft and silky, I was thinking. She liked the last one I gave her.' The heat of a blush rose past his neck as he remembered the flimsy fabric Nijinsky had held aloft.

'She has plenty, believe me; she doesn't stop shopping. How about something very French?' He raised his cane, directing Walter's attention along the street. Perfume shops – he had passed several on his walk from the station.

'Splendid, that will be spl—' He blushed. Couldn't he think of anything better to say?

Inside the *parfumerie*, Walter was confronted by shelf upon shelf of labelled bottles. He didn't have the slightest idea where to start, but neither did Alexei.

'Something for a young lady?' Walter asked the assistant, in his best French.

'For a Russian ballerina,' Alexei added, deliberately thickly.

'Oh. You are dancers. Superb!' The assistant clapped her hands, and Walter did not correct her. 'You have a fragrance in mind?'

'Rose, something with roses.' Walter was firm in that, fashionable or not.

At a shelf, the assistant selected two bottles.

Alexei sampled one, drawing a wooden stick dipped in a fragrance across his own inside wrist, lifting it to Walter's nose. 'Do you like it?' Another sample was smeared on the inside of Walter's wrist and Alexei raised it to his own nose and sniffed deeply. 'I like. I sense a rosebud here, ready to bloom!'

Teasing eyes met his own and he felt his face glow. At that moment, Walter wanted to float away, hand in hand with Alexei, somewhere above this city that was proving so magical.

With his selection carefully boxed and gift-wrapped, they headed back to the theatre, where Walter hid his gift amongst his textbooks, pyjamas, toothbrush, and the decent suit he had tried to fold. He meant to look smart for Nina's premiere and their birthday.

As Walter knelt, fastening his crammed case, he asked, 'Has Nina arranged somewhere for me to stay, do you know?'

'With us!' Alexei looked surprised. 'Your sister never bothers with – um – details. You stay with me and Nicholai.'

'Ah, I… I…'

Alexei looked anxious. 'Hotels are expensive, but if—'

'No!' Walter could hardly breathe. 'That will be—'

'Splendid!' Alexei finished.

'Walter, *darling*, you made it!'

Walter jumped to his feet and watched an elegant young woman pushing through a group of dancers, musicians, and singers about to prepare for the evening.

'Nina!' Walter held his sister at arm's length, then kissed her first on her left cheek, then her right, as he'd learnt was the thing to do.

'Where shall we eat? I'm famished.' She linked arms.

'Not so fast, please,' Alexei said. 'And your suitcase, Walter.'

He was borne away on a tide of bodies. Hilda, he knew, other names flowed in one ear, out the other.

Dancers, he discovered, could devour massive meals.

'How's Ma?' Nina remembered to ask as they were paying the bill, but he could say little, just as he'd said little about school, doubting she'd be much interested. His eyes roamed the gathering, settling on Alexei, laughing about something with an English dancer – Anna, he recalled.

At the lodgings the Russian boys shared, they found quilts and blankets in a cupboard. Walter lay on that makeshift mattress in the gap between two narrow beds, tossing and turning, the sounds of the city drifting in through a wide-open window:

hooves on cobbles, the drone of motors, a church clock striking the hour and half hour.

Nicholai snored lightly, but when he turned to Alexei, he found his eyes on him.

'Can't you sleep?' Alexei whispered. 'You can have my bed.'

'No, no. It's perfectly all right. I wouldn't dream of it.'

'Dreams only come in sleep. It's hot, no?'

'Yes, I am a little hot.'

'Those pyjamas…' Alexei's hand reached over and touched the cloth at his shoulder. The Russians, Walter noted, slept in their underwear shorts.

'I suppose I could…' Walter sat up and unbuttoned his pyjamas shirt, fanning the fabric. He would not remove it but having the shirt open helped a little. Still he tossed.

'You're keeping me awake.' Alexei sighed. 'Come.' He pushed back his sheet, rolled away to face the wall. Soon Walter was lying with his knees fitting snuggly behind the dancer's, leaving the problem of where to put his upper arm. Still he fidgeted.

Alexei reached back and drew it over him. 'Better?'

'Yes,' he replied, breath unsteady, not trusting himself to say more. It was torture, but a sweet torture and he could not control the stirring in his loin. He jerked back, mortified.

'You know, I'm sure I can get to sleep on the floor. So sorry… so very sorry…' He slipped out of bed and back to his nest. Alexei stretched out a hand and laid it on his shoulder. Walter allowed it to rest, then seeing Alexei did not remove it, covered it with his own hand and eventually slept.

20

ABOUT NOW, NIJINSKY WOULD BE PARTNERING Karsavina in the waltz. Soon *Sylphides* would be over, and it would be their turn.

Nina secured her black wig with another hairpin, then flicked all four braids behind her shoulders where they trailed to her waist. Selecting a greasepaint crayon from her make-up tray, she peeled a little of the wrapper to reveal scarlet pigment. Carefully, she infilled the triangles she'd outlined on each whitened cheek. In the reflection, a doll-like creature stared back: enormous eyes, brilliant red cheeks and lips, the mirror catching twenty such female faces in various stages of readiness, each fighting for space in the dressing room.

'Oh Lord, if it's half as hot onstage.' Hilda – costumed top to toe for Act One – fanned the neck of her tunic, funnelling the breeze down to her belly.

'I'm putting off the moment.' Nina glanced at her own costume over a chair: the red flannel tunic a riot of orange and green shapes. It made her hot just looking at it.

'Did you manage to get a seat for Walter?' her friend asked.

'Not a chance!' Nina pulled a face. 'Double the price and still it was sold out, even in the slips. But if I'd told Walter that, he'd never have come.'

'Oh, Nina! He's very sweet to travel all this way.' Hilda and the other English girls had a soft spot for Walter. At supper the night before, the group of them had adopted him as if he were family.

'He's watching, but from the wings. Alexei's going to sneak him backstage. Walter didn't seem too fussed about it actually. It's the music he's set on hearing.'

'He'll hear it all right!'

They shared a nervous laugh. What had been a four-handed rendition of the score on two pianos in rehearsal was now a full-blown orchestra. At yesterday's dress rehearsal, the squawks from the pit had been alarming, the conductor seemingly at odds with the composer, while onstage Nina silently recited her counts, battling to stay in time.

After patting her face with blending powder, she set the hare-foot puff down next to a small bottle of *Bois de Rose* she would dab on her wrists and behind her ears. She had been touched by Walter's gift – first thinking it was for the premiere before realising it was their birthday – and had not thought to buy him anything. In fairness, rehearsals had been slavish. Walter, she understood, was travelling home on Saturday, giving her just tomorrow to sort something out.

Two weeks earlier, on arriving in Paris, she had been at a reception. The conversation had turned maudlin as they talked about Isadora Duncan.

'Poor, poor woman. Two children dead.'

'I heard she likes her drink. I wouldn't be surprised if she's drowning her sorrows. I would be.' Nina raised her glass.

'Drowning! Nina,' someone scolded her. 'That's not very nice.'

She bit her lip.

What had affected Nina was the suddenness with which life can end. An automobile on the bank of the Seine without its handbrake full on, a slide into the water, sinking, sinking, little faces pressed to a window. Even girls who'd never seen Duncan dance became weepy.

She had stalked to the hotel reception, champagne in hand, and immediately dashed off her message: RITE PREMIERE 29th. BIRTHDAY. COME.

When she didn't receive a reply, she dug in her heels. What had begun as a sentimental response to another family's tragedy became a determination to have Walter here.

'Honestly, who *wouldn't* want to come to Paris?' she stormed at Alexei.

'Bet you can't make him come,' he said.

'You watch!'

'Bet you… Price of a theatre ticket.' They shook on it.

She fired off another message, in truth only half expecting her brother to turn up.

Seeing him backstage, so gauche, had made her want to hug him. Besides the chance of getting to know him better, having him here verified her, confirmed her success. If only she could be sure of not mucking up in those tricky counts. Even in dress rehearsal, she had blundered, earning a hiss from the dancer next to her.

In the corridor, shrill female voices indicated a performance gone well. The pit-a-pat of pointe shoes on the floor, flashes of white tulle tutus as airy sylphs hurried to dressing rooms to become pagan Russians when more than forty dancers would beat the earth.

'Break a leg!' Hilda said.

'Break a leg!' echoed through the dressing room.

While stagehands changed the backcloth from woodland glade to Russian Steppes, Nina found a place in the wings to warm up – *pliés*, crisp *tendus*, small jumps to get her legs and heartbeat pumping. She peeped through a wing. There was

Diaghilev in tails and top hat, hair pomaded, walking the stage with an eye on the backdrop – the smell of fresh paint still about it – ensuring every crease was removed. Beyond the front curtain, squeaks of instruments warming up indicated interval was ending. At applause, the conductor would be taking his place at the podium, while beyond, in the auditorium, the audience was settling. Monied subscribers and celebrated artists doing well for themselves would be in plush armchairs at forty francs a ticket. Nobility and select society from the historic district, Faubourg Saint-Germain, to their dining-style chairs in first-level boxes. Students and artists who *weren't* doing well took two-franc seats with barely enough legroom in the steeply sloped upper levels and seats to the sides with restricted views.

Nina made her way to the upstage left wing to where Doris waited, and others hurried up: seven red-costumed women ready for their entrance. She fanned her armpits. Did she exude the smell of fear? A pity Mim wasn't with them, but she was in a group with shorter dancers that included Hilda. Barbaric bearskin-clad dancers were filing onstage into opening positions. Off to her side she glimpsed a pale face close to a wall. Walter?

A hush, the audience falling silent, and she imagined the conductor's baton raised. At a long wail from the largest of the woodwind instruments, she shivered despite the woollen costume and suffocating heat.

❧

Walter shivered. A rising and falling high note – can that really be a bassoon? – now horn… clarinet… an eery soundscape painting a mythical Russia. Unfamiliar snatches – mere hints – of melodies he couldn't quite catch before dissolving. Trills, off-chords, and shards of metallic horns.

He pressed further into the wall as if to disappear into the fabric of the theatre. He should not be watching from here, but in the chaos of backstage readiness, he had been swept into this alcove. Alexei had thrust him there, warning, 'Don't move!'

'But—'

'Tell them you're an English aristocrat – your seat mistakenly given to a German count. Who's to argue?' Alexei reached out to straighten his tie. 'There. You're looking very smart.'

Seeing Alexei turn away, Walter grabbed him. 'Aren't you staying?'

'Something to see to.' Alexei hobbled off.

He quashed his disappointment. He wanted Alexei to explain the story of the ballet, tell him which were his parts – when he would be well enough to dance again. More than anything, he wanted Alexei by his side.

Hand over hand, stagehands hauled on a rope. The front curtain rose. That bassoon again. Those phrases and whispers of melody. Cello strings. Pounding chords. From the stage came the sounds of soft shoes thudding, first lightly, then with more insistence as men in heavy tunics took up the pulse.

New sounds – over and above the musicians and dancers. Whistling? Was that booing?

'Shut up!' a man bellowed from the auditorium.

It shocked him. Theatres and concert halls were chapels with rituals – the congregation there for an act of worship. Did they normally behave this way in Paris? Alexei was not here for him to ask.

Earlier, he had seen members of the audience sweeping in, and he milled around the foyer, gathering impressions and stories for Rose and Mr Reed, so he could say he'd been here. Were these sumptuous, top-of-society people acting like this?

He tried to imagine a man in a tailored tailcoat, hands forming a megaphone, booing. Catcalls and whistles continued. Such loutishness must, surely, be from the cheaper upper seats.

Through a middle wing, he caught glimpses of pointy hats edged with fur bobbing up and down, clenched fists in the air, bearskin men still beating the stage. There, waiting in the wings, he saw Nina – at least, he thought it was her – among identically dressed girls. He watched as, hand in hand, a line of seven scarlet dancers skipped onstage in front of hills and clouds. Whatever he might have to lie about, or elaborate, when he got home, he could honestly say he saw Nina onstage.

But what to make of the score. Unlike anything he'd heard. He wanted those idiots in the audience to shut up so he could concentrate.

A squeeze on the shoulder and Walter tensed, sensing he was about to be ejected.

'Come.' Alexei cocked his head.

'We can't stay?'

'I've a better place.' Alexei hobbled away, and Walter followed closely, afraid he'd lose him in the dim light with bodies pressing around him, rushing in and out.

'Sorry!' Walter almost tripped over a little man running – Nijinsky, he realised in horror – in white tights and a curly wig from the last ballet. Alexei grabbed his arm, tugging, and Walter just had time to watch Nijinsky grab a chair, place it out of sight of the audience and jump on it, yelling, conducting the dancers, 'Odin… Dva… Tri…' Then the stage door closed behind them, muffling all sound.

Along a corridor, Alexei almost leaping with the aid of his cane, down a flight of stairs, through a door, the orchestra close again, judging by the volume. Above Walter's head came thuds of feet. He was under the stage and Alexei was fumbling with a key, opening a door.

'Alexei?' Walter laughed. 'This is perfect right here. I can hear everything!'

'But here is better.' Alexei thrust Walter in, found the light switch and closed the door behind him. A dim light flickered and spread.

They were in what seemed to be a storage room, little more than a cupboard. There was a broad-headed broom, buckets and mops, chairs, folded piles of black cloth – curtains still to be hung? It wasn't musty; this theatre was brand new. Walter turned to face the dancer, standing three feet from him, tense and watchful.

'Have I made a mistake?' Alexei said.

Walter could only stare, knowing his face reflected his anguish, his desire.

Alexei gave a small nod, softly saying, 'I want you to always remember your eighteenth birthday.'

Walter knew what to expect. Knew it, feared it, longed for it. But this was wrong. All church teachings he had ever received said so. And so did the law.

'Would you like my present?' Alexei's voice was guarded, head tilted, a querulous gaze, small wrinkles forming about those grey eyes.

'Yes. Yes, please,' Walter answered without hesitation, before he could change his mind.

'I wasn't sure.' With the tiniest of smiles, Alexei took his hand with a small squeeze. He turned the key in the lock and Walter wondered if this was the first time he'd been here.

Together they hauled a massive, folded curtain from a pile and spread it out, shifting things in their way. On a shelf were cloths, little more than dusters – they spread these out by way of a sheet. Thank goodness he had bathed in preparation for later that evening with his sister. His body would not smell sour. That mattered. Thank goodness he could still hear the music so, later, he might speak about it without making things up.

Draping his suit jacket over a broom handle, he began unbuttoning his shirt, eyes devouring Alexei, who was out of his trousers. Anxiety gnawed his gut. Would he know the right way of doing things when faced with needing to do *something* with Alexei?

Above him came sounds of dancers pounding feet; beyond the door came the mournful moan of a trumpet and a fresh mash of orchestrated sounds.

'The rival tribes are fighting,' Alexei said, 'but we are loving, yes?'

Walter nodded, unable to speak at the impossibility of what was happening.

∼

Nina cast her eyes around the dancers hunched forwards, feet in frenzied stamps. Where was Mim when you needed her? This was every man and woman for themselves.

They had reached the Dance of the Earth section, and Nina was doing her best to keep up. Yells and catcalls, and actual whistles – to think that people had brought real whistles with them, clearly intent on disruption. *Bastards!* She'd like to strangle them. Thundering kettledrums – *thrump… thrump* – sound rising above the noise from the audience. Would someone call a halt? Diaghilev? The theatre manager? She could barely hear the orchestra over the shouting. Her eye caught the conductor's arm in staccato up, down, up, and from the prompt side came Nijinsky's shrieked counts.

She leapt, legs and elbows forwards, hands to ears. Rapid stamps: one, two, three, four. Spin… spin… braided hair flying, tunic billowing, sweat showering. On and on the pulse drove her forwards. She could no longer hear the music but trusted her body to find the rhythm. *Rat-a-tat, rat-a-tat…*

Circling, pounding the stage. Turning inwards now, and with the other pagans, forming a tight circle. She could hear the breath of every panting dancer near her, could feel the heat of their bodies. Sweat ran between her shoulder blades, down her back. Beneath her wig, clammy hair clung to her scalp and sweat dripped from forehead to nose. She was in a furnace. She was on fire.

Soon would come a screeching, strident chord and she would punch the air.

Soon the curtain would fall on Act One and she would race back to her dressing room to shed this soaking costume for a clean white one for Act Two.

Walter lay on his back. The warmth of Alexei's breath and probing tongue in an ear, the wetness of tongue on his neck, downwards, now at a nipple, a hand cupping his balls, gently applying pressure. He was moaning and couldn't stop. He allowed himself to be rolled on his side, Alexei's knees fitting snugly in the back of his own as if they belonged there. He yelped as Alexei pressed his stomach to his back, the hardness of his... his *thingamabob*... utterly thrilling. Alexei reached around to encircle his. Ragged gasps ripped from his mouth at the sensation of long, smooth, sliding motions. When Walter reached back, longing to grasp this man's penis, his hand was slapped away, and Alexei jerked back.

'No, my gift.' And Alexei kept on giving.

'Ooh!' Walter arched his back, angry with himself this had not lasted longer. 'Sorry, sorry... I couldn't help—'

'Shh,' came the reply and Alexei clutched him tighter, moving... moving... breath jagged.

Here was Nijinsky as Faun, that last moment in the ballet,

that final moment of ecstasy and release. If this most carnal thing was in Nijinsky's act too, it couldn't be so very wrong, could it? If Diaghilev could love Nijinsky – everyone knew, Nina said – then why not him? Why not Walter Roberts?

There was someone at the cupboard door, rattling the handle, calling, '*Auelqu'in a vu la clé?*'

'No,' two stagehands replied. They didn't have the key, hadn't seen it.

Alexei put his finger to his lips, neither of them moving.

It was interval, the orchestra quiet, a low rumble of arguments and conversations from the auditorium, and from the stage came clunks of heavy shoes.

'Stagehands,' Alexei said. 'Changing the backdrop. And the floor needs sweeping. Bits of beard and fur all over the place. Hairpins...'

Soon the ballet resumed. So many pounding feet made the floor vibrate, dislodging dust above them.

Alexei lay on his side, hand propping his head while his other idly stroked Walter's chest and stomach.

'They're choosing the sacrificial girl. That girl didn't choose her fate, but you, Walter, seem happy with yours.'

He turned over and crushed Alexei to him, mouth open, lips mashing into Alexei's, a more-than-willing participant.

Above and beyond, pagan rituals of spring continued. *Oomp, oomp,* the incessant kettledrum. He heard horns and oboes... strings... eerie blocks of melody he'd heard earlier but now disconnected and fitted again. Within the cupboard, he added blissful moans and there were whispered words in Russian he didn't understand.

'Listen... wait.' Alexei cocked an ear. 'She's dancing to death. It will soon be over.'

He lay, encircled by an arm, his head resting on Alexei's chest, listening to the steady beat of a heart.

The Rite of Spring ended. Walter heard male and female voices raised: 'Bravo! Magnifique!' Hands crashing in a thunder, trying to outdo boos – like so many bulls – and derisive insults: '*Merde! Honte á toi!*' And surely, Walter thought, those cries of "Shame on you!" were not directed at the orchestra and artists, but at each other. There was no way of knowing. Walter imagined Nina defiantly taking her bow amidst this unrest: head dipping but heart strong. Musicians started to make their way from the pit. Beyond the cupboard door he heard their footfall, laughs of relief, comments like "those bastards". He feared someone would again come – this time with a key.

No one came, and they stayed.

Weber's music drifted through the cupboard door as Nijinsky and Karsavina – so Alexei said – danced the gentle dream that was *Le Spectre de la Rose.*

If ever Walter associated music with love, he'd thought of music such as this one playing now. Or arias: Puccini, Bizet, certain works by Bach, sweeping Liszt, Tchaikovsky. A dozen – no, a hundred – melodies could be summoned: music that tried to speak of love. No longer. Forever after, it would be Stravinsky's score that ripped through to his soul. This is what love felt like: a primeval soup. He gazed at the pale-skinned youth next to him: dancer's body as perfect as those Greek and Roman Adonises in the British Museum.

He reached out and touched Alexei's neck, feeling the movement of his Adam's apple. 'You're so beautiful.'

'And you, young Walter, are delightful.' Alexei laughed, kissing him lightly on the nose, the spell broken. This was the old Alexei, slightly arch, aware of himself. Walter wasn't sure if he were jesting and if any of this meant a thing. He dared not ask.

Alexei gently pushed him aside and they silently dressed.

The rags they had tried to spread under them had shifted and the black curtain was smeared with sticky whiteness. They wiped what they could, then folded the fabric to hide the outcome of their actions. Now it was over, they were just two young men skulking in a cupboard.

'You go first,' Alexei said. 'You remember how to get out?'

'I think so.'

Walter scampered away, once more a frightened boy.

21

Nina sped towards where Walter and Alexei stood, a little apart from a gaggle of dancers on the pavement, both of them smoking.

'There you are! I've been looking all over. You could've said!' She greeted them with a peck on a cheek. What a pity Walter had to witness this debacle – hardly the triumph she had imagined. 'Poor darlings, I'm so sorry.'

'Sorry?' Alexei breathed smoke through his nose, and Walter's lips were twitching, undecided whether to smile. Clearly the evening had been horrible for him, and he didn't like to say so.

'Poor you…' She poked Alexei's chest. 'You missed the premiere. Missed all the fun. Oh my goodness, what an absolute riot. You know someone yelled, "Get a dentist!" Then some idiot shouted, "Two dentists!" Honestly, I didn't know whether to laugh or cry. But you heard it. You saw it, right? From the wings?'

'Yes, some.' Alexei shrugged. 'I will test my foot in class tomorrow. Maybe next performance, I'll dance.' He flexed and rotated his injured foot.

'And poor you!' She turned to Walter. 'You'll hate me after this. Just hate me!'

'Why should I?' Walter looked perplexed.

'It's a rotten shame. I'd wanted it to be special, hoped I'd slip you in somehow – like before. But, oh goodness, the security, like the crown jewels. Anyhow, there were no seats to be had.'

'Don't worry, Nina, I've had a splendid time.'

'You mean it?' Her brother was being scrupulously polite – as always. 'Which part did you like best? The parts with the boys dancing, or us girls circling around Maria—'

'Maria?'

'Oh, I thought Alexei might have said. Her.' She indicated one of the chattering group, already walking away. 'She was the chosen virgin, the one quivering like this for ages.' She stood like a wooden puppet, toes turned in, head tilted, hands flat to her thighs. 'We girls were prancing around her. Remember?'

'Oh yes… I do now. I think—'

'I *love* the bit when we drop to the floor, face first.' She could not shut up, intoxicated. 'Walter, tell me, did you find the dancing ugly? Some do, you know; they think the *whole* thing a dreadful mistake, and that Nijinsky must be crazy, and—'

'Not ugly exactly.' Walter frowned. 'I'm not sure how to describe it.'

'And what did you make of the music? If you could only hear it over all that jeering and stamping. Frightful!'

'Unforgivable wretches.'

'Did you *hate* it? The music I mean!'

'It was… it was startling.' Walter smiled. 'You're doing so well. I'm so proud—'

'You mean it?'

Her brother nodded. 'Thank you for insisting I come. I will never forget this evening.'

She knew Walter's taste, and this was not what she

expected. She had expected it to jar. 'Really! You truly liked it?'

'Oh, yes. And you. Especially seeing you, knowing how much you've wanted this.'

An idea came to her, and she clapped her hands. 'Oh! I know exactly what to buy you for our birthday. *Exactly*! I had no idea, but now I do!'

'Oh, what is it?'

'No, no, no. You'll have to wait and see.' She laughed, relieved to have solved the problem.

Her eyes went from her brother to Alexei, who had now joined the group arguing where to eat and who was missing. She tugged Alexei's shirt.

'Thanks ever so much for looking after him.'

'Any time. Come.' Alexei hooked an arm into Walter's, she took her brother's other arm, then the three of them joined their boisterous group.

Supper: so much rich beef stew, so many bottles of wine none of them could afford, so many creamy desserts. Afterwards, the whole gang trailing to Bois de Boulogne, burning energy. Here they played games of tag and leapfrog, Mim cartwheeling gleefully across the grass. They had *done* it, they all agreed. They had got through the birth pains of that ballet and were jubilant.

Nina sought out Walter, and clasping both hands with her twin, spun round and round till they landed in a heap.

'I'm so pleased you're here, little brother—'

'Stop calling me that. Only by half an hour, so Rose says.'

'Twinny then.' She laughed. 'I'll always remember tonight. You know, one of the Jewish boys said eighteen is when you become an adult. Twenty-one is way too old, don't you think?'

Walter lay back, head resting on his arm. 'Mr Quince oversees my affairs till I'm twenty-one, and I can't vote till—'

'At least you'll be *able* to vote!'

'I see why you'd want to – vote, that is.' Her brother raised himself up onto an elbow. 'You know, the army would sign me up now, certainly wouldn't wait till we're twenty-one – any of the lads here – should it come to it.' He gestured to where boys sported with girls and with each other, laughter spilling into the night.

'Too young to vote,' she said, 'but not too young to die.'

Not meaning the conversation to become sombre, she reached for Walter's hand, and they lay side by side on their backs.

'Look at the stars, Walter. We'll remember this.'

He squeezed her hand. 'I will never forget – I told you. I'll remember everything about tonight.'

The talk around them was turning to food again. Dancers! Always hungry. There might not be any sleep tonight, but still maestro's morning class must not be missed. Cecchetti would not stand for that, nor would Diaghilev… or, for that matter, Grigoriev, and she could not afford a fine. She'd spent far too much on clothes and was in debt to more than one friend.

❧

When Walter arrived back at the lodgings with Alexei and Nicholai, the sun had risen. The dancers showered before heading to class.

'See you later,' Alexei said. 'Please make use of my bed.' He was friendly but there was no glance, smile, touch, or words to indicate there had been anything between them.

Walter collapsed onto Alexei's bed and, with the smell of its usual occupant lingering on sheets and pillowcase, slept a deep sleep. He woke late, head fuzzy, then set out for coffee on a cloud of exhaustion, ecstasy, and anxiety. He would fill his hours sightseeing.

In Notre-Dame, with midday mass in progress, he slipped into a pew. If he missed last night's ballet, then here was different theatre. At the candle-lit altar, among crimson and gold attired celebrants, one of them swung a thurible from its chain, fragrant smoke wafting from within. With his Latin inadequate, following the mass was impossible, but the power of worship enveloped him. The choir – not a French hymn he knew – divine. At rumbling timbres from the bank of organ pipes, he knelt, hand to forehead, and prayed. For what, he wasn't entirely clear. For forgiveness for having sinned? For receiving tokens of love from someone he had no right to expect them of. Guidance…

Soon he was due to meet with Nina "and some others", she'd said. He had not dared ask who. When he made his way to the café, he found it easily enough, but was early and, not fancying sitting by himself, walked further before circling back. He paused, surveying the occupied tables on the pavement.

Nina's group was easy to spot. Two tables had been pushed together. A dozen young men and women, all slender, fashionably dressed, chattering in a mix of languages. Everyone seemed so mature, so sure of themselves, and he felt callow. He searched the faces and wasn't sure whether to be relieved or disappointed that Alexei wasn't there. Maybe that made things easier. He walked up and tapped Nina on the shoulder.

'Walter!' Nina was on her feet – 'The French way!' – greeting him with a light kiss on both cheeks. 'Make space.'

Chairs scraped as people shuffled along, and someone grabbed an empty chair from another table. He squeezed next to Nina, half listening to their gossip, an outsider to this life. Soon, a white-aproned waiter appeared, notebook and pencil ready. Decisions and changes of mind. Soup? Stew. Who was having cake, coffee, tea…?

Nina tapped his knee. 'I've part of your birthday

present but didn't have time to wrap it.' She bent to retrieve something from her bag and placed it before him: Stravinsky's transcribed arrangement of *The Rite of Spring* for four-handed piano.

'Where did you get it? I mean, I didn't know it was even available.'

'Just published. It's not too difficult for you, is it? Really, I have no idea about these things, but when you said you *liked* the music.'

'Yes, yes, I do!' He opened a page at random and looked at the frenzied clusters of notes across the staves, topped with long trills.'It looks terrifying, but I'll learn it. I'll most certainly put my heart and soul into learning this and get someone else to play with me. Oh Nina, nothing could be more perfect.' He kissed his sister's flushed cheek.

'I'm so relieved; I wanted to salvage something from that ghastly premiere.' She laughed. 'So, what have you been up to?'

'Oh, walking. Seeing the sights, you know. Notre-Dame is wonderful.'

'So they say. I've not been. Should I?'

'For the... *theatrical* experience, if not the religious, yes.' That was fair, Walter thought. The rituals between priest and congregation, the incense, those massive stained-glass windows Bakst would surely love for their kaleidoscope of colours.'I rather think cathedrals are like theatres.'

'In that case, I shall make the effort. But speaking of theatre, ballet is off the menu tonight, but opera is on. I'm not keen but you may be, so I've tickets for *Boris Godunov* – Chaliapin's singing.'

'He's the best.'

'He would be, naturally, otherwise Diaghilev wouldn't be presenting him.'

'How much do I owe you?'

'No, no. The *other* part of your birthday present.'

'More? Really, you shouldn't.' Nina didn't have much money, and even with her connections within the company, she'd have paid a lot.

She laughed airily. 'I called in my bet with Alexei.'

'A bet?' It came out as a choked whisper. A sticky pink rising from neck to cheeks, eyes welling, ears ringing as he imagined them laughing about making a man of Walter, or some such talk. And how did Nina guess this about him – his partiality?

Nina, misunderstanding his reaction, placed a hand on his, smiling. 'It's all right. I've enough to pay. Please don't worry.'

He pulled back. Was this the way theatrical types behaved? He bit his lip hard to stop tears spilling.

Still Nina continued: 'I was right, you see. You *did* come after all, and I'm so glad. It's been such fun!'

As relief flooded through him, dizziness overcame him, and he put his hand to his head fearing he might collapse into the soup being placed before him.

'Walter?'

He collected himself. 'Thank you so much. That's thoughtful. I didn't think you'd be keen on opera.'

'Oh, I'm not going; I'll be tucked up in bed. Honestly, I'm beyond exhaustion.'

He frowned. Maybe Nina had not said "tickets" but only "ticket", and he imagined sitting by himself for his last evening in Paris.

'You're going with Alexei. He insisted on that as part of paying up. Says he can translate what's going on if you get lost in the plot.' She laughed. 'I think he said he was going back to catch up on sleep, then you two boys can enjoy the delights of hours of *very* heavy Russian opera.' She rummaged in her pocket, extracting a ticket with fanfare. 'I hope you enjoy it. Now, let's eat before it gets cold.'

There could never have been such a golden summer afternoon.

In the foyer, Walter stood among so many chatting people in their evening finery – just as he remembered at the Opera House. If there was a difference between fashion here and London, he couldn't say: women's hairdos equally elaborate, gowns as rich, men in black tails just as dashing.

'Alexei!' He pushed past an older, thick-waisted man to reach the slender young man by the staircase, striking a nonchalant pose with his walking cane. 'Alexei, I'm here.'

'So I see.' Alexei looked him up and down. 'You look, as you like to say, splendid.'

'And so do you!' Walter knew his stare was that of a devoted puppy.

'I have to say, for all my many accomplishments, I've never been to an opera in my life. So if I fall asleep...' He poked Walter in the ribs, tickling a little. 'That should do it.' They stood grinning at each other. 'I am told Diaghilev is particularly fond of Mussorgsky's little piece and spared no expense. But then, he never does. Shall we go in?'

What an instrument! Fedor Chaliapin's voice as rich as the furs, brocades and golds of his costume, the chorus like an Orthodox choir. Magnificent, all of it. Walter didn't understand a word, but the *Russianness* was palpable. Next to him, Alexei leant over whispering, 'A lament, Russian misery, it goes on, you see. Insoluble... Only so much melancholy one can stand... God help this idiot, he's trying to write the history of Russia!... Here come more starving peasants...'

Watching, he waited to feel the warmth of Alexei's breath in his ear with another whispered aside. The last time he was certain he'd gently blown in his ear. When it felt to Walter that too much time had passed, he leant across, taking the opportunity to touch Alexei's arm.

'What's happening here? What's he saying?'

At the second interval, they stood outside the theatre where Alexei opened a silver cigarette case, offering. Like so much else in his life, smoking was about learning "how". As they strolled up and down, Walter copied the way Alexei held his cigarette between his fingers, admiring the way it clung to his lower lip.

Alexei blew a soft stream of smoke upwards. 'You know, Walter, I've done well this evening. Two and a quarter hours of being sung to, yet still another act to go.' He yawned. 'Ballets are never so long, thank our gracious Lord.'

'Are you tired?' Walter was contrite. 'I know you've class tomorrow. I meant to ask if you managed all right this morning. Your ankle…'

Alexei nodded. 'Improving. I must attend class. I want to, naturally. In a few days, it's *Rite* again, and this time I want to be *onstage*.'

"Rather than underneath", Walter could have finished, glancing at Alexei to see his eyes were serious, smile guarded.

'You, Walter. Do you have regrets?'

'No! How could I ever…' Walter gazed at Alexei. 'It was beautiful.'

'Beautiful, yes. I thought so too.' A smile stretched Alexei's lips, and his eyes shone.

They strolled five steps this way, five back, smoking in silence. The pavement was thinning, the audience sweeping back inside. Alexei sighed, stubbing out the remains of his cigarette under the heel of his shoe.

Walter was emboldened. 'We don't have to stay if you don't want to. If you're tired, that is.'

Alexei hesitated. 'Tired? Possibly – I can tell you now,

it won't end well – but not tired of living.' He seemed to be weighing up the situation. 'You're so young.'

'Eighteen!'

'I don't want you ever to hate me—'

'Never! Alexei, I could never…'

'All right… all right…' Alexei squeezed his shoulder. 'Where we were last night was very nice, I thought. Not the cupboard, though that too.' He laughed. 'I mean the park. Might we walk there and hope we don't meet a troupe of dancers who refuse to go home to sleep?'

'That sounds spl— I mean…'

Alexei chucked under his chin. 'You can say it. I agree it's a splendid idea. Stupendous!' They walked on. 'Let me show you something.' From his breast pocket, Alexei removed a folded Ballets Russes programme with yesterday's date, 29th May. 'I'm keeping this.' He refolded it, returned it, and patted his pocket. 'I have a sentimental side, you see.'

Walter couldn't reply.

Hidden by the darkness of the night, amongst trees of the Bois de Boulogne, Walter kissed Alexei's lips tasting of tobacco, of wine, of life. Jackets abandoned on the grass and starched collars ripped from throats, Walter pressed his body to Alexei's. Through his thin cotton shirt, he felt two beating hearts… *tump, tump.*

Fingers fumbled at crotches, stubborn flies, grateful hands took hold of penises swollen with desire, pumping… *tump, tump…* timpani in rhythm.

'You first,' Alexei breathed, before kneeling and burrowing his face into Walter's groin. As his lover's mouth enveloped him, he gasped, clutching Alexei's blond angelic head to steady himself: not to keep from falling, but to stay anchored. At any second, he might float upwards. The gasp from his throat became a howl to the heavens.

Here was something impossibly wonderful. Here was an upheaval, an overturning of anything before.

These days in Paris marked the end of his old self, and Walter felt the first fluttering of the man he was destined to become.

22

Rose plumped down onto her seat at the Theatre Royal. On one side sat Molly, at her other, her son: the entire family turned out to watch her girl dance with those Russians. If hearts could swell, then hers felt huge behind her whalebone corset. Thank goodness one Banbury had the sense not to lose her head over a man and find herself in the family way. 'You don't have to worry about me, Ma!' Nina would say when Rose trotted out her story of thwarted ambition.

'All right, Molly?' Rose turned to see Molly rummaging for her spectacles. Why it mattered, the Lord only knew – but Molly refused to wear those bottle-bottomed specs in public. Not popping out to get groceries, that didn't count, but in her finest for a real night out. Today was special.

They'd just watched *Narcisse* – fluff but with very pretty music – and Rose feared the next wouldn't be her cup of tea. She had wanted to see one of the other programmes, the one with *Les Sylphides*, but no, Walter had insisted on seeing *The Rite of Spring*.

Oh, my Lord! She was loathe to call this screeching sound "music" – it set her teeth on edge. Glancing at Walter, she saw he was watching the conductor, listening rapt. She nudged Molly and the two of them pulled the corners of their mouths down, raising their shoulders. That was another thing Walter had insisted: best seats. Bloody hell, she'd thought when they booked, he might be swimming in Arthur's inheritance, but there goes the money she'd been saving for a seaside outing with Molly. But what could she do? Front stalls it was. She couldn't deny him; he'd just finished his exams, and she was so proud. She reached out and squeezed his arm for no reason other than that she was glad he was there.

With the raising of the curtain, Rose focused on the scene before her, trying to make sense of all the disagreeable dancing that unfolded. Was she getting old? Was the world moving too fast?

Seeing a line of girls skip on, she nudged Walter. 'Is she there?'

'Fifth in line,' he whispered, and she turned to Molly. 'Fifth one.'

It was as she feared and didn't get any better. Rose sighed, knowing that nearby at the Hippodrome, there was a skit called *Danse du Printemps* that friends had told her was hilarious, about the difference between ragtime and springtime. That would have been preferable and tickets a darned sight cheaper! She comforted herself, knowing *Prince Igor* would end the evening with a burst of energy. Then she would see Nina at her best, and she wasn't averse to Adolf Bolm leaping about. She'd get her money's worth then.

Who could have thought skinny Nina Banbury from Whitechapel could transform into Nina Rosova. None of Nina's ballet teachers had seen anything special in her, other than fodder for panto and revues. She looked out for her daughter as she endured the rest of the ballet.

Watching the sacrificed girl leaping about, resisting death, her heart tugged, thinking back to her own girlish dreams. Hadn't she lost her beloved ballet to motherhood? A little death in itself. She'd been ground into the earth by forces stronger than herself.

Rose's thoughts turned to Sid. On Sunday, he was due back from Southend, no doubt with a souvenir. Molly's one remaining porcelain shepherdess was sharing shelf space with a China donkey, a latticed plate with a pier in the middle, a painted seashell and the rest. Nina had sniffily picked up the donkey and called it "tatt".

She was enjoying having Nina home for a few weeks and looking forward to seeing Sid. These days, the Black Horse was an attractive haunt. 'Stout for my stout-hearted lady,' Sid would say, placing a creamy-topped glass of dark ale by her. 'Stout in other ways too,' she might say.

Just thinking of it made her salivate. Lots to look forward to.

⁓

In her heavy white tunic for Act Two, Nina posed in her group, looking to where Maria stood centre stage in that peculiar frozen puppet stance, preparing to dance to death, all those bearskin men slowly circling, heads down, feet sliding, flat-footed. Not long till she'd be changing into her *Prince Igor* costume. Ma and Mo would enjoy that. Why Walter wanted to see this programme was anyone's guess. She'd have thought once was enough. Mind you, she had surprised herself, beginning to like the dratted thing.

Her spirits were high. Just this morning, during class, Maestro Cecchetti had said, 'Good Nina, very good.' He had never complimented her until now, and hearing this made her feel truly part of the company, not an imposter. That afternoon, meeting Grigoriev to collect her fortnightly pay, she took pleasure in signing the ledger with her adopted name, with a flourish.

'As you're here,' he said. 'We're finalising contracts for the next tour. You're available, I trust.'

'Yes!' came her swift reply, while pocketing all those sovereigns and smaller coins. *South America here I come.*

She smiled, elated. Life was good and she intended to live it.

❦

Walter couldn't take his eyes off one dancer – white-costumed with a high conical hat edged with fur – sometimes linking arms with the fellows in his group in small bouncy steps, pausing to paw a foot on the ground like a horse. His eyes moved to the chosen maiden, stock-still in the middle of the stage. Nina, he knew, was in the group of girls kneeling nearer the footlights, to his right. He focused on Thomas Beecham, the conductor's body, elbows lifted, baton hand moving in forceful upbeats, face sheened with sweat. He was doing a magnificent job keeping the orchestra together. Walter's eyes rested on the violinists' bowing arms sawing the strings, then back to dearest Alexei. All the dancers were on their feet circling the chosen one, and from the orchestra pit just in front of him, repeats of a melody from the piano music Nina had given him. It was a gift he would treasure for ever.

Another gift was having the Russians – Alexei – in town for these summer weeks. They had met several times in a group with Nina and her chums, and three times Walter had paid for hotel rooms. He had little money but was determined to see as much of this golden creature as he could. Soon the company would leave for another leg on their tour, and he would be bereft.

'Only this moment,' Alexei had said, more than once. 'We can't see tomorrow, so we must enjoy here and now.'

Walter smiled to himself as he watched the ritual play out on this London stage, thinking of another ritual, several weeks earlier under that Paris stage.

He loved this ballet, this score. After the interval, he would, again, watch Nijinsky as Faun raise a scarf and give himself to a sublime moment of lust. Another interval, then *Prince Igor*, when *his* Russian prince would be amongst the leaping horde of savages. And after the performance was over…

The hotel room was booked. 'An old school friend visiting,' he'd said.

INTERLUDE

1914

23

In Monte Carlo after a South American tour, Nina finds letters at the theatre. She pockets Walter's and opens Ma's.

> *Hoping you are well and having better weather than we are. Nothing but rain and more rain here, the wettest March on record, so they say.*
>
> *You might like to know I bumped into Edith the other day – haven't seen her for years. You'll never guess, she got herself arrested, but said it was worth it spending a night behind bars! She was outside Buckingham Palace with the rest of those ladies who want the vote. I remember her such a sweet polite girl, with those starched pinafores and a big bow in her hair. Well, such a change. She was dressed ever so severely. Her hat was the plainest thing imaginable and with her hair scraped back in a bun no man is likely to find her pretty!*

Her childhood friend *was* always neat, her mother wanting to paint a careful picture that masked harsher truths. None of her other friends had been interested in seeing Isadora Duncan or attending Mrs Holt's bare feet dancing classes with her. It doesn't surprise her that Edith has thrown her lot in with the suffragettes. As she folds Ma's letter, she decides she might look Edith up when she's in London. "Home", though?

Last summer, during their London season, she'd stayed with Ma 'n' Mo but the house looked increasingly shabby and threadbare. The butcher's boy she'd known all her life was now working in the shop with his father, and the pallid youth had said, 'Home for good, Nina? Thinking of settling down?' while slipping an extra cut of beef onto the square of paper and wrapping it. 'Just a welcome home,' he'd added. She thanked him and hurried out. And the same with the grocer's wife. 'Lovely to see you, Nina! Goodness, look at you!' And the woman had rushed from behind the counter to appraise the cut of her dress and feel the stuff of the fabric. 'A dressmaker in Paris,' Nina explained, to be met with, 'Paris! Well, I never!' The woman gave detailed updates on her brood of growing and grown children, while Nina fixed a smile.

She has moved on from East London, has travelled far.

Leaning with both elbows on the stone balustrade – the terrace and theatre at her back, Mediterranean Sea stretching into the distance – she savours the sea air, and smells of fried seafood and freshly brewed coffee drifting from a nearby place. A smile touches the corners of her lips, and she thanks her good fortune.

Michel Fokine is back as choreographer, and star dancer, Nijinsky, dismissed. If only Sergei Pavlovich had been with them in South America, none of this would have happened. But then Diaghilev hates travelling on water – this iron-willed man who's unafraid of any *artistic* challenge… She sighs. That Romola de Pulszka had weaselled her way into the company, got her claws into their star dancer. Married him! Odd as that seems. Such a strange fish that one. So, yes, inevitable, he should be banished. She imagines Diaghilev charging Grigoriev with the firing and new hiring.

It's thrilling to be rehearsed by Fokine in his own ballets. He only speaks to her to give instructions or a terse correction – they'll never be chums. There's a pecking order and she's way down the rank.

The Legend of Joseph is her favourite Fokine ballet, in no small part due to the new lead, a boy her own age. Léonide Massine is fresh from St Petersburg. 'Fresh meat for Diaghilev,' it is rumoured. Even so, Nina has a crush on him. Those luminous eyes! He isn't an exceptional dancer, and she sees Fokine's frustration as he simplifies a sequence he has in mind. She decides if Cecchetti can be tasked to make something of Massine, she can work hard under their teacher to make something of herself. Hilda is a rising star, something she is trying not to envy.

With class and rehearsal ended, Nina strolls along the promenade and remembers Walter's letter in her pocket. The date is from two months ago, but Monte Carlo was the next stop he could be sure to reach her.

Just a line to thank you for your last postcard. Please keep them coming. Since Christmas the weather has been vile…

Why must everyone in England obsess over the weather? Nina thinks.

…but otherwise, everything is going swimmingly. I'm enjoying my music studies and making enough to get by. None of the "prodigies" will ever have the makings, but as long as their mamas continue to pay for my time, I will do my best.

I'm enjoying working with the quartet – a college get-up. We have strings (cello, viola, violin) with me on the ivories. We're working on a piece by Schubert amongst others, hopeful we will be ready for the concert I told you about.

Nina frowns. This has missed her somewhere. Receiving post on tour is unreliable at best.

One of the chaps at college – our violinist – has invited me to stay with his family over Easter, and I think I might go. I don't know Oxford and I look forward to exploring it. Kit's father is a don at Balliol, and I understand the whole family are rather clever, so I mustn't let the side down.

I look forward to seeing you in summer, and please give my news and best wishes to those in the company who might like to hear from me.

Your loving brother, Walter

She should, she decides, write to both Walter and Ma. There is a kiosk nearby. Her eyes slide past newspaper articles about Austrian troop movements and the French army on the march to Piedmont, then she turns her attention to a rack of postcards. Rifling through pictures of the terrace and seafront, she tries to recall which of them she's bought before. Passing coins and sharing words, she is pleased with how easy it is to chat. Her French is fluent, though Russian remains foreign. She licks stamps to the corners and begins to write Ma's address.

'Nina! Are you joining us?' The call comes from a café where she sees a group of dancers, plates of cakes and steaming cups before them. That will keep them going till post-performance supper. She heads over and pulls up a chair.

'Don't you just love how Madame Karsavina never

complains? Ever. And the poor lovely is dancing every night,' someone is saying.

'Not dim either. Very thoughtful and you have good conversations with her,' Hilda says.

'I wouldn't know,' Nina says, arched eyebrow. She's not chummy with their ballerina, whom Diaghilev calls Tata, while she calls him Serioja. Such intimacy is restricted to an inner circle. She sees Hilda blush. Her friend is in between the masses and those picked for greater things.

'I'll tell you something,' Nina says, moving on, 'if I ever have a baby girl, I'll call her Tamara. Not that I'm planning to any time soon. If ever.'

Around the table her friends hoot, finding that hilarious.

Alexei teases her, 'I pity the man who loses his heart to you. You'll consume him.'

'Oh, I don't know,' Hilda says. 'I'd rather like to see you in love, Nina. See your heart melting. Look at them…' She gestures around the table, and the boys there put on winsome faces. 'Who's it to be?'

These are men and women she rehearses, performs, and dines with, day in, day out. There isn't anyone she sees as a lover. They're like family.

Hilda and Nicholai – Kola, as everyone calls him – have become lovers, and she watches him now, leaning in, placing a hand on Hilda's. Nina hates how jealously he guards her friend, and she's said as much.

When Nina imagines a lover who may suit her, she imagines someone who won't interfere with her life, but she won't make the mistake of falling for a married man like Ma did. So far, her heart hasn't melted for anyone.

The train is halfway to Paris. Nina puts aside her book and walks along the carriage, stops where Kola and Alexei have an upturned trunk beside them, shuffling a pack of cards.

'Can I join in?' She knows the answer will be yes, so opens a window wider to let out the fug of tobacco. These boys are something else.

'Make room!' Kola says, rubbing his hands.

'I'm going to win this time.' But she probably won't.

Three hands of poker later, she owes all of them.

'How's that brother of yours?' Alexei asks, so she repeats what was in his letter.

'Oxford. Have you been there?' he asks.

'Never, but I've heard it's lovely. I'm sure Walter will enjoy himself.'

'Kit. An unusual name.'

'Short for Christopher,' she says.

Alexei smiles. 'In Russia, pet names may be longer. So Tamara may be Tamarochka – but I wouldn't go calling Madame Karsavina that.'

'I won't.' She laughs.

'And you, my dear, would be Ninochka.'

'Ninochka,' she repeats in a deep voice, pushing out her lips. 'I like it.'

'Ninochka, then. When you and Walter come to visit me in Petersburg—'

'What?'

'Oh,' Alexei waves a hand, 'I've just invited you. After our London season. Our holidays.'

'I'm going cycling... I'd love to visit the Mariinsky, of course, but a visit to St Petersburg isn't on the cards.'

'Why not? If Walter can holiday in Oxford with his new friend, Kit, he – and you, Ninochka – must visit my family.'

'Oh Alexei.' She laughs. 'But are you going home?'

He nods. 'I must. Papa has business things to discuss, and I'm keen to see the little ones.' Alexei had two younger brothers and a baby sister. 'And Mama is, naturally, worried about the state of the world and wants her big boy home for a while.'

'A little unnecessary, isn't it? Being worried, I mean.' Nina hasn't read an English paper in ages and feels out of touch.

'Quite unnecessary, but mothers…' Alexei shrugs, and turns back to their game.

The entire Paris season leaves audiences wanting more. Here is total theatre, intoxicating dance and design. Nina is drunk with pride at being part of it.

On Saturday after class, she thanks Cecchetti with a respectful curtsey. 'Merci Maestro.'

But before she can leave, he calls, 'Nina! *Un petit oiseau, 'e say to me, aujourd'hui est un jour special…'*appy birthday, *ma rose anglaise.'*

She colours in delight, accepts everyone's well wishes then bobs another curtsey to Diaghilev as she leaves. He has watched class today, keeping an eye on the talent he has invested in: Massine.

He catches her eye, saying, *'Joyeaux anniversaire.'*

'Merci beaucoup, Sergei Pavlovich.'

'Dansez bien ce soir, puis celébréz. Dans cet ordre.'

She laughs, and he smiles.

'Quel age?'

'Nineteen, Sergei Pavlovich.'

'So young.' His gaze moves from her to Massine, who is going over a troublesome step with their teacher. She thinks her director looks old as he hoists himself to his feet and joins Cecchetti.

That evening, in her dressing room, she has greeting cards festooning her mirror – from Ma, Walter, some of the dancers. Thankfully, Alexei had reminded her to cable Walter and to include greetings from him. She'd not forgotten her twin, but there is never time. Her gaze moves to a Ballets Russes playbill postcard signed by Diaghilev in his customary bold handwriting in thick black ink. How delicious!

When the performance ends, Nina pours out into the street with her friends. They buy her cocktails, wish her happy birthday. She is heady with it all.

Late into the evening, she is with Hilda, Doris, Anna, Alexei, Kola, and so many others at the same park where they'd sported last year after *Rite's* premiere.

'Let's do the opening of Act Two,' someone says.

'Nooo,' someone wails. 'Can't remember a thing.'

'Let's,' Nina says, already pushing her friends into a circle.

The boys who aren't in this bit become a clapping, singing orchestra, while she tries to recall all those lunges, thrusts and punching movements.

'I want to do the end,' Hilda says. 'Be the chosen one.' She begins trembling.

'Me too!' Nina joins her friend, knees knocking.

'And me!' Alexei scrambles into the circle.

Two sacrificial maidens, one sacrificial man. Trembles turn to leaps – abandoned jumps, arms flailing – all of them shrieking, replicating shrill violins.

All the while, other girls are dancing something – she's not sure what. And the boys are doing a stamping, grunting kind of dance.

'What are you doing?' she manages between jumps.

'Dance of the Earth,' one of them says.

'That's Act One!' she says.

'Who cares!' comes the reply.

'We need Mim,' someone shouts, but Marie Rambert is no longer with them.

It's chaos. They dance a jumble of remembered bits from

the ballet, then one after the other, they fall to the ground laughing, defeated.

She sees Alexei lifted high in the air by some of the boys, re-enacting the final moments, his arms and legs floppy, head thrown back. A dead boy.

'Me next!' She feels strong hands under her back, her feet leaving the ground. She is airborne, arching her back, limbs flailing.

'Die!' she is urged. 'You've been sacrificed.'

'Never!'

With feet back on the ground, she calls for attention. 'I've a secret,' she says.

'Do tell!'

'I'm in love!' Her eyes glisten, her face splits into a massive grin.

'Who?' they beg, but Nina shakes her head, teasing.

'Shan't say!'

Alexei grabs her, tickling under her arms where, from experience partnering her, he knows will set her off giggling.

'Ninochka, it will be death by a thousand tickles if you don't say.'

'Wait! Wait!' she begs, seeing others crowd nearer, wiggling fingers probing her ribs, all to torture her into submission. She pushes free, rushes from friend to friend kissing them on the lips, boys and girls alike, before throwing her arms wide, crying, 'Don't you know? *All* of you. I love you all!' Her eyes glow, and they see she means it. They form a tight huddle, and she holds on tight to these friends.

ACT 4

1914–1917

When Stravinsky was looking for deep rhythms of the earth, he uncovered patterns that were more fearsome and less predictable.

<small>THE RITE OF SPRING, THE MUSIC OF MODERNITY, GILLIAN MOORE.</small>

24

WALTER DREW TO THE SIDE. WHAT LOOKED LIKE AN entire garden of red roses bobbed past, obscuring the carrier, a call-boy, his voice piping, 'Outta the way… Sorry, Guv… passing through.' The blooms, arranged in a basket, would be the nightly offering to Madame Karsavina from a would-be lover. 'The Aga Khan, no less,' Nina had said. But he was not backstage at Drury Lane Theatre this interval to offer homage to the company's esteemed star.

Amongst the clamour of artists and staff, one voice pierced him: 'Must get this stuff off,' and his stomach clenched. For a moment, he watched Alexei still in his *Scheherazade* costume: baggy Eastern trousers, caught at the ankles, his gorgeous head bound by a turban, normally pale face and throat coloured dark brown. Walter's heart began to thump. A year had gone by since he'd seen him. There had been occasional postcards, but Nina had been the conduit through which news was channelled, such as it was, and he had no idea if the spark was still there.

Seeing the dancer about to head into a dressing room, he plucked up courage. 'Alexei, it's me.'

Alexei turned slowly, his hand on the door. 'So it is! How lovely to see you, Nina's brother.' A smile crept across his face.

'You didn't come to see me after the show earlier in the week. I was terribly disappointed, but I had a delightful time getting to know your mama. There's a lady who likes to party.'

'I heard. I couldn't come till tonight. Sorry.'

Truth was, he could have come with Rose but lost his nerve. After hearing that Alexei had asked after him, he had not been able to stay away.

'Couldn't? Hmm!' Alexei frowned. 'Well, you're here now, and look at me, ready to serve and be *your* slave.' Alexei dropped to the ground prostrating himself, and Walter blushed not knowing how to respond. How ill at ease he was with these theatrical types, so different from the musicians he spent his days with, Kit the exception.

The foolery lasted only seconds. There was another ballet to prepare for.

After the performance, Walter joined Nina's gang where, over supper, they shared stories: Nina's adventurous, his studious and dull. When the party spilt into the street – Nina to Rose and Molly's, others to their lodgings – Alexei slung an arm around his shoulder.

'Which way are you heading?'

'Pimlico. Not far from Victoria. The District Railway...' He pointed. 'That direction, the Thames—'

'I should like a walk. And a chance to catch up.'

His heart hammered.

The three of them walked together to the Strand. Casually, he and Alexei waved off Nina at a bus stop and set off in the other direction. It felt to Walter that it wasn't just he who was unsure and cautious, only that Alexei was able to present a confident front to the world. Walter often imagined the armour needed to fit himself out might involve a pipe and bushy side-whiskers. The armour Alexei deployed so successfully was flippant theatricality.

Somewhere along Millbank overlooking the Thames, they stopped to smoke, and Walter again felt the thrill of his friend's hand cupping his own shaking ones. He remembered that same jelly legged sensation to have that dear face no more than a foot away from his, eyes searching. Sometime later, in a shadowy stretch between gas lights with no one about, and no passing cabs, they kissed. And it was lovely.

'I wasn't sure,' Alexei offered. 'It's been a long time.' He touched Walter's hair. 'It suits you this way.' Walter had changed from a near-centre parting to a side parting, dark hair oiled to his scalp. Alexei's fingers drifted down to his close-shaved cheek. 'Have you made friends, Walter, in this new life of yours?'

'Well, fellows from college. And girls now, of course, not like school! In classes – Music History, Harmony and so on. And I'm getting to know students in my Ensemble Class, particularly those I'm working with.'

'I am jealous of these friends. I want to know everything.' Alexei linked an arm in his. Two smartly attired young men enjoying a stroll.

'Well, Clara plays viola in the chamber group I'm in, she's very good, and Sarah plays cello, and there's Kit – he plays violin.'

'Kit, yes. You wrote to Nina of him. Is he a special friend?'

'He's good fun. He's been kind and welcoming—'

'Welcoming?'

'Not like that. He likes girls,' he blurted out.

'I like girls too, sometimes.'

'Really?' Walter was taken aback. He had thought it a question of black or white, girl or boy, now here was a new thing.

'I'm going home for the holidays,' Alexei said. 'Nina thought I was fooling when I said you should both come. But

I mean it. If your friend Kit can invite you to Oxford, then I don't see why I can't invite you to meet my family. Petersburg in summer is wonderful, and I should like to show it you.'

Walter laughed. 'Impossible.'

'Why? Trains aren't so expensive, and you'd stay with us; we have room. Mama is fussing, worried by those rumblings in Europe we hear so much about.' Alexei shrugged. 'Nothing to do with us.'

'Nothing to do with us,' he agreed. The other day, the papers reported on the assassination of Archduke Franz Ferdinand and his wife in Sarajevo that had led to riots in that far-off land. 'Even so. I've promised Nina we'll go to the seaside. She's taken up sea bathing, she tells me.'

'She certainly has! You should've seen her in Monte.' Alexei chuckled, then sighed. 'If I can't bundle you up in my luggage and take you home, we must make the most of our time together before I leave. Yes?'

'Yes, please.' He blushed, knowing he sounded like a child.

As they walked on, arms linked, Walter felt the heat of Alexei's skin beneath the cloth of their jackets and was nourished by it.

They paused outside a lodging house advertising good beds for single men only. 'Not here,' Walter said decidedly.

'No, I refuse to share a dormitory with a host of grubby men. We might be grubby, but not that kind.'

They walked on, found a cheap hotel, and after some inducement about being old school friends short of cash, followed a wheezing woman in worn-down shoes up two flights of stairs to a room with a narrow bed.

Over the coming weeks, Walter became familiar with cheap hotels in and around Soho, Islington, Kings Cross. Less and less, they felt the need to explain why they were booking one room.

During one of those shared nights, he dared half whisper, half sob, 'I love you.'

Alexei smiled. 'So sweet, my Walter, I will treasure that always. To be loved is very special, and I know you don't say that lightly.'

Walter waited but the words he longed to hear were not forthcoming. Instead, the Russian opened a silver case, lit a cigarette and passed it back and forth. Walter couldn't bear it, just had to know.

'And do you? Do you care for me?'

'Oh yes, I do, very much, and just so you remember…'

'Ouch!' Walter bolted upright. 'What did you do that for?' Alexei had pressed the lit cigarette on his chest near his left nipple. 'That hurt!' He gazed at the angry burn.

'I want you to remember me. I may, once or twice, have said "I love you" to someone and at those moments believed I meant it, but with you…'

'Say it then. Say it.'

'If you wish. I love you, Nina's brother.'

'I have a name.'

'I love you, sweet Walter.' And there was sincerity in those grey eyes. Gently, Alexei kissed the burn blister. 'You'll carry this scar for your entire life. Just so you don't forget.'

'Never.'

The last Saturday in July – the final night before the Ballets Russes broke for summer – was a time for the dancers to let their hair down.

'Find a good place,' Nina had said. 'I expect I'll go mad and dance till dawn. I'll be bringing the usual gang, so pick somewhere that stays open all hours. Diaghilev's hosting his party at the Savoy – principal dancers and the upper-crust lot. Wouldn't mind being invited, but we must amuse ourselves in whatever club will have us.'

It was Kit's idea they go to The Cave of the Golden Calf. 'I'm a member. Your sister and her chums may enjoy it.'

And it was Walter's idea that Kit should accompany him to the Russian Ballet beforehand. 'There's Nina.' He pointed her out to his friend when she shot onto stage. His own eyes were on another dancer. Aside from showing off Nina and her theatrical friends to Kit, he had an idea that Kit and Nina might hit it off.

"Maple Leaf Rag" drifted up from below. 'C'mon.' His sister raced down the steps to the basement club, Kit pausing to chat to the doorman. He followed with Alexei, Hilda, Kola – a flock of vibrant, impossibly glamourous men and women.

In the fug of the basement club, on a low stand, a pianist, trumpeter and trombone player rattled through a ragtime tune.

'Oh, wonderful! Just look!' There was Nina, eyes blazing, clapping her hands, delighted to see the thrashing dancing couples. 'Who's going to dance with me?' She didn't wait for an answer but grabbed a hand of one of the boys from their group, nudging to make space. Immediately, she was bobbing in a bouncy two-step, hips swaying, a flick of a foot, her partner twirling her, lifting her off the ground. Walter loved her exuberance, never less than full-on.

He felt Alexei's hand on his shoulder, guiding him through the crush, passing a table where women sipped cocktails of vicious green, pausing every so often to speak in high voices.

Couples bobbed and skipped in Ragtime Swing, Turkey Trots, men and women glowing with the joy of dancing, of being together. Seeing Alexei dance with one of the ballet girls, Walter longed to cut in: push her out of the way and step into Alexei's arms. Together they'd whirl for all the world to see. But, of course, he couldn't. Wouldn't.

'Come on, up you come.' He was pulled to his feet. First with one girl then another, sometime changing partners mid-way.

'Walter!' Alexei handed him the lady he was dancing with – not someone he recognised – while Walter handed over Doris of-the-big-feet. Not that he had noticed, and she didn't trip him up. She was a lovely dancer, as you'd expect.

The band played on. "The Entertainer", "Maple Leaf Rag", defying anyone not to have a good time. Scott Joplin's compositions were hardly on Walter's study course, but they were wonderful, full of the rhythms of, what Walter understood to be, low-life America. A world of brothels and saloons, of black impoverished lives, reaching into this gathering of Londoners where the only black face in the room was the trumpeter.

Kit was a hit. While the dancers among them were all slender, he had the look of a sleek, well-fed seal, sure of himself, dancing first with one, then another of Nina's friends. Stories of mad parties his mother had hosted spilt from him. His voice had the same confidence his fingers and bowing had when playing the violin: that of a man born to rule.

'I think it was last summer,' Kit was saying. 'Yes, yes, must have been, you should have seen it. All that glitters...' He gestured to the scene around them. 'Mother was a regular and decided my time had come.' Kit's mother, Walter had found when he visited Oxford, was not a drab academic type but a bohemian woman of letters. She was, she'd told them, a frequent visitor at the Golden Calf with her set of friends. Kit was cut in the same cloth. 'That was the night when I, a thing of barely nineteen,' Kit said, 'was being seduced by one of Mother's friends.'

Shrieks of laughter from around the table.

'Do tell!'

'Oh, she was high on something.' And Kit began mimicking a forceful accent. 'Christopher, you are by far the handsomest man in the room, and by blazes, I mean to make love to you!'

More shrieks and laughter as Kit told how he averted a desperate plight by hiding out in a cupboard with the ragtime performer – 'A fellow who could knock back whiskies. I tell you, when he next jigged about onstage doing some number, his joints were well lubricated.'

Nina grabbed Kit to his feet. 'Well, I don't want to make love to you, but I do want to dance.' And little by little, everyone paired off. Walter cast his eyes around to see who he might invite to dance when Alexei caught his arm, staying him. Amongst the swirl and twirls of dancers and jagged notes, they remained at their table, Alexei sliding along to sit next to him, thighs touching.

'I'm leaving at noon tomorrow,' Alexei said.

'Tomorrow! I thought the day after. Can't you delay?'

'Can't. Trains are becoming unpredictable and solidly booked. But we have the entire night, and I don't expect to sleep.'

'I'll see you off, then.'

'To share a farewell kiss, on the platform?' Alexei shook his head.

'I'm going to miss you.'

'But you wouldn't come to Petersburg,' Alexei reminded him. 'I'll be back in September. You make sure you take time off.'

'Oh yes. I'm giving thought to where we might holiday before you head to Germany.' This was where Alexei would rejoin the Ballets Russes. He began to feel bereft, knowing this time tomorrow, Alexei would be gone. For a long moment, he held Alexei's gaze.

Deep into the night, beneath garish lights, flocks of glittering peacocks celebrated being young.

'Walter, we should have a go at this sometime.' Kit, fresh from the dance floor, mopped his brow. 'You could do all right, if you let yourself loosen up, and I'm sure I could manage on the fiddle. What do you say, old chap?' He drew in a chair, Walter between him and Alexei.

'Are you serious?' Walter had to laugh. 'You imagine we'd hire ourselves out to clubs.'

'I was thinking we could surprise Mother at one of her soirees. That could be fun.' He slapped his own thigh. 'Don't be a stick in the mud.'

'What is this?' Alexei looked puzzled.

'Oh, you know, a fellow who's not up for adventure. So, what do you say? Are we working up a ragtime number or two?' This time he slapped Walter's thigh. 'It'll be jolly.'

At his other side, Walter felt Alexei draw close, a firm hand at his back. 'Walter is no stick in the mud. Come.' Alexei was on his feet tugging Walter to his. The pianist, alone now on the stand, began a new rag, "Weeping Willow", and before he could object, Walter was arm in arm with Alexei dancing a funny, tender two-step. And he didn't care who saw. As other dancers realised what they were doing, they pulled back to give them space, with hoots and laughter of encouragement. He felt himself rising into the air, as Alexei lifted and spun him, the lights a kaleidoscope. For precious seconds, he was airborne. It didn't last. Such moments never do.

'Oomph.' Alexei pulled a face. 'Not as light as I thought.'

For an exquisite minute or so, Walter felt Alexei's hands resting on his hips, allowing his partner to guide him this way and that, his feet skipping in time to the beat. All too soon, girls in their group would cut in to claim a male partner each.

'When I am back,' Alexei whispered.

'Yes,' he replied, feeling Alexei was a rock, and dreading to be prized away.

25

Nina kept her eyes on Alexei and Walter as they jittered and jigged to the honky-tonk. While others saw only the fun of it, she was acutely aware of a spark when eyes met, or hands caressed. More than hints of attraction. Breaths of longing and belonging. Alexei had mastered the art of acting, but she could read Walter like a book.

How had she missed knowing this? How long had this been going on?

In theory, she didn't mind. After all, she was with the Ballets Russes! From Diaghilev down the ranks there were *liaisons amoureuse*, couplings and uncouplings, men and women, men and men, and she wouldn't be surprised if there was something going on between their devoted female dressers. In *theory*, she didn't mind at all. But when it's your own brother... She watched him smiling shyly, his face longing, and every ounce of her wanted to protect him.

This evening, she had seen how Kit might suffocate Walter and within a short time had formed a view on him. Now she was horrified that Alexei might hurt him. Walter's heart was weakened from that childhood bout of scarlet fever. A physical thing, of course. Palpitations and so on. But it must be protected from harm.

She glared at Alexei. She'd seen enough of his flirting. Word was around: 'Don't bet on Alexei.' This was not about being supported in *arabesque*. Hearts – *human* hearts, not those printed on playing cards – were at stake!

And now Hilda and Kola were all lovey-dovey over glasses of champagne. Engaged! It enraged her to see her friend throwing herself away on this up-himself Russian. What on earth did Hilda see in him? Thinking about this tarnished their charmed night when she wanted everything to be perfect.

Grabbing her bag, she pushed her way through the crowds, racing upstairs and out into the evening air. A moment to herself.

A slender moon barely lit the scene. Horse-drawn cabs clopped past, two peak-capped chauffeurs chatted between parked cars – a Beaulieu and a Daimler. Which would she choose if she had the money? A man, evening dress dishevelled, stumbled to clutch a streetlamp and she wondered if he might throw up. People sidestepped, just in case.

Walter and Alexei. Nina tried to get her head around it. What was it that rattled her? She reached for her cigarette case, selected one, placed it between her lips with shaking hands. Why on earth should she mind? She flicked her lighter and found it would not fire. Repeatedly she tried to get a spark. 'Dratted thing!'

'Allow me, ma'am.' A flame appeared just beyond her nose, and she sucked in, the tip of her cigarette glowing.

'Thanks.' She noted the dark colour of the hand that cupped the lighter. The trumpeter.

'My pleasure,' he said before stepping back. They stood smoking, looking at life passing by.

'Love your playing,' she eventually offered.

'Thanks, ma'am.'

'What's your name?'

'They call me Charlie.'

'Well, They-Call-Me-Charlie, where're you from?'

'Who's asking?' He looked at her sideways.

'Nina Rosova when I'm being fancy; Nina Banbury on home turf.'

'A Londoner, heh?'

'Born not far from here,' she gestured in the general direction of Leicester Square, 'in the Alhambra Palace.'

'Palace! I've seen Buckingham Palace.'

Nina smiled, tempted to string him along, but when he looked earnest, she came clean. 'It's a theatre – skits, funny acts and so on – and I was born backstage. Now it's the Alhambra Theatre. They dropped the *Palace*.'

Now he chuckled. 'Well, well. That's some story.'

'American?' she prompted.

'Sure. Small town in Louisiana most folks ain't heard of. I guess Chicago's home now. Lived there some years.'

'Now you're here.'

'Now I'm here. Got a contract for a couple a months yet—'

'Congratulations, you deserve it. Ragtime's so popular, I'm sure good musicians are in demand.'

'But you know, I'm thinking I should book a passage. With everything as it is right now, I don't know I'll be getting home any time soon.'

'What on earth do you mean?'

Charlie looked at her frankly. 'There's goin' to be fightin', ma'am, and I—'

'Don't be absurd! There can't be.'

'I reckon there can – ain't you been reading the papers? And I'm standing here wonderin' which side I want to be on.' He chuckled. 'Not fightin'; other folks get to decide that. I mean ocean-side. Here or there.' Charlie stubbed out his cigarette. 'Nice talking with you, ma'am, now I'd best be gettin' back.'

Slowly Nina inhaled, then softly blew. She smiled, seeing a smoke ring hover in the air before dissolving. Idly, she noted the wobbly legged man had vomited, leaving a liquid splatter on the pavement, and was now being helped into a cab. 'I'll be charging you extra if you soil my seat,' the driver said. She noted one of the chauffeurs opening the back door of the shiny Beaulieu. A top-hatted gent handed in his lady, who hiccupped, covering her mouth with a gloved hand, giggling. 'Oh dear, it's gone to my head!'

Fighting? What rot.

Earlier that very evening, Grigoriev had gathered the company onstage where Diaghilev was to address them. Her director looked so solid and dependable as he'd walked languidly onstage, then, a chair having been found for him, sat, monocle close to an eye, hands on the gold knob of his cane. *Dependable*. Dressed in freshly pressed opera suit, shoes polished, his voice steady and reassuring. He spoke in French, of course, never English.

'We continue to show the world what it means to make great art and you, my dears, all of you, with your passion for dance, contribute to our success.' He had beamed that wolfish grin. 'I thank you all and wish you a good holiday – you have earned it – and look forward to seeing you in Berlin on the first of October. It is all arranged, and we have many weeks of engagements ahead of us.'

It was *arranged*! Nina inhaled the last of her cigarette, flinching at the bitter taste. Diaghilev knew everyone who mattered. He knew what was going on. Charlie did not.

With the sole of her silvery evening shoe, Nina ground the butt of her cigarette back and forth then followed Charlie back down, no longer thinking about Walter. Foremost in her mind was to find out who'd be in London at the end of September and to fix her travel for Berlin.

26

ROSE SLIPPED ONE ARM IN SID'S, THE OTHER HAND holding onto her hat for dear life as her skirt swirled against her ankles, threatening to trip her.

The Saturday matinee at the Pier Pavilion had just ended and they were strolling – if you could call it that – along the Eastbourne Esplanade. Later, they'd get a bite to eat before Sid's evening show. Molly had given up on being entertained and retreated to their guest house. It had been foul weather, buffeting winds and rain with more to come, skies leaden.

'Blooming Margaret Cooper and her flaming piano,' Sid said. 'I hardly got a look in.'

'Give over your grumbling – you had your moments.' He was billed with "Other London Artistes", after all. 'Miss Cooper just looked a bit cross when you went into your patter before every song—'

'They loved it!'

'And your suit, love. Don't get me wrong, I like it,' Rose ran a hand over the green and orange check covering his chest, 'but by the look on Miss Cooper's face, she might have thought it, um…'

'Lowered the tone, you're wanting to say.' Sid pulled one of his faces and she had to laugh.

'Maybe best if you change into your other suit this evening,' she said.

When he'd told her he was singing with Miss Cooper at the Pier, she'd said to Molly, 'Right, pack your bags, we're going to Eastbourne.' Last year, they'd not managed to get away for the long weekend – those expensive tickets to see Nina perform had put an end to that. This year, Rose was determined to enjoy the bank holiday weekend – she and thousands of others down from London. As often as not, these were their only days away.

'The National Anthem was heartfelt, wasn't it, Sid? Did you mind us joining in?'

'I thought that was a lovely touch, given the circumstances.'

At the end of the show, she, Molly and everyone else had stood, joining the onstage professionals: Miss Cooper at the piano, a chap on the violin, Sid's baritone and a young lady soprano. Rose had sung fervently, hand to her bosom, "God Save the King", praying that this palaver would stop before it got started.

From where she stood on the Esplanade, Rose looked out over the iron-grey sea, knowing France and Belgium were just across this narrow stretch of water. She drew Sid close, listening to the waves. A deep, resonant wallop – followed by the suck of pebbles on the beach, a distinct *hiss*. Again, a mighty slap of water.

'Look, Sid, just as they break, the waves seem to get untidy, all those splashes and froth... I want to get my dressmaking scissors and snip off all the extra bits...'

'Blimey!'

'...or maybe I'll leave them. Maybe they're pretty, all frilly and lacy.'

'What's got into you?' Sid squinted at her.

'I don't know.' Rose tried to laugh off her mood. 'You know

something?' She patted his chest. 'You wear this suit again this evening and you *keep* making those jokes. If Miss Cooper objects, you tell her from me that people need a laugh.'

'All right, love. All right. Yesterday was fun, wasn't it. I'm minded trying one or two of those gags. Thought I knew them all—'

'Me too!'

Yesterday, they'd been to the pictures: *Keystone Cops*. They'd laughed their heads off at the slapstick. And those chases! She'd tapped Sid's arm, seeing a car full of policemen cross a railway line just dodging a train.

'You think they do their own stunts, Sid?'

'Looks like it. They're fit, those fellows – even the fat ones – all that running and tumbling. What do you fancy doing tomorrow?'

'There's a band playing. That might be nice.' But still she felt an ache in her stomach. No amount of music or films could change the way things were looking.

The next day, she, Molly and Sid gathered on the pier with thousands of others, many clutching newspapers from London.

'General mobilisation… over *there*,' someone was saying.

'Germany's done it – gone and declared war on Russia. It's definite.' A man prodded a finger at a folded page.

'*Appears* so,' a woman frowned at the paper in her hand, 'but I'm not sure what's happening over there.'

Over there were the words Rose clung to. Over that water, that great moat that protected them from stupid things over there.

'We'll be next,' a woman said.

'Not long, I'll wager!' an authoritative male voice boomed. 'That bloody kaiser!' And Rose watched as he shook his cane – a sword against an invisible enemy.

Suddenly, Rose wasn't sure she was in the mood to trot off to the bandstand and search for deck chairs dry enough to sit in. And yet. She looked at Molly, grey hair scraped into a straggly bun, her Sunday hat jammed on her head, leaning on a walking stick. At sixty-four, Molly, who'd been Rose's prop forever, was needing props herself. Molly's mind was sharp, but her eyes had constricted to what she'd called, 'Being in a black tunnel with a circle of daylight ahead.'

Perhaps, Rose thought, a brass band was a good idea. It might jolly them up. She nudged her companions. 'Coming, you two? The bandstand.'

'Think I'll stay a while,' Sid said. 'See what I can learn.'

With her arm in Molly's, Rose pushed through the crowds – 'Excusie, excuse us.' – back to the Esplanade.

'I fancy fish and chips later,' Molly said.

'If you like.'

On Monday, Rose was in a dither. Stay or go home?

Everyone was jittery. The woman who'd served breakfast spilt tea over the cloth, apologising. 'Dreadfully sorry. I've sons, you see.' *I've got a son too*, Rose wanted to say. She learnt there was to be an extended bank holiday for three days. Not that it had occurred to her to take out her meagre savings. But from the talk, others might, and there were fears of runs on the banks.

Early evening, Sid escorted her and Molly to the train station where they found travellers squeezing into carriages, porters pushing trolleys with trunks and cases. When she attempted to pass through to the platform, she was stopped by a flurried station attendant. 'Full. No more seats.'

'But we booked!' Rose held out her tickets.

'Priority to others. Try tomorrow.'

'Priority for who?' Sid was indignant.

The man didn't answer, turning to ward off a crush of would-be travellers. 'Get back! Back!'

'Oh well, Sid, you got our company another day.'

By Tuesday, Rose badly wanted to be home. She hovered around the Post Office for updates from London, then walked to the seafront watching vast rolls of looped barbed wire being unrolled along the beach. "The key bit" over there, she learnt, was just above France. She remembered nothing about that tiny country from her dancing days. Did they even have a national dance? Regardless, it was Mr Asquith and the government that were now in a dither.

On Wednesday came *The Times*. BRITAIN AT WAR.

It had happened while she had slept. On the strikes of Big Ben ringing eleven – midnight in France – that was it. No turning back.

Late that evening, she gazed at the moon, left side in shadow, suspended over the inky sea. Somewhere out there, boys were killing each other. Husbands and sons were dying. Close to where she and Molly stood, along the coast at Beachy Head, searchlights probed the night sky and the horizon.

'What do they look like?' Molly raised her chin, squinting.

'Like bloody big footlights… and imagine a stage unlit. God only knows what they think they might see. Not fairies.'

'Remember that time we watched an aeroplane flying. Such a slow, flimsy thing. You think they've got better? You think that's what they're looking for?'

'Like matchwood stuck together with sticky paper. You'll never see me in one. No. I'm betting on our navy. *Rule Britannia, Britannia rules the waves*,' she sang. 'Our navy's the best.' Though, she acknowledged, a British mine layer *had* just been sunk, but the French fleet had "caught German warships like rats in a trap", she'd read to Molly, and they'd raised a cheer.

'And now our army lads are in, they'll sort them out.' Molly nodded. 'Not Walter, naturally, not with his heart.'

And, patriot that she was, Rose was ashamed to agree. 'Not with his heart.'

'What of Nina?' Molly asked. 'What of her plans now?'

'I don't know. Still at the seaside. Norfolk? With Walter and their chums.'

'If she's home, she'll be wondering where we've got to. Should have sent a cable.'

'Didn't think. To be honest, I'm not sure where she is.'

Shafts of searchlights wove and swayed in the sky. 'Right, Molly, come hell or high water, tomorrow, we're getting home. Sid's staying; concerts must go on. This fighting won't last long.'

Union Jacks stuck out from windows above shops on Whitechapel High Street. When they turned into Alie Street, Rose drew Molly's attention to bunting strung between two houses.

'Remember three summers ago?' she said.

'The coronation?' Molly nodded. 'Lovely, wasn't it.'

She sighed. 'Happy times.'

Inside the house, there were signs of Nina – dishes stacked by the sink, today's papers open on the table – but she wasn't there.

'I'm ready for a lie down,' Molly said, putting on the kettle. Rose made space on the table, moving aside the papers, trying not to read headlines, trying not to think. For some reason, she fetched two cups and saucers they usually kept for special occasions.

Hours later, the outside door opened and slammed.

'You're home!' Nina had spotted their coats on hooks. Her steps sounded along the corridor, then her daughter was before her, hair in a tangle down her back, eyes wild, blouse unbuttoned at the throat. 'Where were you? I've been looking everywhere—'

'Couldn't get back. We're fine.'

Nina stood there clutching her blouse at her throat till a button popped off, revealing more of her tormented breast. 'Oh, Ma!' Tears spilt down her cheeks, great sobs threatening to choke her. 'It's over. It's over!'

Rose shot to her feet, daring to hope. 'What's happened? Is there good news? Are they stopping all this?'

'What? No, Ma.' Nina looked confused. 'It's ramping up and spoiling everything. Everything.' Her chest rose and fell in her effort to control her sobs. 'The autumn contracts are cancelled. We're not going to Germany after all.'

'I should say not!'

'Why should ugly war stop beautiful things happening? Creative things.'

'Cinemas are open. Sid's still singing. Theatres and halls haven't closed.'

'Oh, just perfect. You, Sid and I can get up a routine – The Bouncy Banburys and Singer Sid! We'd go down a treat in Great Yarmouth.'

Rose bit back from saying, 'Why not, if it pays for your board and lodging?' She could picture herself kicking up her legs again.

'*Arty* things, Ma. My company!' Her daughter looked bereft. 'What am I going to do? It was my life. I can't bear it stopping.'

'Mr Diaghilev will think of a way around things, I'm sure.' As she patted Nina's hand, she thought this mess in Europe might be beyond even him, regardless of how strong-willed he was.

'The dancers, Ma! So many – Karsavina, Fokine, and lots of others – back in St Petersburg. Can't get out of Russia now the German border's closed. And Grigoriev's there.' Nina slumped into a chair.

'Give it a few months. We'll be back to normal in no time.'

'That long!'

Rose was reminded of that time, nineteen years earlier, when she had been thrust, unprepared, into the pain of birthing and motherhood. Now this.

'Whatever's ahead, Nina, we must face it. What choice do we have?' She held her daughter's gaze.

27

ON NEARLY EVERY HOARDING OR PUBLIC BUILDING, Walter was challenged by the war minister's glare. Hard eyes above Lord Kitchener's moustache stared directly at *him*, finger pointing at *him*. YOU ARE THE MAN I WANT, scolded one. Another: JOIN YOUR COUNTRY'S ARMY!

It was mid-October, and he was on his way to Victoria station. He had arranged to meet Mr Reed at a small Surrey railway station, Box Hill and Westhumble, for a countryside ramble.

'Let's make the most of it,' his former master had said, and Walter wasn't sure if he meant the weather or the simple pleasures of peace. Maybe it was hinting at his enlisting.

Thinking of *that* was enough to make his heart thud and palms go clammy. The papers reported heavy fighting around Lille and Ypres, and no amount of plucky reporting fooled him. Men were dying out there in their thousands.

Seeing a long queue at a recruiting office, he quickened his step and crossed the street, ignoring a muttered, 'Skiver.' Pausing in a doorway, he forced himself to watch those braver than he. These youths would be clerks, shop boys, lads working on trains and buses, all volunteering to swap civvies for khaki. Most had a woman at their side – a matronly mother or slender sweetheart or wife. On hearing, 'Still thinkin' on it, are you, sonny?' he turned aside from the old man's gaze, sliding further into the recess of a doorway. He stayed long enough to see four males, boys, step through the welcoming jaw of the recruiting office door. Long enough to watch a uniformed youth step out, looking jaunty, puffing out his chest, handing a neatly folded pile of his old clothes to an older woman. She fumbled, an old jacket slipping to the pavement. There followed a hasty embrace, then son and mother parted.

Hurrying away, he glanced at posters glued to the recruiting office. THERE'S ROOM FOR YOU. ENLIST TODAY, one told him, with a picture of a train carriage packed with uniformed men, knapsacks holding whatever it was soldiers carried. His own daypack held sandwiches and a flask of tea.

The only marching he had volunteered for was at the very start of hostilities, at an anti-war rally at Trafalgar Square. There, with so many others, he had raised his voice in a futile call for peace. So many words lost in a wind that had suddenly changed.

The army had claimed Alexei, and Walter was sick with worry. Conscription was compulsory in Russia and Alexei had not escaped the net.

Such a palaver getting here, his friend had first written from St Petersburg – Petrograd now – *So many stops and turning back at the border, but here I am, and I am very glad I did not persuade you to join me for a holiday. That might be a little difficult in the circumstances.*

In his next letter, Alexei said, *Fokine's at the Mariinsky and I am hoping to be included in his plans. Uplifting ballets are the order of the day, and I am very good at being uplifting, wouldn't you say?*

Walter had written back, saying how much he was missing him and how wonderful that he was dancing, but before Alexei would have received it, Walter received another.

I am seeing rather more of the outside of the Mariinsky than inside, Alexei wrote. *You see, my lovely young body is more use to the corps of the army than the corps of the ballet. I am with the Second Army, so you must imagine me as the hero prancing around in a different kind of theatre. While dancers with the Imperial Theatres are exempt, I, sadly, am not under contract with that illustrious institution.*

Alexei spoke of drills in the square, changes and shortages in the city, and Walter could only guess at what he meant.

May I write to you, my Walter? They may not reach you from where I'm going (No secret, somewhere in Prussia, but where even I cannot say). But you must write. Tell me lovely things. Funny things. Or quote some poems, I should like that. Mama knows to forward letters from particular friends, and she has connections with the Embassy so this should ease letters back and forth. I am betting on it! And Walter, Alexei had ended, *you, my good fellow, must continue with your music. That is an order. No, better, a promise – I am increasingly disliking orders. I refuse to even imagine you mired in this.*

That had been a month ago. Walter had written every few days talking lightly of how, in concert halls, no works by German composers were played. Hoping Alexei was keeping warm, telling how he'd laughed like mad at that little fellow Charlie Chaplin. He had no idea if his letters would get through to Alexei's home, never mind forwarded to the Front.

Daily, Walter pored over newspapers and journals, even – he braced himself – the weekly *Army and Navy Gazette*. He would skim over battles on the Western Front for news of the Eastern Front. In early September, he'd read of a battle of Masurian Lakes and rushed to an atlas to find it. It was here that Germans under General von Hindenburg had encircled the Second Army – Alexei's army – and it had been a disaster. He read of blasts so strong that uniforms and boots were stripped off the Russians, and Alexei's pale naked body floated before his eyes. He read of bayonet fighting and tried not to imagine Alexei's soft flesh skewered. Russian losses were heavy. Had Alexei been there? Was he alive?

He sent a telegram to Alexei's home address in Petrograd but had no idea if it had been received. No reply had come.

Eyes lowered, Walter strode towards Victoria railway terminus, eager to escape London, eager to escape his thoughts.

The North Downs was a landscape Walter could lose himself in.

Walking along the ridge of Box Hill with Mr Reed, they paused to listen to a fieldfare chack-chacking in a hedgerow and stopped to watch a flock of redwings, snatches of scarlet under wings, alight on a holly tree at the edge of a wood.

'Beautiful,' Walter said, and Mr Reed agreed.

'The birds are still here, thank the good Lord. What would we do without them? Butterworth *bottled* scenes like this in his compositions.' Mr Reed began whistling "The Banks of Green Willow", and Walter joined in.

Below, in the Mole Valley, they looked upon a patchwork of fields, each bounded by woody hedgerows, where cows grazed. In other fields, he could make out black dots where crows and blackbirds picked amongst wheat stubble, where summer crops had been harvested. There was no sign of winter ploughing beginning.

Mr Reed tutted. 'Foolish to suppose we don't need horses here.'

'Or men,' Walter added. 'For all kinds of work.'

Mr Reed glanced at him. 'Not every man need sign up.

Poor horses don't get a say in the matter. By the way, I saw Forster recently.'

'Two years above me? Choir?'

'He's back, you know.'

'Back, sir? I mean, Mr Reed.'

'Ah. I thought perhaps you were keeping abreast of the Old Johnians. Home within weeks of being out there. Well, most of him. Somewhere in a field in Flanders is his right arm. You all right?'

Walter had stopped. 'I remember he had a beautiful voice.'

'He didn't give a jot for it – or the choir. Used to make you younger boys laugh singing naughty words—'

'You knew!'

Mr Reed smiled. 'Captain, you know.'

'He would have been a good leader.' He was remembering a time when Forster helped him over a box horse that was way too high for him. 'That's it, Roberts. Good man,' he'd said, catapulting Walter up and over.

'Why not visit him?' Mr Reed went on. 'Queen Alexandra's. Millbank. He'll be there for a while I should think.'

'I might,' Walter said.

'Do.' Mr Reed squeezed his shoulder.

They walked on. At one time, Walter had imagined himself living in Paris and had chaffed to leave school for a large city. He was enjoying London life, to a point, but if he had dreams of some future "Walter's house", it was a cottage in a southern England village – Kent, Surrey, Sussex – surrounded by gentle hills of pastures, lanes made narrow by thorny hedgerows. And birdsong. That mostly. Sparrows and starlings abounded in London, but their chatter could not compare with the choral countryside.

'Are they partridges I see?' Mr Reed squinted to a field below, where a flock of large brown birds foraged in wheat stubble. 'Look out, I say.' Mr Reed brought his hands up to hold an imaginary rifle, pulled his trigger finger and made an explosive sound in his throat. 'Hunting season's upon you, fellows.'

28

WALTER WALKED ALONG MILLBANK, HESITATING AT the military hospital entrance before plucking up courage and entering.

'The doctors are doing their rounds,' he was told. 'Shouldn't be long. Perhaps you'd like to wait in the garden.'

Outside, white-uniformed nurses wheeled patients back in from an afternoon airing. One was in no hurry, squatting at the side of a wheelchair, lighting the occupant's cigarette. It was then Walter realised the chap could not light his own. How could he, when both arms had been blown off, shirt sleeves knotted below the shoulders. An involuntary shiver passed through him.

The wheelchair procession passed. Men smoking, chatting, even managing to laugh. Why, he could not imagine. He could not help taking a gruesome limb count: one foot on a platform where two should rest, trousers knotted at both knees, a lopsided rug covering a patient's lap, no second thigh. And their faces. All damaged. How could they not be? Blasts and shots were indiscriminate. Here, a cheek shot away, there a bandage over an eye socket. And those eyes that had escaped the blind and flash of hot metal looked old beyond their years. What a price to pay to protect civilised values.

Visiting Forster could wait.

Walking along Millbank, he stopped at the magic place where he and Alexei had kissed overlooking the Thames. That night they had both worn spats, both dressed to impress. He closed his eyes, remembering those high-arched slender feet. Did Alexei have strong boots and warm socks for those precious feet? Did he *have* feet… limbs? Was his beautiful boy even alive?

He choked back rising sobs for Alexei and all young men being butchered in countrysides where nature should flourish. Could he ever volunteer for something so ugly as this unfolding war?

He hadn't seen Rose since that mid-summer performance. Nina, he had seen. One afternoon in late September, they'd met on one of her days off. One drink led to two and they'd got progressively drunk on vodkas and beers, commiserating about the state of things. Nina, separated from the life she loved, accepting contracts in one revue or another, and he feeling that continuing to study was out of step with the times. 'College is doing its patriotic best,' he told her. 'Focusing on Elgar and Hubert Parry. I rather relish the utter Englishness of it all.'

'I couldn't say. Music is music as far as I'm concerned. As long as I can dance to it.'

'You remember Kit?' he said. 'I thought you and he might hit it off.'

'I took a dislike to him for some reason. Why?'

'He applied to the War Office. He's a second lieutenant now, officer training down at Swanage. Loving it, he says. "Best thing a chap can do."' Walter toyed with his drink then spoke the words that'd been haunting him. 'You think I should? Apply for a commission?'

'No!' Beer sloshed as Nina thumped down her glass. 'You are not a fighter. I should hate – absolutely *hate* it – if you did. I couldn't bear it if something happened to you.' And Walter was relieved to hear her say so. 'All the local lads I knew growing up, in our street and around, have gone. Let them be the ones. Not you. Not any of *us*!'

'Us?'

Nina toyed with her glass, her eyes as bold as ever. 'Have you heard from Alexei?' And he began to stammer. Nina placed a hand over his mouth. 'Oh, don't give me that. I guessed about you two, but be careful; arty people tend to land behind bars.' She'd be thinking about Oscar Wilde, who'd been packed off to prison for gross indecency the year they were born. Still the law hadn't changed. 'But I don't want to see you hurt. Battlefield or bedroom.'

So he hesitatingly told her he and Alexei loved each other, and she nodded, saying, 'As long as he really does.' He had assured her of that before unburdening himself. 'But I'm worried sick, Nina. I don't know where he is. He's having to fight—'

'Oh, Good Lord. I'm so sorry, Walter. You know, I had been feeling jealous. I'd assumed he was at the Mariinsky, with Fokine. Stupid!' She bumped her forehead with a clenched fist. 'Alexei will be all right. He'll play his hand well; he always does.'

'You think?' A glimmer of hope passed from Nina to him, and back again.

They'd parted before blackout made it difficult, him saying, 'Stick to it. At least you're dancing.'

Nina saying, 'And you. Music, study.'

When Walter received a letter from Quince and Fairfield, he did not recognise the writing. But it was Mr Fairfield, whom he'd never met, requesting a meeting, as *Mr Quince has suddenly departed.*

Once at their office, the clerk – a new fellow – directed

Walter to the door to his right. 'Mr Fairfield's expecting you.'

In the past, Walter had been directed to the left-hand door, which was partially open. Inside, he could see the shelves were empty of books and the cabinet free of the decanters he had become accustomed to seeing. He was about to ask when the clerk waved him through. 'Just knock and go in.'

In all these years, he had never laid eyes on Mr Quince's partner. And not a moment too soon, seeing the desiccated old man, peering from behind his paperwork.

'Sit,' Walter was directed. And he waited for the lawyer to finish scratching an inky sentence, sign the document slowly, then add it to one of the stacks.

'Good afternoon, Mr Fairfield, I'm Walter Roberts. I'm sorry to hear Mr Quince has died, we—'

'Died? If he were dead, I would have said so. He *departed* – suddenly – and I have inherited much of his oeuvre.' Mr Fairfield frowned at the stacks.

'Is he well? Where is he?'

'The outbreak of war, you know. He decided to throw in this life. He's gone to live with a daughter and her family, anticipating a time her husband will be called up—'

'That's not certain. Married men, I mean.'

'Nothing is certain. I thought I knew my partner of nearly forty years, yet he has run off to join, not quite the circus, but to a *farm* near Norwich, I ask you…' The lawyer picked up a file labelled "Arthur Roberts" and without wasting time, began flicking through the records, letters, receipts, concluding, 'We have two further payments to make, as I see it, then our business with you is concluded.'

'I believe that's correct, sir.'

Mr Fairfield rose, so Walter stood. 'Before you go, Mr Roberts, what do you want doing with this?' He stooped and picked up the old shoebox of Rose's keepsakes.

'I'll take it with me.'

'Good. One less thing to be rid of.' He extended a bony hand. 'Good luck in your life.'

Soon after his meeting with Mr Fairfield, Walter set off for Whitechapel. 'Fancy coming for Sunday?' Rose had said. 'We'll all be there.' At Alie Street, he laid out the contents of the shoebox on the kitchen table.

'Oh!' Rose gasped, grabbing the photo. 'Look at me.' Walter watched her face soften with longing. 'Just look at me, Sid.'

'What a beauty, eh?' Sid put down the *Illustrated London News* long enough to admire the photo before Nina snatched it.

'I've never seen this. You were so pretty, Ma. I'm nothing like you.'

'She was a beauty!' Molly said. 'Let me see.' She took up a magnifying glass and peered closely. 'We've taken good care of that cape down the years.'

Nina rested her hands on Molly's shoulders, peering over. 'I've never had a fancy man. Perhaps I should. Our dad gave you lovely things.' Walter caught her eye as she directed his gaze to knickknacks cluttering a shelf, and he suppressed a chuckle as she rolled her eyes towards Sid. '*Lovely* things, Sid,' she repeated, poking the man who had become a fixture in their mother's life.

'Eh?' Sid looked up from the paper.

Rose dipped into the shoebox, drawing out the bisected shawl. 'Remember this, Molly?'

A smile spread across the older woman's face. 'How could I forget!'

So Walter heard, again, the story of how Rose had been wrapped in it and deposited outside the Alhambra's stage door.

Nina fingered the fabric. 'I remember my piece was a tatty scrap.'

Rose snorted. 'Not to start with! You used to suck it while crawling around. It got absolutely sodden and filthy.'

'I was forever untangling tassels you'd managed to wrap around your fingers,' Molly added. 'Or you'd sit there pulling the blasted things off. You were a destructive child!'

Walter listened to their laughter as they reminisced over a past he did not share.

Soon the talk turned to the war, Sid pointing to one illustration of a driver leading two horses and a laden cart, bursts of bright lights around them. FEEDING THE BRITISH LION IN HIS DEN, read the heading.

'Goodness, don't they look like stage lights?' Rose pointed to flaring beams directed downwards from the sky. 'What on earth…?'

'Clever, those Jerries.' Sid tapped the paper. 'Parachute lights – magnesium – so they can see when to detonate the shells. In the air, you see. God help those poor bastards below. Better news here,' and Sid turned a page to where a British Destroyer was shown ramming a German submarine.

'Yes!' Rose shook her fist. 'Told you; it'll be over by Christmas. Got to be. Now, clear the table.'

Sid handed Walter the paper. Before setting it down, he saw simple wooden crosses marking graves of French soldiers near Aisne, a line of gun carriages pointing towards an unseen enemy, an officer standing in a waist-deep shell hole. And this war was not yet four months old.

'Wash your hands, son,' Rose said. 'Let's eat while it's hot.'

Walter stared at a page titled THE FIELD OF HONOUR AS IT IS: DEATH ON THE BATTLEFIELD. Men's bodies lay strewn across a grassy field, a grove of trees beyond. He imagined the rattle of machine guns mowing them down.

These same horses, now harnessed two abreast in groups of six hauling gun carriages, would once have been harnessed to threshing machines. He imagined lots of things as he looked at those fallen men. Most of all, he imagined one man. Alexei. He did not share Rose's optimism this carnage would soon end.

'Walter!'

At the table, Nina and Rose were placing plates of roast beef and gravy, potatoes, turnips and cabbage. Sid was tucking a napkin into his collar.

'Coming.'

He set aside the war.

29

It was a Friday night when Nina paused at a greengrocer's shop in Frith Street, her eyes shifting to *the* door next to it hiding stairs leading up to living quarters. Ma had pointed it out to her, saying, 'This is where your life began, you know.' One day she should show this spot to Walter. They could have a laugh about it.

She walked on, then, drawn by sounds of a gravel-voiced female singer, pushed open a shabby door.

'… *That's just the bestest band what am, my Honey Lamb…*'

It had been almost ten months since she'd listened to "Alexander's Ragtime Band". A lifetime ago.

The cheery rhythm tugged her.

'…*Come on along, come on along, let me take you by the hand…*'

It was long past closing time, but it didn't stop anyone – just drove these new Soho clubs underground. Literally. She'd have a drink and smoke, and, if her weary legs were up to it, a spin around the floor. Already today she'd performed in five unprepossessing halls. Seven tomorrow.

Downstairs now. Raising a match to a cigarette between her lips, Nina paused, taking stock of this seedy little club. An ample-figured singer in a spangly gown belted out the song, a middle-aged chap pounded the keyboard. And the trumpeter – what was his name? – why on earth was *he* still around? The stringy black fellow was looking very swish in a checked waistcoat and spats, body swaying, giving himself to the music. Charlie! That was it.

She made her way to the bar, squeezing between men and women in civvies and raucous, khaki-clad soldiers home on leave, some with army mates, others with girls – at least for tonight. She eyed one couple, cheek to cheek, the girl's make-up and low-cut dress suggesting she'd be someone else's sweetheart tomorrow. She didn't judge them – man or woman.

Nina warded off military men keen to dance, starved for female company. 'Later, perhaps,' she said to one. 'Not right now,' to another, unpeeling an arm from around her shoulder. She didn't have the heart to be rude. Who knows if they'd be alive a week from now.

A sentimental song began – lots of good ones coming from America. '…*Your silvery beams will bring love's dreams, we'll be cuddling soon…*' and Nina watched the amorous couple, thinking if they went any further, they'd be having sex right there.

Before long, the pianist stood. 'We'll be back!' Then the singer stepped down from the stand and Charlie wiped the mouthpiece of his trumpet. Nina waited till he reached the bar.

'What are you having, Charlie?' He stared at her blankly. 'Thought you'd be home by now. Chicago, isn't it?'

'Okay!' His mouth stretched into a grin. 'I remember. Back before… You look different.' He eyed her from top to toe.

'I suppose I do.' She touched her newly bobbed hair and stretched out a foot. In the past months, she'd had Ma raise the hemlines of all her dresses to mid-calf. Their freedom of movement was about the only good change the war had brought. 'So, what can I get you?'

'A lady paying.' He hesitated, humming. 'Well, if you insist.'

'I do. What's it to be?'

'Okay if I go for a whisky?'

Drinks in hand, they found standing space at the far side of the club.

'You haven't said why you're still here,' Nina said.

'Oh, you know. With all these U-boats about, I got to thinking I might get hit. Can't swim, see.'

'Chin up. If that were to happen, you'd likely freeze and drown soon enough. Look what happened last week.'

'Yeah. Poor bast— excuse me, ma'am.'

Nina touched his arm. 'But nothing like those effing bastards that did it! And I'm not apologising for saying so.'

Charlie stared at her, wide-eyed. 'Yeah. You can say that to me.'

'And don't call me "ma'am". I'm Nina.' She clinked her glass to his. 'Here's to those poor souls.'

'You'd think the German U-boats would know the difference between battleships and—'

'Deliberate! *Any* target now.'

Some days earlier, well over a thousand passengers and crew had perished when a lurking U-boat torpedoed the liner *Lusitania*. Charlie was right to be cautious.

'So, Charlie, you'll be around a bit longer?'

'Looks like it. Plenty of work. And you know something else…' He pressed his lips together, humming.

'Yes?' she prompted.

His look was direct. 'Till I came over here, I never had no white man – surely no white lady, till now – buy me a drink.' He grinned. 'I could get used to it.'

'Huh!' She knew nothing about America, let alone what

it was to be an American Negro. Looking around the club, she realised that Charlie was one of the few black faces in the room. 'Huh,' she said again.

Soon the pianist was reseated, the singer stepping back on the stand.

'Gotta go,' Charlie said. 'But you gotta stick around. I owe you a drink. Okay?' He held up index fingers of both hands. 'Okay?' He was suddenly less sure of himself.

'I'll be here. Go on, blast the stockings off these ladies.'

The following week, Nina went to Charlie's club with a group of friends. She gazed at him with increasing interest. He was older than them, maybe late twenties. She found herself wondering what those expert lips would be like to kiss, what that swaying body would be like to feel next to her. When the band called the final song, she rushed up to the stand begging the piano player, 'I want to steal your trumpeter; please allow me.'

Charlie looked from her to the bandleader, who shrugged. 'Up to you.'

Nina held out her hand. 'Don't disappoint a lady.'

'Not about to.' He laid down his trumpet.

On the crowded floor, with a reduced band playing "Ballin' the Jack", they danced, one of Charlie's hands on her waist, the other clasped in hers as he bobbed her back and forth in a foxtrot. He had, as she expected of a ragtime musician, a fine sense of rhythm.

'Isn't this great?' she said.

'I think so too.' He twirled her under a raised arm and brought her into a closer embrace, and above the fug she inhaled the scent of his body.

'You know, Charlie, at the end of the month I'll be twenty – having a small party. Might you come?'

'You're inviting me?'

'Definitely. Do say yes.' She held his eye.

'I'll see – if I'm not working, that is. Sure you're sure?'

'I'm sure.'

Since Nina had a twin in her life, birthdays, she insisted, should be double the fun.

'You must come!' she demanded of Walter. 'You tell Mrs Whats-her-face you can't teach Precious that evening; it's only one Monday.'

On Saturday, their actual birthday, she was busy with shows. On Sunday, they marked the occasion with afternoon tea, Ma 'n' Mo presiding. Monday night was the real party with anyone old banned from attending. She'd hired a hall above a pub in Whitechapel, doing a deal with the landlord to stay past closing time.

'Bring food to share,' she'd told everyone. 'Walter's lot are bringing a gramophone and stacks of records. I've warned him I won't tolerate anything boring. Let's hope!'

She arrived early with Edith, arms laden with spring tulips, lilies, roses, and they set about decorating. The two of them had rekindled their childhood friendship, finding they still had much in common.

'This will do,' Nina said, sticking bunches in beer glasses as Edith set about decorating with swathes of coloured cloth over any surface that looked bare. 'Oh Lord.' Nina flinched as she tested the keys of an old piano, sticky with spilt drinks. 'Poor Walter.' She wiped her hands. 'You know, I think you two will get on. He's not at all like me.'

'We'll find out.' Edith laughed.

Before long, Nina was greeting guests and what had been a dim room smelling of stale beer was full of dazzling young people, perfumed and pomaded, smelling simply delicious.

A gramophone appeared, carried between Walter and one of his friends, followed by a girl with a stack of records.

Soon a ragtime song filled the room. 'Marvellous!' She clapped her hands seeing couples begin to dance and drew Edith to where Walter presided over the gramophone. 'Walter, this is my old friend, Edith – doing wonderful things for the war effort. This is who Ma's working with now.'

Walter extended his hand. 'Rose mentioned you yesterday. Pleased to meet you. What are you working on?'

'Nurses aprons. Thousands!'

Edith and her Women's Suffragettes had turned their Knightsbridge office into a workshop, and Edith had appealed to Ma. 'I'm losing the battle. All these girls need directing and I haven't the faintest idea. You used to make lovely costumes. Can't you help me?' So Ma swapped gaudy pantomime outfits for regulation army shirts or uniforms for the Red Cross.

Nina excused herself, confident Walter and Edith would get on, on *some* level. They were both earnest types. She glanced back, trying to read Walter's face, not sure if he could be tempted by any girl. But if not Edith, then who?

'Charlie!' She pounced the moment he stepped inside. He'd been playing at a tea-time session. She allowed him to set down his trumpet case, then, with both hands, drew him straight into a turkey-trot, knocking into everyone.

'Charlie, meet…'

'Say hi to Charlie…'

She'd heard rumours of the Fast Set's "Dances of Death" parties. No morphine needed here to dull the pain of war. Dancing and laughing with friends were enough to make her buzz.

'I'm so happy you made it.' She beamed at the American.

He squeezed her waist. 'Happy to meet your friends. You organised this yourself?'

It wasn't just the party she'd planned. Being twenty seemed a good age to lose her virginity and she liked Charlie very much. He may not be bold enough to make a move, but she had no such qualms. She had the key to Hilda and Kola's flat. They were on tour and had said, 'Help yourself,' and she meant to.

'Are you hungry?' she asked, remembering to be a good host. 'I think there are some sandwiches and cakes left... Something... Boiled eggs, sliced ham? You might find some wine left... And Walter. You must meet my twin.' She began to lead Charlie away.

'Later.' He drew her into an embrace, and as they danced, she drew stories from him. She learnt he was one of six, that his father had left, that he had too, seeing no future in their rural backwater.

Sometime around eleven, over the shuffle of feet, chatter and laughter came the sounds of an explosive *whoomph*. Walls vibrated and the gramophone needle skidded across the record. Quick-stepping dancers froze.

'Shit!' she heard herself say.

'Holy shit!' Charlie said.

Friends whose mouths had been open in laughter and song were now screaming. 'Back! Back!' someone yelled.

They cowered at the far wall, as, following another massive thud, shards of glass flew into the room from the shattered window.

'I'm sorry,' was all she could think to say, as if this were her fault. 'So sorry.'

Another explosion. While a calm had befallen their little party – all of them alert, listening – from through the jagged glass came human screams and buildings rumbling as they crumpled, and sirens screeching into the night.

'Nina!' Walter pushed his way through to her. 'Are you hurt?'

'No. I'm all right.' She looked around wildly.

'Our turn now,' someone said, and Nina repeated in wide-eyed terror: 'Our turn.' She clutched Walter. 'Ma 'n' Mo! They might've been bombed.'

'Get out! All of you. Out!' It was the harried-looking landlord who had panted upstairs, beckoning.

Nina started for the door, but Charlie grabbed her. 'No, sir! We're not going out in that!'

'No… Right… I suppose… Gawd help us.' The man tugged his hair.

As another bomb exploded, everyone screamed, ducking, hands to heads.

But maybe this thing was moving away. Nina cocked her head, trying to decide. She didn't fancy being trapped inside.

'I'm not staying in. I want to see.'

'Best go up then, and don't blame me if a bomb drops on ya.' The landlord pointed.

Nina charged out the door, hand in hand with Charlie and Walter, only breaking a grip to race up narrow stairs and out onto the roof terrace. The rest of her party followed, some clutching drinks.

'Will you just look at it!' Charlie's voice was awed.

She was looking. Couldn't take her eyes from where criss-crossing searchlights highlighted a solo performer – the entire night-time stage to itself. A massive greyish-white cigar-shaped craft moved silently across the night sky. She – all of them – had seen photos from raids up the east coast these past months. But nothing could prepare her for the sight of the enormous thing.

'Our turn now,' she said again.

Each sickening thud reverberated through the soles of her shoes. What had been a clear night was foggy as buildings crumbled and dust rose with each bomb from the Zeppelin.

Some streets away came an explosion and belching flames.

'Gas pipes,' someone said. A siren, then another, as fire trucks navigated clogged streets. She scoured the outline of rooftops. *Our house...*

'Oh, Charlie!'

'You all right?' Charlie placed an arm around her shaking shoulders.

Walter next to her, hands in his pockets, gazing upwards, spoke quietly. 'I tried to enlist, you know.'

She spun to face him. 'Why, Walter? Why would you?'

'Stand in my shoes,' he said. 'Last week a woman stepped in front of me – pretty smile. "Here, take this," she said. I was expecting a religious pamphlet. Instead, I felt a white feather in my palm—'

'Oh, that was mean!'

'And her look. "Aren't you ashamed to be in civvies?" And I was... Oh, you needn't worry.' He sounded bitter. 'I rather thought they'd turn me down – dicky heart – and I'm ashamed to say, I felt relief.'

'I couldn't bear it if you—'

'Died?'

She nodded, dreading to say it.

He looked at her thoughtfully. 'You know, it's not so much death I fear – though, of course, one doesn't welcome it – it's horrendous pain and disfigurement that frightens me. And as for choking on poison gas, gasping for breath—'

'Stop it, Walter.' She clutched his arm.

'But worse than anything that might happen to me,' his gaze shifted skyward, 'is imagining bayoneting a chap, guts spilling...'

'Please stop!'

'To be capable of even doing such a thing. That is not to be endured, and I can't bear it.'

She shook him. 'You must stop this, Walter. You aren't going to fight. You must not! I forbid it!' Now he turned to face her, looking relieved to be forbidden. 'Oh, Walter.' She hugged her twin. 'What will it take to stop them? This is too ghastly.'

Edith was by her side. 'There might be others. Do you think?' Nina drew her close, her arms encircling her friend and Walter, then she tugged Charlie's sleeve, drawing him in.

30

On that rooftop, Nina felt suspended, between dark heavens and burning earth, between youth and adulthood. For an hour they waited, then, with the sky clear, began to drift away into the disrupted night.

'Edith, come with us, our house is closer than yours.' Her friend nodded. 'And Charlie, Walter and I must get through this, but you should go home. You might find buses or trams.'

'I'll see you home,' Charlie said. 'I'm not leaving.'

The four of them made for a strange party. She and Edith in their pretty dresses, Walter, feet in spats, clutched a pile of records he refused to leave. Charlie, trumpet case in one hand, the other on her elbow.

'Watch your step,' he said. Her party shoes, Nina found, were not for picking over fallen slabs of sooty bricks, beams of wood, shattered glass.

They passed a cascade of bricks tumbled out of a gap that had been a terraced house. Scrambling over rubble, four men clawed with bare hands, tossing bricks aside, voices choking: 'Nelly… Nelly…' It was every bit as she'd imagined, but worse for being real. Adjoining homes looked like dollhouses – walls removed to reveal the intimacy of a bed, a wardrobe toppled, roof timbers strewn, ragged curtains hanging awry.

Tongues of flames shot from a building, firehoses making little impact.

'This way,' Nina redirected them, only to come across another barrier.

'Back! Back!' A policeman blasted a whistle, trying to control the tangle of vehicles – horse-drawn and motored – and people.

'Got to get home,' she shouted. He didn't hear or care, and they weren't allowed to pass.

Church bells tolled three o'clock before they turned into Alie Street.

'It's there!' Nina broke into a run. 'It's us!' she shouted, bursting through the door.

Ma, in her pink flannel dressing gown, faded orange hair hanging down, rushed forwards. 'Oh, thank the Lord.' Ma's relieved eyes moved from her to Edith and Walter and beyond, a frown gathering. 'Who's he?'

Nina heard Charlie mumble, 'I'll be off.'

Keeping her eyes locked on Ma's, she reached back and grabbed his arm. 'A friend, Ma. Charlie.'

And with only a second's pause – Nina was relieved it was not longer – Ma stepped back. 'Best come in. Streets are no place to be.' Ma hugged Walter, stroking his hair. 'Oh, son, this has given us a fright, eh?'

And there was Molly, grey hair hanging down her back, blue flannel dressing gown unbound to reveal her nightdress. Nina crushed her in an embrace.

'Here I am, Mo. Can't get rid of me.'

'Oh, love, worried sick we were. Made Sid go out. Couldn't have him sitting around not knowing about you.' Mo's squinted hard at Walter. 'Oh, lad, you're a sight for sore eyes, no mistake. And is that you, Edith?'

'Hello, Molly. Yes, it's me.'

'And Mo,' Nina steered Molly forwards, 'this is Charlie. A friend. A special friend.'

Charlie grinned. 'Special, I like that.' He removed his hat. 'Pleased to meet you.'

As dawn came, Nina idly rolled an empty bottle of cooking sherry Ma had rummaged from the larder. She, Edith, Walter and Ma remained at the table, eyeing the final Marie biscuit, while Sid and Charlie sat in deep conversation on the sofa and Molly slumped in her comfy chair, her twisted foot raised, jaw dropped, snoring, a bottle of stout beside her.

Nina's eyes drooped in exhaustion, half listening to Walter. 'I think I'll be going,' he was saying.

'Not sure how easy it'll be. How about I put on some bacon and eggs?' Ma said.

'Oh, that's a great one, isn't it!' Sid was saying.

'I guess,' Charlie said.

Sid began singing, '*It's a long way to Tipperary*—'

'Sid, please,' Ma shouted across at him.

'What? It's a beautiful song. Forget the marching. I was just telling Charlie here that my ma's family came from there.'

'Not from Tipperary!'

'Ireland though, Rose.' He began again, '*It's a long way to go...*' He did have a good voice, Nina admitted. Charlie was whistling, clicking his fingers. Then Sid was on his feet, grabbing Ma. '*...To the sweetest girl I know...*' Then Walter's tenor joined, '*...Goodbye Piccadilly, farewell Leicester Square, it's a long, long way to Tipperary, but my heart's right there.*'

Walter was very pale, tears in his eyes. She squeezed his hand. Still no word from Alexei or his family.

Nina caught Charlie's eye. 'Families!' She rolled her eyes.

Charlie was on his feet. 'Yeah, families. How about a dance, birthday girl?'

This was crazy. Just crazy. She in bomb-dirty party clothes, stockings ruined, shuffled arm in arm with Charlie next to Ma in her dressing gown, arms wrapped around Sid in his open shirt, old trousers held up by braces. Edith pulled Walter to his feet and the two of them joined in.

Molly had jerked awake.

'...*It's a long way to Tipperary*...' Sid and Walter sang.

'All together now,' Molly called, waving her arms in time.

And the whole ruddy lot of them were at it, singing about that bloody place in Ireland and the girl left behind. Sobs rose in her throat only to catch and turn into hysterical, exhausted laughter.

'All right?' Charlie asked.

She leant her head against his chest, crying again as they swayed.

That summer, Charlie's narrow bed in a dingy house in Southwark became an oasis. Here she discovered what it was to explore another's body – not as a dancer working out where to place hands, but as a lover. Charlie's body, so stretched and wiry, pleased her.

'Don't forget to eat,' she scolded, 'you'll disappear down a drain.' She luxuriated in the feel of warm hands exploring her contours. Seeing his pupils dilate, she experienced the intoxication of power over another. In the heat and sweat of intercourse, she would moan.

'Hush!' Charlie put a hand over her mouth. Always too loud. Charlie's bed was a fecund spot: not to produce children, but to talk about ideas and what they wanted.

'Oh, Charlie, the travelling, the dancing. I want that again, and—'

'War can't last forever.'

'—for Diaghilev to see something special in me.'

Teasing fingers traced the hollow of her throat. 'Want me

to have a word with this Mr Diaghilev when I see him? Better. I know some fellas…'

She tugged his hair. 'And you, Charlie?'

'How about a smart club. Y'know, *real* smart. Six-piece band, grand piano. That'd be nice. Chicago maybe.'

At the back of her brain, she tucked away the discomforting thought their dreams might take them apart. She hugged him to her. Right now was the only thing she could count on.

The following months brought raid after raid: more and bigger Zeppelins, lit by more powerful searchlights, fired at by bigger-capacity guns: Lewis machine guns, Nina learnt. She paused to look at fresh gaps in the ground leaving holes in people's lives. And over *there*, not far from where she'd journeyed by train to Paris, it was carnage. No longer in the thousands, tens of thousands, but *hundreds* of thousands slain. Thankfully Walter was exempt.

She, normally a woman of sunshine and laughter, became a mole-ish thing, scurrying between dance bookings, emerging after the last show onto dimmed streets, buildings cowering like cringing dogs waiting to be whipped.

That autumn, Hilda received a cable from Diaghilev. He was in Geneva, getting a company together, inviting Hilda and Kola.

'That's wonderful,' Nina told her friend between gritted teeth. Hilda was to be billed as soloist Lydia Sokolova. 'Tell Grigoriev,' Nina said, 'if there's space in the *corps de ballet*, to count me in.'

But no telegram arrived, and she bit down her disappointment and continued to find contracts in halls she'd come to loathe. They belonged to an old world – Ma's world – and she was a woman of the new world that must, surely, be forged from this tumult.

Astride Charlie, she vented her anger at shattered dreams and a war she couldn't escape. She and Charlie had sex till she was raw, or Charlie complained she was using him as a punching bag. Her frustrations at the injustices of life in general – hers in particular –corroded the best parts in her, exposing her smouldering heart.

31

WALTER TOOK IN THE POSTMARK AND UNFAMILIAR writing – communication he longed for and dreaded. He fingered the paper, summoning the courage to open it, then, stilling trembling hands, carefully opened the envelope. Two pieces of paper: a much-creased, many-folded printed sheet, the other a letter.

Dear Mr Walter Roberts,

I am Alexei Samokhinn's mother.

Following your numerous letters I can no longer ignore responding. You were obviously a good friend of my son, and I apologise for not writing sooner.

We received news our son was missing within a month of his leaving. For the past year or more we kept our spirits kindled in the hope he may have been taken prisoner, but all our enquiries have come to nothing, and we are resigned to his loss.

The other week I found the courage to go through his possessions and in doing so found this programme, with a note attached saying I must send it to you. Again, my apologies for not writing as I should have done, but my heart has been heavy.

The playbill was from the Paris 1913 Ballets Russes season, with dates and ballets listed. It was the one Alexei had shown him that night of the opera when he had folded it, slipping it into his breast pocket. In the margin, next to *Le Sacre du printemps*, Alexei had written: REMEMBER.

Immediately he went to the piano, an old upright that had been left in the Pimlico apartment, too heavy to shift. He placed the playbill where he could see it and opened a hand-written solo piano score for *The Rite of Spring*. His fingers began the tremulous opening sequence, building to the crescendo, exploring the trills and dissonance. This score, as with the two-handed score, was one he worked on daily. *Thud, thud, thud...* he threw himself into the percussive, strident insistence.

'Alexei!' The name ripped from his throat. 'Alexei!' He pictured a bearskin pagan, pounding the stage and the earth. Alexei stretched naked in bed, pale skin luminous, eyes bright and impish. Alexei lying in a war-torn field, his bones and blood emptying into the dirt.

On he played, flicking a page, working himself into a sweat, not stopping at the parts he stumbled over, grappling with his own arrangement, determined to bring the colour of a full orchestra to the room. He gazed from score to playbill, eyes on the single word: remember.

He was reaching the end – the climax, the sacrifice – remembering being in that cupboard with thuds of dancing feet above him, remembering the thrill and warmth of Alexei. With a slide of his fingers along the keys with his right hand, he finished with a left-hand chord, then closed the piano lid.

Rupert Brooke dead, poems unwritten. Music George Butterworth would never compose. Who was *he* to shy away from duty? What did his life matter?

He'd stayed on at college because everyone expected it of him, and he kept this rented room, as the address Alexei had. Now there was no reason to stay, and he knew what he must do. He supposed the military no longer cared about such imperfections as weak hearts, and he no longer cared whether that heart carried on beating.

It was to Wandsworth recruiting office that Walter presented himself, enlisting with the East Surrey Regiment, which would form a part of the 120th Brigade.

Nina howled seeing him in uniform, balling her hands into fists beating his chest.

'Sorry, Nina. I had to. After I heard—'

'Poor darling Alexei. And if *I* find it hard to bear, I know what *you* must be feeling. Really, I do Walter. But even so. I don't want to lose you! Christ, Walter, must we risk all our young men? Are you going to tell Ma, or should I?'

'I rather hoped you would talk to Rose.'

'Coward! Not that way.' She glared at him. 'I wish I could cry, but I'm too angry.'

Training followed in the English countryside in fields he might have rambled through. Nights in huts, reading, writing, sleeping on canvas beds, days becoming acquainted with every armament he was likely to come across. And horses. That was a surprise.

'How is it, Roberts, a man of your class hasn't learnt to ride?' The training officer looked dumbfounded. 'Basic requirement, lad. Better here than thrown in the deep end over there.'

So he learnt, and discovered he could do it well enough for whatever might be required of him. There was a rhythm to it, and a certain pleasure to feel strong, sweaty horse flesh between his thighs.

Throughout these months, he found a camaraderie he had never experienced. They pitted themselves against each other – stealth as much as strength – and their regiment against other regiments in mock attacks, football games and field sport larks. He managed to come third in a sack race. 'Sure but steady!' He laughed, hopping past a heap of more competitive men who had collided and fallen. 'Go, Edwards!' He waved his cap, cheering on another of the East Surreys being pipped to the post by an East Kent man in the half mile race. The day in late May was beautiful, and with men cavorting around, he made a vow to do whatever was in his powers to protect any man in his charge. His gaze moved beyond a line of them straining in a tug of war to the open landscape of Salisbury Plain. And he would do whatever was in his power to protect this precious country.

Kit wrote from Egypt, where he was grappling with camels as much as the enemy. Walter enjoyed hearing from him – always so confident, always ready to bat away the heat and flies and a *jolly inconvenient bout of the runs. No dignity in that, I assure you!*

He wrote to Mr Reed, who made him promise to write regularly once he was "over there". *Keep up your work,* his former master wrote. *Take inspiration where you can. I advise you take notebooks, jot ideas.* And poetry volumes, Walter added to the list of essentials.

Nina wrote, *Don't be shocked, but Charlie and I are living together. Life is too short to worry about such things. I don't want children, so doing my best to avoid that. I liked hearing about sports day. Well done you!*

It was early June when Second Lieutenant Walter Roberts of the 13th Battalion East Surrey Regiment visited London during a week's leave. He made his way to Whitechapel, where Rose was expecting him.

'You look so handsome.' She brushed a hand over his shoulder, the epaulet of a commissioned officer, and handed his peaked cap to Molly.

'You keep this polished, mind.' Molly held the cap close, peering at the regiment insignia.

'And my brass buttons,' he told her. 'When I'm back I will be a champion polisher. Perhaps you'll entrust your ornaments to me.'

'Never!' She laughed.

'I'm so proud of you, son. Molly and I'll be knitting and sending you whatever you wish for. You just shout out.'

'I will.'

'Tell you something. I can look Mrs Dowson in the eye now. Three of hers… two now, after Harry was hit. Such a nice lad, he was. And Mrs Whitehead, always on at me, asking about you with a look on her face.'

He could picture Rose in Whitechapel's markets and shops, and the competitive gossip of women who had, or had not, sacrificed their "best boys", husbands and sons, or been bombed out of their living rooms and beds.

'Well, Rose,' he smiled, 'you can hold your head up high.'

'You write now, and anything for Nina, send it here. Who knows where she'll be.'

'And where are you off to?' Molly said.

'South coast tomorrow. From there to Le Havre.'

First Molly embraced him. 'I wish you hadn't joined the 13th Battalion. It sounds unlucky. Let's hope it's not.'

Then Rose. 'Bless you, and God keep you safe.'

He inhaled kitchen smells in her hair: fried onions and meat. If her earthiness had offended him when he was a boy, it now gave him comfort.

'Be sure to write,' she said.

At the corner of Alie Street, he turned to see Rose and Molly at the doorstep, Rose waving a handkerchief, calling, 'Bye… Bye.' Then he was beyond them.

Along with hundreds, sweltering in the same woollen uniform and heavy kit, Walter marched along lanes through the Flanders countryside, fields lush in the fullness of summer. Passing through villages he sang "Tipperary" and other ditties to make the miles speed past, distant artillery *crumps* and *booms* growing louder as they drew nearer their destination.

In those first days at camp, amongst intensive drills, training in trench warfare, and inevitable parades, there was a memorial service for Field Marshall Earl Kitchener – drowned when the vessel that carried him hit a mine.

'Shit can happen to the best of 'em,' someone remarked.

He bowed his head as their chaplain read a prayer, giving thanks to Kitchener's leadership and courage; raised his voice as they sang, "And did those feet in ancient time…"

It was odd, Walter thought, how well school had prepared him for this life.

He became a new boy all over again.

D company, his company, had been placed with the more experienced Black Watch. They followed their Scottish counterparts to the stretch of trench they would be defending. Amidst craters, churned earth, and stumps of exploded trees, he caught glimpses of large swathes of red poppies and blue cornflowers.

The Scot followed his gaze. 'Aye, it's a flower heaven. Where there's muck – blood and bone.' And so many explosives, Walter knew, leaving traces of nitrogen. 'Keep your head down, lad, or you'll be fertiliser yourself.' They dashed along a narrow connecting trench, knowing snipers would be on the lookout. He would not be a tall poppy.

On his first day in the trenches, he discovered war tasted of soil and blood, smelt of a festering soup of fear and sweat, with overtones of hot metal. And it sounded like nothing on earth should ever sound.

Instinctively, he ducked as a shell landed yards from where he was hunkered down. Behind sandbags lining the top of the trench, his men were at their mortar gun, loading, firing, reloading across the stretch of wasteland that belonged to no man while, high above, swallows ignored this human folly.

At another shell, the ground shuddered, dark sods and exploding shrapnel erupting into the air. Grit landed in his eyes; lips tasted earth. At an anguished howl, he turned to see a face near him covered with blood, a kilted highlander from the Black Watch sinking to his knees. The screaming man was clutching his face.

'I've got you, laddie.' Another of that battalion scampered to the Highlander who could only gargle through a shattered jaw. 'Can ye walk? Get him out!'

Another kilted man hauled the injured one to his feet, staggering along the duckboards, telling the dazed and moaning soldier he would be "right as rain".

A high-pitched whine took up residence in Walter's head, ear to ear, and would not leave. Whizz-bangs – light shells fired from small calibre field guns – like so many exploding firecrackers, shocking in their suddenness. A rattle of machine guns. Their own, vying for the higher ground. The other team, Huns, determined to hold on to the advantage of a ridge. Never-ending whines, whistles, booms, thuds, and Walter became a bit player in a diabolical orchestra led by a conductor he would never see. His inexperience – all their combined inexperience – was dreadful to witness.

One day, in a lull, one of his soldier's saluted. 'Lieutenant Roberts. It's Webb, sir. We're not sure what to do with him.'

Walter followed, pushing past the line of men at their stations to where Webb – a former shop boy, almost certainly not eighteen – slumped against the revetment, face frozen, jaw clamped, hands pressed to his ears, legs threshing, trouser crotch soaked.

'He's been like this for some time, sir. We moved him out of the way, but as it's quieter now, thought you best know.'

'Thank you, Bolton.' Walter laid a hand on a collapsed shoulder. 'Webb. Can you hear me?' Webb's eyes rolled one way and another, unable to focus. 'Help him to his feet,' Walter said, and willing hands tried with a cheery "up you get!" but Webb couldn't stand, legs skittering. Seeing this youth known for his smutty jokes reduced to a whimpering, drooling half-creature was shocking to see.

Walter sucked in his breath. 'Take him away,' he ordered. 'The rest shouldn't see.'

'Casualty clearing station, sir?'

'Obviously! I don't mean a knacker's yard.' Immediately the words left his mouth, he regretted them.

'Yes, sir. Up you come now. We'll get you sorted.'

'You'll be right as rain tomorrow, Webb,' Walter added, his voice louder than necessary.

As two of his men hoisted Webb from under his armpits and dragged him along broken and muddy boards, flailing legs hitting anything they met with, Walter considered he'd become a convincing liar. Most days he was tasked with writing official letters to families who must be told their loved one had died. He rarely told the truth – too brutal – better to find uplifting words. Let the family know they had a hero to mourn; tell them it was a quick death.

Intermittent shelling marked the night, stretches of relative quiet between. From the ground, beams danced in a dark sky ready to pinpoint planes, while from that same black heaven, brilliant flares flashed, hoping to catch unwary patrols below. Somewhere in the distance, a dog was barking.

At dawn, he was relieved of his position. He passed men,

271

razors delicately scraping cheeks, tin helmets turned into shaving bowls, peering at tiny mirrors balanced on ammo boxes.

'Well done,' Walter said. 'You've done us proud.'

'Sir,' came exhausted responses. 'Yes, sir.'

Others sat leaning against the revetment, clutching tin mugs of tea, scooping bully beef from the can – supplies delivered up the line.

'Another day under our belt,' Walter said in what he hoped was a cheery voice. 'What's for breakfast, Collins?'

'Dog biscuit.' He waved a dry clump. 'But I'd eat anything, me.'

'And me.' He made his way to the dugout where he knew food and rest waited for him and where he would report to Captain Mills.

Another day, still on this earth.

32

'Ma?' And Nina was flying at her the moment she came through the door. 'News!' It looked like a telegram clutched in her daughter's hand, but Nina was jigging so much Rose wasn't sure. 'Read... read!'

'Heaven's sake,' came Molly's voice, 'let her get in.'

'Just a minute.' She took off her jacket and handed her groceries to Molly. 'Shocking bread queue... Now.'

'From Grigoriev. Finally!' Nina uncrumpled the paper, pressing it into her hands.

8 SEPTEMBER SAILING BORDEAUX NEW YORK. AMERICAN TOUR TILL END FEBRUARY. CAN YOU COMMIT?

'Oh, love!' Rose hugged her daughter. 'Go! Better than staying here.'

'But all those subs.' Molly was looking from her to Nina. 'I can't help thinking...'

'No, Mo, if my time's up, it's up.' Nina skipped from foot to foot. 'I'm off to America, dancing for Diaghilev!'

'And Nina, you must write to Walter. He'll love to hear.' Rose had his regimental address and wrote every two days. And to Sid. She was no longer Miss Rose Banbury, but Mrs Rose Wood, or Mrs Sid Wood, as she liked to say. There had been a small ceremony before Sid joined up. 'And thinking of our men. What about Charlie? What does he think?'

A frown formed between Nina's eyes. 'Doesn't know yet. Give me a chance. I just dropped in to see you—'

'The telegram. It arrived here, you see,' Molly said.

Rose nodded. Her daughter was no longer in the present but hurtling towards the time she'd be gone. She spared a thought for Charlie.

Shortly before Nina left, Rose went to see *Battle of the Somme*. Edith had been already, but insisted, 'It bears watching again. May I come with you?' Nina and Charlie wanted to see it, but Molly begged off. 'It sounds nasty, and we've enough of that.'

Camera people had been out filming troops at the Front. Now, at cinemas in London, and up and down the country, millions went to see their men at war. The previous week, Mr Reed had sent a note: *Bill Monroe's playing at one of the cinemas. I'll let you know which. Do try and catch him as he'll want to hear of Walter.*

Her party arrived early. She placed her bag and jacket on a seat, then made her way to the piano to the side of the screen. Not having met Mr Monroe, she assumed the middle-aged man rifling through sheets of music must be him.

'Mr Monroe? Sorry to disturb you. I'm Walter Robert's mother.'

'Oh, delighted!' He was on his feet, large frame looming, two paws grasping her hand. 'How is your son? How is dear Walter?'

'Alive, and well, I hope.' That was the best she could reply.

'Thank the good Lord. You know, each day I accompany this film, I think of him, and all the other St John's boys I knew so well.'

Knew? Did he refer to the past when he'd taught them, or were they dead?

'That's kind. Thank you.' She squeezed his hand.

'Today it's just me, I'm afraid. Sometimes we've a small band, but it's hellishly difficult recruiting musicians. And to be frank,' Mr Monroe leant forwards conspiratorially, 'we've a *score* we're meant to follow. Slavish, if you ask me. I prefer to improvise and some of these formally trained musicians are so, so, *stiff*. But there we are. I'd better sort these.' He sighed, tapping the pile of music.

'And I'd better get back. Nice to meet you, Mr Monroe.'

'Please pass on my very best wishes to Walter. Tell him he's in my prayers.'

Rose hurried to her seat.

Walter's regiment hadn't been filmed – but even so…

A battalion of metal-helmeted men marched through a village, motorcyclists weaving past outrider horsemen and village dogs trotting out to see what the fuss was about.

She whispered to Nina, seated to her left, 'I know it's not, but it *could* be Walter.' She glanced at Mr Monroe, hands drumming a fast march. Far rather it be Walter at the piano. At a camp – boxes unloaded from horse-drawn wagons, a pile of stacked shells – she whispered, 'That's what Sid'll be doing.'

Sid was on transport duties, ferrying supplies and ammo from trains to lorries. 'Those tents. I hope Walter's keeping warm.'

'Shush, Ma.'

When a massive howitzer fired and rebounded, she *felt* it, Mr Monroe ratcheting up the tension with terrific crashes that had her and others crying out in shock. It was, the caption said, firing at German trenches. That gave little comfort. The same would be coming back in Walter's direction.

'What's a "plum pudding"?' she heard Charlie ask Nina. In

a trench, uniformed men placed a metal ball atop a mounted gun before firing.

'Not that!' Nina said.

'That's one son of a bitch,' Charlie whispered, seeing an enormous cannon winched into position, loaded with a metal projectile, then adjusted to an angle and fired. Smoke filled the air as Mr Monroe struck defiant chords. Before long, she was staring at a crater, deep as a house, an officer standing at the edge dwarfed by it.

'What kind of earth-ripping machine is this?' she whispered.

'A mine, Ma. Our side. Now hush!'

'Oh, dear Lord!' Her hands flew to her face. Cheers resounded through the picture house while on screen there was mayhem: smoke, barbed wire, men falling… Feeling a grip on her arm, she turned to see her daughter's frightened face.

It was hard to watch, the bag of toffees she carried, from habit, in her pocket going uneaten, and she wasn't minded handing them around.

She glanced to her right to see Edith staring at the screen, tears flowing down her cheeks. Rose reached for her hand. Maybe she had a sweetheart over there. She'd not said.

'Christ!'

'Oh, My Lord!'

Cries rang through the cinema at a pit strewn with bodies: uniformed men, limbs flung this way and that. More men, sprawled in mud, one slumped in a restful position.

Rose gasped, clutching Nina's arm. 'Are those men dead? Are they *real* men?'

'What do you think, Ma? We're not at the Alhambra!'

'Thank God they're Jerries.'

She noticed Nina gripping Charlie's arm as if to nail him down.

Trees without branches. Houses without roofs. Mr Monroe playing that sad lament, "Flowers of the Forest". She dabbed her eyes, longing for the melodrama to move to a happy ending.

Now, *this* tune she knew. She rocked in her seat, humming along to "Till the Boys Come Home", while on screen, young Tommies cheerfully went about polishing arms and ammo. Mr Jacobi's scores came to mind, stitching melodies to those onstage ballets. The film only needed a good old gallop as a finale. If only Mr Monroe could play one of those. But not yet. This horrid real-life show wasn't done.

They trailed out of the cinema – audience jabbering in a can't-quite-believe-what-I've- seen kind of way or walking stiff-legged and stunned.

Nina looked at her as she waited for Charlie to light two cigarettes. 'Well, Ma?'

'I'm a bit wobbly, I've got to say. But I'm glad we've seen it together. My goodness, how brave our men are. We will win. We always win. Our Tommies will beat those Jerries, no question, but oh, what a sacrifice.' She patted her heart.

She had more than Walter to worry about. 'Told Sid not to go volunteering for anything daft and to keep his feet on the ground. Poor Basil.' She sniffed. The morning papers had delivered news of Basil Hallam's death. The music hall star was in an observational air balloon when something went wrong, plunging him to the ground. Onstage, he'd looked so dashing in top hat and tailored suit, posturing as he sang, "*I'm Gilbert the Filbert, the nut with a 'K'. The pride of Piccadilly, the blasé roué…*"

'Did I ever tell you I stole his cravat?' Nina said. 'Least, I said it was his. Got a bit for it.'

'Nina!' Edith punched her arm. 'I remember that.'

Rose looked aghast at her daughter.

'Would've been worth a fortune now he's dead… Oh, Ma, don't look like that. Got to find something to laugh about.'

She watched her daughter inhale, relishing the heat in her throat. Rose had never smoked, couldn't see the point of it.

Nina prodded her. 'What do you think will happen if we don't win?'

'Oh, we will. We simply must!' Rose was adamant. 'You saw all those Jerries lined up. All those prisoners? They looked happy to be out of the trenches, don't you think?'

'But what weren't they showing, Ma? I got to think of Isadora Duncan. No artifice, lay bare the truth and so on—'

'Too much truth may be hard to take,' Edith said.

'No doubt that's why it was filmed in summer,' Nina said. 'Winter's coming. Walter's first…'

That was an uncomfortable thought. Rose preferred to keep a thin veil between herself and reality.

'Charlie?' Nina was watching him through narrowed eyes, sucking on a cigarette. He'd been quiet. 'And don't dare tell me you would enlist if you could.'

'Sugar, you know I would.' Charlie looked regretful. 'And I can't see how we can stay out of it. Can't see how President Wilson can hold back. Just don't seem right. If *we* join, *I* join. I can do more than blow a bugle for the dead.' He raised an imaginary rifle and bent his trigger finger.

'Honestly!' Nina knocked his arm away.

If America joined, the war might be over sooner. If America joined, Charlie would join. Hobson's choice.

Rose looked at their sombre faces. 'I fancy a cup of tea and something sweet. My treat.' That drew smiles. She tried not to think about Walter, nor of Nina's upcoming voyage with those lurking subs.

'Lyons then,' Edith suggested. 'They're good value. There's a teashop near.'

'Let's see if they've got Battenberg cakes. My favourite.' She was hoping the marzipan wouldn't be spread thinly.

'Rose! That is not patriotic of you.' Edith was wide-eyed. 'Rather too German, don't you think? Perhaps treacle tarts?'

'Yes, Ma. We can't possibly.'

For a moment she was crestfallen, till everyone laughed.

'All right, you lot. Come on.' She linked arms with her daughter while she had the opportunity.

33

Buildings that had been tiny from a distance now pierced the sky.

'I see her!' Nina shrieked. 'There she is. Liberty... Very Isadora, don't you think?'

'How do you mean?' Doris said.

They were crammed at the rails of the *Lafayette* – Doris, Hilda, Kola, and other passengers – everyone happy that the grey swelling Atlantic was behind them.

'She reminds me of when I saw Miss Duncan perform. Those same heavy draperies, standing solid, arm raised. Oh, I just love her; I'm sure I'll adore America! I can't wait to get started.'

'I expect Monsieur Nijinsky will be there to greet us,' Kola said.

'Bound to!' Hilda agreed.

When Nina set foot on firm ground, she absorbed everything that was new. Accents brasher, even, than Whitechapel costermongers. Manhattan's downtown skyline beckoning to be explored. And people seemed bigger too – more robust, surely, than worn-down Londoners.

'Where is he?' they said, standing on tiptoes, searching among the jostle of dockworkers and disgorging passengers.

But no one was there to greet them, certainly not Nijinsky.

Nina looked at Kola's crestfallen face, knowing he faced his first challenge.

'Not sure where we should go,' he said.

'Let's go to the Met,' Hilda suggested. 'Someone will know where we're staying.'

'Yes, yes. Good idea.' Kola looked relieved, and the two of them hurried away to find a porter.

No one uttered a word but she, and all of them, were thinking the same. Grigoriev would never have allowed this. But he was not with them – Kola allotted the role of rehearsing and organising. Worse, Diaghilev was not with them, banned from directing this second tour. Earlier that year, on the first tour, there were one or two backstage spats.

'You know, I saw him actually strike a stagehand with his cane,' Doris said. 'Just imagine, this gum-chewing fellow sauntering up to Mr Diaghilev. "Hey, whaddaya think about trying…?" No, "Excuse me, Mr Diaghilev, I wonder if…"'

Nina smiled at the imagined scene, knowing their director hadn't always seen eye to eye with America's democratic ways. He was staying in Europe with others of the company, with Nijinsky in charge of the artistic side over here. Somehow Nina felt cheated. Being *in* Diaghilev's company, with him *there*, ever watchful, was what mattered.

Sitting on her suitcase waiting for Kola and Hilda to return with instructions, Doris caught her eye, raising a hand with fingers crossed. Nina did the same.

During rehearsal, another argument was underway.

'But I don't want *that* role.' A principal dancer stamped her foot.

'You'll take what *I* say,' Kola thrust his face close to hers, then twisted away. 'Anyone seen Nijinsky?' Seeing shakes of heads, he cursed.

'Nina.' A dancer came to her in tears. 'You were in this ballet, please tell me what I have to do.' So Nina helped rehearse new dancers into smaller roles she had danced. But no one could magic something out of air for *Till Eulenspiegel*.

'What was Diaghilev thinking of to allow this?' an exasperated dancer asked. 'Kola's fetching Nijinsky from his hotel bed.'

Each day, rehearsals were a nightmare.

'Vaslav, for pity's sake, man!' Kola strode towards the choreographer and shook his shoulders. 'Pull yourself together and get this damn thing done. I beg you!'

'Don't touch me!' Nijinsky, pallid skin greying, jerked back, his fingers fussily brushing at his shirt.

'Please. Just make something... Anything...'

'Full ballet. Forty minutes. Impossible to just "make". I am no cook!' Nijinsky drew himself up. 'I create. Talk to Monsieur Diaghilev, tell him—'

'Oh, we are!' Kola yelled. 'Daily! Telegramming back and forth. Me and Mr Kahn with Sergei Pavlovich. Grigoriev replying. On and on!'

But Nijinsky shrugged, his face sullener than before, drawing into himself, absorbed in his own thoughts.

Despite ongoing rehearsal difficulties, Nina found an energy and directness about New Yorkers.

It's got a buzzy feel about it, she wrote to Ma and Mo. *I love the food mainly because it's not rationed. And I'm not missing blackout and bleakness. Americans have no idea what it's like at home...*

On the back of a Coney Island postcard, she wrote to Charlie: *I ate a hot dog! I'm a real American now, eating with my fingers! I could live here, you know...* Thinking of Charlie tugged her heart. She missed him but wouldn't miss this adventure for anything. Anyone.

She included a four-leaf clover pendant in Walter's letter, posted via Ma. Though it was October, she wished him a Merry Christmas, telling him: *We're about to open in New York with Nijinsky's new ballet Till Eulenspiegel, which is a mouthful to say, and a German story to boot, but let's not dwell on that. I think it'll be funny, if only we knew what to do!*

In what was supposed to be a dress rehearsal, she watched Nijinsky pick up his jacket and stalk out. 'God almighty!' Her words – all their curses – hovering in the air, a toxic smog smothering them. '*Rite* all over again, but far worse!'

The person who eventually walked back in was not their choreographer but the Opera House manager.

'My dear dancers,' Mr Kahn said in his German accent. 'We have a situation we must address. We are sold out and can no longer postpone this much anticipated new ballet. I ask you, I appeal, is there any way you wonderfully talented dancers can pull this ballet together?'

Which is what they did, hazarding a guess, making things up in all the sections they were clueless about, stitching together the threads of *Till* to premiere to discerning New York audiences. Taking her curtain call on that mighty stage, she bowed graciously, thinking, *If people only knew how fragile this artifice was...*

At the end of October, along with forty dancers, protective Russian mothers, a full orchestra of musicians, costumers, crew, Nina crowded into a customised twelve-coach Pullman – the Ballets Russes Special – people in front carriages, scenery and costumes packed into rear freight cars.

Here she sat next to Doris or one of the other girls, chatting, reading, darning pointe shoes and stockings, pondering what the dining car was serving for lunch. Her bunk was above Doris's. In that curtained bed, the only patch to call her own, she took up her pen.

You ever seen a circus? she wrote to Charlie on the postcard. *All those wagons and cages parked to stuff elephants and lions in before trundling off to the next stop. That's me.* She wrote of her excitement of seeing his country, and where they were travelling, pausing before adding, *Missing you, Nina. XX.*

Missing Charlie hadn't been calculated for. She'd toured so much – a Dorothy on her yellow brick road – knowing Ma and Mo would be there when she got back. Home, yet *not* home. She hadn't figured out where she belonged. Just as she hadn't figured how Charlie fitted in her life.

Her last night before leaving London, snuggling next to Charlie in a big bed he'd bought, Nina teased him. 'No dilly-dallying while I'm out of town.'

'Not me. Couldn't ever.' He smiled that smile that melted her. Mouth stretched wide, the corners of his eyes wrinkling. He was a caring and faithful lover. For some reason that had surprised her, and she was further surprised to discover his faith. He'd sought out, and found, an evangelical church where, he'd told her, 'Mine's not the only black face in the pews.' He wasn't one of those chaps getting his kicks from drugs and sleeping around. Her criticism, which he'd heard, was that he wasn't ambitious enough.

Now she tapped a buttock. 'By the time I'm back, I want to see your name in the entertainment column.' She stretched an arm, tracing words in the air: 'Charlie Jackson and his band appearing at…'

He laughed. 'That'll be the day, but we can dream.'

'You're smarter than you make out.'

'Yeah, well.'

That was another thing. He never thought he was good enough. While he didn't have much by way of a formal education – 'Who bothers schooling black kids?' – he was well read, knew more than she did about many things. Still, he would back off from an argument – even with Sid! When Sid pontificated about the war, Ma would say, 'Is that a fact?' and Charlie would just nod and press his lips together. Sid had become a leech and had both Ma and Mo kowtowing to him.

'Yes, Charlie, you can do it. Make it happen!'

'Yes, boss!' He mock-saluted and she knocked his hand away.

'I've got to be up early, no more talking.'

'Yes, ma'am, if you say—'

She locked her mouth on his, drawing him close.

One stop became six… sixteen, then onwards through flatlands towards Houston, momentum building. Always, the press was briefed well in advance with stories of their exotic appeal, of their fabulousness.

On hearing the Pullman sliding to a halt, Nina peered out to see cameras fixed to tripods and a crush of reporters and Houston dignitaries gathered to greet them. It was the principal dancers that mattered: Nijinsky, of course, but the ballerinas particularly. They travelled in their own front coach.

'Wait, sweetheart!' Nina imagined an anxious Olga Spessivtseva's mother saying while fastening a string of pearls around her daughter's throat.

'Really, darling, we can't have this.' Someone would frown on seeing Lydia Lopokova about to descend, her fur coat glamourous but her hair a shambles, just as Lydia would jam an elegant hat on with a pert, 'Better?'

And Nina. And Doris. And Hilda – all of them, no matter how little money they earned, were putting on a show. Nina ran a comb through her hair, applied a lick of bright lipstick, checked her sparkly green glass earrings were firmly clipped on, then draped a silk scarf artfully over her shoulder.

'Ready for your entrance, darling?' Doris teased.

'Absolutely, darling,' Nina said.

Now they were so many wizards – phony Russians, shams – not for their own glory but in name of art and enterprise.

Nina Rosova took her time to pause at the carriage door, before extending one elegant foot, one silk-stocking leg, after the other. Then she was on the platform, smiling, graciously extending a hand, purring in a Russian accent, 'Delighted to be here, I do hope you will come to our show.'

34

MEN WALTER HAD KNOWN BECAME STATISTICS TYPED up in the battalion's diary for Lieutenant Colonel Newton to sign off. He would watch Captain Mills take another sheet of paper, down another tot of whisky, before formulating the right words for a grieving family. But there never were right words. One of his men had accidently died, having fallen asleep onto his own bayonet.

'How on earth…?' Walter began, irritated at this senseless loss.

'Bone-tired, sir,' a distraught fellow explained. As they all were – everyone. An exhaustion that seeped into the very bones.

Through Mr Reed's letters, he kept up with the plight of Old Johnians: names of boys who'd been above him, his year, and younger. He learnt Chilcott had died an *honourable* death. Maybe his old friend had met his fate undertaking valorous action, or possibly he'd topped himself. Men did. Walter forced himself to write to Chilcott's parents offering his sympathy, reminding them how kind they'd been to him, and sharing some memories from school days.

He learnt of maladies new to him. Gums bled, and he could barely eat, his mouth so sore with ulcers. With disgust, he unpeeled socks to find fungus leaving his feet stinking and skin peeling. In December, he succumbed to a fever that'd lain low half his company, spending two weeks in a field hospital dosed with quinine, aching, too dizzy to stand.

He learnt to live with what, as a boy, Mother had called "dirty creepy-crawlies", forbidding him to play with a poorer family living nearby. Lice colonised every part of his skin and he itched his crotch and underarms until they were red-raw. Baths, when they were scheduled in a period of rest, were welcome along with a change of underwear and a freshly steamed uniform. But it was impossible to dislodge louse eggs from the seams of his trousers and jackets, so he'd sit in his underwear, trousers turned inside out, running a heated knife blade along the seams hearing the satisfying cracking of louse eggs. 'Die, you bastards,' he'd growl.

Once he woke to scampering across his face. He shot upright and saw the thing watching him unafraid.

'I'll get you if it's the last thing I do!'

These rats were massive, their food supply – dead men and horses – endless. They were there en masse, flourishing just like poppies. He lit a cigarette and, with another fellow, watched several rats having a good go at a dog's corpse.

'A rat heaven, wouldn't you say, Roberts?'

But for men, it was hell. He and his side were not winning against pests, sludge, nor the enemy.

One night, he, with four others, were charged with assessing the lengths of coiled wire between them and enemy trenches. Under a slight moon, they crept into the expanse of no man's land, elbows and knees digging in.

'Down!' he hissed, as another flare threatened to reveal them, inviting machine gunfire. The churned ground he pressed himself into stank of evil. Scarcely breathing, he could hear the enemy talking softly as they rolled out more coils. So close. If they were to look in his direction, they would surely pick out shapes of men flat to the ground. For what seemed an age, he lay belly down on the sludge, pinned to the spot, then slithered back, sodden and frozen.

With chattering teeth, he reported: 'None the wiser, sir. If there are gaps, we didn't spot them. They're doing a good job out there.'

Was life reduced to this? Was any of it worth it?

In late December, he was at Camp 112. The days were raw, ground a slush of not-quite frozen sods. One morning, he was about to organise a work party for draining and cleaning duties when he heard his name and saw their chaplain striding towards him.

'A little bird tells me you have a fine voice, Roberts, and you were a chorister.'

'As a boy.'

'We're getting up a little concert – Christmas Eve – and I'm rather hoping you'll sing.'

'I play piano. I can sing but—'

'Well, a piano may be too much to ask for – the portable one I'd my eye on has been commandeered. Never mind that. We have some comic turns lined up, but you know, despite a wish to keep things light, I do feel something sentimental might go down well.'

'Of course. What have you in mind?'

'I was thinking something poetical.' The chaplain waved his hand. 'Perhaps early on, and we'll finish with something rousing. Don't breathe a word to a soul, but I have a little surprise for Christmas evening.' He tapped his nose. 'Cinema, you know. Chaplin.'

'The chaplain?'

'Not the man of God; the little comedian. He will raise the spirits, I should think.'

On Christmas Eve, Walter lined up for the church parade: brass buttons, insignia and boots all polished. He wore new underwear, a freshly laundered shirt and thick overcoat against threatening sleet. At a special service at Dernancourt church, puffs of icy condensation issued from so many singers. 'Silent Night, holy night...' Wishing this *were* the case; that there wasn't a makeshift hospital up the road; a military cemetery filling so quickly.

That evening, he sung unaccompanied in the chaplain's spirit-raising concert. He chose two songs from Butterworth's "Shropshire Lad" cycle to Housman's poetry: "Loveliest of Trees", singing of a cherry tree in bloom in spring woodlands.

After applause, he heard, 'Such a fine voice, Roberts.'

'Beautiful.'

He began the next.

'*When I was one and twenty I heard a wise man say, "Give crowns and pounds and guineas, but not your heart away... "*'

Strange, what he tended to think of as mawkish now resonated at a deep level. He strove to keep his voice steady.

'*"... Give pearls away and rubies, but keep your fancy free..."*' His voice soared over the heads of men – scrubbed Christmas faces, oiled hair – sitting in rows before him, and he hoped they'd live to find happiness with sweethearts. His young heart he'd given to Alexei. Could he ever love again?

Before he could walk back to his seat came cries of, 'Off with him! Make way!' Towards him came a pantomime horse, two pairs of sack-covered soldiers' legs capering. On its back, a well-padded "woman" brandishing a rolled umbrella. Where they'd got the dress and make-up from was anyone's guess. The skit was met by bellyfuls of laughter, everyone finding joy in something silly.

At midnight, officially Christmas Day, he retreated to his cot to open presents he'd been keeping for the occasion. Socks

– more, but always welcome – and a box of toffees from Rose.

Dearest son, she wrote. *I hope this finds you well. Everything is hard to come by, so our small offering is all I can manage. No goose for us this year; it will be slim pickings.* In fact, he was eating very well, a result of overordering rations by those fearful of being reprimanded. If he were to die in the course of duty, it would not be from hunger.

He opened an envelope dated mid-October Nina had posted from New York by way of London. He smiled at the card with a jolly, red-costumed Santa Claus, the message wishing him "The best of all Christmases". Inside, she had enclosed a tiny four-leaf clover pendant.

Dearest Twinny, I hope this finds you well…

Why did all his family begin letters this way?

I just want to wish you a Merry Christmas and all that, and if I don't post this now, it will never reach you. We're about to open in New York with Nijinsky's new ballet Till Eulenspiegel…

Having read his sister's letter, he kissed the pendant and tucked it in a breast pocket.

Edith had sent a card and letter, as had Clara, whom he'd played with in their college musical ensemble. Both wrote regularly, and he was always pleased to hear from them. He mused at their diligence, deciding these good-hearted young women thought him a worthy cause.

He unwrapped Mr Reed's gift. An illustrated book, *British Birds with their Nests and Eggs.* In an enclosed note, he had written, *Dearest Walter. You'll see many of these where you are. Come spring look out for some of these little fellows. You are always in my prayers, dear boy. Stay well. Edmund Reed.*

It was warming to read the word "dearest". *God willing I'm alive in spring,* Walter thought as he lay on his canvas bed, curled tight under blankets.

35

Beyond the Pullman coach window, Nina gazed at exhausted farmland: shacks without a lick of paint on shingled roofs or wonky planked walls.

'One storm would flatten that one.' She nudged Doris, sitting next to her. 'Do you think Dorothy's Kansas farm looked like this?'

'If it did, I wouldn't be hurrying home,' Doris said.

Men, women, and children – white and black – toiled in the sun, dragging bulging sacks. Still cotton crops. Was this the kind of upbringing Charlie had?

At a crossing, the train slowing, she watched an old man ease his aching back, hands resting on a plough. His black face was etched with wrinkles, grey hair frizzled. She'd have given anything to read his thoughts while watching their carriages trundle past, not touching his life in any way. What was real? What mattered? Were their ballet shows just a fake Emerald City? She was confused by it all.

At Tulsa, she and Doris dragged heavy suitcases first to one then another boarding house looking for the cheapest.

'Just look at us, a couple of old drudges,' she grumbled at yet another dismal front door. Then, having found an affordable room, they handed over precious dollars to a care-worn woman. She claimed one saggy bed as Doris plonked down her suitcase.

'Something must be done!' Nina said to her friend. 'It's all right for Hilda and the principals – Nijinsky's being paid a fortune; a *thousand* dollars a performance, I heard – but what of us!'

'Adolf paid for my dinner last night.' Doris kicked off her shoes and dropped onto her bed.

'Me too. Lydia paid for dinner *and* gave me a bit extra for new knickers.' Whenever clothes were packed off to a laundry, she discovered not everything came back.

Doris sat up. 'I've had enough. I'm writing to Mr Kahn. He must understand this is not possible. Has he any idea what it's like? Any idea that thirty-three dollars a week isn't enough to pay for rooms and food?'

'Do it!' Nina thrust a pad of cheap stationery towards her friend.

'All right!'

Dear Mr Kahn, Doris wrote, *I am writing on some of the girls' behalf, also my own. It is concerning our salaries…*

Nina had written to Edith about the wages, to which her friend had replied with a diatribe: *Really, Nina? I'm surprised. This is feudal. Doesn't Diaghilev keep up with revolutionary happenings in Russia?* He kept up with – was ahead of – art trends, Nina thought, but if he could save money, he would.

That evening, at curtain call, she heard clapping like the light patter of a rain shower rather than thundering, blocking out all sound.

'Dismal box office.' Kola shook his head. 'Better next stop, I hope.' And back they packed into carriages reeking of colognes, perfumes and hair pomade mingling with the stale smell of cigarettes and unwashed clothes.

As the weeks wore on, Nina wrote fewer postcards and

letters back home. She didn't have spare money – no extra forthcoming – nor the inclination to tell the truth: that the tour was a fiasco. Nijinsky refused to dance or barely danced, the audience clamouring at the box office.

'We paid to see Mr Nijinsky,' a shrill-voiced women said, 'are you gonna give us our money back?'

'What kind of a scam is this?' A fellow loomed over Kola, grabbing his lapel.

This was not the glory she had imagined.

In Los Angeles, while Nijinsky took himself off to see Charlie Chaplin on set, she risked Kola's wrath by skipping company class. She'd spotted an advert for Denishawn Dance School and was curious. Ruth St Denis's husband, Ted Shawn, had called Nijinsky's dancing "decadent, freakish and degenerate European art". That got her thinking.

She made her way to the address, dropped a dollar bill in the jar and took her place outside – novel! – with a clutch of other barefooted girls in practice clothes.

Mr Shawn arrived in a comfortable shirt, long trousers, bare feet. When he cast an eye over his waiting class, chatting easily here and there, his eyes rested on her.

'A new girl today. By the look of you, you're a dancer.'

'Yes, sir, I'm with the Russian Ballet.' She didn't bother putting on a fake accent. 'I'm from England.'

'England! Okay! Welcome. We've never had one of Diaghilev's girls here.'

She nodded. 'But years ago I studied with Mrs Holt – she followed Miss Duncan's style.'

'All right,' he grinned, 'and so you know, I'm Mr Shawn, or Ted, but never, ever, sir.' He wagged a finger. 'And your name?'

Here on grass covered with a wooden platform, she was led through floor exercises of breathing and stretching, then free-flowing expansive sequences not unlike those she'd learnt under Mrs Holt's tutelage in a chilly London church hall. But under the brilliant blue Californian sky, moving barefooted across the space, she experienced something grounded, more muscley in style, more, well, *American*.

'Thrust, lift your chest. Go on now, feel the weight of your arms… reach… reach!'

She followed an intense black-haired dancer with a head that looked too large for her small frame.

'Okay, Martha. Good. Good. That's it. Extend your legs!' Their teacher praised Martha constantly but sometimes his words were for her. 'Be yourself, Nina! Feel the muscles of your feet connect with the ground. Let the movement travel up you.'

She was enjoying this. Los Angeles was added to the places she imagined living. With Charlie? Maybe New York. Chicago, perhaps. *Not* in the south.

Nina leapt, following Ted's instructions. A warmth radiated upwards, outwards, forcing itself from muscles to skin.

'Okay, Nina. Attagirl!'

Her face lit, lips stretching into a smile of bliss. For the first time in weeks, she felt truly happy. With each leap, she pushed the earth away with her feet.

36

Mid-March, stationed at Little Dale barracks, Walter grabbed the opportunity between drills and tactics practice.

'Sheely, come!' Walter held up his copy of *British Birds with their Nests*.

Lieutenant Sheely shot up from his cot. 'Rather,' snatching his field glasses.

He had to get away and Sheely was good company.

'I do believe...' Sheely picked up a broken eggshell, then peered up at a downy nest just visible within the prickly hedgerow. 'Yes, if I'm not mistaken it's a long tail. So soft and mossy. What a cosy home for her chicks. Do check it out – the tits.'

Walter thumbed through his book.

'Told you so!' Sheely's face shone. He moved closer only for mother bird to burst into a "back-away" song.

Wrapped in long coats, they sat quietly on a log. Sheely got out his sketch book and watercolours, delicately copying the eggshell, smudging blue speckled paint, before dipping his brush into a tin of water and dabbing the tiniest of black spots. He shifted position to where mother bird's head showed above her nest.

'Shh,' he said, and began to capture her likeness.

Walter watched his face, so calm, absorbed in creating something lovely. The opposite page was filled with vivid blue robin eggs, and a scarlet blur of a robin's breast captured during yesterday's outing.

'It's the little things, isn't it, Roberts. I do hope I'm around for nesting season proper.'

'What, you greedy chap,' Walter said. 'Another *whole* month—'

'Give me two!'

They shared an uneasy laugh.

The following day, Walter watched a dangling corpse carried in by two puffing men. 'Sniper got him, sir. Silly bugger stopped to watch a fuckin' bird.'

Walter noted the neat hole in the back of the skull, the front shattered. 'Lay him down there.' Words barely audible. Kneeling by his birding companion, his shaking hand touched a bloodied cheek. When sobs rose, he thought he would choke.

That evening, he carefully wrapped Sheely's notes, sketches, and diaries to send home to his family.

Twice now he'd formed close bonds with other officers only to see those men killed, and it tore his heart.

It was dark, a new moon just visible, when Walter picked his way in a single file around one corner, then another, in the labyrinth of shallow trenches, following sounds of labouring breath and footsteps. At each enemy flair exploding in the sky, garish ghostly outlines of a line of men ahead flickered and faded. Soldiers: a sandbag on each shoulder or carrying three shovels and a pick with two cast-iron grenades apiece dangling from belts.

On and on they trudged till they reached the Fifteen Ravine. He lowered his burden, stretched aching shoulders, then took out his shovel and set about digging an adjoining trench, heading north-west. Faint sounds of picks striking earth indicated that men working towards them from another trench would soon break through. Six hundred men, digging deep, cracking the earth, releasing it from winter hibernation.

In a moment of stillness, between rattles of machine guns and sniper fire, he heard a faint *whoo* of a prowling barn owl. Spring was arriving at this landscape of fields and wooded copses.

He hoisted a sandbag next to another along the ridge of the new trench. It was shallow but would provide protection of sorts for those stationed here, guns pointing out. Walter hoisted up the second sandbag, wedging it in firmly.

To the back of them, Gouzeaucourt and Gauche Wood had been secured. The north-east push continued. Today's game was to get past enemy posts and capture Villers-Plouich, a tiny village south-west of Cambrai, situated in a dip surrounded by five low wooded ridges. He knew the settlement was there, several hundred yards beyond barbed wire rolls and enemy trenches forming the defence line south from Arras.

The Ds were providing right support for B company. Fun and games, boys. Them against us. May the best team win.

Captain Mills, eyes bright with nerves, moved up and down the line. 'We can do this. I have every confidence in you.'

'Sir!'

'Got those Huns on the run. Who said the Hindenburg line couldn't be broken. One more push and we'll have them.'

'Yes, sir!'

Almost zero hour when, like so many innocent children, they would follow an imaginary piper. They would march in formation or fling about in twisted dances of death, sacrificed for the greater good.

Walter thought of those dancers he'd watched waiting in the Theatre de Champs-Elysées wings. Stretching a foot, practising small jumps, waiting for their cue. Alexei had stood next to him, his breath warm in his ear as he whispered, pointing to a group of men in bearskins, 'I should be in that group.' Nina was in a brilliantly patterned costume, fixing a hairpin to her wig. Earlier that day, she'd said, 'I've practised over and over; now it's in the hands of the fates. Wish me luck, Walter. I'm dreading doing something stupid and letting everyone down.' As did he. He touched a left side breast pocket where he kept Nina's keep-safe clover leaf. It would take more than this tiny scrap of metal to protect his heart from a bullet, but he hoped his heart was strong enough and he'd do his duty, leading men as he had been trained to do.

About him in the pre-dawn, a *corps de ballet* of identically dressed men made slight adjustments to their costumes: tightening a helmet strap, checking bootlaces were knotted, touching a dangling grenade, envisioning a release and throw action. He watched men's lips move in prayer and tongues moisten lips, suddenly parched. Anxious heat radiated from his comrades. They huddled, knowing there would be sacrifice – *don't let it be me*. He closed his eyes, wishing that if death were to come, it would be quick. In this ancient ritual of war, he was, as Nina had been, in the hands of the fates. Each had been drilled in their manoeuvres. She, with a lunge and thrust of a fist. He, charging, bayonet-tipped rifle at his right hip, thrusting hard metal into a sack of straw. He and his twin had rehearsed over and over.

Now his performance.

At a signal, he watched a line of men crawl up and over, knees and elbows hugging the ground. This forward line was tasked with blasting through the wire. His platoon was not in the first row of this ballet.

Staccato cracks of sniper fire. Muffled shouts in German. They'd been spotted.

'Best of luck, men,' were the last calm words he spoke that day, then he scrambled out with them.

He ran, stumbling through shell holes, skirting a comrade screaming on the ground. Eyes front, brain rehearsing the moves he'd learnt from chalk diagrams and coordinates on maps. He ran, lungs reaching for breath. Brilliant flares like stage lights. Yellow. Red. Green. Green again. Yellow. A burst of grenades: his team's. Machine guns rattling into action. A chorus of howls of pain, yells of encouragement, and curses in his own language and that of the other side.

He ran, and through a tangle of cut and blasted barbed wire, he raised his rifle, finger on trigger, to see a man about to lob a grenade. Holding his breath he squeezed. With a grunt, the figure sank gracefully to his knees, clutching his chest as if in prayer, '*Mutter… Mutter…*'

Thud. He landed in a deep trench, a raving man, joining a chorus of, 'Hands up! Fuckin' Jerry.'

'*Nicht schiessen!*'

'*Nein… Nein!*'

Too close for firing, he was in what seemed a wrestling match. At any moment, he imagined a sickening stab of a blade. He and two of his men ganged up on one war-befouled man, bayonets threatening, all of them screaming, 'Hands up! Hands fuckin' up.' The man's hands shot skywards, and Walter was saved from finding out if he could disembowel a living man.

Terrified German youths who, moments earlier, had been ready to kill them, now cowered, hands on heads, anxious not to be sacrificed. He gave them no further thought, leaving dozens of prisoners to others to take charge of. His objective lay ahead.

Into a pre-dawn gloom he raced, houses nearer. This village they must take, and the ridge beyond.

Flashes of gunfire flared from gunners positioned in destroyed houses and strong posts. From his side, a steady rat-a-tat of Lewis guns aimed at enemy emplacements, where German gunners did their best to thwart them. Them against us. Us against them. A fizzing whine passed his ear. So close.

'Lieutenant Roberts… here!'

Charging into an alley, he pressed against a whitewashed wall, willing ragged breaths to settle. His eyes darted upwards to windows and into doorways alert to shifting shadows and the barrel of a sniper's rifle.

They gathered, like so many reeking alley cats off night-time prowls, and slunk through cobbled streets towards their rendezvous, rifles ready. He visualised the layout of the village from those chalk drawings. Street by street, house by house, shot by shot, they advanced.

One of his men stationed at a street corner peered into the town square. 'There, sir.'

Dozens gathered, and Walter sought out Captain Crocker, leader of the right-side party. He saluted. 'Reporting for next stage, sir.'

'Roberts. Thank Christ!' Flecks of foam gathered at corners of the captain's mouth. Nostrils and eyes wide, he had the look of a harassed stallion. 'Casualties?' he barked.

'Four, sir.' He was thinking of Leo, who had followed his father into the motor industry and who could be relied on to fix any engine. Of Albert, leaving a wife and two little ones. Of Tom, straight from school. Of John, whom, three months earlier, he'd dragged from freezing, stinking mud on a night patrol.

'Twenty-six here then.' Captain Crocker calculated units of energy for this machine.

'Correct, sir.'

The captains convened and just as hurriedly splintered into three groups with Walter, bound for Highland Ridge. Higher ground. Enemy ground.

It took no time at all for the village to be secured, then Walter followed Captain Crocker. The ridge ahead was low, barely a ripple on an otherwise unremarkable landscape, but they wanted to take it from the other boys. Own it. Say this is ours. But the other boys did not want to give it up. Come-and-take-it-from-us machine guns taunted from German-held positions.

Walter heard Captain Crocker's scream, saw him throw his arms wide, chest lifted, watched him fall.

He raced on. The sounds of his breath ragged in a chorus of damned and be-damned – grunts, groans, howls and yowls. Men fell, blood emptying from them, precious breath and guts spilling onto the earth.

He was aware of his body lifting off the ground in an ungainly buck, a piercing whine filling his ears. His face smashed into hard ground, jaw forced wide, neck forced back as his helmet rammed into the ground. Pitch black. Earth forced into his nostrils and throat. Eyes clogged. Boots caught his ribs as others stumbled over him. He, a fallen man, now an obstacle for those still in the race.

With desperate fingers, he clawed clumps of earth and grass from his throat, gagging and spluttering. Blinking, blinking, he wiped at grit that scoured his eyeballs, then, fumbling for his canister, poured precious water over his eyes till he could see. Throbbing pain wracked him.

Keep going. Don't Stop. The ridge wasn't far ahead.

On his knees, he forced his right foot forwards, but when he tried to scramble to both feet, he was met with unimaginable pain. A howl issued from his throat as he fell again. Lying on his stomach, he contorted his body till he could see his left boot twisted awkwardly, and through the split leather, he saw what remained of his foot. He jerked back and with his face only inches from the ground, retched, till all that was left was strands of soily slime. Above his head, machine guns and snipers raked the air. A shell, landing with an explosive blast, sent up a fresh shower of soil and shrapnel, giving rise to a fresh chorus of howls and grunts of slain and stricken men.

Keep going. But he could not. Neither could he lie here in a no man's land between village and tree-lined ridge, with so many boots pounding onwards and so much artillery focused on this stretch.

Dragging himself, head lowered, elbows jabbing into dirt, he inched forwards till he reached a hollow: not a natural feature of the landscape but earth gouged open. Into this he slithered. With his head below gunfire line, he huddled next to another soldier.

'Can't feel m' hand.' The man spoke through his teeth, shaking uncontrollably, clutching his right arm from where a hand dangled limply. Walter's gaze travelled up the torn and bloodied sleeve to where the shattered arm bone attached by slender sinews to the shoulder. There was a gap where ribs had once protected organs. Nestled within, possibly along with a piece of shrapnel, shiny soft tissue moved, a lung, determined to keep on. *Lord have mercy.* On seeing this, his own injury became that much less. He wondered if he would die alongside this man.

'What's your name?' Walter managed.

'Sergeant Wilks, sir.'

'First name. I'm Walter.'

'Harry.' No more than a whisper. 'Fingers, see, won't move.' His eyes appealed.

Walter wiggled closer. 'I see, yes. Where's your medical kit, Harry?' It must have been blasted away. Walter undid the straps of his own pack, fumbling for a small metal tin with two morphine syrettes. He hesitated before jabbing one into Harry's good shoulder – the only shoulder. He used his remaining syrette on himself. Oh, the relief. Such relief.

Bubbling blood leaked from Harry's mouth, guttural sobs and laboured breaths.

'I'm a saddler... need m' hands... see.'

'I see,' Walter repeated. He drew the man's juddering head onto his chest, trying to hold it still. The only thing he could think to do was to sing.

'*Amazing grace, how sweet the sound that saved a wretch like me...*'

It became a lullaby – a soothing song as he cradled this man's head close to him, swaying... swaying. He sang it once, then again.

'*...Through many dangers, toils and snares...*'

Nearby a tree, struck by an explosive, burst into flame. Walter continued, his voice raw, as scorched as the destroyed tree.

'*...This grace that brought me safe thus far...*'

By the fifth rendition, the head he held clamped in his hands had stopped shaking. Through Harry's shattered shoulder girdle, a lung became still, and he felt a soft expulsion of air from Harry's throat. He didn't stop singing until he reached the last lines: '*I once was lost but now I'm found, was blind but now I see.*'

Except he didn't believe a word of it. There was no creator, only a destroyer, and he was lost.

He closed Harry's soulless eyes then began stroking hair, matted with soil. 'There there,' he wanted to say, 'you'll be right as rain.' Sobs rose through his throat for them both. Sobs turned to howls. 'Why?' He raised his head. There could be no answer. Heaven didn't exist but hell did.

A high explosive sent an eruption of soil and searing metal that made men howl again. A body landed just beyond his hiding hole, one leg sticking over.

'Got you!' Walter assured the man, tugging on a foot, dragging him to safety. But he found himself clutching a leg, thigh bone glinting white within its torn and bloodied fabric. With a cry he threw it aside.

Another shell smothered him in sods and Walter scrabbled to keep his head above the mire, his helmet providing some armour. He couldn't tell if shrapnel had hit him and was disinclined to scoop away the dirt, of what might be his grave, to find out.

Throughout the morning, blooms of grey smoke and dark soil stained the blue sky. Acrid smells of spent shells hung in the air. Whines, whistles, and rumbling thuds filled his ears.

Eyes closed tight, he sought those scores and songs he loved, methodically going through them, clusters of notes dancing on staves. Where Housman's poems of the Shropshire countryside had been set to song – George Butterworth, Ralph Vaughan William – he croaked: '*Is my team ploughing, that I used to drive…*' When his voice gave out, he went deeper into himself.

Great shells exploded – a deep thunder, resonating timpani. A whizz and bang of small shells like brass. Staccato spurts of sniper fire. The distortions ugly, without melody, without purpose or structure. Stravinsky did better.

He forced himself to remember the score of *The Rite of Spring*, imagining his fingers spread over piano keys, alert to the difficult parts he was apt to stumble over. He would not cheat and skip over these bars but doggedly repeated them, angry he was not concentrating, until he knew he had remembered correctly. Half buried, he saw the arbitrary sacrifice in *Rite* and in the killing ground around him. Ancient rituals. The randomness of who lived and who died. Dissonance. Dissonance.

Deep under the earth that covered most of his body, his leg was on fire, the effect of the morphine now gone.

Through the afternoon, he became aware the bombardment had slackened, and there were fewer men passing. They must, he rationalised, have secured the ridge. With quieter skies, birds began to take to the air. In past months, it had comforted him watching them soar, feeling them a link to heaven. Now he felt nothing.

Come nightfall, with pain gripping him in a vice, he couldn't find anything to keep his mind occupied. His world had narrowed to his own groans and those of fallen men lying somewhere beyond. He cried in self-pity, longing for the pain to go. For water. For oblivion.

Deep into the night, he was shivering uncontrollably, wondering if he'd live to see dawn. Hours passed as he tried, but failed, to seek solace in the stars and moon. They looked almost ludicrous, like sequins on discarded cloth.

Then came a new sound. Men's voices. English.

He opened his mouth to yell and found he had no voice. His body was entombed in dirt that seemed to have set into concrete around his ribs, or perhaps he was too weak to move. A torch beam caught his waving hand, and he heard, 'Over here!' and the clump of boots.

He felt his body convulse on being released from his grave, felt himself being lifted and lain on a stretcher, hurried away. They were asking questions, but he couldn't speak, only move his mouth, fish-like.

'Not to worry, sir, we'll soon have you sorted. We'll get you to a dressing station in a jiff,' one of his carriers grunted as he trotted on.

How futile. He could never be sorted.

At dawn, he was loaded into a field ambulance with others who had survived this slaughter, all heavily dosed with morphine. Wheels bumped along rutted tracks and above the whine of the engine, he imagined he heard a bird. He turned his head, and there, contained in a small cage, was a tiny yellow bird greeting the new day. They were right, these doctors. Hearing a canary sing could lift a man's spirits, even if he were dying. As the little bird trilled, Walter closed his eyes, drifting into darkness.

37

Rose hadn't heard from Walter since Easter and tried to hide how wretched she felt. Nina was keeping in touch – her latest letter from Paris.

'*Diaghilev adores him. Have you heard of Cubism?*' she read aloud to Molly.

'I know everything there is to know about queues, but what's queuebism when it's at home?' Molly said.

'Spelt with a "C", like an OXO cube. And I've no idea.' She turned to a second page where Nina had sketched Picasso's so-called costumes. 'Probably this.' She handed it to Molly to peer at through her magnifying glass. 'She says they're cardboard, to look like skyscrapers. And the music's got foghorns and typewriter sounds.'

'World's gone barking mad,' Molly said. 'How long's she there for?'

She skimmed the letter. 'Doesn't say, but there's mention of Spain.'

A letter from Sid had arrived – grumbling about a sleety spring – so she knew mail was getting through from the Front. She'd given him short shrift, replying that she and Molly had worn gloves and coats inside, cursing those dratted U-boats sinking coal ships. In any case, Sid was better fed than she was. The queues these days! And poor Molly wasn't up to standing for hours to buy a bit of margarine or a loaf of bread. But what could she do? Rose hadn't time to line up at shop after shop with her ration book; she was overseeing all those girls at Edith's sewing factory. She didn't dare complain about her lot, not with those poor souls blown to smithereens at the Silvertown Munitions factory. Hundreds killed and maimed. Better working in central London on parachutes and uniforms than down at the docks with TNT and ammo.

She was becoming a fretter, needing to know where people were and that everyone was looked after and safe. By and large, Molly was all right: her life contracted to house, neighbours, and local shops. Sid she wasn't worried about. He seemed to be having a right old time, with just enough danger to give an edge to his stories, but away from the Front. In each letter, she read of some derring-do, never knowing whether it was real or not.

Walter though? She had written wishing him a happy birthday – still a week away – enclosing another pair of woollen socks, a bit wonky, but never mind; he would appreciate Molly's effort.

That Friday, early evening, Rose listened as her sewing girls chatted about plans for the weekend – a dance with a sweetheart, the latest Charlie Chaplin – all the while dawdling, eking out their piece of work, not wanting to start on a new garment.

'Go on then.' She jerked her chin. 'Start packing up.' Edith wouldn't mind, she had too much on her plate to care.

'Thanks, Mrs Wood.'

Just then, a blast of a maroon siren sounded, and hands that'd been scooping aside cloth, cleaning woollen fuzz caught under bobbins, or placing wooden lids over sewing machines now hurried to fetch belongings. 'Oh Lord, what can this be?' All of them more curious than afraid.

Out on the pavement, as the last girls hurried away, Rose peered up at thick low cloud, not knowing what lurked up there. The sensible thing would be to stay in, but she felt safer outside. In the event, nothing happened.

Next morning, while queueing at Whitechapel Market, first at one shop then another, she had plenty of time to learn about the previous evening's goings on. The blanket of cloud over London meant bombers had turned back to hit coastal towns.

'Huge planes, Rose. A whole lot of them, not just one or two! We ain't got anything to touch 'em!'

'What can we do?' she asked their butcher as he wrapped her purchase, and he could only shrug. She imagined lying awake in the coming nights, fretting, wondering where the safest place in the house would be. 'What can we do?' she repeated.

Arriving home, Molly called out, 'Any sausages?'

'Yes,' she called back. 'Oh, thank goodness.' Spotting a letter on the doormat, she couldn't put her shopping bags down quickly enough. But the writing was not Walter's. She ripped open the envelope and slid out a letter quickly skimming. Thank God it was not from the War Office, no *"it is my painful duty to inform you"*.

'Oh!' She leant against the wall, sliding down to sit.

Molly hovered over her. 'Is it bad? Rose?'

'He's lost part of a leg...'

'Lost?'

'Cut off. Amputated.'

'Ah, Rose. That's terrible. Read what he says.'

'That's the thing, Molly, he doesn't say. It's a nurse in one of those hospitals.'

'Oh, blessed boy. Is he here?'

'No. Still over there. And he's not talking. Or can't talk.' She looked up at Molly from where she sat, knees bent, back propped against the hallway wall, planted to the spot. Somehow, she was to blame – had to be. She was his mother.

'Up you get. I'll put on the kettle.'

Across the old brown teapot and chipped cups, she shared the news.

'*Dear Madam,*

'*I am nursing 2nd Lieutenant Roberts. Walter. Please let me assure you that, though injured, he will live.*'

'There's a blessing, Rose.'

'*Someone from his regiment delivered a bundle of letters to us he had kept, so we discovered your recent letters and understand you are his mother. Please excuse me for having read them, but it was the only way.*

'*Due to shrapnel injury to his left foot and ankle, a doctor had to amputate mid-calf. This is healing nicely, but we are more worried about his state of mind as in the weeks he has been in hospital, he has not spoken and his hands are too jittery to write, though he's shown no interest in doing so.*'

'I don't like the sound of this.'

'What else does she say, Rose?'

'Not much. *I understand 2nd Lieutenant Roberts will be transferred to a military hospital in England and you will be notified. Kindest regards, Nurse Sibyl Gibson, No 22 General Hospital, Camiers.*'

So, when all was said and done, Walter was a cripple, had jitters and wasn't talking. Worries and questions crowded in.

'Will he be able to walk upstairs – to bed?'

'Will he want to live here, do you think?' Molly looked dubious.

'Where else? He must, for a time, till he, until he... gets better.' A new thought occurred to her. 'Why hadn't his regiment written? Surely, they have a duty to let next of kin know when something like this happens.'

'I don't know. Perhaps when he's settled in a hospital here, they'll contact you.'

The fighting near Ypres had been vicious with many thousands slaughtered, and there was no end to it. The transports were busy – fresh men to France, the worst of the injured back. Somewhere in this mass of comings and goings was her son, and she wanted him home.

There followed a flurry of telegrams: Nina set to abandon the tour and head home, Rose persuading her otherwise. No point in Nina getting under her feet with nothing to occupy her.

Molly steadied her nerves by stockpiling meagre rations, out every day with a neighbour who had a good nose for supplies. Rose was happy to see Molly kept busy now she no longer needed to knit warm things for Walter.

She trekked down to Kingston to make enquiries at the East Surrey barracks, but no one could say when to expect him, or even if he was here. 'The paperwork. So much to keep up with,' an administrator told her. 'We always notify family, but I'm happy to take your details again.'

Where was he? Where was her boy?

38

NINA SHIELDED HER EYES AGAINST THE GLARING SUN
where spectators crammed into the steeply raked bullring.
Below and to her right, in better, shaded seats, were three
straw-boatered heads – Diaghilev, Massine and Grigoriev –
here to absorb something of the essence of this spectacle that
might be put to purpose in a new ballet. Somehow the Ballets
Russes was surviving the war. Soon they'd be leaving Spain,
risking torpedoes on a crossing to Brazil.

Hearing about Walter had battered her. Ma had telegrammed,
but still no news where he was, and she couldn't stop thinking
of him. She imagined what might have happened, each time
thinking up yet another torment her brother had endured. She'd
written a harsh letter to Ma saying *you shouldn't have let him go!*
But that was unfair. No woman could stop a man from signing
up, and she was coming to dread telegrams. Yesterday's:

*ENLISTED. SAID I WOULD. WILL KEEP YOU
POSTED. CHARLIE.*

She'd been tempted to fire off a hasty message – IDIOT! I
FORBID YOU – only to reconsider. For a full ten minutes
she'd waivered, only to cable back:

PLEASE TAKE CARE. ALL MY LOVE. NINA

He'd soon be heading to bloodied fields somewhere near where Walter had been – or still was. Maybe Walter was not recovering; maybe he'd got worse, wound infected. Had died! Ma had no idea where he was and didn't seem to want her back, which hurt. *Best stay away,* Ma wrote to her, *nothing for you here right now. Spain's safer.*

While *she* wasn't in danger, the odds were stacked against the bull. It stood, legs planted, uncertain as to what to do. Its chest heaved, a thick slick of blood forming a shiny saddle across its withers where sharp sticks stuck into flesh. She had thought she'd love the spectacle: matador's crimson and gold costume as rich as anything she'd seen onstage, the skill with which he managed the red muleta – the cape an extension of his right arm – in long sweeping passes. But…

A horseman cantered forwards, jabbing the beast with a pike of some sort. 'That'll egg it on,' Kola's voice. With a ripple of the matador's cape, the bull charged. She sucked her breath, horns barely missing the man's taut frame. A collective "olé" that could raise a roof if there'd been one.

The matador turned his back on the bull in a stiff-legged, arched-back strut, then swivelled, legs apart in a "dare you" stance, while fluttering that huge cape. At the bull's charge, came a roared, 'Olé,' and a babble she didn't understand, sun-scorched faces bursting into masks of pleasure, hands waving handkerchiefs. The bull twisted, quick for such a bulky beast. Another charge. Another elegant turn of the man's body, cape in a gliding pass, horns inches from a thigh. Could he smell the heat of the beast? Beneath the tightly fitted brocade jacket, his heart must be hammering, fearful that something might go wrong. All it would take was a twist of that massive head.

A twist of fate might have a horn rammed in his groin, tossing him up, no more than an annoyance. *Let me get back to my quiet field*, the bull might think.

She lowered her head, hands covering her face.

'Nina?' A hand stroked her back and she looked up into Hilda's concerned face.

'I'm hot. That's all.' But it was everything.

'Rehearsals have been exhausting. You should rest.' Hilda fanned her with her own fan.

'*You're* the one who should be resting.' Her eyes went from Hilda's rounded stomach to Kola sitting next to her. He pressed his lips together, refusing to understand. As well as dealing with the heat and her growing pregnancy, Hilda couldn't so much look at another man without his lashing out. She would never get herself into such a fix. In turn, she rubbed Hilda's back.

'That's nice.' Hilda leant into her hand.

A glint of steel as the matador raised an arm, the purposeful thrust of a sword into a powerful neck. The beast toppled, not dying immediately, then lay prone. Life here. Life ended. Minutes later, she watched its hind legs roped and its carcass dragged by two harnessed horses, a sweep of blood across the sandy floor.

'I'm not so sure I'm enjoying this,' she said.

She was tired of theatres of war and theatres in general. Tired of bloody spectacles.

But the Spaniards adored spectacles – not just in bullrings – so night after night at the Teatro Real it was the dramatic ballets – *Cleopatra, Scheherazade* – that drew bursts of appreciative *olés*. She heard them above the music as she and fellow ladies of the harem flung themselves into the arms of leaping slaves. Or cheers for Hilda's bacchanale in *Narcisse* – a part she was learning for when Hilda could no longer dance.

And travelling. She was tired of that too but had to keep going, less a choice than necessity, driving her on with the circus she'd joined. Dancing took her mind off things. When she was onstage fully costumed and made-up, her stomach no longer felt hollow. She didn't ache for people no longer in the world, or somewhere else in the world she couldn't reach.

This is what she had always wanted. Wasn't it?

39

It took Rose a second or two to recall that Mr *Angus Fairfield Esq.* was Mr Quince's partner in their legal firm, the one she'd never met.

Dear Madam

East Surrey Regiment have indicated your interest in knowing 2nd Lt Walter Roberts's whereabouts. It is my pleasure to tell you he is being cared for at Queen Mary's Hospital, Roehampton…

'He's alive! Oh, he's alive!' She crushed Molly to her.

Molly pushed her away. 'He's written?'

'No, the lawyer—'

'Mr Quince?'

'The other one. Hush! He's at Queen Mary's. Says, *As per 2nd Lt Roberts's instructions, the East Surrey Regiment requested my services in contacting his next of kin, Mrs Beatrice Wallace, née Roberts, should events require. My clerk dealt with the matter, doing extensive investigative work to discover her whereabouts…*'

All the joy at knowing Walter was just miles away was sucked out knowing he must have deliberately – *deliberately* – chosen to notify a woman who was never his kin, who had never loved him, while her heart overflowed with love. She continued, voice wobbly:

'*Following a second correspondence with the East Surrey's, I am reminded of your relationship and regret we did not contact you earlier.*

Please accept my apologies and sincere wishes you find your son in good spirits.'

She could hardly breathe. 'I'm his mother, Molly,' she sobbed. 'I thought he'd grown to love me. Why would he do such a dreadful thing?'

'Don't take it to heart,' Molly said, 'he must've had his reasons. But it's hard to imagine what they are. Ask him when you see him.'

'Yes, all right. I will.' But she was knocked back. 'Perhaps on Saturday. But I'll feel a bit strange knowing this. Will he want to see me?'

'Of course he will,' Molly said. 'I'll bake something nice for you to take.'

Rose tried to put thoughts of Walter and Mrs Wallace/ Roberts out of her head as she left the house and headed to Knightsbridge, where a fresh order for several hundred army shirts waited to be filled. At Park Mansion's Arcade – suffragette premises turned clothing workshop – she knocked on the door to Edith's office to find the younger woman, pencil behind her ear, another in her hand, going through columns of inventory.

On hearing her news, Edith's face drained of colour, and she was around her desk in a flash squeezing her hands.

'You must go and see him, Rose. Take time away from work.'

'No, I'll wait. I'm stung, Edith.' Her eyes welled up.

'If there's anything I can do? In fact, may I come with you?' Edith, Rose noted, was blushing, and it made Rose wonder.

'I'd best go first to get the lay of the land. Then we can go together.'

Edith hugged her, then they both set about their work.

It was mid-morning. A sudden siren caused feet to pause on treadles, heads to jerk up from feeding fabric under rapid needles. There had been no raids for months, and never at daytime.

Edith shot out of her office. 'Quiet! Quiet!' She raised her hands. 'Quick, as smart as you can.'

Bodies in motion, colliding as bags and hats were gathered, and dozens of frightened women headed out and towards Knightsbridge Underground.

Running was pointless, even that short distance. Her chest heaved with the effort, and amongst all the thoughts rampaging through her mind was that she would throw away her corsets. She could hardly breathe. People sped past, giving the Germans a piece of their mind: 'Brazen. Absolutely brazen!' And as to their own air defences, 'Where are our bloody planes, eh? Someone stop 'em!' From the eastern edges of London sounded a faint *rat-a-tats* of anti-aircraft guns.

And above the sounds of her own gasping breath and so many yammering Londoners all in a tizzy came a steady drone, a drumming sound. Clutching her arm, Edith pointed up. Twelve biplanes in a "V" formation swooped past, German crosses on the underside of wings. These, then, were Gothas. The beasts that had rained down death on Dover and Folkestone a week earlier. That German Kaiser, that villain, was even more evil than von Rothbart, the magician in *Swan Lake*, and that was saying something!

Like migrating geese, these machines acted as one as they banked, changing direction, then, without waiting to land in some field, they began to shit on her city. She watched small black turds detach themselves from undercarriages, becoming bigger, each one heralded with a whistle followed by a blast. 'Jesus Christ,' a man's voice caught in his throat. 'What kind of explosive is that?' Pulverised brick and concrete shot skywards. Her own cries of dismay added to screams of those nearby, everyone with hands to their mouths. Shock does that, Rose found. Makes you act like a mime: wide-eyed and slack-jawed.

'Hurry, Rose.' Edith tugged her.

'You go on,' Rose managed to say, 'you see to the girls.' If her number was up, so be it. She wanted to stare her bomb in the eye and curse the lot of them.

'Around St Paul's,' someone panted, 'and the East End is my guess, but why? No munitions there. Just people.'

'Molly!' The name shot from her mouth. Under this was her house. Was Molly home or with neighbours? Or shopping? Rose tried to remember if she'd said. Molly liked to go out, knowing the streets like the back of her hand, barely needing her cane for guidance.

It didn't take long to drop dozens of bombs.

She did not see those fat geese fly away, the sunny clear day now blanketed in a grey fog of burning and dust. To think that aeroplanes had only been invented a few years ago, now these foreign Gotha dragons were slaying them. Thank goodness the King'd had the good sense to change the family name from Saxe-Coburg-Gotha to Windsor.

There'd be no buses going where she needed. She set off walking towards Piccadilly, fear making her heart heavy, feet leaden.

At Leicester Square she sat on a garden bench, easing her feet, feeling her toes chaffed by cracked leather of old shoes. She looked at the statue of Shakespeare, leaning on a scroll that read, THERE IS NO DARKNESS BUT IGNORANCE. Too right! She glanced at the Alhambra, tempted to pop in, undress, and loosen her undergarment. No. Best get on.

Hoisting herself up, she continued walking. When challenged, she argued with one policeman after another, one fire warden after another, insisting, 'It's Molly, you see. I've got to get home to Molly.' She'd seen it all before. Only this time was ten times worse. So much dust. She took out a hanky, pressing it against her nose.

Through the clanging and clatter of ambulances and police vehicles and people shocked into hysterics, she trudged on. *Bloody corset. Bloody shoes.*

There was a bus, windows shattered, passengers – bodies – grotesquely draped over windows like so many *Petrushkas*: that final tableau, puppet dangling over the fairground stall roof. *Dear God!*

'You all right, son?' She sat on a curb, an arm around a distraught boy, no more than five. A quick check showed he was largely unscathed.

'Ma... Ma...' He could barely get the words out. She followed his gaze, only then clocking the body lying nearby: a middle-aged woman, dress cut to bloody ribbons. She turned his face away.

'Don't look, son... What's your name?'

'J-Johnny.' Barely a whisper.

'Where do you live? Shall I get you home?'

No answer. Shock. Cuddling was all she could think to do.

Together they watched his mother's body being lifted and carried to a waiting vehicle – not an ambulance, no need for that. When the boy went to follow, he was told, 'You stay here.'

'Sure I can't take you home, love?'

Soon a man ran to them. 'Johnny... Johnny...' An uncle, he said, and the lad went off docile as a lamb, hand clasped by the older man.

On that journey home, she encountered mangled bodies and horses laying twisted, still harnessed to vehicles. And everywhere rubble. It was difficult to find a path home. Her throat was parched.

She learnt a bomb had dropped on a primary school with dozens of children killed. 'Poor wee souls,' she gasped, 'poor sodding parents.' How could the Kaiser do this, with his cousin, their King, not far away in Buckingham Palace? And there was their other cousin, the Russian Czar, who'd been arrested along with his family. Royal families, what were they about? And men? All men. Perhaps Nina and Edith were right to insist women should vote. Maybe they'd stop this folly and set things to right.

The sun had set when she reached her street and, oh, the joy at seeing their house standing, every bloody brick of it, windows intact. She hurried in, shouting, 'Molly, you here?… Molly.' But the house was silent.

She longed for a cup of tea, had not drunk since breakfast, but the gas was out. And the electricity. She guzzled cup after cup of water – somehow the pipes were intact – then set out again.

Door after door she knocked. 'Have you seen Molly?'

No one had, but they all had their stories – what they'd been doing, who they knew who'd been hurt, whose shop had been destroyed. She asked at shops around the corner, and further afield, only to be shouted at by Mr Walmsley, a normally mild man: 'Do I look like I know where she is?' His window was shattered, his mannequins toppled over, floor and shelves thick with blasted glass and bricks. 'Go home, woman!'

So she did.

She couldn't bring herself to go to bed, but she took off her corset, threw on a dressing gown and sat in her easy chair. How odd. Looking at Molly's vacant chair, this was the first time in her *entire* life she'd been alone at night, and she didn't like it.

As a small child she'd shared a bed with Molly in a one-bedroom flat, then with Nina and Walter on the scene, they moved to a two-bedroom place. With baby Walter gone to live with Arthur, she'd slept with Nina who was a right old fidget. Here in Alie Street they had the luxury of three bedrooms. She shivered. Suddenly this house was much too big.

Through the night she could find no peace, likely creating a hole in the rug with her pacing, while outside, sirens wailed. London was awake.

She jolted from a doze. Dawn now and someone was knocking.

'Coming!' She hurried to find her neighbours on the doorstep, a young couple, recently moved in.

'All right, Mrs Wood? Just wanting to check.'

'I don't know where Molly is. I'm desperate, don't know what to do...' She spilled out her worries. But what could *they* do? Couldn't even offer a cup of tea: no gas at theirs either. Better to be doing something.

In a daze she dressed, and amidst the carnage of the High Street, she found a temporary canteen. The bliss of hot tea and buns.

'Have you seen Molly?' she asked everyone she knew.

It was afternoon, at a makeshift-morgue, she found her.

It had happened at the market, all of them caught unawares.

While Walter had lost a foot, it was Molly's thick-soled boot that identified her. A chair was found, and she remembered to thank the young man, then sat and held Molly's grubby hand, the dear face streaked with dried blood. Rose tried to tidy her bodice where it'd ripped. Molly wouldn't like to be seen like this.

She is maybe three years old, backstage at the Alhambra, standing barefoot on the Green Room table as Molly, head bent, pins in mouth, fixes a frilly orange ruffle to the hem of her dress. There are others in the room, sewing and repairing, and she is singing, keen for their attention. Molly hobbles off to fetch something and a devilish thought takes her. She begins cavorting on the tabletop, imitating Molly's uneven walk. One of the sewing girls giggles. Emboldened, she begins to sing, 'I'm a goblin, I'm a goblin.'

'What a mean girl you are, Rose.' Someone wags a finger, but she hears one girl giggling, so ups her game.

Now she sings louder and hunches, pulling a face. 'I'm a goblin, an ugly old goblin,' dragging her foot behind her.

'Take care, my girl, or Molly will chuck you out in the street.'

But she continues, thinking she's funny, loving the attention.

At a stinging slap on her bare leg, she spins to see Molly, face pink, lips free of pins.

'Nice girls don't poke fun at those less fortunate. Perhaps I should give you away.'

This, more than the unaccustomed slap, stops her in her tracks.

'I'll say. Best give her away!' one of the girls says. 'If I were you, Moll, I'd bung her into a box and toss her outside.'

'There's an idea,' Molly says. 'I just might.'

Her chin quivers. 'Oh, 'olly, don't do that.' And she's crying, terrified at being left alone. 'Don't give me away. Please, please don't give me away.' The horror of it makes her shake and sob.

Molly touches the dimple in her chin. 'You're a pretty little girl, Rose, and don't I always dress you nicely?'

She nods, looking down at her dress, floral colours merging through blurred eyes.

Molly speaks softly: 'But little girls have got to be pretty inside too.'

She loves Molly more than anything in the world and

knows she's hurt her. She throws herself at Molly, wrapping her arms tight around her neck, nearly toppling her over.

'Don't put me in a box, 'olly. Please keep me.'

'There, there,' Molly soothes. 'As if. As if I'd ever give my Rose away.'

Aged forty-one, she was not ready to let go of this woman who had guarded and guided her from day one, determined to take care of the baby girl left on a freezing pavement.

Her dimpled chin quivered, and warm tears washed down her plump cheeks. 'There, there.' She patted Molly's hand. 'There, there,' she comforted herself.

INTERLUDE

1917

40

He'd thought he had a rendezvous with death but finds himself living.

He tries to wriggle his toes.

He revisits favourite rambles in the countryside, knowing this will never be the same.

People sit by his bedside. He recalls Rose and Mr Reed. Other names are a struggle.

'You remember Edith, don't you, son?'

He stares at the earnest young woman whose face is familiar, tries to smile but not sure he has stretched his lips.

'Back on leave, old chap.' A ruddy-faced military man, about his age, settles cross- legged next to his bed and chats about life in the desert. It takes an age, the name refusing to come. Then out it burbles: 'K... K... *Kit!*'

'That's it, old chap.' His visitor beams.

He tries to piece together his recent past.

These things he knows:

His iron bed is fourth along one wall. There are twenty in this ward. It is not unlike boarding school but the fellows – each in regulation pyjamas – are older and chopped about.

He's at a military hospital that specialises in amputees,

he surmises, looking at limbless specimens hobbling along on crutches or being wheeled past.

He has one good leg ending with a foot. The other stops short.

He finds this imperfection ugly and doesn't like looking at it.

He's encouraged to sit up and chat with the other fellows. He refuses, stubbornly closing his eyes and his mouth. He's irritated by their cheeriness, wanting to shout: 'Cripple. Cripple!' but it's better not to speak.

He's told he must be fitted with a prosthetic foot. He resists, but realises he must, so submits to doctors and nurses measuring and insisting. He's forced to confront that amputated limb, the scar still raw and ugly. 'It'll heal in time,' he's told.

He finds the wood and leather attachment cumbersome. The carved foot does not look real. There is a clever mechanism at the ankle to allow movement and where the stump of his shin slides in, it is hollow. There are straps to attach. He feels like a horse being harnessed and finds he has made a whinnying sound. It hurts when he puts weight on it, feeling his face drawing in.

He hears nurses and doctors whispering. He registers that one of the doctors wearing a white coat is a woman. They're not concerned for his missing foot, but worried his mind is missing.

He shares their fear he won't find himself. *Where's Walter? Where are you hiding?*

He dreams he is floating on fluffy cumulus clouds in a blue sky – a recurring childhood dream – tethered only by the sounds of Mother playing on her grand piano. It is peaceful and he wishes he could stay up there, but always he wakes.

He watches a woman being escorted along the ward. He sees her upright carriage, notes her careful choice of tailored blue suit. She is somehow familiar. They stop at his bed.

'A visitor for you,' the nurse says.

Mother is at his bedside saying, 'How are you, Walter?' And he is back to being a sick child with scarlet fever. She reaches out an ungloved hand to briefly touch his forehead then sits with hands resting on her lap. She smiles and it is a compassionate smile. 'I'm so sorry to see you like this. I felt great sorrow on hearing.' She touches his pyjama sleeve. 'I'm so very proud you have done your duty.'

He holds her eye, mouth moving, trying to say something. Maybe he says, 'Y-yes.' He manages to nod. She understands. He thinks back to that day at Wandsworth recruiting office, filling out forms and addresses. It was a spur-of-the-moment decision. He had not thought it through, but in the event of his death, he wanted Mother to acknowledge him, be proud of him. Perhaps consent to a headstone next to Father's, though likely his body would become pulp mulching Flanders mud or, if recovered, laid to rest in foreign soil.

In the event, it is his broken body and broken mind that has been returned to England, and he wishes Mother could not see him now. Better a dead hero than a broken man. This had not figured in his mind when writing *Mother, Mrs Beatrice Wallace, formerly Roberts* in the next of kin section.

Mother comes again. Rose turns up at the same time. He lies in the bed, the meat in the sandwich, two very different women either side: one he had longed to claim him, the other he had been reluctant to claim for himself. He could try to say something, but being silent is easier. He listens to their light conversation. He doesn't hear much as they move away from his bed and pace up and down. When Mother leaves, she touches his cheek, saying, 'Goodbye, Walter.' He doesn't expect to see her again.

Rose visits. Always chatty. This time she takes out something soft and puts it in his trembling hands.

'Remember this, son?' She shakes out the fabric and he sees tangled tassels and purple silk rippling. 'My mother would have wrapped me in this. I loved playing with it when I was little. Remember, I wanted you and Nina to have half, so you could find me when the time came?' He does not respond, so she urges, 'Remember, Walter?'

And he is forced to unclench his teeth: "Ye… yes."

Rose seems satisfied. 'All these threads bind us, whether we like it or not.' She sits silently, then says, 'You hurt me, putting *her* name down. She didn't want you. I always wanted you. How could I know Arthur would die like that, or that *she* would turn her back? I was lucky; Molly loved me, God rest her dear soul. Children need love.'

A fresh wound stabs him, and he knows he must apologise. It's an effort to raise a trembling hand. She's quick to see the gesture and clasps it. He wills his mouth to form words, sweating with the effort to speak. He thinks he says something, but Rose is frowning, leaning forwards, 'What is it, son?'

'Sorry.' He believes he has spoken. He sees Rose's lips quiver.

'Oh, Walter. Life is such a messy thing, eh?' She brushes hair away from his sticky forehead then holds his hand and tells him what she's up to. Little things. Ordinary things.

He begins to look forward to visitors., begins to accept the changes he must endure, though it is hard. So very hard.

He struggles to balance on crutches, bones turning to jelly.

'That's it! One step,' two nurses encourage him, standing close, either side. Sweat pours down his face as he tries to control jerking limbs. He collapses on the floor with a cry of despair. 'Up you get; we'll leave it for today.' Arms reach under his armpits, and he gratefully retreats to bed.

'You need fresh air,' he's told. He allows himself to be wheeled outside – but only when it's dark and no one can see him. A nurse tuts.

One evening, Rose takes control of his wheelchair, and they set off around the hospital grounds. Searchlights sweep the sky. He can't take his eyes off them, his head tipped back. She manoeuvres around a corner, wheels jamming in gravel. She persists and they set off again. He cranes his neck, face skywards, eyes on those beams of light.

She notices. 'I'm sorry, Walter; I didn't think. Perhaps we should go in.'

He shakes his head. 'No.'

'I would have thought,' she hesitates, 'they might remind you...'

'F... Footlights,' he says.

'Yes. Rather!' Rose laughs. 'Better than... But never mind that. What will this new world be like, eh?'

ACT 5

1918–1921

Blast furnaces lit up the sky – the Mariinsky and Theatre Street left behind for ever, these were the footlights of a new world.

THEATRE STREET, TAMARA KARSAVINA

41

As much as Nina tried, sitting with legs curled under her, she could not fill the emptiness. The threadbare chair with garish cushions shrieked for Mo's ample bottom. She missed Mo terribly. What was the point of blackout with these German bombers raiding, bold as sodding brass, during daytime?

And there was Walter's missing foot – she'd been prepared for that – but it was everything else that was a shock. Walter's body was given to sudden jolts, arms and legs shooting out like a puppet. He, always slender, was sallow, skin stretched over cheekbones, pock-marked scars mingling with freckles. Above dark, bruised shadows, his blue eyes were troubled pools.

'Oh, Walter,' she had cried, on seeing his haunted face, 'I'm so sorry.'

And he had turned away, rejecting her embrace, as if disgusted with the wreck he had become. 'A… a… cripple,' he had stammered, and Ma had taken her aside whispering, 'At least he's talking.'

Walter had come to grief, she learnt, fighting to take one of many small German-held ridges leading, months later, to the push to take Passchendaele. The senselessness of the losses appalled her. Now she was tortured with yet another man in uniform. As far as she could make out, Charlie was within spitting distance of where Walter had been.

Bon joor my best girl. See I'm learning new words, Charlie wrote. *These French folk sure were pleased to see us, such a fuss when we swung past towns. Trying to knock out those Goddam Jerries – toot sweet – but not so easy. I've lost a few buddies, sad to say. Can't say much about what we're doing but not surprised Walter's nerves are bad. Give him my best, he's a good man. You might like to know a bunch of us got up a band, so you see it's not all bad. Look after yourself. Write back soon.*

Her cupboard of cheery stories was bare.

When Walter was released from hospital, she helped him move into Alie Street. There were difficult stairs to navigate, then pausing at the door to Mo's bedroom – his now – he sucked his breath, which set Nina sobbing.

'Poor dear. She was just out to buy a bag of spuds.'

Walter placed his cane against the table and spread his arms. 'S-sorry.' *An offered hug. Finally.* With her arms wrapped around him, she felt his insubstantial frame.

'And I'm sorry, Twinny, for you and… and…' Then the tears started.

They settled on Mo's bed – Walter's bed – and he waited for her sobs to subside.

She stroked the patchwork bed covering – so many scraps Ma or Mo had brought home and stitched into a quilt.

'Oh, Walter, it was horrible not being at Mo's funeral – couldn't even say goodbye. And ghastly imagining the grim things you've been through.' She held his eyes. 'You must say. You must tell me if it helps… Walter?' But he turned away, so better not to press him. 'It feels like the worlds gone to ruin, and no matter how far I travel, I can't switch off from, well…'

'Everything,' Walter said.

'Yes. Everything.' She placed a hand on his and they sat side by side in silence for some minutes.

'T-tell me, about you?' Walter asked.

'Pitiful dancing contracts in pitiful halls.' She groaned. 'But for a few precious hours each week, I have class with Maestro Cecchetti.'

'Here?'

'He's set up in Shaftesbury Avenue. I'm loving seeing the old gang – oh, Hilda passes on her best wishes – but all of us look sorry sights: faded practice clothes, ballet shoes held together by willpower.' Was Walter interested? Hard to tell. 'Just yesterday, Maestro surprised us, saying, "My dears, Monsieur Diaghilev, he ez working so hard and soon, beata Maria, we may 'ave news."'

Was that a glimmer of a smile from Walter as she imitated her teacher's accent?

She was sleeping in the small bedroom that had always been hers. Ma had long ago brought a large bed into her own room, and on those occasions when Sid was on leave, Nina closed her ears to the sounds of bouncing springs.

One night, she woke to hear howling and, rushing to Walter's room, found him curled on the floor next to his bed, sweating, shaking, sobbing.

'What should we do?' She panicked, turning to Ma.

'You're safe, Walter.' Ma was by his side, arms around him. 'Don't just stand there, girl!'

Nina squatted, adding two more arms to the job of holding the broken man together.

'It helps to cuddle him,' Ma said, and Nina realised this wasn't the first time.

'G… g… go away!' her brother begged, hating to be seen like this.

On these occasions, they held him, insisting he was safe, helping him back to bed, then Ma would put the kettle on. Tea, a panacea for all ills.

Once, seeing Walter slumped in Mo's chair, she sat on an armrest, a hand on his shoulder, asking, 'Will it help to talk? About what happened, I'd like—'

'No, no.' He turned away, and she resisted pushing him.

Each time she tried coaxing him, she met with rebuffs.

'Why? It doesn't change the past.'

Thinking a different tack might work, she asked if he fancied going to a concert. 'No.' And when she encouraged him to join her and her friends at a club, he didn't bother to reply, merely stared aghast. It irked her that she couldn't drag him out of the doldrums.

Once she blurted out to Ma, 'He's got to learn to stand on two feet sooner or later.'

'Nina, what a thing to say!'

'I didn't mean... Oh, gosh.' Then she was laughing because if she didn't, she might cry.

Sometimes after one of Walter's turns, Ma would climb into bed and cradle her twin as if he were a baby. That was odd, but when she said as much to Ma, the answer was, 'He needs me, Nina, and you know I need *this*. Finally doing something for him.'

Edith was a regular visitor, first to see her, then, so it appeared, increasingly to spend time with Walter.

One evening, Nina saw Edith to the door. 'Thanks so much; it's so kind of you. Ma and I appreciate your help. Walter can be hard work.'

At that, Edith looked surprised. 'I don't think of it like that, I assure you! I'm fond of Walter so it's a pleasure to help him find himself. I wrote to him regularly when he was—'

'Did you?' That surprised her. Neither had said.

'He's been sharing favourite poetry with me – not my forte. I'm discovering much about him.'

How much, Nina wasn't sure. 'Does he talk about… you know…'

'About what?'

'Oh,' Nina wasn't just thinking of Alexei, 'the war, I mean. He's so closed about it. It must've been horrid.'

Edith shook her head. 'When he's ready to, I hope. It seems those who returned don't wish to – not just Walter.'

Nina was comforted. He had two willing listeners, should he wish.

Another evening, she, at the back of the house in the kitchen with Ma, heard Walter's uneven gait manoeuvring downstairs. He'd be venturing out for an under-cover-of-dark walk.

At the sound of the front door opening and closing, Ma's eyes followed Walter's path, and she said, 'I met her, you know.'

'So who're we talking about?'

'Beatrice Roberts, as was.' Ma's voice rose, surprised this was not obvious.

'Walter's moth… When?' Nina's eyes became saucers.

'Would've been October.'

'That long!' Ma had kept this from her. 'Why on earth didn't you say?'

'I had a lot on my mind, and you weren't here, then, well…'

'Where, Ma? Does Walter know?'

'I hadn't planned it. She was there when—'

'Where?'

'—when I visited him, hospital, so yes, he knows. Now, are you going to let me talk?'

Nina leant against the draining board, crossing her arms. 'Go on then.'

'Once I knew where Walter was, I'd planned to see him, but there was so much to think about with Molly dead, and those ghastly bombs wouldn't stop, week after week. It was terrible, Nina, and I was alone here. Enough to send me mad. Anyway, I wasn't sure he wanted to see me.'

"Course he did!'

'When I did visit the hospital, poor lad, he was in a bad way, then—'

'You've said, I know. But what about *her*?'

'—and then the whole ward was quarantined.'

Nina nodded. Walter had been on the edge of death all over again. There was a nasty flu going around and had people wondering if the troops had brought it home.

'One day I got there to find a woman sitting by his bed.'

'Her?'

'So I parked myself the other side and we had a little chat by Walter. Good as dead, he was, for all the conversation we got from him. A bit awkward to start with.'

Nina was goggle-eyed. 'What was she like?'

'I expect we both thought the other was much as we imagined. She's a respectable sort – pays for good tailoring. Said she was sorry to see Walter in this way. And she was, I could see that.' Ma sighed. 'We walked up and down the ward, away from Walter, but you know, I didn't want to talk about him, apart from saying I'd be looking after him and she needn't worry. Not sure she would. What I really wanted to talk about was Arthur.'

'That was ages ago.'

'To you. I remember everything as if it were yesterday. Your father was special. I wanted her to know I wasn't a floozy, but as chance would have it, I'd dyed my hair a few days earlier – cheap orange stuff on the black market – so she probably thought I was.'

'Oh, Ma!' Nina burst into laughter. 'She probably did.'

Nina pictured them, one woman austere, hair neatly pinned,

the other a thatch of orange frizz and a loose-fitting dress. Ma was dressing differently now, more bohemian, no more heavy corsets.

'You know,' Ma said, 'I felt sorry for her, strange as that may seem. Arthur and I always enjoyed a laugh. Suppose that's why I get on with Sid. And I don't see her as a jolly sort. Could be wrong, but… And another thing, I felt sorry she missed out on being a real mother, so I made sure she knew Walter got plenty of mothering from me. I wanted to rub that in her face.'

A lick of jealousy touched Nina's heart, only to dissolve. 'I'm sure you made a good impression.'

'I hope so. I'd like to think so. I wish Walter would put thoughts of her aside.'

'You know he's sorry. He didn't do it to hurt you.'

'And I wish I could get him to laugh. Tried taking him to *Chu Chin Chow*. Seen it three times, but he's not having it.'

'Good luck – getting him to laugh, I mean.'

Her brother, this new Walter the war had spat out, was an enigma she was struggling to know. When she'd asked when he intended to take up his music studies again, he shook his head. When she asked when he'd start playing piano again, his barking "Ha!" was harsh.

She hated what this war was doing to them all. At the slightest provocation, embers of resentment might be fanned and she would flair up. On the one hand she felt mature – sophisticated even – yet suspecting what her twin had endured made her dancing ambitions seem childish.

'Childish? Never!' Ma looked like she'd been slapped when she said as much. 'Pretend worlds matter – now, and more so when all this is over. You mark my words.'

By June, newspapers were saying the war couldn't last long, yet fighting around Amiens sounded as vicious as ever. Charlie wrote when he could, saying little that might upset her. But one time he wrote: *It's been quite something being with so many guys from home, and I'm thinking that when this is over, I'll go back. Chicago, I think…* Nina's blood ran cold. She hadn't seen that coming, imagining she and Charlie would set up home, at least in London.

She was finding herself irritated that Walter's recovery was taking so long and hating herself for feeling that way. It was a full year since he'd been back. He was better, but morose, refusing to engage with music. Instead, he was teaching at a local secondary school, not well paid as he wasn't qualified, and it was exhausting, him travelling to and fro.

'Why do it?' she asked, seeing him drop into a seat after another day teaching boys who couldn't wait to leave school.

'I've got to work.' He blinked at her. 'It's something I can do. In any case, it's only for a few more weeks.' He rubbed a hand along his left shin, and she knew he was longing to take off that dratted false foot but would not until he was alone.

Then came a day she never thought would arrive. Not finding Ma home, she burst into Walter's bedroom without knocking.

'Walter! Such news!'

He was at his desk, marking exercise books, and you'd think she'd seen him naked, the speed at which he picked up his prosthetic leg and tried to stick it back on.

'Sorry, sorry, Walter. It really doesn't matter, you know. I don't care in the least.' She skipped up and down. 'It's happening!'

'The war? Ending?' His eyes yearned for such news.

'I wish. No, not yet. But, oh, Walter, I'm going to be dancing with Diaghilev again. Here in London.'

'Ah. I see.' Walter smiled. How good to see him smile! 'Congratulations. If I can't be happy about my life, I can at least share your happiness.' He stood one-legged, balancing against his desk, and she wrapped her arms around him in a tight hug, feeling how unsubstantial his body was beneath his cotton shirt. She longed to press her energy into him, wanting her twin to be nourished. To flourish.

42

COULD HE STILL PLAY? FOR WEEKS, WALTER TOYED with the idea. *Cowardy custard*, a voice taunted.

While visiting Miss Reed, along with Mr Reed, he left brother and sister chatting and went to the parlour. He eyed the piano, then cautiously approached it as if it were a land mine, wires taut, ready to explode at the merest touch. Cautiously he sat but found his hands shaking so much he could barely attempt a note. As he was about to put down the lid, it seemed that Alexei was right there, elbow leaning on the piano in that louche way of his. 'What of your promise, Nina's brother?' His hand fluttered to his chest where a circular dark patch of skin was hidden by his shirt. With a shuddering breath, he reached for a cigarette, never far away.

A hand pressed his shoulder. 'Well, Walter?' Mr Reed at his side. 'We can start slowly, you know. Go over those pieces you played as a boy. I'd enjoy that.'

Liking the idea, he nodded, knowing it would require enormous effort. He had no strength, body nor mind; the war, still spitting and spluttering, kept him in its grip.

He need not speak of atrocities, grateful that those more eloquent were doing so. Poetry that had inspired him in his school days now forced him to recall, and others to confront –

if they cared to read those journals and slim publications – the muck, shock and revulsion that was Flanders. He grieved for those poets who had not returned. 'Waste!' He would pound a pillow with clenched fist. Those who had made it through, thus far – Sassoon, Graves – and were able to confront and share, crafted word pictures, laying bare the futility of the whole hateful thing.

In July, he moved from Alie Street to lodgings in Pimlico near where he lived before.

'I'm not going to let you slip away,' Edith said, laughing, at his door unexpectedly. 'And I'm not convinced living alone is good for you. You busy? Let's take a stroll.'

So, they walked slowly: he one more amputee to give way to on the pavement, to avert one's eyes from, she a drably dressed woman he'd no need to doubt.

'You'd think, after everything, they'd jolly well give the rest of us our say.' She was stung that women must be thirty to vote. 'Honestly, we've kept the country going these past years. There's no turning back.'

He smiled. 'I put a note up at the local shop for a woman to clean for me, and you know, I wasn't exactly overwhelmed with enquiries.'

'Better things to do.' She laughed, gesturing to where a motor bus trundled past, a uniformed female conductor clinging to the upright pole, looking official in a knee-length skirt, leather bag over one shoulder. In that Roehampton military hospital, amongst the male medics, he'd encountered a female doctor, which had surprised him. This was a new world with women firmly entrenched.

'How's work?' he asked.

'Loving it. They've little money, of course. I'm furthering worker's rights and I'm doing it for a pittance.' She'd handed over her sewing work. The Labour Party now, an organising job. 'Heaps to do. We've a big campaign to drive up union membership, can't allow momentum to flag. This ghastly war must end soon.'

Nothing was slowing – certainly not Edith.

'I love being out there, turning up at lunchtime at factories, giving them my talk and leaflets.'

'I can just picture you.'

She went on to talk about Labour Party common ownership ideas she found interesting. He listened, allowing the brightness and certainties in her mind to reach into the shadows and doubts of his own.

Leaning on his cane, he eased the pressure on his damaged leg. 'I think I must turn back. Better still, a bus.'

'Here's me being selfish talking on and on, enjoying your company,' Edith said. 'Let's cross the road.'

'I can see myself home, you know.'

'I know you can.' She tapped her bag. 'I forgot the coffee I bought for you, so if you invite me in… I'm not offering to clean your place, so don't bother asking.'

'As if!' He was learning to laugh.

Weeks earlier, Rose came out of the kitchen looking flustered. 'Oh dear, I'm either daft or going dilly. Put a lump of coal in the oven and almost chucked the rice pudding in the fire!' On hearing his loud snort of laughter, Rose began to weep. 'Oh, son, that's a sound for a sore heart.'

He listened as Edith clattered about his kitchen, calling, 'Where do you keep cups? Any biscuits? I should have bought some. Next time.' Then appearing with two cups of coffee, she moved an overflowing ashtray from the table, asking, 'Did you always smoke so much?'

'I seem to need them,' he said. Having something to do with his hands calmed him, as did the immediate feeling of relief. Before long, he craved another.

'Well, I don't know, never been keen myself. Creates rather a fug, and I can't think it can be healthy.' She patted his hand.

Edith was a stalwart friend and fond of him, though how fond, he wasn't sure. And his feelings?

Easy to picture sharing toast and marmalade over a breakfast table, giving each other hasty pecks on the cheek before heading off to work – he a teacher, he had decided, she a political firebrand. Might that be enough? When he tried to imagine the two of them naked in bed, lusting after each other, his fantasy would disintegrate. Surely with more effort, he might will himself to desire her. She had not married and might welcome an approach. He frowned at such an inappropriate thought: he a broken man, she an energetic campaigner set on changing the world.

Edith fished a newspaper out of her bag, flicking to the entertainment section. 'I'm wondering if you fancy a visit to the cinema.'

Maybe it wasn't such a foolish thought: him and Edith.

43

AT THE APPOINTED DAY IN AUGUST, NINA TURNED UP at a club room in Shaftesbury Ave to find the floor being swept. Seeing the state of it, needing a good mop, she feared for her ballet shoes, which she couldn't afford to replace. But never mind that. Familiar faces! All of them early, longing for Cecchetti's class to begin and getting stuck into rehearsals. She dumped her bag and rushed forwards, a beaming smile stretching her face, arms flung wide.

'Darling, how wonderful to see you!' Kisses, hugs, and shrieks, greeting those she knew. And, like the old pro she was, putting fresh recruits at ease. 'Don't worry, it will all make sense; Grigoriev's very methodical.' Not like when she'd first joined the company in Monte when snooty Russians barely gave her the time of day. Times had changed, with the company a veritable stew of nationalities.

'My dearest darlings.' Now *here* was a Russian accent she hadn't heard in *so* long. Lydia Lopokova stepped into the room, wearing her practice tutu, arms flung wide. 'I made it! At any moment, I thought we go *pooph*!' The Channel crossing was perilous, mined as it was by the Germans. More shrieks, and Nina joined a cluster, welcoming their little ballerina, who'd had such a gruelling time. 'I dropped my luggage and came straight over.' Lydia laughed.

'No doubt *her* cushy lodgings will sort her out,' a waspish whisper in her ear. The luxury of the Savoy was only for principals – Massine, and so on – but Nina didn't care; it was being here that mattered.

Later, with Grigoriev rehearsing them, she heard a breathy, 'Shh, he's here,' and there was no doubt who *he* was. Coming through the door was the man she'd not seen in far too long.

'Sergei Pavlovich.' Curtsies from the girls.

'Sergei Pavlovich.' Bows and clicks of heels as the boys acknowledged their director.

A press of hands with Massine; a kiss on the hand to Lydia.

The war, she noted, was taking its toll on Diaghilev, his languid walk that little bit slower, and while immaculately dressed, as always, she could not help but note the sheen of a suit worn thin. As he sat watching rehearsals, legs crossed at the ankles, she spotted a hole in the sole of a shoe. Did he know? Did he not care if people could see? He somehow looked exhausted, those heavy bags under his eyes darker.

Nina strove to lighten his load, leaping and streaking in remembered patterns. By the force of her will, she would do her bit to make dear Sergei Pavlovich a happy man.

Their premiere was postponed again and again: soloists not yet arrived, Grigoriev and Diaghilev sending frantic telegraphs across Europe; lost scenery needing reproducing; essential costume boxes lost, finally retrieved at a railway station warehouse.

In early September, Nina stepped onstage at the Coliseum in the first performance of their twelve-week contract. Ballets were slotted between, 'Performing dogs and acrobats,' Diaghilev was heard to say, but at least he was keeping his enterprise before the public. If it was a climb down, he never showed it – while she was present – but she had to laugh at his little snobberies. Mr Stoll, the manager, had agreed to thousands of sequins being removed from the drop curtain. 'Those must go!' she imagined her director saying. And, he would be thinking, *If we are to dance in a music hall, we will not be common!* He'd insisted on a new lighting rig: *his* dancers would be lit with the subtlety, he demanded.

Amongst the principals that stayed with them, Hilda was making appearances as a soloist. Acknowledging she would never be as favoured as Hilda was tough. Still, she persisted in her dream along with other English girls who'd been taken on. Nina Rosova kept good company amongst recently Russified names: Granzieva, Muravieva. Appearances mattered.

Just as your war horses and mules will be hard at it, I too am back in harness, she wrote to Charlie. *Let me tell you one review spoke of our "elegant poetry in motion from the chief principal dancers down to the humblest members of the troop…" And we are a big troop of more than 70 filling the stage. We cut quite a dash, and the public are loving having us back. Hoping you are keeping whole and well, from moi, a humble member of the troop.'*

Being onstage doing what she loved most took her mind off all the rest.

In November came the news.

'It's over!' A male dancer costumed for *Carnival* rushed into their female *corps de ballet* dressing room flourishing *The Times.* 'An armistice, it says. The Germans have surrendered, as far as I can tell. It's over. Do you hear? Over!'

At momentous times, what does relief and joy sound like? Feel like? What memories lodge in the brain?

Nina had been peeling back ragged paper from a well-worn stick of Leichner greasepaint, exposing what remained of the stub: a No. 2 flesh-colour she was applying as a foundation. The distinctive smell of this warm colour always thrilled her, the smell of preparing to perform. Since the war, it'd been hard to get hold of, being German, now it'd be on the market again. What a stupid thing to go through her mind.

Charlie! 'Charlie! He's coming home!' No longer would she have to tamp down gnawing anxiety, refusing to consider the unthinkable. She longed to throw herself at him, be lifted and wrap her arms and legs around him, and hear his, 'Hey, sugar. How's it goin'?' She would peel away his stinky old uniform and, body to body, re-establish the rhythm of lovemaking they were so good at.

Reflected in her mirror, so many half-dressed dancers spasming, arms and legs disjointed, faces distorted. Thrusting back her chair, she was on her feet whooping, joining a crazed dance of peace.

'We must celebrate!'

'Let's find Grigoriev.'

'No, Diaghilev!'

Dashing from their dressing room, a trickle becoming a stream as other doors flung wide, artists flowing into the corridor. Dancers and musicians, a uniformed Canadian Concert Party, Margaret Cooper – who Sid used to sing with – shimmering in a blue ballgown. 'I was singing at the start of this damn thing, and I'm here at the end,' Nina heard her say. All the acts preparing for the matinee with backstage crew, squeezed together, a mighty river, heading for the stage. Where else to gather?

Mr Stoll was there, and among this hive they sought out Diaghilev, a solid presence, unruffled and unconcerned.

'Oh, Sergei Pavlovich, how are we celebrating?' her director was asked by a breathless dancer.

'*Nous danserons, come nous le faisons toujours.*'

'Yes, yes, of course we always dance. But something special. Afterwards? A company party?'

'*Vous pouvez, bien sûr, naturellement.*'

'We *will* be, but what about you? All of us? The company?' Diaghilev shrugged.

'Next week then, Sergei Pavlovich? Surely then? We must have a party then!'

Nina waited, seeing Diaghilev biting his tongue, thinking on it.

Next week would mark the thousandth performance of the Ballets Russes since Diaghilev launched it. That, along with the end of the war, was worth celebrating. Nina waited impatiently for their director's answer. She was already imagining herself at a fabulous party, flowing with champagne among his high-society sponsors.

'We perform,' came his sonorous reply, always in French. 'I am not fond of anniversaries. Why look back when we can look forwards?' A shark-like smile stretched his lips, a rare glimpse of his teeth, and Nina could sense that within his massive head, a brain was churning, fresh artistic challenges and possibilities. Now the war was over, the world – his European, artistic world – would open again. 'Come! We must not keep our public waiting.'

Later, costumed and posed onstage, she watched the curtain rising and felt its significance. A veil was lifting. Darkness had not swallowed them. She, and many others, had survived to walk towards the light and she couldn't wait to see what the future held.

44

Unable to find grace in God, and with the church having sanctioned that uncouth war, Walter turned to worldly refuges.

In Burlington House, the Royal Academy of Arts programme stated, *To give unto them beauty for ashes.* Isaiah. Perhaps the Bible did have something to say to him. And in those rooms with over a thousand watercolours and oils – waterfalls, children at play, donkey rides – he marvelled that there was still such a world. Only in the sculpture room, with models commissioned for memorials, did he freeze, heart thudding, and had to sit. At the newly named Wigmore Hall – Bechstein no longer– he listened to recitals graceful in finesse and elegance.

Then Charlie got in touch, all excited. 'No way am I missing this, and you're coming, whether you want to or not.'

'Take Nina,' he deflected. The revue didn't appeal.

'She's outta town, up north, Manchester. Anyway, *you* must come. These guys are touring from New Orleans. The real deal.'

So, with a group of Charlie's American friends – 'Guys who've come back from hell,' Charlie said – he went to opening night of a revue at the Hippodrome. The comedy star, George

Roby, had a string of corny jokes – 'Large dog for sale. Will eat anything. Loves children.' – which raised a chuckle, but this wasn't the attraction. It was a café scene with the Original Dixieland Jazz Band.

Brassy sounds smashed from the stage: metallic whoops and slides, fingers dancing on brass keys, pounding honky-tonk ivories. Next to Walter's left ear, one of Charlie's friends let out a piercing whistle and to his right, Charlie moaned, 'Oh man. Oh man!' A fever rippled through the auditorium in a way he imagined it had been for the premiere of *The Rite of Spring*. But here, no one questioned the rightness of the music for this time. At the end of the set, he was on his feet with every other man and woman. His clapping was a restrained response, while wild whoops and cheers rang out around him and stamping feet juddered the floor.

Charlie's face shone. 'Woo, man! *This* is what life's about. Can't you taste it? I want more!'

Walter *could* taste it, if only for a moment, before sinking into a fog.

'After, I'm goin' backstage. Goin' to be a party,' Charlie said. 'Comin?'

He declined. 'The leg, you know, need to rest.'

Kit and Clara and other old friends urged him, and Mr Reed insisted, 'I beg you, don't allow my years of investment go to waste. You must. You simply must.' So after much persuasion, he was completing his disrupted final year of study but doing so reluctantly. A cuckoo in a nest.

Using a cane, he limped along a corridor at the Royal College of Music. Hearing shrill chirps and chit-chat, he drew to the side, allowing freshly fledged young men and women clutching instrument cases to scamper past. While his body might be a few years their senior, his soul was eons older.

His ancient eyes followed them, then he carried on towards a practice room.

Clara, violaist in their student piano quintet, had, in that previous life, been sweet on him. When he was serving, she'd kept up a steady stream of letters, and he'd written back because, well, he hoped he might reciprocate tender feelings. She was newly married, having given up on him as husband material but not as a friend. And he was grateful.

'Walter, I thought we might try this today.' Clara produced a score. 'I think you'll get on well with it.'

By that, Clara meant it wouldn't be too challenging. It was a piece by Marco Anzoletti he could see she'd transcribed.

'Let's have a go, shall we?'

As he took his section from her, he fumbled and, with dismay, watched the sheets scatter. 'Clumsy, so clumsy!'

'It's all right.' She stooped quickly, placed them on the music rest, and arranged her sheets on the nearby stand. Taking out her viola, she rubbed her bow with rosin, tuned, then drew back her bowing arm.

This was their routine. In exploring ways to best engage him, to feel himself into the music, they had discovered if he listened first it helped. As she played, his eyes followed the dots and lines on the staves in front of him, remembering how the piano blended with strings. Every so often, he glanced at her standing, instrument tucked under chin, a vision in a pale-blue dress. He felt a fleeting pang of regret – if he could have loved her, they'd have been well matched musically.

Clara lowered her bow, looking at him. 'Ready?'

'A little slower,' he suggested, before interlocking his fingers, clicking his knuckles, and placing tremulous hands on the keyboard. It had distressed him hugely when he had first sat at a piano. The impact of his fingers striking the keys startled him, inky notes on the staves threatening to skip off the paper. He could not create order. Mr Reed had kindly guided him back to basics. Under his old tutor's guidance, he progressed to playing Satie's *Gymnopédies*, *Moonlight Sonata* and other favourites of his childhood and youth. Now Clara was guiding him: nothing discordant that might rattle him, but romantic, good for the rich viola.

For five minutes he stumbled through until, defeated, he lowered his hands to his lap.

'First time.' Clara smiled. 'Well done.'

She chatted about an exhibition she planned to see, the spoilt brat of a child she was teaching, then she picked up her bow. 'From the top.'

This time, he stumbled less, turned one more page. Progress.

Before they ended their session, Clara said, 'Now for our fun time. Let's give "I'll Say She Does" another go. A-flat major,' she reminded him. They'd vetoed all war-related songs – sugary, sentimental, or otherwise. In her soprano, she began:

'*I've got a brand-new sweetie, better than the one before. Oh, she's got everything and a little bit more...*'

He placed his fingertips on the keyboard, trying to connect the ragtime rhythm he heard in his head. No sheet of music now. By ear. Such a struggle to find the bouncing beat. You needed speed for that, which he just didn't have in him. Everyone but him seemed to be bouncing along: people and songs alike.

'*When she dances, does she twist, does she do a lot of things I can't resist...*'

Al Johnson's song didn't suit Clara's classically trained voice, but it was cheerful. They made an odd duet: a pianist groping to find the thread of his life and his well-meaning friend who, he suspected, still harboured feelings for him. Feelings she would, one way or another, have to let go. Having cultivated a thick moustache, he slightly resembled the normal man he feared he could never be. Outwardly he might pass as such, if inwardly he flailed in a morass of uncertainties. How to change essential nature? How to bloom into a different flower?

While Clara had married, Edith had not, and he continued to consider possibilities in that direction. She was a constant in his life. An ideal companion. They'd fallen into a routine – Wednesday evenings at his place, her bringing provisions ('Chops today.'), the two of them side by side in his tiny kitchen peeling, chopping, chatting. Saturday afternoon or evening an outing. ('*Monsieur Beaucaire* is on at the Shaftesbury, good reviews, fancy that?')

Days before his twenty-fourth birthday, he, Nina, Edith, and Rose were amongst a crush of Empire Day celebrants at Hyde Park: massed military bands and choral singers giving voice to peace and thanksgiving.

Shine upon us as we sing this 24th of May. Shine upon our brothers too, far across the ocean blue... Without so much as a look, he felt Edith, standing on his right, slide her hand into his... *As we raise our song of praise, on this our glorious Empire Day.*

He held himself together, but Elgar's music – *that* song – was his undoing:

Land of Hope and Glory, Mother of the Free, How shall we extol thee, who are born of thee...

When it ended, all four of them openly wept tears of happiness and grief. Everyone seemed to have a hanky at the ready. Rose crushed each of them to her bosom saying, 'I'll never forget this day for as long as I live.'

'I do wish Charlie had come,' Edith said.

'Yes. Why didn't he?' Rose asked.

'Isn't well.' But seeing the set of his sister's mouth made Walter wonder.

45

<small>CHARLIE!</small>

Nina had dressed in a favourite blue skirt with a soft loose-fitting cream blouse, fixed her hair, and breakfasted. Only then calling out to Charlie.

'Ugh?' He squinted before closing his eyes.

'You don't want to miss the parade, do you? And I'm heading to the theatre straight after. Come on. This is for you and everyone who fought.'

An eye opened. 'Empire Day, right?'

'It'll be huge.' She pulled back the blanket.

Charlie sat up and placed his feet on the floor, wrists dangling on thighs. 'Not mine.'

'Not your what? Hurry up, Charlie, won't you. We're going to be late. It'll be hard enough finding the others, and Walter won't want to stand for long.'

'Not my *Empire*,' he said.

Where had this come from? 'What on earth do you mean?' She sat down next to him. 'It's a massive party—'

'Not mine, sugar.' Charlie looked at her. 'I don't wanna go, but say hello to the others.'

'Really, this is so… so…' Once he'd told her what his "black doughboy buddies" said about the war clearing the way for people like them. She rapped his shoulder. 'You're getting a chip as big as a block of wood. This isn't like you.'

'Maybe it is like me. Or maybe I'm changin'.'

'Huh! What'll I tell Ma and Walter?'

'Tell them I'm not feeling well.' Charlie drew the covers over him.

She stalked out, angry he was spoiling family arrangements. How foolish to make a song and dance about bloody old Empire Day.

Ever since those Americans had hit town, that Dixieland jazz band, Charlie had been in a fever. If, with the ending of the war, Walter had gone into himself, Charlie had become a party boy, hanging about with musicians from home. Jazz was spreading like a heat rash.

'We're invited,' Charlie said one day. 'Said to come along after work.' Charlie's evenings at the club finished later than hers at the Alhambra. She hesitated, thinking of morning class, afternoon rehearsal, next night's show.

'Just for a short time,' she agreed.

At a large house in Belgravia, with a porticoed entrance, she and Charlie handed coats and hats to a waiting servant before being escorted to the reception room.

They stood inside the door, a jazz recording just audible above laughing, chattering guests. Dancing couples two-stepped past; others lounged on velvet sofas: party creatures, cigarettes dangling, glasses in hand.

'Nice!' Charlie whistled, his eyes on the glittering chandelier hanging from the high ceiling. 'Though you're used to hobnobbing.'

'Hardly. It's just Diaghilev's inner circle, not us…'

'It's Daddy's house,' she was told by an impossibly glamourous young woman wearing a low-waisted pink satin party dress. 'Do help yourselves.' She waved vaguely towards a cabinet arrayed with bottles, decanters, and glasses, before turning to greet more guests. 'Darlings, you're late!'

Charlie rubbed his hands. 'Booze. You bet.' Nina followed and poured herself a glass of champagne. His was a generous whisky.

Whinnying, well-brought-up young women – judging by their perfect enunciation – threw themselves at the American musicians.

'Just love your accent,' one shimmering creature fawned, draping herself over one of the men. And didn't he soak up the attention, head thrown back, a proud roar.

'He's happy,' Nina said, as the American tipped back his head a second time to slug back whisky. She watched him pull the woman onto his lap – a high-pitched squeal – before her playful protest was cut short by his mouth clamping down on hers.

'Nick. Clarinet players for you. Good at that.' Charlie grinned. 'He likes making out. They all do.'

And you? He'd been arriving home at dawn, sleeping well beyond the time she headed out to class. 'Been jamming with the boys,' he'd say when asked.

Charlie read her face. 'Hey. Look at them… Look at me.'

'You're a handsome man, Charlie. And there's nothing wrong with *my* taste.'

'Yeah, well… But do you see me getting gigs like these guys, or parties like this? Just the way things are, I guess.' He shrugged.

She squeezed his arm. 'Even *they* say you're good enough.' Charlie had said as much after one of their sessions.

'Chas, my man!' It was Tony, the drummer. 'See you've got your girl with you tonight.'

'Yeah, this is Nina.'

'Hey, gorgeous. Whatcha doin' hanging around with a string bean like him?' Tony slapped Charlie's back, winked and moved on, calling, 'Hey, sweethearts, don't be shy, come on in,' to two shimmering girls paused at the door.

'Let's dance.' She plonked her glass down and drew Charlie close. "Ja-Da" was the jitteriest, jaggiest number, and they were off in a tight one-step, manoeuvring around the floor with a dozen or more laughing couples jostling for space. As she danced, she noticed Billy, the band's piano player, seated on one of the squishy sofas, talking loudly with a girl. He held an open small silver container, and Nina watched his fingers pinch some powder and sniff. Then the girl's turn.

She considered herself sophisticated but felt uneasy. Never one to be out of control – the discipline of ballet demanded that – this way of living was not what she wanted for herself, *or* Charlie.

'Let's not stay too long,' she whispered in Charlie's ear.

He was beginning to move to a different rhythm, his heart hankering for a different country. Her heart was still nailed to Diaghilev's cause. Right now, that cause was the creation of a new ballet *La Boutique Fantasque*.

Diaghilev was in his element overseeing details of designs and lighting. He thrived on it. Derain's design – set and costumes – created great slashes of vibrant combinations. While being fitted for her can-can costume, she admired the tarantella costume waiting for Hilda's fitting, dark bodice with brilliant green skirt, contrasting trimmings and apron. *Ma will love this.*

Earlier, she'd seen Diaghilev pouring over Picasso's designs for another ballet project. He was looking ahead, next year, the year after. She detected a restlessness in him surrounded by an ever-younger clutch of artists and hangers-on – so many shards of shimmering steel around the magnet.

One day after class, she remained, sitting on the floor, small sewing kit by her side. She was criss-crossing the ends of new pointe shoes with darning wool when she heard footsteps and distinctive voices approaching.

'...*la fille anglaise, je pense,*' Massine was saying.

'*Oui, oui. Je l'ai regardée,*' came Diaghilev's rumbling baritone.'*Elle sera ravissante dans le costume blanc moelleus.*'

Nina paused, needle raised. Should she cough? She'd seen the sketch for the white fluffy poodle costume. *This part was to be created on her!* Perhaps she wasn't to be one of the can-can dolls...

'*Excellents pieds,*' Massine said, as they passed along the corridor without coming in.'*Je commercerai à travailler avec elle demain.*'

She stretched her toes, regarding her feet. Not very high arches but here was Massine saying they were excellent! What ideas might she bring to tomorrow's rehearsal with Massine? What character quirks might her delightful poodle have?

Next day after class, there was no call for her to rehearsal. She gave no more thought to it, as schedules altered, but stayed to watch Massine rehearsing with Lydia, their lead can-can doll. All the while, Rossini's joyous music spun from the fingers of their rehearsal pianist. Nina laughed out loud seeing Massine, lifting Lydia, his face the picture of insouciance, hers a rounded doll-like innocence. This would bring the house down.

Others began slipping into the rehearsal room, Vera sitting quietly by her.

'I'm just so *thrilled* to be here and being noticed!' Vera gave the sweetest smile, not a trace of artifice in her. 'I'm working with Monsieur Massine when he's ready.'

Nina gulped, heat flooding her cheeks. *English* Vera, so new to the company, was to be given a solo in *La Boutique Fantasque*. Nina pictured her dressed as the white poodle, those *excellent* feet tiptoeing on pointe. Quietly she got up and left. Perhaps Massine would ask her to do cartwheels in the can-can number. She was good at that.

When she told Hilda of her error, her friend burst out laughing. 'You silly sausage. For now you'll have to be happy learning my tarantella, on the off-chance I fall under a bus. And I don't propose to do that. But your time will come, I see Massine noticing you—'

'I doubt it!'

'Trust me. He does. There hasn't been the right part for your, well, *particular* talents. Unbridled energy and so on.'

'You know, Hilda, when I was in Los Angeles, I did so enjoy Ted Shawn's class. My energy *was* unbridled.'

Hilda studied her. 'Maybe that's your future. Now this rotten war's over, it's possible, isn't it? What does Charlie want to do? Does he want to go home?'

Yes! Nina sucked her teeth. 'We'll have to see.' Where to settle was an ongoing discussion.

One Sunday morning, lazing in bed together, Charlie had said, 'What exactly's an anarchist?'

'What?'

He continued twisting a strand of her hair between his fingers. 'Just something Nick was saying. About jazz being a revolution. About them being musical anarchists... I guess it's not sticking to rules, right?'

'I suppose so.'

'Says he likes to murder syncopation... Says I should catch the steamer with them when they leave. Says—'

'New York!' She pulled away.

He drew her back into his arm, her head on his chest. 'No, no, don't worry. But it got me thinking.'

That got *her* thinking. Where *did* she belong? The old world of Europe and ballet or the new world of jazz and modern dance. Nina wriggled free and, lying on her back, spread her arms and legs – one leg straddling Charlie.

'What're you doin?'

'Seeing if I can span the world. One foot in London, the other in New York.'

'How about Chicago?'

She extended one toe, reaching further. 'Maybe. Or California. What do you think?'

Charlie was silent for a time.

'I'm not sure you'd even want to be with me over there – couldn't be for the most, laws against it and all. But, just say we married here – not saying we should – but just say…' His fingers played a silent tune along her leg. 'Even then, I can't see it workin' out most places. White folks'd look down on you, and I'd as like get my head busted for being an uppity nigger.'

She flinched. 'Surely the war must change things.'

'Must, or should, sugar.'

The tips of Charlie's fingers continued in their slow, thoughtful tune.

46

WHEN POLITICIANS CALLED FOR PARADES AND squeezing Germany till her pips squeaked, it made Walter want to weep. And he did.

Away from soothing musical sessions with Clara, he was digging deep, working through his emotions through composition. He was no longer a romantic. No longer nostalgic for a past he knew was gone.

He had a piano at his lodgings – hauled there by a gang of sweating, cursing fellows – and his worktable was spread with sheets of scribbled staved music paper and jottings in notebooks.

Amongst his scores there was Nina's gift of Stravinsky's *The Rite of Spring*. It lay untouched, taboo, yet it taunted him. The music was a soundscape to his life. That first astonishing ritual with Alexei, feasting on his beauty, the scent of his skin, the feel of his touch. And what could never be erased from memory, quivering in a hole gouged from the earth, the world exploding around him.

When Edith visited, she picked up a theory book of Arnold Schoenberg's he'd left open. 'Gosh, not exactly riveting. Each to his own.'

Walter smiled. 'He's experimenting – fewer tones.' He didn't want to bore her. 'I've been working on small sequences led by pitch, rhythm, dynamics—'

'Do play some for me!'

'No, no.' Walter backed away. 'I improvise, you see.'

This was private. He could not share how he swayed, sweated, howled as, with stammering fingers, he relived scenes from his life, both beautiful and wretched. Dared not share sounds, harmonic and jarring, that rose from the keyboard, piercing him. When he had something worth keeping, he would pause to write it down, jotting dots and dashes on staved paper. He doubted he would share this work – tutors at college being somewhat traditional. So not with them, or anyone else. Not even Edith.

Seeing she was hurt, he said, 'Honestly, I don't think the mess is playable. Not yet. But if I have something, you have my promise.' He looked at the book. Here was a compositional form being formulated: something half-broken, angry, honest; something that might suit a soul-wounded musician-soldier finding his place in a new world.

When he had met Nina, she had asked, 'Finding your feet yet?'

'Trying to,' he replied. 'How are things with you and Charlie?'

She shrugged. 'Usual.'

'And work?'

'Busy! That time in Spain stimulated Massine and Diaghilev. Why waste a good crisis – war – when something lovely can be created? And *Three-Cornered Hat* is such a sunny, funny ballet. De Falla's score will have you clacking that foot of yours. You know, I should find a matching castanet for your good foot. Two blocks of wood will do the trick!'

Hearing Nina laugh was wonderful. He couldn't, yet, see the sunny side of things, but he promised to see the ballet, 'With Edith.'

He looked up to see Edith studying him. 'Penny for your thoughts?'

'Nothing, nothing.'

'You know, Walter, neither of us have had a holiday in so long. Maybe blow away some cobwebs at the seaside for a day or two?'

'Yes, I should like that one weekend. Good idea.'

'Let's not wait too long.'

He and Edith had trundled on, seemingly happy with the equilibrium they had established. This would shake things up.

'Yes, let's go soon.'

He pictured walking (short walks of necessity) along a promenade. Not on sand – unstable with those sudden soft dips when he'd be liable to stumble. But perhaps he *should* venture out. Worst that could happen is that he'd land face down in the sand. He allowed his imagination free reign, picturing them arm in arm. Bolder now, him saying something like, 'Look here, Edith, we get along terribly well. Do you think we can make a go of it?'

And she would say…

What *might* she say?

47

Having Sid home was lovely, but he'd changed, Rose discovered. Over there, he'd been transporting supplies and ammunition by lorry and wagon, then bodies to cemeteries.

'Scooped up as best we could. Not pretty sights or smells. Something I'd rather forget.'

'Once you're back on the boards, you'll get over it.'

'Not sure I want to go back to that, truth be told.'

'Not sing? That's what you do. That's your life.'

Sid stroked his moustache. 'You're fond of the seaside.'

They were in the kitchen, and her eyes slid to the souvenirs on the shelf he'd collected for Molly.

'To a point,' she said, curious.

'I was thinking, pier towns, you know, Southend, Eastbourne, Hastings. Maybe Great Yarmouth – went down a storm there – got a soft spot for the place. What do you say?'

Rose held her cup with both hands then took a cautious sip. 'Let me get this straight. You want to leave London? With me?'

''Course with you! We're married, ain't we? And why not live somewhere else?'

Rose could think of many reasons. She was a Londoner with Whitechapel her home for her entire life. Even during the worst of the raids, she'd never once considered leaving. While she loved the bustle of Covent Garden market with all that produce coming in from the countryside – and given half a chance could gorge on fresh cream and butter – farms were a foreign land.

'It's so quiet, Sid. The only things you hear and smell are cows.' Years ago, she, Molly and Nina had been on a walk through a field and those oafs had terrified her, drawing near. Molly couldn't run to save her life, and Nina would have been three or four. All those drooling munching jaws and sloppy poos buzzing with flies. 'No, Sid, I'm not keen on cows.'

'Who's said anything about cows? Seaside ain't the countryside. Towns with fairgrounds and pavilions.'

'And I suppose donkey rides. I like them well enough.'

'There you go then!'

'But Nina and Walter, Sid, I—'

'Heaven's sake! You've got your own life. They're not kiddies.'

'So you always say.' She felt his glare.

'Listen, Rose.' Sid placed his cup down on the saucer, with a clatter. 'Nina'll do what suits her, and when a man's been through what Walter has…'

'What you got in mind? Once you've shipped us out south.'

'Or north. Essex, Norfolk.'

Her voice wobbled, trying to be brave. 'So, what've you been thinking about?'

'A pub. Owning a pub. In time, I thought we might buy one.'

'My goodness. When did this start?'

'Over there. I was doing mucky work, and London's mucky. I fancied breathing clean air, nowhere *too* small, not ruling out the boards completely. Just want to move on.'

'I don't know, Sid.'

But Sid had been thinking this through. 'I'd have to save, we both would, so it'll take a while. But I'd like to start looking about.'

Will take a while, she noticed he said, not *might*.

'Well?' he said.

'All right. No harm in looking.'

Sid gave her the biggest grin. How might she dodge this bullet?

Some weeks earlier, enveloped in a velvet cuddle of the theatre she loved, she'd watched *La Boutique Fantasque*. Now, with Sid up-country scouting some place she preferred not to think about, she was again at the Alhambra watching another premiere, *The Three-Cornered Hat*, with Walter, Edith and Charlie. With Mr de Falla's score and Mr Massine's choreography, she defied anyone not to adore this ballet. All those clicking heels, clacking castanets… She remembered Arthur admiring her Spanish dancing in the Alhambra's *Don Q*. And how in that little flat on Frith Street she'd turned temptress, whirling and twirling a silky scarf. How could she leave London with such riches as this? How could she turn her back on her past? She'd always want to be in reach of this place.

Charlie had booked a table in advance for an after-show supper, making her recall all those delicious evenings with Arthur, only now she sat wedged between Edith and Charlie and the other youngsters. Waiting for dishes to be served, Nina chattered non-stop.

'Did you spot Leon hamming it up as he was dragged off? Then I felt my headdress wiggling, and thought, *oh my stars, please, please stay put, can't face a fine…* Oh, Sergei Pavlovich glanced at me on his way to Tamara's dressing room, and I swear he smiled!'

Soon everyone had said what there was to say about the performance, and Nina was coming back to earth.

'Tell me, Charlie, how are things?' Rose risked asking. Nina had invited him, so that meant they were together again, or at least on speaking terms. And "things" was general enough.

'Going good, thanks. Pretty good.'

'*Really* good, Ma. Go on, Charlie,' Nina said, 'you say.'

'Ah well…' The American smiled shyly. 'I've my own band—'

'My idea!' Nina chipped in. 'Just last month.'

'Playing at a new club, Dalton's, close to the Alhambra.' Then everyone was congratulating him. 'Come along one night,' Charlie told Walter.

'Yes do!' Nina said. 'Some of us can dance. You'd like that wouldn't you, Edith?'

'Rather!'

It delighted Rose that there was still a whiff of the dancing girl in Edith. Young people should dance.

'There we go then.' Nina clapped her hands. 'And you, dear brother, can tap your foot or analyse the music or whatever it is musicians do. But Edith and I will be dancing.'

'Even if with each other.' Edith smiled.

For a moment, conversation paused, all of them thinking of those lost young men.

Nina gripped Charlie's arm. 'There's a future here for Charlie, I keep telling him. We can't get enough of latest fads from over there – films and music. He can do well here, no doubt about *that*.'

'Yeah, well…' Charlie fiddled with his glass, and Rose sensed a tension. 'There're good scenes cooking in America.'

Nina jumped in. 'Charlie can be big in London—'

'A small pond for my music, sugar. Far rather be in a big pond with big fish teaching me to swim better.'

And with Charlie's sigh, Rose felt how difficult it was for all of them to find a new path.

'I tell her,' Charlie went on. 'She can come.'

'*She*, the cat's mother!' Nina's voice was tart.

'I mean,' Charlie spoke softly, eyes on Nina, 'I'd like you to try living there, if we can figure out how.'

'Might you, Nina?' Edith asked. 'Could you consider it? I can imagine you fitting in. Not that I've visited America, but you enjoyed touring there, didn't you?'

Nina's hand darted to Walter's cigarette case. Rose watched a frown form as Walter lit her cigarette, Nina cupping her brother's unsteady hand. With a breath in and out, Nina began cautiously.

'It's a funny place, America. Some of the cities I liked well enough—'

'You liked New York,' Charlie reminded her.

'I did. And I'd get work easily enough.' Nina held her cigarette away from her mouth. 'I haven't talked about some things. Like when we performed *Scheherazade*, we had to tone down the orgy scene, had to stop colouring our boys in brown paint. Audiences didn't go for white girls dancing with negros, even make-believe ones—'

'How beastly!' Edith cut in.

'Goodness!' Rose said. 'It's just a ballet.'

'You might think so, Ma. And not just onstage. Some of these Southern towns wouldn't dream of having Charlie attending a theatre with me. It opened my eyes—'

'Sugar,' Charlie appealed, 'better not—'

'To the way they treated…'

'People like me,' Charlie finished.

Edith was all in a lather. 'America is so, so modern in many ways yet in others it's backward and wrong-thinking. I can't stand it when people aren't open-minded. Such a dilemma for you both. I see that.'

'Thanks, Edith.' Charlie smiled in gratitude.

Nina on tour was one thing but considering her packing up to live in America saddened Rose. 'America's so far away.'

'Don't bother yourself, Ma. We're here for a good while. Charlie's contract is for six months, and they're bound to extend it. As for me, there's no way I'm leaving.' Nina laughed. 'Have I told you? We're opening at the Empire in autumn, then after that we might be back in Paris. Diaghilev's heading over to sort things at the Opera. So, no, America's not on the cards for me. At least, not yet.' Nina gave Charlie one of her looks.

Rose eyed the dessert menu, wondering if she had room for an ice after that Beef Wellington, when Edith tapped her glass.

'I – that is we,' she glanced at Walter, 'have an announcement. Without fuss and fanfare, we want to let you know we've decided to marry.'

And you could have heard a pin drop.

'Marry, did you say?' Rose needed to be sure.

Edith nodded. 'Yes, marry.'

Charlie was the first to congratulate them, leaning over to pump hands, Edith looking very practical, and Walter looking, well, Rose tried to make out his face... like a card player not wanting to reveal his hand. Inscrutable. That was the word. Nina's face was anything but. Her daughter was flushing from pink to beet-red, until she couldn't hold back. Then it was as if a bomb had landed – hot metal shards flying.

'You can't *possibly*! How can you *think* of it! In fact, *are* you thinking?' Her daughter pushed back her chair as if this was something she could better battle while standing. 'Not thinking straight, that's for certain. This is the *craziest* thing. It'll never work. *Never!*'

'Sugar.' Charlie touched her hip, Nina pulling away as if scolded. She planted her knuckles on the table, leaning in.

'Edith. I'm surprised at you. And Walter, does Edith know about—'

'Hush, Nina!' Edith spoke firmly, glancing at diners at nearby tables who'd stopped to listen. 'This is between Walter and me.'

'Walter,' Nina appealed, 'say something. Anything to make me say "congratulations" and really mean it. You know I wish your happiness as much as my own. Go on. Say something.'

Rose sat in this whirl, not quite keeping up. She rather liked the idea of Walter and Edith marrying for all it surprised her. It had to be said, they didn't strike her as the most romantic of couples, but they'd stay put and not go gallivanting. She might then become a grandmother, which Nina had been clear was not on her horizon. Edith then. She was already fantasising. Nina and Walter were staring at each other, one twin with smouldering eyes, the other's face a mask.

'Well, Walter?' Nina said.

'As Edith said, this is between us. We're very fond of each other...' At this, Rose's antennae wiggled. Hadn't Arthur said as much to her? What about love? Why wasn't Walter speaking of love? 'We're keen to make a go of it and get on with our lives. Edith doesn't mind my leg—'

'Not in the least!' Edith cut in, and Rose knew that'd be true. 'It's what's in here that matters.' Edith tapped her head. 'We can make it work. A modern couple. I'm sure I'll be a good wife, and—'

'I know *you* will be.' Nina's words were for Edith, but Rose saw her eyes locked on Walter's.

'We're very close companions,' Walter said. 'That's a sound basis.'

But what about *love*, Rose wanted to shout, but Nina said it for her.

'No, Walter. No, Edith. I'm not going to congratulate you. This is stupid! You don't marry because it's convenient!

That's how it seems to me – particularly for *you*, Walter. As for you, Edith… Why?' And Nina was glaring at Walter through teared eyes. 'Edith's my friend. I need to know you love her.'

'We've a strong affection—'

'Affection!' Nina grabbed her bag, heading for the door.

Edith rose to follow. 'I'd better…'

But Charlie shook his head. 'Leave her. That's best.'

'Well,' Rose said. 'Well, I never.' She turned from one unsettled face to another then reached for the near-empty wine bottle. 'Can we squeeze out a bit for a toast?' She poured and raised her glass with a dribble in it. 'I wish you both happiness.'

'Thank you, Rose.' Walter nodded.

'Thank you so much,' Edith said.

What an odd evening this was turning out to be.

48

It was through Kit's connections Walter heard of a temporary teaching position at St Hilda's College, Oxford.

'Right up your street, old man. If they don't gift it you, there'll be hell to play.'

Walter was not altogether sure whether Kit's father hadn't had a hand in it. There was no way of knowing.

The interview was straightforward and the position his – replacing a tutor not yet recovered from the flu that'd killed so many. For a while he would live in Oxford, Edith still in London.

'You won't mind my being away?' he'd asked.

'Not one bit! The train doesn't take long, and I'm sure there are perfectly adequate places for me to stay.' By that she meant cheap places, the Labour Party somewhat exploiting their many workers and volunteers, to his mind, though Edith wouldn't have it, insisting "every scrap of money must go to the cause". That cause being forming the Government. 'I've never been punting,' Edith said. 'I'm sure I can manage if you can't. Or one of those rowing girls can pole us along. They'll have muscle.' Edith approved of the women's college, saying, 'It's only a matter of time before the powers that be accept it as a full member of the university.'

With the start of Michaelmas term, he began tutoring – choir, composition, music history – and playing and composing in the breaks. The environment of Old Hall was everything he could wish for. The library provided something of the peace he no longer found within any church. Situated by the river, he'd see St Hilda girls straining at the oars of a skiff or walking across to the Meadow. The other direction brought the town centre, his lodgings not far away.

'Meet people; make friends; get out and about,' Edith charged him with, and he set about them diligently.

On occasions he woke drenched in sweat, jaw clamped, but slowly, the trenches were releasing their grip on him. He joined a poetry society and by Hilary term (he was getting used to the rhythm and names of this quaint place), the quintet he played with was shaping up. Life was shaping up. He was shaping up.

A small concert was being organised, raising money for the Red Cross and injured soldiers' families. 'As a cripple of the war, it's the least I can do,' he said, and the organiser, an earnest female teacher from his college, blushed, not knowing how to reply. 'That was clumsy of me.' He managed a smile. 'I have both hands, so I'll be delighted. I'm sure our group can get something together.'

They did. Schubert's "Trout" Quintet, 4th movement – not one he particularly enjoyed either playing or listening to, but it was a bubbly piece. As his hands flitted along the keys, a fisherman's feathered lure, he was astounded at the speed of his fingers, grateful to have reached a point he could again play in public when a year ago it had felt hopeless.

At the last playful notes, they received a smattering of applause. He and the string players – violin, cello, double bass, viola – stood, bowed, before packing their instruments and leaving the small stage. A young woman in a green evening dress stepped forwards, her accompanist settling at the piano he had just vacated. He should stay and listen, but having heard her rehearsing earlier… An amputee was excused so much. 'Playing up a bit,' he might say, or, 'Thanks awfully, but I think I'll rest up.' And always people nodded, always said they understood.

After parting company with his fellow musicians, he headed out, leaning on his cane, sheet music in a shoulder bag. He *was* feeling tired so need not feel guilty skulking out.

'Excuse me!' He turned to see a sandy-haired fellow at his side. 'I had no idea you played! Brilliant.'

'Not really, but thanks.'

'Saw you at Poetry Soc.'

Walter couldn't recall. 'Sorry.'

'You were nodding off. All those *dancing daffodils* and such. Better Wordsworth than poems of war and gore. Hah! Rhymes nicely.' He thrust out a hand, forcing Walter to rebalance and extend his own. 'Harvey. David Harvey.' His Welsh accent was slight, the lilt pleasing.

'Walter Roberts.'

'Saw it on the programme. Who were you with?'

'East Surrey's. You?'

'Royal Welch. Seventh. Not much by way of scratches unless you count a broken arm and ribs. Fell off my horse, you see. Mind you, the medics saw plenty of me. Trench fever and every damn blight—'

'Oh yes. All that. Unavoidable!'

'But here,' David tapped his head, 'never goes away.'

'No, it doesn't. I knew men from the Fusiliers. The Second.' He didn't trust himself to say more.

'May I carry that?' David touched the satchel.

'I can manage, but thanks.' Walter smiled a little stiffly. 'I hope to see you around. Next Poetry Soc?'

'I seriously doubt it. I was dragged along, you see. Could've been me nodding off and we can't have that.'

'Well, I should be on my way.' Walter turned, and even as he took one, two, three steps, his brain was seeking a reason to remain.

David called after him: 'I say, are you keen on history by any chance?'

Walter turned. 'That depends.'

'You don't think you might accompany me to a public lecture, do you? Benedictine Monastic History. I can't promise it'll be gripping, but we can nudge each other awake.'

'When?'

'Short notice. Tomorrow evening.'

'Tomorrow… Yes, that should be all right.'

'Excellent! I'm a modern history man myself, but he's a visiting scholar and we're all being encouraged.'

Having David next to him was unsettling. It felt to Walter as if a lever that'd been jammed shut was now released – just a little – allowing a magnetic current through his skin. No more than a tingle, but he was alert to it, conscious of the effect on him. He wasn't in the least bit tempted to nod off, but he realised he was no longer as attentive to the speaker at his lectern as he had been earlier.

Afterwards, they went to a pub along with others from David's crowd. It was noisy, difficult to talk, but over a pint, he learnt David was studying recent history at Balliol.

'A perpetual student, I'm afraid. I'd started my doctorate before the war, now I'm rather starting over. Having been through the rot, I'm keen to look at what brought us here.'

'That sounds a handful. More than one thesis.'

'I fear you may be right, but what can I do? I must try and make sense of it all.' David looked around. 'You may find me here in ten years' time still beavering away, trying to get to the nub of it. Oh dear. Already I feel much too old to be amongst all of you young things.'

'Hardly!' Walter looked closely at David's face: small lines around eyes, creases forming between nostrils and corners of the mouth. He might be late twenties, perhaps thirty, taller and broader than himself.

'And you, Walter? Aside from being a brilliant pianist—'

'Far from!'

'Tell me what you're doing.'

Walter talked of the classes he was teaching and of his own attempts to compose.

'I should like to hear you play your own pieces.' David's hazel eyes were bright.

'Oh no. I don't share my work. It's not melodic – not the kind of music you hum along to.'

'Pity. I'm a good hummer. Try me!'

'And I'm not sure it's good enough.'

'One day, Walter, one day, perhaps you may decide they are good enough, or failing that, that I'm good enough to share with.' David raised his glass.

And Walter was stumped. There was nothing behind those casual words, yet he felt them keenly. He took a breath then continued. It must be owned.

'I'm here for the year, on trial. My fiancée lives in London.'

'Fiancée. I see.' Walter wasn't sure if the uplift at the end of David's sentence showed surprise or was his natural lilt.

'Yes, so I'm not sure where we might settle. Here or there.'

'I see,' David said again.

Over the coming weeks, Walter met David occasionally, sometimes with a group, sometimes just the two of them, discovering common bonds. Both from Welsh teachers' and preachers' stock (his paternal grandfather; David's father). A love of the countryside. David was, he declared, 'A Welsh Marches man', promising, that, come summer, he would introduce Walter to those landscapes that featured in the poetry he loved. 'You can recite Housman to me,' David said. 'I shan't mind.'

'And I shan't be able to walk far, so you're safe.'

'Oh, you're not so heavy, I shouldn't think. I may piggy-back you.' And David laughed.

In March, Walter went to London for a weekend. On the Saturday evening, he, Edith, Kit along with *his* fiancée, a debutant from Berkshire, met at the club where Charlie played. It was one of the many short-lived clubs that rose only to fall as authorities cracked down on what they saw as "well-springs of iniquity". Seeing Charlie fronting his band gave Walter joy. He caught the musician's eye, signalling they'd speak later, and made their way to a table.

Walter's group made odd bedfellows. Kit was still at the War Office.

'Mopping up, old man. Paperwork. No end in sight.' He had put on weight and Walter imagined him as a pen-pusher behind a leather-topped desk for the remainder of his career. Then Kit surprised them. 'I'm thinking of standing for Parliament.'

That led to a heated discussion. Kit, a Tory, with Edith's politics a pole apart. His fiancée said little, twiddling with the stem of her glass. Walter left him and Edith to spar, turning his attention to the band. Charlie had talent for this music that refused to stay still. Before long, Kit's soon-to-be wife pushed back her chair.

'Enough of this; come on, you.' And Kit was led to the dance floor.

'And you too. Come, Walter, I insist.' Edith was standing, extending a hand, and he rose because he must at least try.

Amongst all those jittering, jerking dancers, he felt inadequate. 'I feel rather awkward,' he protested.' She leant in and kissed him, before twirling under his arm. 'You see, you can do it.'

With the band on a break, Charlie joined their table. Introductions. Asking after Nina and Rose – Walter had little to say about either woman – but all of them interested in Charlie, telling him how good he was.

A woman, dressed in a sequined gown, approached, cocktail in hand, placing the other hand on Charlie's shoulder. 'You joining me or what?'

'Sure,' Charlie gave an embarrassed smile, 'in a minute.' And the woman tottered unsteadily away. Shortly after, Charlie made his excuses.

Walter didn't ask if Charlie was still planning on leaving London for America, but he assumed the relationship with Nina was over. But Charlie had asked after her, so perhaps it wasn't, or perhaps he was being polite.

That Sunday, he and Edith visited the British Museum before his train. In the Parthenon gallery, while Edith exclaimed at the craftmanship, he admired a reclining male torso, missing head, lower arms, lower legs. While it might have recalled an amputated or mutilated soldier from his nightmares, it didn't. This naked marble was not mud-encrusted, was not death. It was *life* Walter saw here: full-fronted nakedness, rippling torso muscles, relaxed cock and scrotum, marvellous to behold. He felt a familiar tingle between his legs.

'When are you coming to visit?' he asked Edith suddenly. 'Do make it soon.'

49

It was early April when Edith visited. Easter. Walter was spared introductions as David was visiting parents in Brecon. Both declared they were very sorry not to meet.

'Next time,' Walter promised.

There cannot have been one nook or cranny in Oxford's ancient streets that didn't delight Edith. 'You must love being here. Have you decided?'

That choice lay with him. The post at St Hilda's that had been temporary was offered permanently. Pneumonia had set in, and the music professor, young as he had been, had died.

'They need a decision from me soon,' Walter said.

'I think you should, Walter. I wouldn't mind leaving London and I can see myself amongst all these blue stockings. There must be something useful for me to do.'

With the commencement of Trinity term, Walter talked with his principal, Miss Moberly, gratefully accepting the offer of a permanent position. 'And we're grateful, Mr Roberts,' she said. 'The gals do so enjoy your tutoring.'

After summer, following their marriage, Edith would be moving to live here, and Walter knew he must resolve the degenerate aspect of his nature, that stubborn boyhood phase he'd determined to leave behind. It would, he decided, be better if he didn't see David. Yet they continued as before: sometimes a crowd of them, sometimes just the two of them at a concert or the cinema. And in those dark halls, elbows on arm rests, tweed jacket sleeves touching, Walter could not turn off the current that raced up his arm, over his chest to nestle in his heart. Worse, when knees touched, as often they must, the current went straight to his groin.

One Sunday afternoon, he bathed early, slung on his dressing gown, settled at his desk, staved music sheets piled neatly, a glass of whisky by hand, prosthetic foot abandoned. When alone, he was more comfortable without the thing. His suit was laid out on the bed, shirt freshly ironed. Later, David was calling, they were expected at a friend's place. But first, a tricky section he was grappling with. A juxtaposition of two chords, the imagined sounds in his brain unwilling to become dots on paper. He was rubbing out the run of semi-quavers, A flat, C flat, G flat, back to C natural, when the door burst open.

'Sorry to be late!' And David was in the room, putting his knapsack down. 'Oh!'

Two sets of eyes, startled, all confusion and apology.

'Later, I thought.' Walter dived for his prosthetic, inwardly cursing it, cursing David.

'So sorry. My note...'

'Ah,' they said in unison, eyes on the folded slip of paper David must have pushed under the door. He closed it now and picked up his note. 'So sorry, they changed the time... didn't think to knock.' David took cautious steps into the room he had visited twice before.

'It's quite all right,' Walter managed. But it wasn't in the least. His heart was hammering with the distress of knowing David must have glimpsed his stub of a leg protruding from beneath the flannel gown. Hateful, imperfect, ugly thing. His hands shook with the urgency to attach the damned apparatus, all the while tugging at the hem of the dressing gown to conceal this imperfection, and trying, unsuccessfully, to twist away from David. He fumbled, then, with dismay, watched the bloody thing clatter to the floor.

Heads bashed as he and David bent together. An unseemly scuffle. David had it, was examining the carved oak foot, the metal hinge and leather straps.

'Ingenious. The things that can be done these days. Lighter than I thought.'

And Walter couldn't speak, could only hold his hands out. 'Please.'

But David didn't hand it over. 'So how do I attach it?' Eyes met. 'I'd like to.' With one hand, David reached behind the back of Walter's knee, firmly holding the curve of his calf muscle, staring frankly at where the tibia and fibula had been amputated, a flap of skin folded over. 'They've done a neat job with this.' And Walter could only shudder, close his eyes and grit his teeth. 'It's all right, Walter. Truly. There are far worse things; we both know that.'

He met David's steady gaze, loving those small creases at the edges of his eyes, noticing a small mole at the hairline of unruly, tawny hair.

'No need to hide this, or *anything*, from me.' Captain Harvey would have been a dab hand at putting men at ease, preparing them to face what might come.

Walter submitted, stretching out his damaged leg, pointing to an old woollen sock on the floor. 'I put padding under; stops it rubbing.' He found himself telling David about Molly and her knitting.

Walter rested a hand on David's shoulder, feeling his firm grip under the knee as he positioned the prosthetic in place.

'Rather like harnessing a horse.' David smiled. 'I'm well practised at that. First time's bound to be a little clumsy...

There! There. I believe I've done it.' He buckled the strap, sat back on his heels, smiling in triumph.

Walter lips stretched into a smile of relief. 'I'll get dressed, won't be long.'

'Wait!' David placed a hand on his thigh. 'You know, I don't think we'll be missed. Old Flothers can make toasted crumpets and tea for the others.'

'But it's his birthday, isn't it?'

'I expect there'll be cake. I've a bottle of wine with me. We can go if you wish, but what do you say we give it a miss?'

He weighed up the situation, hesitated. 'Happy to. Miss it, I mean. I can m-m-manage tea, p-possibly biscuits.' How dare that stammer reappear! He took a steadying breath. 'And whisky. I believe there's still whisky.' How much, he wasn't sure. He was taking a tot before bedtime, and most afternoons.

David leapt to his feet. 'Tell you what. Don't budge. Not an inch.' He unbuckled his knapsack and produced a bottle of red wine. The empty bag was on his shoulder. 'Give me fifteen minutes – ten – I'll cycle back.'

'I'd rather dress,' Walter said.

'I'd rather you wouldn't. This is your home. Promise you won't.'

Again, Walter nodded. The door opened, banged shut, and he heard leather-soled shoes striking a linoleum stair.

Reaching for the whisky, in a chipped everyday glass, he noticed his hand trembling. The amber liquid shimmered, and he tried to calm the surface before taking a sip. What had been meant to encourage his playing might be needed to fortify his moral courage. As he sipped, he wondered how strong he was. Then he wondered what was so important for David to leave.

He didn't move from the chair; instead, he filled the following minutes, which seemed an eternity, with the knotty problem of those bars of music that refused to resolve themselves to his satisfaction. With a pencil, he tried something new.

Footsteps. Taking the stairs two at a time.

'Quesnel, I was thinking.' David charged into the room, face shining with sweat, removing a bulging knapsack.

'Sorry?'

'Your false leg! Needs a name. Quesnel means "small oak" in French. It is carved from oak, isn't it? What do you say?'

Laughter burst from him. What a joy to laugh. 'I hadn't thought to give the bloody thing a name. I've cursed it often enough.'

David rummaged in his bag, then, to Walter's astonishment, produced a garment – a brown and blue plaid dressing gown – tossed it to the floor, rummaged again. First an old carpet slipper then another landed with a soft thud.

'We should both be comfortable, I was thinking.' David's jacket was off, unbuttoning his shirt, kicking off shoes. And there he stood, in just his underwear, before shaking out his dressing gown and sliding arms into sleeves. 'Here we go!' He stretched out his arms and spun around.

The two of them laughed. Loudly. Freely. Stupidly.

Walter stood to face his friend. 'There's a lock on the door.'

'Quite!' David was there in a second. The key turned.

'Quesnel,' Walter said. 'I rather feel that's better suited for a horse. Besides, it sounds formal considering I'm on intimate terms with this.' He extended his false foot. 'I'm thinking Quinny. Nina used to sometimes call me Twinny.'

'A toast to Quinny and Twinny. Please don't tell me you haven't a corkscrew, otherwise I'll be haring through the streets on my bike wearing this, and I may get arrested.'

'Top drawer, with the cutlery. You'll find glasses there. Tumblers, nothing fancy. How delicious, how absolutely splendid. I'm so p-pleased you're here,' Walter called.

David returned with the opened bottle of wine and two glasses. He looked thoughtful before setting them down. 'It's not always easy, is it? The war. Everything. It's never easy.' His eyes appealed. 'But sometimes… sometimes, we must face…'

Walter stepped forwards and kissed David firmly on the lips. Rarely had he felt so bold. He heard a soft sigh of breath, tasted a salty upper lip, worried his moustache might be scratchy. It was remarkably easy. The two of them stood in their ridiculous dressing gowns, arms wrapped around each other, bodies pressed tight. As their mouths sucked hungrily, he was both physically unable and mentally unwilling to stop. This act of man-loving did not feel either grotesque or unwholesome but as nature intended. At least for him.

'Come.' He led David to his bedroom.

50

FOR ALL THAT MONTE CARLO WAS EVERY BIT AS bright and as fashionable, Nina felt that little less intoxicated, that little bit removed.

Charlie was on her mind – was often on her mind – as she strolled the promenade that morning, smoking her first cigarette of the day. Relationships were difficult – they'd quarrelled, Charlie and her. Before she'd left, he'd said, 'Best quit while we're still ahead. You're way too classy for me, you know that, right?'

'Too classy, or just too white?' The thump on his arm told him what she thought of that. 'You want to see other girls? Is that it?' She couldn't help imagining him in the arms of others, knowing how girls threw themselves at hot musicians.

'Come on, sugar.' He rolled his eyes. 'All I'm saying is that while you're away doing your dancing, you think about it. For now, let's take a break.'

She wondered if Diaghilev had any relationship now Nijinsky had left; if so, he was discrete, though she sensed rising tensions with Massine.

'Moths, don't you think?' Hilda pointed to a clutch of women dancers hovering around the Russian star. Earlier on tour, one ballerina-moth had flown too close and was summarily fired. Keep away from Massine, the clear message.

Soon they'd be in Paris, then London, which held the possibility of patching things up with Charlie. And Walter and Edith's wedding. Coals of simmering anger flared whenever she thought about *that*. She'd not seen her brother and prospective sister-in-law since last August.

It was at Margate. She and Edith had been swimming, Walter sitting in cream linen trousers in the shade, as he resisted displaying his damaged body, so would not swim. Charlie was with them, not a swimmer either. While Charlie strolled along the beach to an ice cream kiosk, promising to hurry back before they melted, Nina grabbed her opportunity. But how to broach it? As she towelled her wet hair, she allowed her words to shoot forth.

'Look, you two. We're all going our own ways soon and I must talk about this – you getting married, I mean.'

'Oh, you want to be a bridesmaid!' Edith teased. 'Of course, how ill-mannered of me not to have asked!'

'You know that's not it.'

Walter had swung his legs off the deck chair and stared at her. 'You think you know me, but you don't. I've told Edith about Alexei—'

'Yes, Nina. I've always suspected this about Walter.' It was Edith's turn to look her in the eye. 'People can love in different ways. Sometimes one needs to explore, find out about yourself. Alexei sounds like he was a radiant and worthy young man for Walter. I'm very glad they loved each other.'

'Ooph! That's generous of you.' Nina let out a long breath. 'In that case, Walter, promise me you really want this, and you won't hurt Edith. You're both very important to me, but I tell you, brother, if you fudge this, if you are using marriage as a, as a *cover*—'

'What are you suggesting?' Walter's neck had gone splodgy and it wasn't from the sun.

'Then I'll never talk to you again.'

'Must you be so dramatic?' Walter said.

'Don't be an idiot.' She landed a gentle thump on the arm. 'But I feel strongly!'

'Nina, listen.' Edith draped a sun-warmed arm across her shoulder. 'You and I have known each other longer than you've known Walter. I know you and I know you mean well, but please believe I honestly think Walter and I can make marriage work. We've decided to wait till next summer when he's had a year to decide on London or Oxford. I'm willing to move.'

'Fair enough.' Nina nodded. 'Fair enough, then.' Looking at them, and hearing them speak, made Nina wonder if they'd shared a bed together. She couldn't help but feel marriage was one of Edith's social experiments. 'I've said what I wanted to say.'

'Good.' Walter looked relieved. 'There's an end to it, and here's Charlie with our ices.'

One lingering look at a shimmering Mediterranean – she might swim later – a final suck on the cigarette stub, then she set off to prepare for Cecchetti's class. Massine had been elevated to ballet master working on *Pulcinella*, involving most of the principals. It was wonderful having Madame Karsavina back with them, among the shifting line-up of dancers tempted from Russia. Might Nina Rosova ever get promoted? Was she destined to be one of the leaping hordes of gypsy dancers or canoodling in a harem? In a few weeks' time, she would be twenty-five and needed to look ahead.

On arriving in London fresh from a successful Paris season, she phoned Charlie.

'It's me. I'm back. Can we meet? I'd like to, if you—'

'Hey…' And with that voice, she was wobbly kneed. 'Sure. Drop by. I'm sharing with two other fellows.'

'You seeing anyone, Charlie?' Fingers crossed.

'Ah, come on…' What did that mean? Yes or no?

She pressed on. 'But do you *want* to get together?'

'I guess Sam and I can swap rooms – he's got the big bed.'

She made her way to the address in Shoreditch, had dressed nicely and popped her birth control cap into her bag, just in case. It took ages for Charlie to answer her knocking.

'Sorry, been napping,' he offered.

Eyes that had once been shining and clear were bloodshot, lanky frame thinner.

'Hello, Charlie. It's been a while.' She kissed him lightly on the lips, drawing back at the sourness of his breath, then stepped inside where she paused and harrumphed.

'Didn't have time to tidy,' Charlie said, picking up and closing a small container – not before she'd glimpsed white powder.

She took in the array of empty bottles and lingering odour of alcohol, tobacco, and unfamiliar smells. 'How can you live like this!'

'Long hours. Just want to relax. You know how it is.'

'I know everything there is to know about long hours.' Her face reflected her disappointment as she removed an ashtray full of hand-rolled cigarette ends, then gingerly lowered herself onto the chair. 'You alone?'

'Others are sleepin'. Can I get you something to drink?'

She settled on a glass of water.

As they chatted, hearing that familiar rumbling voice, she could feel the stirring of what had sparked her love for this man: his passion for music, his warm nature. But not *this*. Looking around the room, her gaze returned to the black

American who was sliding into a life she feared might suck him into a mire.

'Oh Charlie!' She stood, crossed to where he sat, wrists dangling on lanky legs, and bent to kiss him lightly on the forehead. 'You've lost weight. You've got to look after yourself.'

'Yeah.' He shrugged.

'Don't you see? I can't live here. I want us to be together, and you do want that too, don't you?'

His longing eyes answered her.

'But you've got to make changes. Remember, you said I was too classy for you, but, honestly, you're too classy for *this*.' Her gaze took in everything. 'But you've got to want to make those changes, as I can't do it for you.' *And I've no time for this*, she was thinking.

'Yeah,' he said again, not meeting her eyes.

'I hate seeing you like this, Charlie.' She ran her fingers through his hair and met his eyes. 'I do want you, but…' She pulled away.

She left soon after, saying, 'Contact me at the theatre, yes?'

She settled in with Ma and Sid – suffocated by the dreariness of older people and their set ways but not wanting to waste her pittance of a salary on lodging with some of the girls. Besides, Ma liked having her at home. And there was the familiarity of curling up in Mo's chair for a chinwag with Ma, sitting across from her.

Some days after opening, Charlie left a message at the Opera House stage door – hadn't sought to speak with her – the scribbled note on a scrap of paper merely giving the address of Dalton's Club he was playing at. *Come if you want to.* Nina was stung by his casual words. There was no *I'd like you to come.* Had she relegated herself from star position to… what? Could they even remain friends? It hurt to realise they'd drifted so far but as a matter of principle she'd not reached out. *He* was the one who needed to change.

Knowing a real club musician made her popular.

'We must go!' she was urged. 'Book a table under the Ballets Russes name, that'll get us a good spot!' And it did.

Eyes followed her onstage at the Opera House, then she'd changed from her exotic *Scheherazade* costume, cleansed her face of stage make-up and transformed again. This time into a two-tone turquoise silk dress cut on the bias, ending mid-calf, and a silk ribbon band across her forehead, diamantes and fluffy feathers at her right ear. She applied brilliant red lipstick, slipped on her favourite red strappy evening shoes, then led her party of glittering, young dancers through the streets of Soho. Heads turned, eyes following these exotic chattering creatures of the night. Into Charlie's club and to a table near the stage, they were, she noticed, a cut-above the heaving mass of drinking, dancing Londoners out to party. Charlie noticed her, saluting her with a raised trumpet. She meant to impress him, show the gap that'd widened between them. Yet seeing him on the stand – black suit, white shirt, hair slicked down – he looked so handsome, and she remembered why she had passionately loved him.

Charlie's five-piece band took her breath away. A crooning light tenor, brass, piano, and a thrashing drummer, all of them under Charlie's leadership, putting swing and slide into music you just *had* to dance to. As the singer announced "Royal Garden Blues", she grabbed one of the men from her company and joined the other fox-trotting couples on the floor.

Sometime later, she was aware of a ruckus, the band coming to a halt. A table clattered over, two men in double-breasted suits and spats.

'Outta my face, before I take it out for ya,' one shouted.

The other insisting, 'Get yaself another spot.'

'Out! Out of me club!' A determined, slightly built Irish woman set about sorting out the brawl.

The men ignored her, trading blows.

'Ah, no. Not here, ye don't,' the woman insisted. 'Ye can take yourselves out… Fuckin' hell!' She staggered, scattering chairs. 'Out!' she screamed, and two burly men rushed up, ejecting the troublemakers. The woman – Kate, Nina was informed – cooly rubbed her hands together, motioning to the band to play on.

A man near Nina's table shrugged. 'Turf wars.'

'Well, Nina,' one of her gang tittered, 'what den of iniquity have you brought us to?'

Nina shared a wide-eyed look with her friends. 'Rather more than I bargained for.' And they all laughed.

Later, the singer took the microphone. 'The next song's for all the lovely ladies here, especially for the ballerinas lighting up our club tonight.'

Charlie put aside his trumpet, leapt off the stand and was at her side, leaning close. 'Don't turn me down,' he said softly. 'I've told the fellows about you.'

She was on her feet in an instant.

The singer began, cut-glass enunciation, "A Pretty Girl is like a Melody".

It was magic. Two exotic birds turning heads again as, bodies close, she and Charlie rocked together.

'You look a feast.' Charlie's eyes devoured her. 'Too good for the likes of me, I guess.'

She leant in, tiptoeing close to an ear, hissing: 'You make it sound like a man reaching up from the gutter. That's not you, Charlie.'

'Well, yeah…' He didn't know how to respond.

The song was over far too quickly. There was much more she wanted to say. Far more she wanted to do, her body on fire for this man. He was about to jump back onto the stand when she grabbed his arm. 'Charlie. I'll wait. But we're not going to your place.'

The hotel room around the corner was a step up from Charlie's house – just. The sheets on the bed, not fresh. They stood on the threadbare carpet and began circling in a cautious dance, a light-skinned woman in vibrant peacock blues, a dark-skinned man in sombre black and white.

'You look a fine man tonight,' she told him, removing her sparkly headband.

'I miss you,' he said, loosening his bow tie. 'Thing is, whenever I think I have you, you're off again. Leaves a man, you know, kind of empty. Gotta fill it with something.'

'And someone?' She heeled off one shoe, then the other.

'But no one special.' He'd shrugged off his jacket.

'I'm special, Charlie.'

'Oh, I know that. I sure know that. You're my girl – if you wanna be.' Charlie was on his knees, had reached under her skirt to release a stocking. 'Oh, sugar,' he whispered.

And even as she melted with desire, her brain would not let up. 'And so are you – special, I mean. I don't want to see you ruin the gifts you have.' She had a dancer's view on what that meant, her body her instrument. Champagne and cigarettes aside, she looked after herself. 'I've missed you, Charlie.'

Her dress draped over the chair where she flung it, Charlie's suit a crumpled pile on the floor.

'Wait!' She pushed him away and dug around in her bag. 'Damn! Charlie, have you rubber jonnies with you?' He did, and Nina swung between relief and wondering if he *always* carried them.

Making love, the iron bed headboard rattling against the wall, bodies sheened in sweat, released her into a frenzy of moans and shrill shrieks. She determined Charlie was worth fighting for.

'Oh Charlie, this feels so right! I do love you.'

'Me too, but when you're not here I get lonesome. All the fellas take stuff.'

'I'm a dancer. I tour.' Some things could not be given up.

51

THE WEDDING. MY WEDDING. WALTER HAD WRANGLED
with the idea for so long, spurning the possessive, but now it
must be owned.

Nina's rebuke had burnt itself into his brain. And she was
right – he must not *deliberately* hurt Edith. She must be given
the opportunity to back out of their engagement, and that
required admitting to David. While Edith knew of his Oxford
friend, she, possibly, didn't appreciate the depth of his feelings.
Feelings that were unlikely to change. He was being an utter
coward and that would not do.

When Edith next visited, they spent Saturday morning
walking in the Meadow. With heart thundering, he plucked
up courage.

'I had dinner with David the other day. I've spoken of him.'

'Not so much recently.' Edith shot him a glance. 'So, you're
seeing him still?'

'Yes. Quite regularly.'

Edith stooped to pluck a daisy. 'I assumed there might be,
would likely be, casual men friends…' She stood twirling it in
her fingers. 'But is he a special friend? Like Alexei?'

A breath. 'And so much more.'

Edith turned aside, but not before he caught her startled

look. 'I'm sorry, Edith. I – *we*, that is – hope to know each other always.' He ran the back of his hand across his brow. Done. Owned. 'Are you sure marrying me is right for you? I'll understand if—'

'Stop!' Edith swallowed what seemed like an obstruction in her throat before saying, 'May I meet him? I'd like to meet him. I *should* meet him, I think.'

He paused, before saying: 'David says the same. But I'm not entirely sure…'

'Dearest, as I will not be your only *special* friend,' he was assured by her touch to his cheek, 'it's right we all become acquainted.'

'Shall I see what he's doing tomorrow? Too early, you think?'

'Not in the least. Let's make the most of my being here. Somewhere outside; the weather should hold.' She cleared her throat. 'Just in case it's difficult and I feel the need to dash off.'

It was arranged. They would meet at the jetty by St Hilda's. 'As you're bringing the lady, I'll bring the hamper,' David offered.

Next day, Edith took his arm as they walked to the river. She, normally an indifferent dresser, was wearing a becoming cornflower blue outfit – dress and matching hat.

'New?' he asked.

She coloured. 'I popped to the shops yesterday afternoon. Oxford has some lovely ones.' She squeezed his arm. 'Silly of me, but I'm a little on edge.'

Of a precipice, all of us, he thought, returning her squeeze. He waved. 'There he is.'

'Ah.' Edith gripped him tighter.

David was shading his eyes, watching them, and it made him walk even more stiffly, fumbling with his cane. The distance between them was taking ages to close. Then they were before each other.

Introductions and handshakes.

'Pleasure to meet you.'

'And you.'

'And what a glorious day we have.'

'Isn't it?'

'Splendid,' Walter found himself saying, the others quickly agreeing.

David, dressed in cream blazer and flannels, extended a hand to Edith, 'Allow me,' before turning to him, gripping his hand and elbow firmly. And for that second their gazes held, he was comforted by the steadiness he saw in them.

Carefully, right foot followed by Quinny, he stepped into the shallow punt, settling on the hard bench next to Edith, the promised hamper already stowed. David boarded, untied, and with a cheery, 'Off we go,' began poling.

He was reminded of the time, ten years ago, when he had been persuaded by Rose to meet Nina after a ballet class. It had not gone well, and Rose had wrung her hands. 'Oh dear, I'm meant to be the glue to bind you two. I've made a terrible job of it, haven't I? You didn't even get to shake hands. No chance of sticking until that happens.'

He eyed the hamper, knowing it contained a picnic rug, Pimm's, mixer drinks, cheeses, bread and cakes, wondering if his stomach would unclench enough to enjoy their picnic.

'Walter tells me you are a stalwart of the Labour Party. Do tell me what you're up to?' David invited Edith.

'Gosh, well, you know... I was furious the other day hearing about this girl who'd been sacked for talking about trade union things during work hours...'

And Walter listened as she spoke with passion about her work, knowing that David was genuinely interested, as he would be. He smiled, feeling this might bind them a little.

'Tell me, Edith, what do you make of Walter's music? His compositions. He won't play for me.'

'Oh, me neither!' Edith laughed. 'But let's not hold that against him.'

Before long, Edith turned the conversation. 'I can't help feeling a little nervous—'

'Oh good! Not just me.' David laughed.

'Or *me*,' Walter chorused.

'But truly, I am pleased to meet you,' Edith said. 'You're just as Walter described, so I feel I know you a little already.'

'And I you.' David held the pole in the water, steering their craft midstream. 'I want you to know I care deeply for Walter.'

He felt Edith's hand on his thigh. 'As do I,' she said. 'I love him, you know.' That hand squeezed a little.

'As do I,' came from the darling man who was punting.

Words blurted forth. 'And I'm so grateful.' It was such extraordinarily good fortune to find he was lovable. With hands to his heart where that burn mark persisted, he pressed on. 'I offer m-my own deep love… But… it's, it's different.' That wasn't a lie. There was only so much passion any person could generate. At least he imagined so. 'Yes, *differently*,' he asserted.

Their punt slid through the water, all of them silent, birdsong and summer voices about them. David poled on, manoeuvring past a punt with four loud-voiced students.

'Well, there it is.' Edith sighed, patting his hand. He smiled at her, thankful this wonderful woman wished to throw her lot in with his.

'Yes,' David said, laughing. 'There it is. We can pull in a little bit further. There's a terrific spot on the bank.'

By the time they lounged on the rug, two glasses of Pimm's down, Walter felt calmer. It was going well with goodwill on all sides to ease the mood.

In the following weeks, they met on two further occasions, Edith and David getting the measure of the other, all thrashing out what must be navigated.

David sanguine enough to joke: 'Can't I be your best man, Walter?'

Edith laughing: 'Better that you are Walter's "best man" after our marriage, not *at* the wedding. Besides, I should then have a bridesmaid, and I suspect Nina wouldn't relish that role.'

'Ah, Nina,' David said, 'I should like to meet her.'

'Not yet!' he and Edith said in unison. One step at a time.

'It's a small affair. I really don't want a fuss about this wedding.' Or this marriage?

But it was a bigger gathering than he had wished. On the appointed morning, a dozen came to Old Marylebone Town Hall – one of the smaller rooms – Edith in the same summer-weight blue suit, a bouquet of orange blossom and roses, he in a light-grey linen suit, a rosebud in a buttonhole.

'And I brought this for you.' Rose tied a red-ribboned bow at the top of his cane. 'Dear Walter… Dear Edith…' And she was wiping her eyes for no reason.

He watched Nina arrive, in a muted green suit, Charlie at her side, striding towards him. After they'd hugged, he touched the silk multi-coloured scarf at her throat. 'I recall choosing this.'

'You see, Twinny, I'm not always careless. I've kept it safe all these years.' She took a breath. 'I didn't really want to come, you know.'

'But you're here.' He held her at arm's length, holding her gaze. 'Thank you. And you, Charlie.' He turned to the man in her life, *their glue still holding*, his unspoken thought. 'Good to see you.'

'Hey, Walter, good to see you; you're looking well.' Charlie held his right hand in both of his. 'Am I allowed to kiss your bride?'

'Edith!' His soon-to-be wife hurried over.

Edith's family were there. A mother – a thin, nervy woman he'd met quite recently. 'No father-in-law to worry about,' Edith had reminded him, the heavy-handed man, 'Long gone, and good riddance.' A brother and two sisters he barely knew, one with children in tow. And Sid, of course, as well as a couple of Edith's friends. He'd not invited anyone.

Seeing the room filling, people taking their chairs, he took fright. 'So many people,' he whispered to Edith, suddenly terrified at those eyes and ears witnessing him taking his vows.

'Good morning.' The friendly middle-aged male celebrant raised his voice, quieting chit-chat. 'On behalf of Edith Florence Blevins and Walter Arthur Roberts, I would like to extend a warm welcome…'

The minimum was spoken. 'I am,' he replied when asked if he was free lawfully to marry. 'I do,' he replied at the appropriate moment. The register signed, formalities over barely before it had begun.

'A little rushed, I thought,' Rose said. 'You might've had some music.'

Photos followed on the porticoed steps. He and Edith. The two of them with their families. Everyone grouped together. Then it was over.

'Well, I hope you'll be happy.' His sister managed to find the words as she kissed first Edith then him on the cheeks. 'Happy honeymoon, and all that. Where are you off to, by the way?'

'The Lakes,' he said. 'Train's late this afternoon.' He'd promised to phone David when they reached their destination. Truth was, they'd promised to stay in touch throughout the week.

'Have fun,' Nina said. 'Where are we going now? Drinks and so on?'

'Oh, goodness, we hadn't thought.' Edith looked surprised at this oversight, and he felt a stab of guilt, imagining they'd slope off. 'Shocking. We passed some cafés further along.'

Rose overheard. 'Really, Edith *and* Walter, this won't do. I'm cross with you both. If I'd known earlier...'

Nina burst out laughing. 'You're hopeless, you two. A little romance wouldn't go amiss. I only came for the champagne, now I'm denied even that!'

Rose hurried away, calling, 'Florrie,' and Walter saw his mother-in-law – he had to get used to that relationship – flutter her hands as Rose explained. Then Rose was back at his side. 'Right. I know exactly where we're going.'

In dribs and drabs, their wedding party dispersed, travelling by cab, bus, and Underground. In Regent Street, Walter ushered Edith into the Café Royal, saying, 'I used to come here as a child, special treats with Father. And you know, I first met Rose here.'

'Fabulous, isn't it.' Edith looked in awe at the blue ceilings and columns edged in gold.

'The place hasn't changed.' *But I've changed*, he thought.

He listened as Rose sobbed real tears, telling the manager, 'We've been let down; we'll never book *there* again! We're desperate for luncheon for this special occasion. Please... Yes, yes. That sounds delicious... Can it be prepared quickly? Train to catch, you see... *That* much? Can you offer a special price? I've been a regular here for *decades*...'

It could be done. Customers politely requested to vacate seats and move to other tables. Crisp white tablecloths shaken and smoothed out. Silver cutlery clattered and glasses clinked.

A white-aproned fellow – old, but not the same one Walter recalled – held out an arm. 'This way.'

It was Rose who led their party through the crowd, beaming. 'I do love this place. Excuse us.'

At the tug on his sleeve, he turned to see Nina looking at him intently, eyebrows raised. He spoke softly, 'It's all right. You'll see. We'll be fine.'

A knot was forming in his stomach, and he wondered, again, if this wasn't a massive mistake.

52

Backstage at the Liverpool Olympia, Nina rang Dalton's at a time she expected the band to be setting up and got Kate Meyrick on the line.

'Nina Banbury, you say? Listen, pet, I don't allow private calls.'

'If you please, Mrs Meyrick, it's very important I speak with Charlie.' Nina put on her quality voice. 'I'm touring with the Russian Ballet.' It was September and she was back on the road – a provincial tour, lots of old rep – with Massine working on a new *Rite of Spring*.

'Ah, I recall. Important, ye say. Bound to be bad news. Always is.' Kate Meyrick's voice was matter of fact. 'Just this once then and don't make a habit of it... Charlie! Get yourself in here and keep it quick!'

Nina waited, knowing this call would cost her a lump from her wages. From the London end, she heard Kate saying: 'It's that ballet dancer girl, wantin' ye.'

Then Charlie's voice: 'Nina? That you?'

'Oh Charlie. Terrible news. Terrible—'

'What's happened? You hurt? Someone dead?'

'I can't have a baby,' she wailed into the mouthpiece.

'Whoa... How did th...?' Charlie's voice crackled along the wire. 'You sure?'

'Oh, how I hate this! And yes, yes, I'm sure. Haven't had my monthlies and the other night I barely made it offstage before puking! *Everyone* knows.'

'May I have a moment, ma'am?' Charlie's muffled voice suggested a hand over his handpiece, but the sharp-tongued Irish woman reached Nina through her earpiece. 'A kid, isn't it? Got six m'self. Blessed Jesus, you been makin' trouble for yourself?'

'Mrs Meyrick, please?' came Charlie's voice. 'Nina, what you wanna do about it?'

'I'm coming back to London. Grigoriev's given me time off. I'm getting rid of it!'

She heard the flinch in his voice: ''Cos I'm a black man?'

'I'd never be ashamed of having your baby. I just don't want any man's baby – or to get married right now.'

'Okay,' came Charlie's cautious voice. 'I guess that's okay, but can you hold on? I'd like to pray on the matter.'

'Pray!' she screeched.

'I still do, you know. I guess that surprises you.' The idea that Charlie had a place for God in his new life *did* surprise her. 'Promise, Nina, you won't be hasty about this?'

'Can't wait long, but yes, yes. Promise. This is so lousy! Makes me want to join a nunnery!'

Charlie managed to laugh as they ended the call. She steeled herself, imagining the conversation she'd have with Ma. That could wait a day or two till they were face to face. Nina stroked her belly, aware of a slight thickening, as a near three-month foetus began to take shape – a bit of her and Charlie. She couldn't help wondering at the miracle of a baby from such a simple act as having sex. She frowned, wondering why she'd felt the need to phone Charlie. Was there a tiny part of her that thought this beginning-baby deserved a life?

Back in London, Ma's reaction was just as she had expected.

'Oh, Nina. Are the Banbury women fated to go off the rails?'

'What a thing to say! I'm not a train!'

'My beauty was my downfall. But you…?'

Ma was eyeing her, not quite daring to say her sharp features weren't a patch on her own at a similar age. And Ma had been pretty in a rounded, soft way that was fashionable back then, before her body spread and her face coarsened.

'My looks will last,' was the best retort she could make. Which was true. Her eyes were inquisitive, her slender body never likely to become plump. 'Any rate, this'll be gone soon. I've booked in.'

'I don't know.' Ma shook her head. 'After all, you'd have to raise a brown-skinned baby—'

'Ma, please!'

The day before she was due at a discreet clinic, she met Edith for lunch, Edith looking as crisp as ever in her woollen suit.

Nina kissed her on the cheek. 'When are you joining Walter?'

'There's a delay with the house. But I don't mind. We're very busy at work and Walter doesn't mind either.'

Nina would give a lot to know the ins and outs of their relationship, but when she had probed, asking if they'd had good fun in the Lake District, Walter had replied, 'Splendid,' with Edith adding, 'Yes, we walked – or rather I walked a lot and Walter a little.'

They chatted about inconsequential things, then, with meals on the table, Edith placed a hand over hers. 'I don't imagine we're meeting for a sister-in-law chat – though that'd be welcome. But I'm curious why you're back in London.'

'I'm pregnant. Charlie's, of course—'

'Wonderful!'

'No, it's jolly well not!' She lowered her voice. 'I'm taking time away from the company to get it sorted –booked in tomorrow actually.'

'Oh, Nina.' Edith's face went splodgy. 'Please don't do that. Please.'

'You're not going all religious on me.'

'No. No. I don't believe in *that*.' Tears were welling in Edith's eyes. 'But… It's just… The world has lost so many young men. Butchered.'

Suddenly the lamb stew was losing its appeal and Nina pushed it aside. 'It's not like I'm killing an actual human. In any case, if it were to be a boy, why raise it only to be slaughtered in some new war?'

'There won't be another. Not after this one. There mustn't.'

'Who knows.'

'Oh Nina, I would love to have a baby. But… oh dear. I wonder if I ever will. I thought on the honeymoon we'd—'

'Please don't tell me you and Walter haven't—'

'Hush!' Edith glanced around the café. With the fingers of her right hand, she fiddled with the gold band on her left ring finger.

Nina opened her cigarette case, lighting one for herself. 'Well?'

Edith opened her mouth to say something, before taking a breath and starting again. 'I'm a pragmatist – you know that of me – and I approached marriage like women's right to vote or workers' rights. You seek to change how people *think* about things. Only this is about *feeling*. I thought—'

'Edith, you idiot.'

'We do love each other. Truly we do. Walter is the sweetest man, only…'

Nina watched Edith's face dissolve. Beneath "political Edith", Nina saw a woman whose emotional needs were not being met. She had to know. Just had to. She leant across the table, whispering, 'Tell me. Plain and simple. Have you and my brother exercised what the courts like to call conjugal rights?'

That made Edith laugh. 'What a delicious term! One rather anticipated it on marriage. Oh dear. I'm not sure Walter would like me talking about such intimate things, but, what the heck. It remains an *ambition*, let us say.'

'Edith!'

'I do so want a child.' Now Edith leant forwards, their faces nearly touching over their barely touched luncheon. 'The war, Nina. You've no idea how this still affects him.'

'I lived with Walter, remember, I saw him. Is he not better now?'

'I'm not sure they'll ever be really better. It does something to a man. You can see it in him, and others.'

'Oh.' Nina jolted. 'I would have thought memories would be like an illness you get over in time. But can Walter love *any* woman? Intimately. You deserve that, Edith.'

'Walter and I would be loving parents. He's coming up to London soon, collecting one or two things he's stored and taking back. No doubt we'll persevere and before long I'll swoon and melt as they do in the cinema.' Edith's voice dropped. 'Please don't tell anyone we've had this conversation. Certainly not Walter.'

'Certainly not!'

Edith looked thoughtful. 'He's a good man.'

'I know.' He was unlikely to become a drunken brute and clobber her, as Edith's own father had done to her mother.

'Sorry, I was thinking of Charlie. You two could marry—'

'We've talked about it, but…' A frown between her eyes deepened.

Edith placed a hand on hers. 'It's your life, but I'd love you to bring a child into the world to make up for just one of those broken men over there.'

Nina left the café in a state of confusion. She had no moral qualms about ridding herself of an unwanted pregnancy, but what Edith said niggled at her. Did she have a duty to procreate for Mother England? That didn't sit well.

Later that afternoon, she made her way to the 43 Club. As she waited for Charlie, Mrs Meyrick handed her a basin of water and damp cloth.

'Make yourself useful, why don't ye. I'm short today.' So Nina wiped tables sticky with last night's spilt alcohol, while Mrs Meyrick railed about staff. 'These girls, ye know, picky about wages!'

'Hey!' Charlie spotted her first. 'New job?' He grinned as he placed his hands on her waist and kissed her. 'Well?' He looked deep into her eyes. 'You set on keeping your appointment?'

'I've talked with Ma and Edith. And with Hilda. She's here working on a new ballet.'

'Hilda. She's got a kid, right?'

'She reminded me – as if I didn't need reminding – of how difficult it is to be a mother and a dancer.'

'But she *does* do both, all the same.'

'She's a more dedicated dancer than mother. Even *she* says.'

'So?' Charlie's hand stroked her stomach.

She met his gaze. 'I'm doing it, Charlie. I'm not ready to be a mother – a *good* mother. And you're not ready to be a *good* father. Maybe one day that'll be different.'

'Don't like it. But…' Charlie rocked her in a tight embrace. 'Okay, sugar. Okay.'

The next day Nina kept her appointment then got a cab to Ma's house where, sitting in Mo's old chair, a cup of tea next to her, she sobbed and sobbed, her body aching, her mind in turmoil.

'How about inviting someone over,' Ma suggested. 'A lady friend, I'm thinking.'

'They're all on tour. Except Hilda.'

When Hilda found time to visit she had little inclination for sympathy, simply saying, 'Better this way, I'm sure.'

Seeing her friend looking frazzled, Nina asked, 'How are rehearsals going?'

'Working with Massine is easy, he's always very clear about what he wants, and I'm writing everything in notebooks, but still…' Hilda grasped her hands. 'Oh, Nina, if you are feeling up to it, please come and help. I don't know how I'll cope otherwise. You won't have to do anything energetic. Will you, please?' Hilda was calculating the weeks till she'd be centre stage on the Théâtre des Champs-Elysées for opening night. When Diaghilev had decided to revive Rite, he had set the premiere for December in Paris. With the rest of the company touring the North of England, Massine was working with Hilda on the plum role of the Chosen Maiden. Assisting Hilda was the least she could do.

Next morning, Nina made her way to the basement studio in Maiden Lane. She heard the rehearsal before seeing it: a burst of staccato piano from the climax of Stravinsky's score. She waited outside the door, hearing soft thuds as Hilda leapt and landed, Massine's voice counting. At a pause, she slipped in. She was expected, and Massine barely glanced at her from under those black brows while continuing to think and demonstrate a sequence of steps. Hilda was already in a soggy state, strands of hair sticking to her forehead and nape of her neck. Nina settled on the floor by the piano with a notebook of her own. It was fiendishly difficult, and as in that earlier visualisation of the score, Nina could see the conflict between rhythm and melody. *Jeté… jeté…* and more. Surely this was even harder, more athletic than Nijinsky's choreography. To help Hilda, she needed to be analytical – focus on counts and steps – yet she was drawn into those convulsions and tremors, that toil and heat of life fighting death. Days earlier she had ended a life beginning inside her and now these hard notes pounding the keyboard: death. Death. Death. She shivered.

Later that morning, Vera arrived and settled beside her. Small pecks on cheeks, and, 'Hello, darling.' Vera, Nina understood, was destined to become one of their ballerinas and was learning the *Les Sylphides* mazurka.

'How are you?' Vera whispered, her pretty eyes wide with meaning.

'All sorted,' she whispered back.

'You're so brave.' Vera shuddered. And Nina could only shrug.

With the pianist's hands ready to crash down in a fresh sequence of clashing chords, Massine clapped and called a halt.

'No more. We are done for today.' Even he was breathless. 'You have it? You're sure you have it?'

'Yes, Léonide Feodorovich,' Hilda managed with a small bow of thanks before collecting her own notebook and bag.

'Madame Savina, you are ready?' Massine said.

'Yes, Léonide Feodorovich.' Vera gave her warm bright-eyed smile. No longer plain Vera Clark but Vera Savina. 'I warmed up in the dressing room.'

'Good.' Massine rubbed his hands. 'That will be all,' Massine told their pianist, who closed the sheet music. For the *Sylphides* rehearsal, Massine had the convenience of a gramophone and recordings of Chopin's short piano pieces. Nina could not imagine a time when anyone would be able to record sections of *Rite*, as it was beyond most orchestras.

In the little dressing room, with Hilda's and her own handwritten notes as an aid, along with a metronome, they began to work. Hilda would remind herself of what she had learnt, and Nina would keep count, helping her friend. This was a mechanical thing: having the brain and muscles learn by repetition. The art of interpretation Hilda would layer on later. First the skeleton, then the muscles and sinews, then the skin.

The following day, Hilda was in a lather. 'Oh Nina, I just don't remember what count I'm on here. Is it *five*? Or five *and*...? I must sort this, otherwise I'm wrong for the next bit when I repeat it. You see?' Between the bench and coat hooks in the dressing room, Hilda sketched the steps and her conundrum.

'Check with Massine.'

'Oh, I don't want to interrupt them.'

'He won't mind. Better you sort it than wait till tomorrow.'

Nearing the studio door, with Chopin's piano music drifting out, they tiptoed closer. Nina pushed open the door a crack. They had not been seen. Together they watched Massine rehearse their friend Vera, waiting for the right time to step inside. On the face of it, this was a normal rehearsal. And yet. Softly they closed the door and withdrew, speaking in whispers.

'Did you see the way he caressed her arm when he adjusted her position? Am I imagining it?' Hilda wanted to know.

'And he stood *so* close to her.'

'He never does that with me!' Hilda was wide-eyed in shock and some degree of jealousy. 'The way he *looked* at her!'

'And the way she laid her head on his chest—'

'And he kept her there, way longer than needed.' Hilda was almost spitting. 'Those doe-eyes of hers!'

'And what a soft-headed fool.' This Nina meant for their friend. Was Vera unaware of what was happening, was she so foolish to dice with the devil? Handsome Massine was forbidden fruit. All of them knew this on pain of expulsion, excommunication from the Church of Diaghilev. If he caught wind of this, there was no saying what might happen.

'Should we say something to Vera?' Nina said.

'No. We mustn't. In any case, next week we'll be back with the full company. I can't win on the beauty stakes, but I'll make the best of my role, pounding the floor into a pulp. You just wait! Can you work with me tomorrow, Nina?'

'It's Saturday. I've arranged to meet Walter. He'll be here for the weekend.'

'Walter! He knows the score. Please ask him to come. I need to show Massine he didn't make an error in choosing me. I need to show myself.'

And, Nina supposed, Hilda wanted to show Vera she too could excel. Hilda was not especially sylph material, more a reliable clay pot, compared to Vera's fine bone porcelain.

'I doubt Walter will have time,' Nina said. Or interest, she might have added. 'But I'll come by tomorrow regardless.'

Hilda nodded. 'But do ask him. Beg him from me, please.'

'Best give me the key. If he agrees, he'll want to come earlier to practise.'

53

WALTER FELT THE WEIGHT OF NINA'S REQUEST SETTLE on his shoulders. 'Sorry. Rose is expecting us for morning tea.'

'Make it lunch then.' At the end of the phone, Nina's voice rose in that "don't-make-a song-and-dance-about-it" way. 'Ma won't mind. In fact, Ma'll be thrilled you're helping on the ballet front. *Thrilled*. And I'm sure Edith won't give a jot.'

'Besides, I haven't played that piece for a long time. It's fiendishly difficult, I can't—'

'Really, Walter! Hilda doesn't expect concert standard, much less the whole score. I'm sure you can manage that section with one hand if necessary. If I could hum the bloody tune, I would. Please say you'll help. We've got a thing or two to prove to Mr Massine.'

He arrived at Chandos House at ten o'clock where Nina led him down, chatting all the while, then ushered him in to the studio. 'Here we go!

The basement rehearsal room held traces of gamey odour about it, and, to one side, a battered looking piano. Walter rested his cane against it and adjusted the height of the stool before settling, Nina placing the score on the music shelf. 'I'm sure you can find the right place – I'll know it when I hear it. There's a bit we want to sort out before Hilda rehearses with

Massine on Monday.'

He allowed Nina to flick through the pages, coming to rest at the section titled *Sacrificial Dance (The Chosen One)*.

'I'm not sure *exactly* which part, Walter. Perhaps it would be helpful to play from the start.'

He ran clammy hands along his trousers before placing fingertips cautiously on the keyboard. Seeing his hands trembling, he immediately dropped them to his lap.

'S-s-sorry, Nina. I, I can't do this.'

'Why ever not? You know this piece backwards, I'm sure. In any case, you can sight-read most things put before you.'

Walter stared at the cluster of notes indicating where he must place his fingers if he were to begin this thing.

Nina nudged him. 'We haven't got much time.'

He breathed deeply. Foolish to think he couldn't do it. Raising his hands, he forced himself to concentrate on the notes before him and began. Familiar sounds greeted him. He played slowly, cautiously exploring those alarming combinations of harmony and discordance he hadn't played for so long.

He could feel prickles of sweat under his armpits and his sight was blurring. Too much! Too many memories. The discords were not as Stravinsky intended, but from wrongly placed fingers. He stopped mid-bar.

'T-t-terribly s-sorry.' He could barely speak, voice part sob. He cleared his throat. 'I've not played this for years, you see. We'd best...' He gripped the edges of the piano and with his good foot pushed the stool back, only to find Nina blocking him.

'Walter, what's going on?' Her face showed confusion, and that stubborn look, determined to get to the bottom of things. 'Is it to do with Alexei? Is that it?'

'In part. Yes. That's part... of it.' He felt his voice strangled.

'Oh Walter.' Nina was squatting at his side, eyes alert to his misery. 'You still miss Alexei so very much?' Her hand rested lightly on his hands that he had somehow clenched again. 'You miss his loving you?'

So like Nina to speak directly, words directed like bullets. He swallowed.

'Miss him? Truth is, I can hardly remember what he looked like! I wish...' He had to stop. He needed to leave this underground place and breathe fresh air in the open. It had been a mistake to give in to Nina's insistence. He leant on the piano meaning to stand, but Nina was on her feet, her hands on his shoulders. Gripping him, forcing him to stay.

'Walter, listen. These are things I remember about Alexei. He was such fun! Always teasing. I remember his slanting, mischievous eyes—'

'Yes.' He could picture those teasing grey eyes.

'Those chiselled cheekbones—'

'Yes... Yes... But he's become a ghost. So many ghosts...' He turned to look at her, shaking his head, appealing. 'So many dead, Nina.'

She stared at him, perplexed. 'I know, but that doesn't stop you playing.'

He thumped his fists on the keyboard making her jump. 'This piece. Don't you see? It is so cruel!'

Nina was staring at him wide-eyed, shaking her head. 'Cruel?'

'Painful to confront cruelty. Cruel to confront pain. Either way.'

Nina placed a hand on the keyboard, slowly exploring one note, then another. 'I remember giving you this music, that birthday we shared in Paris. One of my better gifts, I'd thought. I believed you *loved* the music. Now you seem to hate it.'

He shook his head. So much pent-up sorrow forced its way from deep within. 'In another subterranean world – under the stage of the Champs-Elysées, while you were prancing about, we—'

'Who? You and Alexei?'

'First loved each other, and—'

'Oh!' Nina threw her head back in full-throated laughter. 'How delicious! While Maria was selected as the chosen one, *you* were chosen. My Lord. So there she was pounding herself into the stage, while you two were—'

'Not like that! Not quite. Not then.'

'Oh. I love this story.' Nina spoke gently. 'Then you should cherish this music. It's about love. And *Rite* is all about fecundity. About life.'

'And death.' How could he tell her about grabbing that soldier's leg only to find the rest of the body missing? Of lying beside men with strands of gut mixed into the dark earth as hell rained down from above. He must try.

'I didn't expect to live, that time in the crater. The stench. Tasting soil and blood. The noise. Ugly. Vile.' He brought his hands down on the keyboard in Stravinsky's crashing chords. 'Death! Death! Glorification of death! Sacrifice! Don't you see?'

'Stop! Stop this!' Nina was wrenching his arms back till he almost lost balance. She caught him only to thump him on the back. 'You didn't die. You're alive! You can't regrow your blasted foot, but you can grow inside. We all must.' Nina had shoved him sideways and was perching on a corner of the piano stool, her arm wrapped around him. He hadn't realised he was shaking. 'Life regenerates, Walter. Isn't this what *Rite* is all about?'

'I'm doing my best. To become reborn, that is.'

'With Edith?'

'In part,' he said.

Nina leapt to her feet. 'Play the bloody music. Music of life. Just play!' She began to spin. 'Play, I tell you!'

And as commanded by his sister, older than him by half an hour, he placed his hands on the keyboard and began "The Sacrificial Dance of the Chosen One". His fingers were supple but the muscle memory and brain memory of this score were rusty with disuse. He stuttered through the fractured sound with its staccato notes and pauses, doing his best, until he could no longer.

He stopped, feeling a crushing of his ribs, and found he was panting.

'Play!' Nina yelled. 'Don't you dare stop!' She glared at him from where she continued to fling herself around. 'You've got to live, Walter. Not a half-life. A whole life. We all must live. Play!'

So he continued. And between staring at notes on the page, he glanced at Nina leaping, arms whirling.

'Keep going!' She was by the piano now, fists beating her own chest. 'Life can be ugly – we know that – but beautiful too.' She was off again, bounding across the room in jumps and lunges that had never been choreographed by anyone, inspired by the moment.

Suddenly, Walter departed from the score in front of him, playing one of his own compositions. This he knew well. The jagged chords, and aching, arching arpeggios flew from his fingers and before long Nina was back at the piano, breathless, listening intently.

When he stopped, she asked, 'This is one of yours?'

'You're only the second person to hear it.' He took a steadying breath. 'I played it for David last week.' How strange to speak his name out loud. He looked at her, attempting to smile. 'He's a-a *particular* friend.'

'Is that so?' She slid to sit next to him and placed an arm around his waist. 'Tell me about this particular man.'

'He's a historian, you know, his subject's—'

'Never mind that. What colour's his hair?'

'Oh, an untamed lion's mane, rippling thick tawny gold.'

'Eyes?'

'Speckled hazel.'

'I imagine he might have freckles.'

'Indeed he does!' Walter was seeing David's face clearly, was feeling his presence. 'We get on very well. He's very kind.'

'Of course, he would be!' Her fingers tickled his ribs. 'Do I get to meet him?'

'He'd like to. He knows about you, but, but, I'm not—'

'Why not?' Nina had twisted to face him. 'Why ever not?'

'Please, Nina. Life is complicated enough.' He turned aside.

His sister placed both hands to his cheeks, forcing him to look at her and, as so often, he was alarmed by the fire in her eyes and the currents of energy that flowed from her.

'Does Edith know of your friend?'

This was not Nina's business, yet having started, it was hard to stop – didn't *want* to stop.

'She does, actually. They've met on several occasions. We're considering—'

'Divorcing? Might you and Edith divorce?'

'No!' Now he was worried. 'Has Edith said she wants to?'

'Edith's only talked about wanting a baby! Oh, never mind what she said.' And by his sister's blush, he could just imagine what Edith might have divulged. Now it was his turn to feel the heat rising to his cheeks. His fingers slowly explored some keys, note by note.

'The house we're looking to lease – Edith will have told you we're waiting for it to become available?' His sister nodded.

'It's a large house, four bedrooms, we have room for a lodger and... and...' He finished at a gallop, 'David, as it happens, is looking for a new place.'

'Oh, my goodness!'

'On the outskirts of Oxford. Quite secluded...'

'Oh!' Nina's voice rose. 'You stagger me. You are full of surprises, brother.' She giggled.

'Edith's idea, actually. She is, you might say, efficient about such arrangements.'

'She is, isn't she. Good on her.'

Now Nina's fingers drifted lazily along some notes. 'The French have a word for this: *ménage à trois*.'

'Really, Nina, I wish you wouldn't...' his voice trailed off. Wish she wouldn't what? Speak aloud what was obvious? Confront him with this part of himself that was not respectable, behaviour that was not sanctioned? Or, as David had urged, saying he had nothing to hide. He felt Nina's sharp elbow in his ribs.

'Will I be welcome, Walter? I hope I may visit.'

He smiled. 'If you wish. I rather think you will be welcomed.'

'And Charlie. Charlie's never been to Oxford. He must come. You'll invite him too, won't you?' Nina laid her head on his shoulder. 'You see, Twinny, amongst the ugliness of our new world, there is much that is freshly minted.'

'And we can find happiness, you believe?'

'It's a struggle, isn't it? Life, I mean.'

He placed his arm around her. 'Edith told me you'd had a t-termination. It can't have been an easy decision.' He felt Nina's body sag a little.

'Goodness, can you see me and Charlie managing a third life, when we can't manage the two of us?'

'And Charlie?' he asked, aiming for much with the question.

'Oh, we'll have to see. He's still set on moving to New York one day.'

'And you? Might you go?' Nina living permanently away alarmed him. He was used to her flitting in and out of the country. In and out of his life.

'You know, when I told Ma I was going to end the pregnancy, she said something about a child being brown-skinned wouldn't help it in life... Something like that.'

'Sid's influence. Take no notice.'

'I wouldn't mind one bit, but I've seen how things can be for black people. It got me thinking, if Charlie and I did set up somewhere in America, even in New York, it wouldn't be easy – *if* we had children, that is – here or there.'

'Prejudice,' he said. 'And law.'

He felt another squeeze of her hand at his waist. 'Besides,' Nina went on. 'I'm still set on dancing with Diaghilev, for now... We're not getting younger, you and I.'

That made him chuckle. 'Twenty-five! I should say we've got plenty of life ahead of us.' And here he was being cheerful – Nina had that effect on him.

'I mean a *ballet* life won't be for ever, though I'm quite keen on this modern dance that's taking off in America.' She kissed his cheek. 'We must regenerate, you and I.'

'Regenerate,' he echoed. 'Yes, we owe ourselves this.'

'You know, once I saw myself as a firebird, now I think I shall be a phoenix – consumed by flame but rising from the ashes. And you must do the same.'

He imagined himself, renewed, soaring into the sky.

'Yes,' he said.

And this was how Hilda found them: brother and sister, bottoms squashed together on a piano stool, ribs against ribs, as compact as they had been when they shared a womb. Then they had been in separate spheres. Now, arms wrapped around each other bound them together as never before.

54

'WELL, ROSIE, WHAT SAY YOU?'

Sid was weary, once jolly cheeks now loose and jowly, shoulders slumped. If she didn't agree to this one, she'd never leave London, and she feared Sid would be leaving her behind.

'It's nice enough,' she conceded, running a finger along a sticky counter, before crossing to the large fly-specked window, desiccated bodies on the sill below.

'And we'd be close to the sea,' Sid urged.

Beyond the bathing huts, the far side of the road, the beach was right there. She let the grimy curtain fall from her hands. 'Hmm.'

A pub in Margate was up for sale, as were other contenders for her affection, but she was picky. One, tucked away in a woody village far from civilisation, gave her the shivers. Another – a pub and hotel – so large she'd have run herself ragged rushing up and down stairs, looking after guests. Then there'd been ones that were very smart indeed and doing steady trades, snapped up by those with more cash than them. This one could be Goldilocks's bowl of porridge, just right.

'We can do something with this.' She glanced back to the corridor from where rickety stairs rose. 'And the upstairs flat isn't so bad.'

'Oh, Rosie.' Sid crossed to her in two strides, a smacking kiss of gratitude for her lips. 'You won't regret it, love. I'm sure you'll be happy here. Happy wife, happy life, eh?'

He slipped his arm into hers, leading her out. From the pavement, they appraised the cracked and faded signage of The Old Cottage Pub, then their gaze shifted to the peeling façade, Sid saying, 'A lick of paint won't go amiss.' Rose was already thinking about colours.

She was picturing herself with a bucket of hot water, scrubbing brush and carbolic soap, giving the inside the once-over, then, depending on the outside colour, she'd have her sewing machine out in a jiffy, running up some pretty curtains to frame the windows. What a pity Molly wasn't around, she would get behind this.

Rose looked about her, considering. The High Street bustled: trams and motors, horse-drawn carts and cabs. It was a funny world, the old squeezed out by the new. Beyond the street, the esplanade pavement and beachfront swarmed. She was happy to see that, liking to be surrounded by people, and there'd be customers to pull through the door.

'We'd get a piano in, wouldn't we, Sid?'

'In the far corner. It'll fit nicely.'

She kissed him and the deal was sealed.

'Come on, I fancy an ice.' She tucked her arm into his and they strolled along the seafront where she looked out to where a deeper bluey-grey horizon met a soft blue sky – very nice – then to the jetty. Why it wasn't called a pier, she wasn't sure. The steel curlicues and fancy fretwork were lovely. And the small turrets would remind her of her beloved Alhambra.

She stopped in her tracks.

'You'll have to move down first,' she said. 'I can't leave till after the New Year, maybe well into spring, depending how long they need me.'

'Understood!' Sid clicked his heels, saluting her. 'I know the pecking order. Ballet, more ballet, and me, the poor old sod at the bottom.'

She rolled her eyes but didn't contradict him.

Rose began preparing to leave Alie Street. The move prompted her to sort through final remnants of Molly's belongings she'd not had the heart to chuck out – a frayed knitting and mending bag, her best hat – then began on her own clothes and belongings. Her eyes fell on three patchwork cushions scattered on the settee, the backing of each cut from that purple shawl that'd once wrapped her small body. Nina's scrap had long since become a dusting rag, but the half she'd passed to Walter had ended back with her. The frontside of each cushion was a riot of colours and texture: squares of crimson velvet, livid green silk, striped yellows and cobalt blues. Monsieur Alias had had no use for these tiny remnants and never minded her taking them home. One cushion was bordered in gold braid, different-coloured pompoms in corners of another. She picked up the third cushion edged with tassels cut from the purple shawl. This one she would keep for herself.

She sat, overwhelmed by the enormity of leaving and knowing so much of her life had passed by. No harm in a little cry.

When Nina visited, Rose took the opportunity to take down boxes from the top of her wardrobe and from a drawer where she kept precious things. She laid two jewellery boxes on her bed. It was time to pass on Arthur's gifts. She opened a faded flat box and displayed her beloved strand of pearls.

'Would you like this, Nina? They'd look nicer on you than me, these days.'

'Oh, Ma. You sure you want to part with this?' Nina lifted

the necklace, placing it around her throat, and Rose fastened it. 'They are lovely, I must say.' Her daughter tilted her head, admiring herself in a mirror.

Below neatly bobbed hair, Rose saw how the line of pearls seemed to draw attention to Nina's chest. She wouldn't say so, but her daughter's figure looked scrawny to her mind, though this flat-chested look was all the rage now. 'You're so slender,' was what she said.

'Worked to the bone, Ma. Besides, Diaghilev likes his ballerinas slim. Not that I'm ballerina material, but I've heard him say female thighs are best covered up.'

'Is that so?'

'Just hates short tutus. Olga will be fine. She's just like Pavlova, only prettier. You'll enjoy sewing for her.'

Olga Spessivtseva was one of the ballerinas engaged for the new, lavish production of *The Sleeping Princess*. Why not *Sleeping Beauty*, she wasn't sure. While the dancer was still in Paris, her measurements were known to Rose.

Rose sighed. 'I'll miss it, down by the seaside, pulling pints.'

'I remember this.' Nina pounced on a little jewellery box, opening the hinged lid to reveal Rose's rosebud brooch. 'So pretty. You should keep this one, Ma.'

'I've worn it every Christmas, theatre outings and so on. Thing is, Sid says he can't afford such things, and the brooch just rubs it in his face.' She touched it, then pushed it away before she changed her mind. 'I'd like you to have it.'

'You're only going as far as Margate. Not the pearly gates.'

'Time to let go,' Rose said.

Nina turned the small brooch in her hand. 'If you insist. Diamonds, aren't they? I can handle small keepsakes. Easy to travel about with. Thanks, Ma.' Nina kissed her on the cheek.

Next, Rose unwrapped tissue paper from her treasured black velvet opera cape, noting with satisfaction that it looked as fresh as when she had first unpacked it. 'And this. I'm not sure I'll have much use for it.' She caressed the fur collar. 'Would you like it, Nina?' Her voice was tentative. 'I'd love you to have it.'

Her daughter wrinkled her nose at the whiff of camphor and lavender. 'It is lovely, but rather old-fashioned. I can't imagine I'd ever wear it.' Then, sensing her disappointment, Nina continued, 'You know me, Ma. Always on the road. I'd hate it to get ragged like that purple shawl of yours.'

Rose shook out the garment then slipped the evening cape over her own shoulders. What had once been created to grace a rosebud figure no longer suited a full-blown flower. She pulled a face at her reflection. 'Can't turn back the clock.'

'Let me try it on.' Nina slipped the cape over slender shoulders, and Rose thought it suited her beautifully.

'You should keep it, Nina. Who else can I pass it to?'

'It is lovely, I must say.' Nina turned to the mirror, admiring the view. 'Tell you what. Why not give it to Edith? She might like it. It can be a keepsake – she can pass it along if… Oh!' Nina's hand flew to her mouth. 'Damn. I've let the cat out of the bag. I was going to say if they have a girl. Oh, Ma. What am I like? Edith wanted to be sure before telling you.'

'A baby!' Rose plopped onto her bed. 'I saw them only two months ago…'

'Would've been after that.' Nina chuckled. 'The child won't lack for loving with a mummy, a daddy and an uncle at hand.'

'Whatever do you mean? That lodger fellow? He mightn't stick around with a yowling baby bothering him.'

'Oh, I think David will!' Nina smiled. 'Yes, see if Edith would like this cape. I'm certain she can accommodate it in her wardrobe as she accommodates *so* much.' Her daughter twirled, pearls jiggling, in the small space between bed and dressing table.

Rose cast her mind back to when she'd last seen Walter and Edith – and their lodger, David – all up in London for a concert. Walter had been keen to attend as Mr Vaughan Williams had been a tutor at music college. 'I think you'll like his music, Rose. And I'd like you to come. Cheap seats, I'm afraid, had to scramble for these.'

It had been quite a party. Those up from Oxford, plus Mr Reed, retired from teaching, up from Leatherhead. It was years since Rose had met the man who had been so influential on Walter. He had aged – hadn't they all? His evening suit shabby, buttons unlikely to fasten across his thickened waist. 'I'm doing nicely,' the former schoolmaster told her. 'Settled with my sister, keeping my hand in, music-wise, conducting choir at the local church.'

At the Queen's Hall, Edith introduced her to David, 'Who lives with us,' and Rose registered his firm handshake and warm eyes, thinking to herself that he seemed a steady sort, not likely to run off with the valuables or forget to pay rent. 'Pleased to meet you,' she offered, he replying, 'Walter's talked so much about you. I'm very pleased to meet you at last.'

She had loved the concert, listening rapt to a soaring violin of *The Lark Ascending*. Mr Reed one side, Edith the other, Walter and their lodger along the row.

As the applause died down, Mr Reed leant across her. 'Walter… Walter! Reminds me of our rambles, hmm?'

'Oh yes, it certainly does. It was masterful.' Walter's voice was shaky, Rose noticed. 'And you know,' he went on, 'I might learn to re-love these pastoral works. "*He rises and begins to round, he drops the silver chain of sound…*"'

'Ah,' Mr Reed said, 'Meredith! "*Of many links without a break, In chirrup, whistle, slur and shake, for singing till his heaven fills—*"'

'"*'Tis love of earth that he instils, and ever winging up and up...* '" Walter stopped, voice choking.

'I do believe this has touched your soul, my dear!' Edith squeezed Walter's hand.

David had offered his handkerchief. 'Well, old chap, I hope your next compositions are ones I can hum along too. I beg you, fill our house with merry tunes. I do love a pretty melody.'

'Me too!' Rose piped up. 'Nothing I like better.'

There had been laughter, with Edith saying, 'Yes, our house must indeed be melodious.'

Rose settled back in her seat. 'What's next up?' she asked Mr Reed.

'*The Planets*; I'm looking forward to hearing Mr Holst's new work. We are blessed to have such composers amongst us. Blessed to be British.'

'Oh, yes!' Rose agreed.

'A baby, then.' Rose looked at Nina. 'When's it due?'

'Not sure exactly. Sometime in the New Year, in the middle of our run no doubt. How are the costumes coming along, Ma?'

'Coming along. Patterns cut. We're waiting for bolts of a particular shade of pink silk to be delivered. It'll be lovely. Everything a ballerina's tutu should be – frilled and flounced, and knee-length. A wedding-cake confection.'

It was such a pity Monsieur Alias was not around to work on this production. She could imagine him holding each of Léon Bakst's meticulously drawn designs, peering through his dark glasses, eyes gleaming with the challenge. It was set in a time he loved: those French kings, those Louises, who went in for long wigs and lots of flummery.

Suddenly Rose clutched her heart. 'Oh, Nina! You don't think I'm a fool to give it all up, do you? Foolish to go so far away!'

'Honestly, Ma! Anyone would think you're going to the moon. What about me?'

'Don't remind me!' She inhaled deeply, trying to suck air into her juddering lungs and stop the ringing in her ears. Too much change. This next Ballets Russes production would be Nina's last. She took the opera cape from Nina, placing it back on the bed.

'Grigoriev says they'll miss me. Told me I'm someone they've been able to rely on. Not enough to promote though, I longed to tell him. Even so, I agreed to wait till after this production. "We need to gather all our troops," he said. Not sure this old-style ballet will be to my taste.'

'Mine though!'

'But with Massine gone, so have my dreams. Foolish men: Massine for falling for Vera, and Diaghilev for chucking him out. He can be such a jealous man.'

Rose looked at her daughter as she slowly removed the pearl necklace. Rose would miss her. Charlie had booked his passage for New Year and Nina was to follow.

'Ma, I'd like to take something with me. I hope you haven't sold or thrown everything out that was Mo's.'

'I kept something back. And you can't say no.'

'What?' Nina frowned.

She went to the living room and returned with a colourful cushion cover over something that Nina couldn't see.

Nina clapped her hands. 'The pompom one. Perfect. I'll find room for that in my travel case and find stuffing for it when I'm settled somewhere.'

Rose touched a white pompom. 'I found this in a dusty corner of a dressing room, from a Pierrot mime artist's costume. The red one was wedged under a wing curtain, maybe a clown wore it.' The origins of the other fluffy baubles were a mystery.

'What else? What's underneath?'

Rose whisked away the fabric to reveal a porcelain shepherdess figurine.

'That!' Nina cried. 'I'll be sure to break it!'

Long ago, the shepherdess's scarved headdress had been chipped, but the rosy-cheeked face was as cheerful as ever. The basque, a shade of violent pink, above a floral petticoat as colourful as always. The figurine plucked some sort of guitar and there was a sheep at her feet, docile as Rose remembered. She and Mo liked pretty things. They provided comfort in a world that wasn't always nice to live in.

She held out the offering. 'Got to take it, love. Keep something of the old for the new.'

'I can't promise it'll survive the journey.'

'Glue it back together then.'

Nina accepted it from her hands.

'We all must get mended from time to time.'

CODA

1921

❦

The Alhambra curtain is about to rise for *The Sleeping Princess* this late November evening. King Florestan's grand hall – massive painted pillars rising to support gilded moulding and domed roof – is, almost, ready to receive its guests for Princess Aurora's christening.

Diaghilev is doing his usual inspection of the stage. In top hat, formal white shirt, bow tie, polished shoes, his body even sturdier in fur-collared opera cloak. Cane in hand, he strides the stage, Mr Care and Diligence in all things stagecraft, leaving nothing to chance. Stage machinery that had jammed on the rising forest on opening night had caused him to weep. Now, three weeks in, not a glitch. Spotting a crease in a canvas backdrop – stagehands on to it immediately – Diaghilev's eyes rest on a golden cradle under a velvet canopy.

Crammed in the wings, the royal party await their entrance. The tall King, in a shoulder-length wig and ostrich-feather hat, a richly brocaded jacket and robe of royal-blue velvet trimmed with ermine. The Queen is equally stupendous. Bakst, Diaghilev knows, has outdone himself. There is nothing that man has overlooked.

Beyond the front curtain, the audience – almost a full house, he is gratified to know – breaks into applause as the conductor takes his place on the podium. Diaghilev leaves the stage to those he trusts to make magic. His black and white figure squeezes through brilliantly clad courtiers who part, making way for the real king of this court.

Amongst these performers waiting their cue, a young woman is costumed as a lady of the court. There is not enough room in the wings, so Nina is with a crush of others snaking up the concrete staircase to the *corps de ballet* dressing rooms where costumes hang in readiness for numerous changes. During weeks of rehearsals in Drury Lane's Drill Hall, Grigoriev has drilled them like units in a fighting army, and she has come to appreciate the beauty of Petipa's strict classical style, which does not quite suit her temperament. This will be her Ballets Russes swan song. She is not sure what her future holds – dance for certain – but she's ready for a change, ready to discover what New York might offer. She moves down the steps as cast members ahead of her take their place onstage. Act One, The Christening, is about to begin.

Watching in a front row of the upper gallery is a middle-aged woman. A single strand of pearls around her neck, a black velvet and fur evening cape at her ample shoulders. These treasured items are having a final outing on her body before passing to the next generation of women in her family.

It is Rose's forty-sixth birthday. Tonight, she wants no company other than ballet itself, but she does have company; her son has insisted. He sits on her right, his friend next to him. Both look dashing: hair slick with pomade, besuited in opera clothes. She's not daft. She understands David has a special place in Walter's life, but until he says something, she'll keep her mouth clamped on the subject. Besides she's not sure what Sid might say.

Edith, her daughter-in-law, heavily pregnant, sits on her left. And her daughter's boyfriend, Charlie, sits next along the row looking distinguished in an evening suit. Her own husband, Sid, sits next to Charlie.

Rose sits forwards, elbows on the balustrade, Tchaikovsky's overture filling the domed auditorium and her soul with its sweetness and promise. Seeing Mr Fittelberg – all the way from the Moscow Opera – in front of the huge orchestra awakens memories of the past. How often had she watched Mr Jacobi swinging his baton?

Her heart flutters in anticipation as cymbals crash and swagged curtain rises. Up until now she has remained backstage in the Green Room with other seamstresses, fixing and fiddling: costumes, a little tight under an armpit here, restricting a leg movement there. On occasion she has managed to sneak into the wings, catching snatches of the ballet from her familiar position, pressed to a wall under a fire bucket.

Soon, she spots Nina onstage among the ladies of the court. Ah! Here come fairies to pay their respects to the babe.

Walter squeezes his mother's hand, whispering that the production is magnificent, even, dare he say, splendiferous. To his right, he feels the warmth and subtle touch of a trousered leg against his thigh, returning the gesture. He'd had to persuade his friend to accompany him. 'You are family,' he insisted, and David had agreed.

Later, he watches prettily costumed dancers waltzing, wreaths of flowers in their hands, and David leans across, whispering that he should take a leaf out of Mr Tchaikovsky's book and write tuneful music. Walter digs him in the ribs.

Here is the moment Rose has waited for. It's time for the grown-up Princess Aurora's entrance. Vera Trefilova – one of the five talented Russian ballerinas Diaghilev has engaged – trips lightly onto the stage: a giddy sixteen-year-old in pink knee-length tutu festooned with roses. Elegantly attired suitors wait to court her. When the "Rose Adagio" commences, goosebumps prickle Rose's entire body, and she wonders how something can be so perfect.

In The Vision scene, she hears Sid loudly clearing his throat and scowls at him for daring to break the spell: delicate

Princess Aurora, the epitome of female beauty that few women attain in real life, Prince Charming besotted in a way real men rarely are.

Memories flood through her. This magnificent concoction of a theatre was made to present such pageantry.

Sometime during the evening, Rose feels Edith reach for her hand and place it on her swollen belly, allowing Rose to feel a jutting elbow – or is it a knee? – and she thinks this grandchild of hers must be responding to the music. In years to come, she will take this child to the theatre to be thrilled by wicked witches, scurrying rats, kind fairies; witness magical scene transformations; where good overcomes evil with the wave of a wand; where a beautiful princess is awakened by a handsome prince... Well, she frowns, Pierre Vladimirov as Prince Charming has a long face, his chin-length wig making him even horsier, but he dances superbly and *is* charming. She grants him that.

Across the footlights, Nina, hand in hand with her partner, runs onto stage. Her feet clad in heeled, hard-soled character shoes make a soft *clop-clopping*. She skips and clicks her heels in a lively polonaise with the rest of her group. She's smiling broadly at the audience, and up to where her family sits. Arms linked, she and her partner spin – a riot of colour as they twirl. There is fire in her heart she hopes burns long and hard.

Rose watches the wedding celebrations, her grin ear to ear. The Prince and Princess skipping about along with Puss in Boots and the White Cat and all the rest of them, the entire cast assembled for a good old gallop.

At the end, the cast gathers onstage, bows and bouquets galore. Rose stands, shouts, 'Bravo.' Can't stop clapping. As she helps Edith to her feet, Rose decides other things she must tell her grandchild is that love and beauty always triumph, that imagined worlds are just as important as the real.

They're going to a private club next, all of them. Charlie knows one that stays open late, 'Where,' Nina insists, 'I'll be dancing till dawn.'

'And straight on to morning.' Walter laughs.

She and Sid won't stay that long, but she will dance. No question. But first…

In the Green Room, she gathers her family for a photograph – management has granted her this after much cajoling – as there may never be a chance when they're all together. Charlie leaves soon and Nina will follow. The background is not a studio set of ruched fringed curtains and potted palms but costumes needing repairs, shelves of fabric rolls and fringing, boxes of artificial flowers and feathers, the warp and weft of Rose's life.

The three women sit. Rose plants herself, matriarch of her family, not the same rosebud she had been for that earlier portrait, but the necklace and opera cape are the same. Behind her stands her husband Sid, robust, heavily moustached, bowler hat, a proprietary hand on her shoulder, his other hand to his chest. Seated on her right is Nina, a defiant tilt to her chin, effortlessly glamourous in shimmering turquoise, slender legs crossed at the ankles, wearing red, strapped evening shoes. Nina's friend, possible fiancé, Charlie, stands behind her, both hands resting casually on the back of her chair. He looks at ease with himself. To Rose's other side sits Edith, both feet on the floor, a placid, about-to-be mother look about her. Behind her is Walter, hands clasped behind his back, a shy smile touching his mouth. Rose sucks in her tummy, smiles, and a photograph is taken. Then Rose insists David joins the group. Sid starts to demand why, but Rose is adamant. The outlier positions himself next to Walter and the men all squeeze in a little closer.

When Rose sees the photographs developed, it is this second photo she has copied, framed, and distributed to her offspring. She tells them it's because of Diaghilev. As the photographer clicked, he happened to be passing, peering in the open door. There he is, a little out of focus, but there all the same, on his way to Princess Aurora's dressing room. Keeping his eye on his dancers. Keeping his eye on the dance.

Glossary

ROSE, NINA, WALTER, ET AL. ARE IMAGINED characters whose lives interact with actual people. Here are *some* of those who make an appearance or are referenced in *Dance of the Earth*. Composers, such as Igor Stravinsky, and artists/designers, such as Léon Bakst are, for brevity, not included in this glossary. Spelling of Russian names vary – below are the ones I've used. A glossary of ballet terms is included for readers curious to learn more.

Associated with the Alhambra Music Hall

Giovannina Pitteri	Ballerina
Emma Palladino	Ballerina
Pierina Legnani	Ballerina
Georges Jacobi	Musical Director, composer & conductor
Carlo Coppi	Ballet Master
Lucia Cormani	Principal dancer & teacher

Associated with Ballets Russes

Sergei Diaghilev	Russian art and ballet impresario, director of Ballets Russes
Vaslav Nijinsky	Dancer & choreographer
Michel Fokine	Dancer & choreographer
Léonide Massine	Dancer & choreographer
Enrico Cecchetti	Dancer & ballet master
Serge Gregoriev	Rehearsal director (former dancer)
Tamara Karsavina	Ballerina
Lydia Lopokova	Ballerina. Later married Maynard Keynes.
Olga Spessivtseva	Ballerina
Vera Trefilova	Ballerina
Hilda Munnings	English dancer, later Munnisova, then Lydia Sokolova.
Vera Savina	English dancer, formerly Vera Clark
Adolf Bolm	Principal dancer
Nicholai /Kola Kremnev	Dancer, married/divorced Hilda/Lydia
Leon Woizikovsky	Dancer, later married Hilda/Lydia
Doris Faithful	English dancer
Anna Broomhead	English dancer, later Anna Bromova
Anna Pavlova	Ballerina, appeared briefly with Ballets Russes
Michael Mordkin	Principal, appeared briefly with Ballets Russes
Theodore Kosloff	Formed a company with wife, Alexandra Baldina
Alexandra Baldina	Formed a company with husband, Theodore Kosloff

Pioneers of modern (contemporary) dance

Isadora Duncan	Influential dancer, choreographer and innovator
Ruth St Denis	Co-founder Denishawn
Ted Shawn	Co-founder Denishawn

Ballet terms

Adagio	A series of slow flowing movements performed with fluidity
Arabesque	The working leg extended straight behind and raised arms extended forwards to create a graceful line
Développé	A gradual unfolding of the working/raised leg
Échappé	A jump from both feet in a closed position to a wide position
Fouetté	A pirouette plus a whip in and out of the raised leg
Grand jeté	A leap from one foot to the other
Tendu	Extending the leg, the tip of the toe remaining on the ground
Pirouette	A spin on one leg
Plié	A knee bend
Port de bras	Arm movements to practice quality and fluidity

Author's Note and Acknowledgements

As a six-year-old living in New Zealand, I began a journey into the world of dance. My ballet teacher, Michelle Robinson, had just left secondary school to assist her teacher, Gwen Gibbs, with the younger pupils. Gwen had trained with Edouard Espinosa, one of the founders of the Royal Academy of Dancing. In this way tradition builds and spreads.

Years later, it was renowned dance critic and writer, Clement Crisp, who fired my interest in the Ballets Russes. He taught 20th Century Dance History while I was studying for my Dance M.A. at London's Laban Centre.

Dance has always been a part of my life, making *Dance of the Earth* my most personal novel to date.

Brenda Brevitt tipped me into this story after giving me a book about ballets at London's music halls, which was exactly where I wanted to start. And thank you for reading the story I spun.

It is telling that many of my beta readers are those I am bound to through bonds of friendship, kinship and dance going back many years. Thanks to: Judy Spence, Tania Kopytko, Bronwyn Judge, Diana Luther-Powell, and Vivienne Hamblin.

I appreciate support from writer buddies, particularly Karmen Špiljek, an additional chapter is due to you. And thanks, Lui Sit, and Rob Valente.

I am grateful to Jane Pritchard, Dance and Theatre Curator at the Victoria and Albert Museum, for advice and those marvellous articles on music hall ballets. Thanks also to Dr Toby Haggith at the Imperial War Museum and to military history enthusiast, Toby Ewin, for checking sections of my story.

Thanks to two editorial services. One prefers to be uncredited, but I'd like to record my appreciation for their insights and staunch support, and to Cornerstones Literary.

Thanks to my partner, Hubert Kwisthout, for reading various drafts, making suggestions along the way, and sharing on-the-ground research, including visiting World War I battle sites in France.

Thanks to The Book Guild for continuing the story's journey into publication.

My character, Rose, says, 'Imagined worlds are just as important as the real.' I couldn't put it better myself.

About the Author

Stories with big themes written as page-turners are Anna M Holmes's speciality. With an extensive background in dance and theatre, Dance of the Earth is a story she has longed to write. Her novels—The Find, Wayward Voyage, and Blind Eye—are all typified by deep research. Anna worked as a radio journalist before embarking on a career in arts management. Originally from New Zealand, she now lives in South-West London.

OTHER BOOKS BY ANNA M HOLMES

Blind Eye
The Find
Wayward Voyage